I0651275

Wakefield Press

Libby Lawrence is Good at Pretending

Jodi McAlister is an author of romantic novels for young adults and adults. Her YA paranormal romance Valentine trilogy is published by Penguin Teen Australia. Her first adult rom-com *Here For The Right Reasons* will be published by Simon & Schuster in 2022. *Libby Lawrence is Good at Pretending* is her first contemporary romance for young adults, published by Wakefield Press in 2022. She is also an academic, and her research interests include romance and pop culture.

Libby Lawrence is Good at Pretending

JODI McALISTER

**Wakefield
Press**

Wakefield Press
16 Rose Street
Mile End
South Australia 5031
www.wakefieldpress.com.au

First published 2022

Cover designed by Stacey Zass
Edited by Jo Case, Wakefield Press
Typeset by Michael Deves, Wakefield Press

ISBN 978 1 74305 904 3

 A catalogue record for this
book is available from the
National Library of Australia

 Wakefield Press thanks
Coriole Vineyards for
continued support

Prologue

His eyes sparkled in the light. One hand was on her hip and one was in her hair and a song was on their lips in the moment that he kissed her.

The music swelled. The lights came down. The crowd cheered.

Their mouths stayed pressed together, intimate, impersonal, through all the clapping. He kissed her like he kissed Annalise, like she was the real princess and not the understudy, allowed one small attempt at glory in a school holiday panto in front of a smallish Sunday afternoon crowd.

He kissed her like he meant it. He kissed her like he didn't mean it at all. It was chaste, romantic, pretend. Until she felt his tongue touch her bottom lip.

She jumped. He winked as he pulled away, taking her hand and looking into the light as the audience demanded an encore.

Something in her thrilled and something in her dropped. Things were very right and very wrong all at once. She nearly missed the first line of the reprise as she tried to regain her balance.

At least she had Nightingale's hand to cling to.

'Good show, you,' he said to her as they filed offstage.

'Thank you,' she replied, lightly, deliberately.

In the blue-lit world of backstage, she was a princess for a few minutes more. 'Oh my God, you nailed it!' someone told her.

'You did so well!' another said.

'Wow, Libby, you smashed it out of the park!'

They all told her that they loved it, that they loved her. She loved it, and she loved them. She wanted more, more, more.

'All right, all right,' Ned said, breaking up what felt like her eightieth group hug. 'It's a kiddie show, remember? Go out there and talk to the kids before they start screaming the place down.'

Nightingale's eyes caught hers over Ned's shoulder. His lips curved slightly.

He's a dick, she reminded herself. *He shouldn't have kissed you like that. You should be furious.*

But she could feel that smile in her veins.

The pins in her wig were digging into her head as she followed the other principal cast members into the foyer, but she didn't touch them, knowing the kids would be horrified if Rapunzel's hair fell off at their feet. She wrapped her long plait around giggling children, around her own neck like a scarf, and took photo after photo. 'One with the prince, one with the prince!' one mother demanded, and Nightingale knelt down beside her with a smile, one arm around a little girl, one around her.

'Did you like the show?' he asked the little girl.

'Yes!'

'What was your favourite part?'

'When you kissed her!'

I will not turn red, she ordered herself.

'Can I tell you a secret?'

'Yes!' the little girl exclaimed.

'That was my favourite part too,' Nightingale said. The girl screamed with delight.

She was sad to unpin the wig, to coil the long blonde plait up like a rope and leave it on the dressing table, ready for Annalise to wear. In the next show, she'd be back to the chorus, and

Annalise would be the princess again, and Nightingale wouldn't look twice at her, let alone flirt with her.

So what? she asked herself.

'Hey, where are you going?' he asked as she walked back out into the theatre foyer. Her face was wiped clean of makeup, her hair still tightly pulled back from shoving it under the stocking cap. He was lounging against the canteen counter with a beer in his hand, looking effortlessly perfect.

'Home,' she replied. 'Show's over, Nightingale.'

'You're not staying for drinks?'

She hesitated. Chorus hardly ever got invited to post-show drinks.

'You're staying for drinks,' he said decisively. 'You don't get to run away after a performance like that one, Queen Elizabeth. Nobody puts Libby in a corner.'

'It was okay? Really?'

He reached out and traced a slow line down the side of her face, fingers dancing over her jawline. 'You know it was,' he said softly.

'Nightingale,' she said, 'what are you doing?'

He smiled devilishly. 'Is it working?'

She gave him the most withering look she could muster, thrilled and terrified that he might work out that the answer was yes.

Post-show drinks went longer and later than she'd anticipated. The techies went up to the bio box and put on a mix of songs from shows past, and there was singing (good) and dancing (bad) and they were all belting out the opening song from *Little Shop of Horrors,* conducting each other with beer bottles and attempting half-remembered choreography from six months ago, when he found her. 'Come with me,' he whispered in her ear.

'Why?' she asked.

He took the vodka cruiser out of her hand and set it down on the edge of the stage. 'Just do it,' he said. She could feel his breath against her skin.

He led her to the Swamp, an old dressing room backstage where so many costumes had been abandoned that the room was nearly half-filled with clothes. He held the curtain aside so she could go before him, but she stalled. 'We can't go in there, Nightingale,' she said. 'We'll drown.'

'Don't you trust me?'

'No.'

'You're sassy, Queen Elizabeth,' he said, grinning and moving closer to her. 'I've always liked that about you.'

'Have you now?' she said. 'And here I thought you barely knew who I was.'

'Oh, I know who you are,' he said, advancing again. 'You're the smart girl.'

Then he was kissing her.

They fell back into the soft maw of the Swamp. She wasn't sure if she had lost her balance or if Nightingale had taken her down with him. His lips were on her lips and his hands were on her skin and her arms were around his neck, hanging on for dear life. Her blood was fizzing and her heart was beating fast and she moaned as his hand slipped under her skirt, his teeth nipping at her collarbone.

'Shhhh,' he whispered against her skin. 'Someone will hear us.'

She pulled his mouth to hers. He tore a ladder in her tights as he pulled them off.

Later, when it was over, when he was gone, she could not find her underwear. The Swamp had swallowed it up.

Chapter One

Libby hated the cold. That was definitely, she told herself, looking up at the theatre, the only reason she was shivering right now.

She procrastinated. She ducked across the road into the café next to the Psych building to buy a coffee, even though the caffeine was the last thing she needed and she didn't actually like coffee that much anyway.

It took all of five minutes. At eight am on a Saturday morning, there was no queue. Terravale University Repertory Theatre was still there when she walked back out. She, encased in coat and beanie and scarf, was still shaking.

Which was ridiculous. She'd done auditions before, and hadn't she always been fine? Plus, there was literally no chance that Nightingale was in there, so it wasn't like anything *that* bad was on the cards.

Perhaps that was the problem.

A hand clapped down on her shoulder. She jumped, nearly spilling her coffee.

'Shit, sorry,' Ned said. 'You okay, Libs?'

'Yeah, yeah, fine,' she said, shaking a few drops off her hand. 'You startled me, that's all.'

'Going through audition stuff in your head?'

She nodded.

'I have absolutely no idea what to expect from the new guy.' Ned reached over and snagged her coffee from her hand, sipped it, and handed it back to her. 'I'm so unbelievably screwed.'

'Oh, come off it.' Had Ned Riordan, the sole remaining king of Uni Rep, really just drunk from her coffee like they were actual proper friends? 'Has anyone ever had a role sewn up as tightly as you've got Benedick?'

'If Nightingale was still here, sure,' Ned said. 'But we're in a brave new world now.'

'Has anyone—' Libby swallowed, her mouth suddenly dry. 'Has anyone heard from him?'

Ned shook his head. 'It's like he's dropped off the face of the earth. He even deleted his Instagram.'

Libby knew that. She'd been checking his social media obsessively.

'Good riddance,' Ned said. 'If I ever see him again, I'm going to punch him in the teeth. But enough about the Prince of Dickheads. What role are you going for?'

'Whatever they'll give me,' she replied, sipping her coffee and trying to settle herself. 'Beatrice would be a dream, but I know everyone's going to audition. Plus, it's Shakespeare, so there'll be hardly any roles for girls. I'm just going to give it a go and see what happens.'

'Don't undersell yourself. You impressed the hell out of a lot of people in your understudy show for *Rapunzel*. You certainly impressed the hell out of me.'

'Thank you,' Libby replied, surprised. 'That means a lot, Ned. Really.'

'I wish it meant more,' he said. 'Who knows what the new guy is after? But next time I'm directing, you're definitely getting out of the chorus. I promise.'

She knew how she should feel. Triumphant. Gleeful. In the context of Uni Rep, approval from Ned Riordan was big.

His had never been the approval she craved, though.

'Anyway, come on,' he said. 'It's freezing, and neither of us are going to get to play anything if we're late.'

She put on the bravest face she had. She would not let Ned or anyone else see how hard it was for her to cross the threshold.

It had been three weeks since that night in the Swamp. Two weeks since the Closing Night of *Rapunzel*, and one week since the Uni Rep group chat had blown up: *OMG, you guys, the committee finally got an accountant in and it turns out Nightingale skimmed eight grand off the top of his show budgets and now he's disappeared.*

It seemed strange, that such a massive change was not written on the building. Nightingale was one of the foundations of Uni Rep: how was the theatre still standing without him?

But the foyer was the same as always, poky, unremarkable, walls dotted with old cast photos over gaudy yellow paint that had been intended to be warm and welcoming but turned out obnoxious instead (with the ever-shrinking Theatre Studies budget, they'd never got a chance to change it). It was the same tiny box office, the same canteen with the same overpriced collection of chips and lollies, the same swinging doors to the auditorium, the same narrow staircase leading to the studio space upstairs. The only change was in the posters in the dusty glass windows, *Rapunzel* torn down, replaced with announcements of the auditions for *Much Ado About Nothing*, the words 'directed by Nightingale Smith' carefully crossed out with black marker.

'Hey, Leung,' Ned said, leaning over and kissing the girl behind the canteen counter. 'How's it going?'

'Oh my God, terrible.' Genevieve rubbed at her eyes, but somehow her perfect winged eyeliner remained intact. 'Three people have already called in and tried to reschedule. I *told* people when they booked their auditions that we're running on a tight schedule! There's afternoon and night shows in the auditorium this weekend, so they *know* all the auditions have to be done before one-thirty, but still! They call! And expect me to fit them in at, like, four pm! Then I'm trying to cross-check the audit of Nightingale's books, and honestly, I only did like one semester of accounting before I dropped it, and I *so* don't have the skills for this, and—'

'Do you want me to come out and give you a hand when my audition's over?' Ned asked. 'I could answer the phones so you could focus on the books.'

Genevieve looked at him pleadingly. 'Would you?'

Ned smiled and kissed her again. 'You knew there was a reason you loved me.'

'Time enough for declarations of endless adoration later,' Genevieve said. She slid two audition forms across the counter. 'Libby, I have a favour to ask, if you're not too busy.'

'Sure,' Libby said, a little surprised. 'What's up?'

'You still have that proofreading side-hustle, right? I have this big essay due for Euro History, and I really need someone to look over my draft. I'll pay your usual.'

'Don't worry about it,' Libby said. 'You're doing a public service with all this audit stuff you're doing on the books. I'll edit for you pro bono.'

'Sounds dirty,' Ned said.

'Shut up and fill in your form,' Genevieve told him. 'Thanks, Libs. You're a lifesaver.'

Libby sat down. She always tried to audition first thing in the morning, because she'd heard somewhere that directors always remembered the first few and the last few people they auditioned in a day. It hadn't worked for her yet – even though she'd been around for more than a year now and everyone knew who she was, she still hadn't managed to break out of the chorus – but everything was different this time.

The doors to the auditorium looked ominous. It felt like Nightingale could come sailing through them at any second, or tearing down the stairs from the studio, or popping out from the back room behind the canteen. *'Hi guys! Who's coming upstairs with me next?'*

His hands on her in the darkness, his mouth on hers. His infectious smile, in her veins, under her skin.

Her hand slipped as she wrote her age on the form, the tail of '19' a long dark slash down the page. The coffee felt like it was curdling in her stomach. Was she going to throw up?

No. No. She was fine.

Which character are you auditioning for? the form asked.

Beatrice, she wrote, in firm capital letters.

What would have been worse? Getting the role of Beatrice because she was the latest in Nightingale's long line of conquests, or being the latest in his long line of conquests and *not* getting it?

'Hi,' she'd said to him in the theatre kitchen, the first *Rapunzel* show back after the night in the Swamp. It had taken every bit of courage she had to say it.

'Oh, hi, you,' he'd replied absently, pulling the frilly cuffs of his Prince Charming shirt out of his velvet jacket and adjusting them.

'Can we—' she'd hesitated. 'Can we talk?'

'I'm busy right now,' he'd said. 'Maybe later.'

Then he'd turned his back and started talking to Annalise like she wasn't even there.

But now Nightingale wasn't here. She was. No one knew about the Swamp except him and her, and he was gone. So if she pretended it had never happened then it really had never happened. He was garbage, and she was *fine*, and—

'Your turn, Libs,' Gen said. 'You can go up now.'

She paused at the bottom of the stairs. She hadn't been up to the studio since ... how long had it been? A month? Six weeks? Before *Rapunzel* had bumped in.

'Gen?' she asked. 'Who did they get to direct in the end?'

'You don't know him,' Genevieve said absently, bent over the books.

'You know how you could find out?' Ned said. 'You could try this thing – it's called walking. Put one foot on the stair in front of you, then another on the next stair, and—'

'Oh, shut up,' Libby said, although that probably wasn't the most sensible thing to say to someone who held as much sway at Uni Rep as Ned.

One foot in front of the other. So much more difficult than it sounded, when you were off balance.

The studio door at the top of the stairs was closed. She raised her hand to knock, but it opened before she could, leaving her hanging, clenched fist in the air.

'Hi,' the guy said. 'Elizabeth Lawrence?'

He wasn't Nightingale. She knew he wasn't going to be Nightingale, but he *wasn't Nightingale*.

One moment. One breath. One second.

Then she dropped her hand and put on her best audition face. 'That's me,' she said brightly.

He held the door open for her. 'Come on in.'

She studied him as he walked around to the other side of the card table that served as a desk. He was tall, much taller than Nightingale, with a mop of unruly brown curls. Perhaps two or three years older than she was. He sat down and put on a pair of black-framed glasses and oh God drinking that coffee really had been a terrible mistake but then he smiled at her and somehow, reflexively, she was smiling back.

'So, Elizabeth,' he said.

'Libby,' she answered. 'No one calls me Elizabeth. My best friend's name is Elizabeth as well, and we've been friends since pretty much birth, so if someone says Elizabeth we never know which one of us they mean, and – sorry, you don't need to hear my whole life story. I'm a bit nervous.'

'It's totally fine,' he replied. 'Will.'

'Will?'

'My name,' he said. 'William Callahan. Call me Will.'

'Will,' she repeated. 'Nice to meet you.'

'So, let's get down to business,' he said, shuffling papers on the card table. 'Have you done any Shakespeare before?'

'Yes. I was in the Uni Rep production of *Twelfth Night* last year.'

'Awesome. Who did you play?'

'A bunch of roles. Olivia's servant, some background towns-people, a sailor when they ran out of dudes.'

He made a note.

'But I've played bigger roles too,' she said. 'I did Queen Margaret's monologue from the third part of *Henry VI* for my Year 12 drama monologue the year before last, and I did really well. Ninety-six percent.'

'Well done.'

'I know it doesn't count because it's high school, but – yeah.' She could feel herself turning red, and tried to will her blood away from her face.

'How much do you know about *Much Ado About Nothing*?'

'It's one of my favourite plays. I studied it at uni last semester, so I'm pretty familiar with it.'

'What do you study?'

'Arts/Law. But it's the Arts bit that I love. *Much Ado* was on Dr Lewis's – Graham – do you know Graham?'

'Yes, I know Graham.'

'Of course you know Graham. What a stupid question. Every person in this building knows Graham. Sorry.'

'Nothing to apologise for. You were saying?'

'Oh! Um. Yes. I took his Elizabethan Drama unit last semester. *Much Ado* was on the syllabus, and I fell in love with it.'

'That's a great unit, isn't it?'

She blinked. 'You took it too?'

'A couple of years ago,' Will replied. 'One of my precious few out-of-faculty electives. Tell me what you love about it. *Much Ado*, I mean, not Graham's class, or we'll be here for hours.'

'Oh God, so much stuff,' she replied, forcing her brain back on track. 'I love that it's funny – like, it's properly laugh-out-loud hilarious. And it's got a heart too. The banter between Benedick and Beatrice – it's classic love/hate, but in the best way. It's so clever and witty and ... I don't know, sparkly, and—'

She stopped. 'Sorry. I'm rambling.'

'No, no, no, go on.' He smiled at her again. His glasses were crooked on his nose. 'Beatrice gives speeches, so ... go on, speechify.'

'I like that Beatrice and Benedick listen to each other,' she said. 'Hero and Claudio say that they're in love, but they barely even know each other. I mean, Claudio has to get his friend to propose for him, like he's in Year Five and he's getting his friend to ask a girl out for him, so it's not exactly surprising that it falls apart so fast. But even when Beatrice and Benedick hate each other, they always listen to each other. They love listening to each other. They're fascinated by each other. They love talking, and sparring, and they play with each other and they mess with each other, and – I am so sorry. I sometimes have a problem knowing when to shut up.'

'Don't apologise,' he said. 'I think it's great you've thought about this and you know what you're talking about. I sure as hell haven't had the chance to think about this as much as I'd like.'

'How long have you, um, been at the helm?'

'A few days. Such a long time to form detailed opinions, I know. I'm really letting the team down.'

'Have you directed before?'

'Once or twice. But this is your audition, not mine. Shall we get on with it?'

'Of course,' she said, mouth suddenly dry. 'Um, sorry. I didn't mean to imply that you had no experience, or—'

'Libby, I promise you, it's fine.'

Maybe it would be better if she didn't get in. She needed to get past the Nightingale thing, and she was never going to be able to do it in a place as saturated with him as Uni Rep.

'You're auditioning for Beatrice, right?'

'Yes,' she said, making herself smile again. 'But any role would be ... fine.'

'I'll make a note.' He handed her a script. 'I'll get you to read this monologue of Beatrice's from Act III, then we'll do a dialogue from earlier on. Sorry if I'm not the most inspiring scene partner – I've done a bit of directing, but I'm not an actor. Do you want some time to read it over?'

'No,' she said, swallowing hard. 'I'm pretty familiar with it.'

His crooked smile returned for a moment, before being replaced with a more clinical, professional director face. 'When you're ready …?'

She nodded, took a deep breath, forced everything away, and began. 'What fire is in mine ears?'

'So?'

'So what?' Libby asked. She dumped her keys on the tiny dining table that sat between the couch and the door to the kitchen balcony, and threw her handbag down the hall in the vague direction of her bedroom. It landed in front of the bathroom door instead.

Ella brandished a wooden spoon at her, sticking her head out of the door to their long galley kitchen. Red pasta sauce, almost the same colour as her hair, dripped onto the linoleum floor. 'So, Elizabeth Two, how did it go?'

'It went fine.'

'Just fine?'

'Fine is what I'm willing to commit to for now. That smells good.'

'Don't change the subject. Elaborate on 'fine', or you're not getting any of my delightful-smelling bolognaise.'

'All right,' Libby said. 'It went … better than I expected? It might be all in my mind. I might just be chorus again. I might not get in at all. I might not even get a callback. But …'

'But you think you have a shot?'

Libby grinned. 'Yeah, I think I have a shot.'

Ella clapped her hands, sending more sauce flying. 'That's so exciting!' she said. 'I'm so psyched for you, Libs.'

She was psyched too. She was psyched enough that for the first time in weeks, Nightingale had been kicked out of the spotlight in her mind, relegated to the background.

She could see herself on stage, in that role. Once she'd got through that awkward opening with Will and got to reading, she'd fallen into the role, and it had felt *so* good. She'd sketched out moment after moment of her playing Beatrice in her imagination on the train on her way home. *He that hath a beard is more than a youth,* she'd say lightly, holding the audience in the palm of her hand, *and he that hath no beard is less than a man, and he that is more than a youth is not for me, and he that is less than a man – well, I am not for him.* The audience would laugh, and she and Ned would sparkle opposite each other, and someone in the audience would press an enormous bouquet into her arms on Opening Night, so big she could barely hold it, and the review in the uni paper would call her performance 'endlessly charming' and 'dynamite', and wherever he was, Nightingale would see it, and he would feel absolutely terrible.

'So tell me about the new director,' Ella said. 'What's their deal?'

'His name's Will,' Libby replied. 'I've never met him before, but he was really nice. He let me ramble about the play for, like, a thousand hours and pretended not to be bored.'

Ella's eyes lit up. 'Do you like him?'

He'd smiled at her when she'd finished her monologue. *Wow,* he'd said, his eyes glittering behind his glasses with what seemed like genuine enthusiasm, *way to set the bar high, Libby,* and for the first time that day, she hadn't felt freezing cold.

'I met him for five seconds, Ella,' she said instead.

'Yeah, but this is high praise coming from you. Is he hot?'

'Calm down. And what do you mean, *high praise*? I said that he was nice and he pretended not to be bored, not that merely entering his presence made me swoon like someone in a period drama.'

'Answer the question.'

'Fine,' Libby replied. 'He's ... not un-hot, I guess?'

'That tells me nothing. Can you find his Instagram or something?'

Libby pulled her phone out while Ella went back to her pasta sauce. 'Oh shit,' she said. 'There are sixty-three messages in the Uni Rep group chat.'

'Is everyone still freaked out about the – what do we call the Nightingale thing? Is it fraud? I want to call it fraud.'

Libby scrolled through the messages. *Who the hell is this Will guy? Do any of us know him?*

IKR? Is he some random off the street?

I don't understand why Graham didn't just ask one of us to do it.

So many of us have been gagging for the chance to direct.

Why didn't they just ask you, Ned?

Literally who is he?

'So?' Ella said, putting the lid on her saucepan with a clank. 'Everyone still mad?'

'No – well, I mean, yes, they are, but that's not what the drama is,' Libby said. 'It's all about Will.'

'Do they want to marry him too?'

'I do not want to— ohhhhhhhhhh.'

'What?'

'You're going to have to reserve all that excitement about me potentially getting an actual role for another occasion, and cancel that wedding you just started planning,' Libby said, feeling like her stomach was being slowly filled with concrete. 'I'm not getting Beatrice.'

'What? No! How do you know?'

'Because Will's dating someone, so she's definitely going to get it. Remember Caroline Lewis?'

'Is she the one that was Mary Magdalene in *Jesus Christ Superstar*?'

'No, that was Rosie Waters. Caro's the one from *A Chorus Line* – "Dance Ten, Looks Three"?'

Ella looked at her blankly.

'Her chicken fillet fell out on Opening Night and she ran offstage crying?'

'Right, yep yep yep, gotcha. Everyone was horrible to her because she should have just kept calm and carried on, right?'

'Well, kind of,' Libby said. 'You can't just run offstage because something goes mildly wrong. You've got to suck it up and improvise and – not the point. Anyway: Caro's on the Uni Rep committee, nominally as one of the student reps, but realistically because she's Graham's granddaughter.'

'He's the president, right?'

'Well, not exactly the president. Kind of ... the faculty supervisor, I guess? He's the reason Uni Rep is allowed to use the campus theatre space for free. It's complicated. And not important to this story. Anyway, according to Genevieve ...' Libby waggled her phone, '... when everyone was in an uproar over the Nightingale thing, Caro was like *hey, Grandpa, here's an idea, how about my boyfriend directs?* and he was like *yeah, cool, seems like a legit solution* and now here we are.'

Here they were. Back where they started. In a place where a dude smiled at her once and she, like an idiot, took it to mean that he was actually vaguely interested in what she brought to the table.

Ella's bolognaise no longer smelled quite so good.

'So he has connections and a girlfriend,' Ella said. 'That doesn't take away from the fact that he seemed like a genuinely good guy. Maybe you still have a shot.'

Libby shook her head. 'That's not the way it works.'

'You do recognise that that's deeply screwed up, right?' Ella said. 'Like, there is something seriously wrong with that. That's some casting couch bullshit.'

'Of course I do,' Libby said. 'But … directors have their favourites, you know? It sucks, but it's not exactly surprising that it's the people they're sleeping with.'

Ella still looked unimpressed, but she didn't press harder. 'I'm sorry, honey,' she said.

'Yeah,' Libby said, sighing. 'Me too.'

She threw herself into work for the rest of the day to distract from the feeling that the concrete in her stomach had hardened into a solid lump. Genevieve hadn't emailed through her essay yet, but she had three others sitting in her ProofItLibby email inbox from students finishing up their winter session classes, as well as an invitation to quote on editing an Honours thesis. She made herself power through all of them, only stopping occasionally to make herself a cup of tea, or, when Ella went to work, to stir the pasta sauce, even though the smell made her feel slightly queasy.

It still wasn't enough. If it wasn't the memory of Nightingale's fingers on her skin, his breath hot against her ear, it was the thought of Will's crooked smile as he looked at her, apparently genuinely interested in what she had to say.

Maybe Ella was right. Maybe it would be different this time.

Maybe that interest had been real, and not an act. Maybe his smile wasn't, *lol it's cute she thinks she has a shot at Beatrice.*

But she'd let herself get her hopes up before. It was never different.

She forced herself to concentrate on the Classics essay she was proofing on heroes in the *Iliad*.

Hero. She wasn't going to get Beatrice, but maybe she could play Hero. Or Margaret. And realistically, Will was going to have a million girls audition but nowhere near as many dudes, so maybe he'd gender-flip some of the other roles. Perhaps she could be an awesome lady Don Pedro or something.

It wasn't what she wanted, but it would still be better than any role that Nightingale had ever given her. He hadn't even done what Ned did in *Rapunzel* and let her understudy. He'd just relegated her to the chorus, every single time. He'd barely even noticed she'd existed until—

No. She wasn't thinking about that night in the Swamp any more. It was over. She wasn't pregnant, the STI check she'd had at the uni clinic had come back clean, and not even Ella knew she'd ever had even the vaguest attraction to him.

Nightingale was gone, and it was a good thing, because he was terrible, and it was going to be one thousand times easier to forget about him without him in her face every day. Plus, even if Beatrice was off the table, working with Will was going to be better. She'd rambled, and he'd listened, and he'd smiled, even.

Nightingale had smiled too. He'd smiled his magnetic smile in everyone's faces while he'd been stealing their money. He'd smiled it at her, and she'd followed him into the Swamp without thinking twice.

Will had listened to her when she told him she wanted to play

Beatrice, and he'd smiled, and he'd kept smiling even though he knew that the thing that she wanted was entirely out of her grasp. He might be new to Uni Rep, but he was just as much an actor as the rest of them.

She wasn't the only one who was good at pretending.

Chapter Two

'That'll be thirty-nine dollars and ninety-five cents.'

'This is such a lovely bookshop,' the white-haired lady said, fumbling for her wallet. She had reading glasses on a chain around her neck, and they kept getting stuck under the strap of her handbag. 'Every time I come in here, I end up buying something.'

'I'm glad you like it,' Libby said, smiling politely. 'Here's your change. Did you want a bag with this one?'

'If you wouldn't mind.' She put her wallet back in her handbag, taking three tries to fasten the clasp. 'I must say, it's wonderful to see young ladies like you reading and not bothering your head about the Netflix and all of that.'

Libby handed her the bag. 'Have a lovely evening.'

'You too.'

The bell on the door jangled happily as the old lady left. Libby glanced at the clock. Five minutes had passed since the last time she looked at it. Glancing around to check there were no customers in the shop, she allowed herself a very theatrical groan.

It wasn't that she didn't like her job. She did. She loved the books. Her co-workers were great. She even liked most of the customers. But the late-night Thursday shift (why somewhere as small as Terravale bothered with late-night shopping, she had no idea) was a killer, especially in winter. It was late and it was dark and the wind was howling outside, a cold salty whip cracking off the sea.

There was one last box of books to process left over from the afternoon. She unpacked it quickly, piling books in haphazard towers on the side counter and fishing around for the invoice. When the bell above the door jangled again, she was elbow-deep in packing beans. 'Good evening, welcome to Terravale Terrace Bookshop!' she said over her shoulder. 'How can I— what the hell are you doing here?'

'Excuse me?' He turned around.

She clapped her hand to her mouth. 'Oh my God, I'm so sorry. I thought you were someone else.'

He raised an eyebrow. 'You thought I was someone else? Where do you live, a soap opera?'

'It's true!' she said. 'You look like someone I know. That I used to know. I only saw you from the back, and— God, I'm so sorry.'

He grunted and turned away, tilting his head to read the spines of the books in the sci-fi/fantasy section. Libby resisted the urge to bury her head in her hands, or possibly put it through the wall. She grasped the edge of the till instead, trying to slow her heart rate.

He wasn't Nightingale. He didn't even look slightly like him from the front. Nightingale's skin was so pale he looked like a vampire. This guy was East Asian.

But something in her entirely refused to believe that it wasn't him – with his back to her, hands in the pockets of his grey overcoat (just like the one Nightingale wore), black hair spilling over his collar (was it longer than Nightingale's? Maybe? Barely? Just?). And then there was that same set to his shoulders, the one that said, *oh, you think I care about a single thing you're saying?*

He was going to turn around. He was going to turn around and the last few moments would turn out to be some kind of bizarre hallucination, because Nightingale would be walking towards her, that wicked smile on his face, and she would melt, or she would scream, or she would melt *and* scream, and—

He turned. 'This one,' he said.

'Sure,' she said, concentrating fiercely on keeping her hands steady as she took *The Fifth Season* from him. 'Good choice. It's a good book. The whole trilogy is.'

'You've read it?'

'I do work in a bookstore.'

He raised an eyebrow – just one eyebrow, perfectly arched, like he was a reaction gif labelled 'why are you like this?'.

'I am so sorry,' she said. 'That thing earlier – seriously, you look so much like—'

'Somebody that you used to know, I got it. You're that Gotye song made flesh. How much?'

'Twenty-two ninety-nine. Do you want a bag?'

'No.'

He tapped his card, then slid the book into the pocket of his overcoat. 'Thanks,' he said.

'You're wel—'

One of the tottering towers of books on the counter chose that moment to fall over spectacularly, littering the floor with books. 'Sorry, sorry, sorry!' she said. 'It's been one of those nights – I can't even—'

The bell above the door jangled. He was gone.

The wind was still howling over the waves when she locked the shop at half-past eight, bringing with it a chilly damp that penetrated through clothes and flesh down to the bone. She loved this walk home in summer, when the sun had only just set and its dying rays spilled over the sea, bathing everything in a warm orange glow, and the little bars dotting the road past the beach were packed. But tonight the streets were empty, and her footsteps were the only sound apart from the whistle of the wind and the distant crash of the grey waves.

It started to rain, first a cold mist and then steady, hard. She turned her collar up and popped her umbrella, angling it carefully so the wind didn't turn it inside out. She wanted to put her headphones in to drown out her thoughts. But she was a young woman walking home alone at night, and she still needed to be alert, even in a suburb that was hibernating for the winter.

What if it had been him?

What the hell *are you doing here?* she would have said.

Queen Elizabeth, he would have replied, turning. *What kind of greeting is that for an old friend?*

You can't be here, Nightingale, she'd say. She would try to keep her voice steady, but it would shake. *You know you can't be here.*

He would walk towards her, that wicked smile of his on the lips that had kissed her everywhere. *I couldn't stop thinking about you,* he would whisper, and he'd be close now, very close, only a breath away, and—

'Libby?'

She had to squint through the rain to see who was in the car idling beside her. 'Will? What are you doing out here?'

'Firstly, I'm being surprised at seeing anyone out in this weather, and secondly, waiting for you to get in the car,' he said, taking one hand off the steering wheel and leaning over to open the passenger door. 'Come on, I'll give you a ride.'

'It's fine. I'm not far from home.'

'And it's dark, and it's raining, and it's freezing,' he said, raising his voice pointedly over the rain hammering her umbrella. 'Get in.'

She paused.

'I'm not an axe murderer. I promise.'

'Okay, okay, you twisted my arm.'

She slid into the passenger seat and closed the door, dropping her bag and her umbrella at her feet. Will's car was much cleaner than Ella's, which was always full of accumulated bottles and food wrappers no matter how often she cleaned it. But maybe Will had just managed to corral his mess better. Out of the corner of her eye, Libby could see a pile of textbooks and papers that had slumped sideways and was now strewn across almost the entire backseat.

'All good?' Will asked. 'Do you need me to put the heater on?'

'I'm fine,' she said. 'Thank you. You really didn't have to do this.'

'Leave a damsel in distress all alone on the side of the road in the middle of a storm?' he said, pulling out from the kerb. 'My mothers would be so ashamed.'

'Firstly, I'm not in distress, and secondly, it's not even raining that hard,' Libby said.

Will raised his eyebrows (both of them, he did not have the same reaction gif quality as the guy from the bookstore) as the rain pelted the windscreen.

'Fine, okay, maybe it is,' Libby said. 'What I'm trying to say here, in the most circuitous way possible – I did warn you that I ramble – is thank you. And please don't axe-murder me.'

'You're very welcome, and you're safe with me, I swear, even though I do realise that *I'm not an axe murderer* is exactly what an axe murderer would say. You'll have to give me some directions – left or right up here?'

'Left. I hope I'm not far out of your way.'

'Terravale is not that big. I don't think there's anywhere that qualifies as *out of the way*,' Will said, turning left at the intersection. 'Plus, I'm running early anyway, so you're doing me a favour. What were you doing out there at this time of night?'

'I just finished work. We stay open late on Thursdays.'

'Where do you work?'

'Terravale Terrace Bookshop.'

'Oh, you must know Catriona!'

'Of course I do,' Libby said, a little startled. 'She trained me when I first started. How do you know her?'

'Uni,' Will replied. 'Well, that and the fact that she dated my brother for about five minutes, but it's really uni. We've been in all the same Stats classes since first year. We had to do a group assessment task once, and you come out of that experience either friends for life or mortal enemies.'

'I take it you're now mortal enemies, then.'

'Oh, absolutely, hundred percent. Catriona and me, it's all blood vengeance and retribution, that kind of thing. Are you going to her wedding?'

'Sure am. I'm looking forward to it. Are you going too?'

'Indeed I am. I guess I'll see you there.'

Libby cast about desperately for something to say next that wasn't *surely you'll see me before that, because you're going to put me in* Much Ado, *right? Right?* 'What about you? What are you running early for at this time of night? I didn't realise anything ever happened out here in the 'burbs after eight pm.'

'Slight time miscalculation,' Will said. 'I live up near campus, but my girlfriend lives around here. Caro? You must know Caro. She has a date night thing planned.'

'Oh, okay.' She kept her tone as light as she could.

Will glanced sideways at her. 'You like her that much, hey?'

'No! I mean, yes. I mean – let me start that again. I like Caro fine. We just—'

'You don't need to lie,' he said. 'I know she's not winning any Uni Rep popularity contests anytime soon.'

'I'm not lying. I just don't know her that well. She's been one of the principals in the shows we've done together – or sometimes the choreographer – and I've just been chorus.'

She regretted the words the second they came out of her mouth. 'Not that I want to stay in the chorus,' she added hastily. 'Because I don't.'

'Libby, don't worry, you don't need to defend your track record to me,' he said. 'I know Uni Rep's got this whole inner-circle cliquey thing going on, but I'm not interested in perpetuating it. I'm going to cast this show off audition, plain and simple.'

'Cool,' Libby said, because she didn't know what else she could say. 'Um, left up here.'

Will flicked his indicator on. 'I wish there was some kind of accepted audition process for crew as well as cast. I have no idea how I'm going to find a production designer.'

'You're not going to use Ackroyd? He's done sets and costumes for nearly every show since—'

'Uni Rep began, I know, but I don't trust him as far as I can throw him. As far as I can tell, there's no way that Nightingale could have pulled off his scam without Ackroyd being in on it, and – sorry, I shouldn't be talking to you about this.'

'I won't tell anyone.'

'Tell whoever you like,' Will said. 'I just don't want to talk shit about your friends to your face.'

'Oh. Don't worry. Ackroyd and I aren't friends. I'm pretty sure he thinks my name is Lily.'

'Seems on brand. I met him yesterday, and he kept calling me Bill. There's no way I'm going to work with him, but Caro says there's no one else, so now I have to work out where you find people willing to design sets in this town for zero dollars.'

'This might be your lucky day,' Libby said. 'I know someone.'

'You do?!' He didn't take his eyes off the road, but she saw his face light up.

'Don't get too excited, because I don't know if she'd agree to do it, but my best friend would do a great job.'

'The other Elizabeth?'

Libby blinked. 'You remembered?'

'The conversation was only a few days ago. Of course I do,' Will said. 'What's her experience?'

'She – Ella, she goes by Ella – is an amazing artist. She's at the Fine Arts school at uni, studying painting.'

'Wow. That's a pretty competitive program, right?'

Libby nodded. 'We grew up in this little town in the middle of nowhere, and we decided we wanted to leave together for uni. We picked Terravale because Ella got into the Fine Arts school. I can do Arts/Law literally anywhere. She's an amazing artist, so she could do sets, and I'm pretty sure she could do costumes too. She made her own Year Twelve formal dress, and it was gorgeous.'

'Can you get her to call me?'

'Sometimes she needs a bit of coaxing to try new things, but I'll do my best.'

'Look, if she's even a little bit talented – and she's not secretly embezzling money from the theatre – I'd love to see what she can do. Otherwise I'm going to end up doing it myself, and that would be a disaster.'

Will pulled to a stop in front of Libby's apartment building. 'Thanks for the ride,' she said.

'Don't thank me,' he said. 'I should be thanking you. You delivered a designer right into my hands in my hour of greatest need.'

'I think there are these chickens, and you're counting them before they're hatched. Or laid. The chickens that were supposed to lay the eggs are still eggs themselves.'

'Don't kill my buzz.'

'Sorry,' she said. 'I'll bully Ella into calling you. I promise.'

'Thank you. Let me give you my number.'

Libby handed him her phone.

'Oh, and while I have you,' he said, typing in his number and then handing it back, 'I'm running a callback at the theatre next Monday at seven. Can you make it?'

'You're calling me back?'

'No, I want you to come and make the tea,' Will replied. 'Of course I'm calling you back. Did you really think I wouldn't?'

'It's just ...' Libby's mouth went dry. 'I know so many people auditioned, and ...'

Will grinned his crooked grin. 'Don't undersell yourself, Libby Lawrence,' he said. 'I'm expecting a lot from you.'

On Monday night, though, she was pretty sure that Will's expectations were unfounded. It had been a long morning in the bookshop, a longer afternoon in her Week 1 Torts lecture and seminar (God, how was she going to survive this subject?), and she'd got drenched in the pouring rain on the walk between the Law building and the theatre. She'd got even more drenched in the five minutes it took her to psych herself up enough to walk round the corner and up the steps.

Nightingale wasn't there. Of course he wasn't.

But maybe he'd been with Uni Rep so long that his absence had left a hole that the universe had decreed must be filled.

That was physics, wasn't it? She hadn't taken any science classes past Year Ten, but she was pretty sure that that was physics. All actions needed an equal and opposite reaction, matter could not be created or destroyed but only moved around, et cetera, et cetera?

Nightingale wasn't there, but someone else was.

The guy from the bookshop was leaning against the wall outside the dirty glass doors of the theatre, smoking. He was wearing a leather jacket, and he looked like a poster for a remake of a movie that would have originally starred James Dean.

What was the appropriate thing to do? Should she pretend like she didn't see him, and just walk straight into the theatre? Smile awkwardly in recognition, and then fake a phone call? Greet him openly and warmly like they were old friends, and then die of embarrassment when he was like, 'sorry, who are you again?'

'Hey,' he said, flicking ash off the end of his cigarette.

'Hi,' she said.

He took another drag. The silence went on a moment too long.

'How are you enjoying—' she started.

'Oh my God, Libs, you're here,' Ella said, barrelling up the stairs. 'Where have you been? I've been waiting in my car for like twenty minutes for you to get here so I didn't have to go inside and hang out with a bunch of people I barely know and make small talk and— Hi, I'm Ella.'

She switched her oversized art portfolio to her other hand and extended her hand to the guy from the bookshop.

He stubbed out his cigarette and took it. 'Roarke.'

'And I'm Libby,' Libby said. 'Shall we ...?'

'Oh, yeah, sure,' Ella said. 'Nice to meet you, Roarke.'

'Nice to meet you too, Ella.' His eyes flickered to her. 'Libby.'

She felt like she should say something, some sort of sassy exit line, but she just made a vague sort of noise and pulled Ella inside the theatre.

Things in there were more familiar, at least. She left Ella in Genevieve's custody – 'Oh, great, you're auditioning to be the new Ackroyd?' Genevieve said. 'That's awesome. Will'll come down once he's got the groupwork going and chat to you. I hope he likes you, because I am super excited about having a designer that doesn't stare at my tits instead of my face whenever he talks to me' – and went with the other called-back actors up to the studio. There were about twenty of them altogether, most of them people she knew, and most of them people who'd played principal roles before. Maybe all that stuff Will had said about shaking up the system and saying no to nepotism had been a bit of an exaggeration.

Caro Lewis was three chairs round from her in the circle.

'Hi everyone,' Will said.

She saw the looks exchanged. Phones vibrated all around the room, and she wondered who was rude – or bold – enough to be posting shit in the group chat while he was literally speaking.

'As you should all know by now, my name is Will Callahan,' he went on, apparently – or least pretending to be – oblivious, 'and I'm the director of *Much Ado About Nothing*. I might have been a last-minute ring-in, but I'm determined to make this show awesome, and I'm counting on the people in this room to help me. Congratulations on making it through to the callback stage. A lot of people auditioned and we've already said goodbye to some very talented actors, so you should all be very proud of yourselves.'

Someone had clearly provided him with the script for Things

You Must Say In A Callback. Everyone applauded politely, because that was what you did.

'As I came into this project rather late in the piece, we're still working on putting a production team together,' Will continued, 'but I'll introduce you now to the people we do have. She's downstairs at the moment, but Genevieve Leung will be our production and stage manager.'

More polite applause, and an appreciative holler from Ned.

'A lot of you already know Richard Lomu, who'll be designing lights and sounds. Hopefully I'll be able to introduce you to our production designer sooner rather than later.'

'Where's Ackroyd?' someone asked.

'Not here,' Will replied. 'Right. Let's break into groups of four – mix the genders up, where you possibly can – and let's get started.'

'Libby! It's late! What are you still doing here? Callback's over! Go home!'

Libby looked up from her Torts textbook, which she'd balanced against the arm of the leather chair she was sitting in. 'I'm waiting for Ella,' she said to Ned. 'She's still talking to Will.'

'Ella?'

'My best friend.'

'Libby dobbed her in to do production design,' Genevieve said, snaking her hand around Ned's elbow. 'I was chatting to her before while you were all being fabulous upstairs. She rules.'

'I still can't believe he gave Ackroyd the flick,' Ned said. 'I'm sure your mate is great, Libs, but Ackroyd is an *institution*.'

'Not all institutions are good, Nedward,' Genevieve said,

poking him in the side. 'You know who else was an institution? Harvey Weinstein.'

'Yeah, yeah, I know, Ackroyd's a nightmare,' Ned said. 'But without him, you and Rich are the only people on the production team with any proper experience, Gen. Sometimes you need a bit of institution.'

'Will has experience.'

They all turned. Caro was standing on the other side of the foyer, arms folded.

'Caro,' Ned said, 'don't get me wrong, because he seems fine, but he's an accountant, not a director.'

'Just because he hasn't directed at Uni Rep before doesn't mean he hasn't directed,' Caro said. 'Just because he's good with numbers doesn't mean he doesn't know anything about theatre. And just because you think you run this place doesn't mean you're not a total arsehole, Ned.'

She wheeled around. The auditorium doors swung shut behind her, and Libby could hear the clacking of her heels on the floorboards as she stormed away.

'Caro really should be a better actor than she is,' Ned said. 'She's got great dramatic timing.'

'I'm missing something here,' Libby said. 'What do you mean, Will's an accountant?'

He hadn't felt like an accountant up in the studio. He'd run warm-ups just as capably as any of the directors Libby had ever worked with. He'd split them into groups to do scene work, and he'd come over and given her a few directions, and they'd just *clicked* in her brain, and she knew in her bones she'd turned in the best callback performance of her life.

'You know how Caro got Will this director gig?' Ned said. 'It wasn't the only gig she got him.'

'Stop making it sound way worse than it is,' Genevieve said, smacking his shoulder. 'Will did us a massive favour. Uni Rep's been leaking money for a while, and we've been trying to push through this motion in committee to set aside some funds to get a proper accountant to look at the books, rather than just me and my one semester of accounting that I barely passed. But it kept getting voted down as an unnecessary expense – mostly because the uni gives Graham basically no money, but also because Nightingale has been in his ear since the beginning of time.'

'He's the one Caro should be calling an arsehole,' Ned muttered.

'Anyway, Caro introduced Graham to Will, because they've apparently been dating for a while now,' Genevieve went on, 'and Graham realised Will is, like, a mathematical genius or something, and he was like, *hey, you're into my terrible granddaughter for some reason, want to look at the books?* and Will was like, *sure*, and now ... here we are.'

'So – wait,' Libby said. 'Will was the one that caught Nightingale?'

'Caught, and then replaced,' Ned said. 'Pretty nifty manoeuvre. You sure you don't want a lift home, Libs? It's nearly midnight.'

'I'm fine.'

'Oh, thank you for looking over that essay!' Genevieve said over her shoulder, as she and Ned were halfway out the door. 'You're a superstar.'

'My pleasure.'

She tried to focus on her Torts textbook, but failed. Not just because there were a thousand pictures of Nightingale staring down at her from the old cast photos on the walls.

Will had caught Nightingale. Will.

Who *was* he?

It was probably only a few minutes until Will and Ella emerged, but it felt like hours. She read the same three sentences in her textbook about fifty times and took in no words at all.

'... really think this will work out,' Will was saying. 'We've got a production meeting at three tomorrow.'

'This is going to be awesome. Thanks so much for taking a chance on me.'

'Thanks for saving my arse – and maybe thank your flatmate, for telling me about you. Hey, Libby.'

'Hey, Will,' Libby said, stuffing her textbook into her bag. 'I take it it worked out.'

'It worked out,' Will said.

'I'm going to be a theatre kid!' Ella said. 'Just like you, Elizabeth Two.'

'If I get in,' Libby said.

It seemed like the perfect opportunity for Will to say 'of course you got in, here's who you'll be playing', but he didn't.

The callback had gone well, she reminded herself. It had gone so well. He'd given her good direction, and she'd followed it. What more could he want?

She saw Will and Caro again through the plate-glass windows as she and Ella drove back past the theatre. They were hugging, Will's chin resting on Caro's blonde head.

She'd been better than Caro in the callback. Caro might have been with Uni Rep forever and had better roles, but she knew – she *knew* – she was a better actor.

Pity it wasn't going to matter.

Chapter Three

Um, did anyone see this? Annalise posted in the group chat while Libby was in her Tuesday afternoon Nineteenth-Century Lit seminar.

It was an ad for a karaoke night the next day at the uni bar. *Cash prizes, bitches,* Annalise wrote. *Who's in?*

Hell yes, Ned sent back.

Me too!

What's the judging criteria?

FFS Bruni, it's not The Voice.

Yeah, but who decides the winners? It's a valid question.

I have to work, but bring the glory home to Uni Rep, guys.

Momentarily curious, Libby clicked on the list of people who were in the group chat. Caro wasn't one of them.

Someone had deleted Nightingale at some stage as well. She wondered who'd made that call. Ned, maybe.

She texted Ella. *Hey, a bunch of Uni Rep people are going to karaoke tomorrow night. Want to come? Might be a cool chance to get to know everyone.*

Will I have to sing?

No. I'll protect you.

Then sure. ☺

The debate over the karaoke judging system was still raging in the group chat. *I'll be there,* she sent, and then put her phone down so she could pay attention to her tutor.

She didn't pick it up again until later that afternoon, during her deathly boring Constitutional Law lecture. There was only a trickle of messages in the group chat, because the debate had apparently been resolved – *okay, since apparently none of you care about ethics in karaoke judging, I called the bar, and they said it's by applause, which seems like some bullshit, but surely we can applaud louder than everyone else if enough of us turn up*, Michael Bruni had written – but she had a new email in her ProofItLibby inbox.

Hi there Libbie, I was wondering if you would be interested in writing some essays for me??? Topics – Sociology (contemporary society) and ethics?? How much do you charge?? I can pay $50 each?? Pls write back asap. – John

Hi John, she wrote back. *Obviously I can't simply write these essays for you, for ethical reasons, but once you've written them, I'd be happy to proofread. I charge $20 per 1000 words and double if you need them back within 24 hours. L.*

She got a new email alert immediately, and sighed. She'd been down this road before when people tried to use her proofreading service for contract cheating. She wondered which slur it would be this time.

But it wasn't.

Hi Queen Elizabeth –

Just thought I'd send you a quick email to see how you're doing. Sorry I didn't say goodbye, but things are messy with me & Uni Rep right now.

I'm doing ok, tho – I've scored a few gigs up here now (turns out people like my singing? Whaaaaaaaaaaat?). Hope you're ok too. I've been thinking about you.

Hit me back when you have time. Tell me all about Much Ado – *did you get in? Who'd they get to replace me? Hope you don't like them as much as you like me. ;)*

Nighty xxx.

She wanted to yell. She wanted to scream. She wanted to punch the wall, or at the very least put her head between her legs and breathe deeply for at least ten minutes.

The Constitutional Law slides swam in front of her eyes. The flimsy plastic table under her elbows felt like it was shaking. She bit her lip until she could taste blood, and then pressed her tongue as hard as she could against the roof of her mouth until she was sure she wasn't going to break down in the middle of the lecture theatre.

He'd only just sent that email. If she replied right now, he'd probably see it straight away.

What could she possibly say?

Dear Nightingale –

Never contact me again.

Regards,

Elizabeth Lawrence.

Dear Nightingale –

You can't just write to me out of the blue like this. You stole $8000. Why would I ever want to talk to you again?

Libby.

Dear Nightingale –

Now you're talking to me? How many girls did you email before you decided to try me?

PS. I know you're just trying to pump me for information about Uni Rep. It's not going to work. I'm the smart girl, remember?

PPS. I'm not pregnant. Thanks for asking.

Dear Nightingale –

I've been thinking about you too.

L. x

She gave herself the same advice she gave Ella whenever she

was dealing with a dude who wouldn't take no for an answer. Delete it. Block him. Never think about him again. He's not worth your time and your energy.

She managed to not reply.

'Libs!' Michael said, when she and Ella arrived at the uni bar the next night, navigating their way around the stickiest patches of the floor to where the Uni Rep people were sitting against one of the walls, right under the *Thursday night: Karaoke and $7 jugs!* sign. They were near the corridor to the toilets, and the vague smell was mingling with the aroma of fried food and stale beer. 'I hope you've brought your cheering lungs. We need to smash this.'

'Um, I hope she's brought her singing lungs, Bruni,' Ned said, leaning over to kiss her on the cheek. 'Didn't you hear her during the *Rapunzel* understudy show? Girl's got pipes. Hey Libs.'

'Hey.' Ned was being so friendly lately. It was nice, but God, it was strange. 'Um, everyone, this is Ella. She's my flatmate and my best friend, and she's the new production designer on *Much Ado.*'

'Hi, Ella,' Ned said. 'Welcome! Gen's told me a bunch about you.'

'I hope it was nice,' Ella said.

'Of course it was. You ladies need a drink? I'm buying a jug.'

Libby and Ella both nodded. Ned disappeared to the bar, skirting nimbly around a crowd of guys watching footy on the big TV in the corner.

They ended up having to shove four tables together to make enough room for all the Uni Rep people who'd turned up. Libby and Ella ended up at one end, crowded in a corner with Ned, Genevieve, and a few others.

'We need to come up with a plan of attack,' Michael said, jabbing his finger into the tabletop. 'One, quality, but two, quantity. We need to stack the karaoke list with our people so that no one else has a chance to interject, but we need to plan beforehand who's going to win so that—'

'God, Bruni, why are you so serious about this?' Annalise interrupted. 'It's pub karaoke. Calm down.'

'Um, maybe because I want us to win? I don't know about you, Lise, but some of us would like to have the spare cash to pay our car regos, and take our beloved Anthonies out for our anniversaries, and—'

'Hate to break it to you, my dude, but I don't think anyone's paying their car rego off their karaoke winnings,' Rashmi said. 'In all that recon you did, did you think to check how much the prize was?'

Michael looked at her.

'Fifty bucks.'

'Shit, really? That'll barely cover drinks!'

'If you win,' Annalise said, snagging the karaoke song list out of his hands. 'I've decided I'm now taking this extremely seriously and plan to defeat you.'

'There's also a wooden spoon prize,' Rashmi said. 'Twenty bucks. So if we want to be strategic about it, maybe we should also send up our worst singer. Try for both prizes.'

'Maybe it's not about worst performance,' Ned said, topping up his beer from the jug. 'Maybe it's about song choice. What would be the least popular thing we could sing here?'

'Probably musical theatre,' Libby said. 'It's a uni bar. No one likes that here but us.'

'Except *Hamilton*,' Rashmi interjected.

'Well, obviously except *Hamilton*, but if we went, like, really clichéd musical theatre? Full *Glee*? Everyone would be like *ugh, drama kids, how annoying* and we'd get totally wooden spooned.'

'I like it, I like it,' Ned said slowly. 'You're a soprano, right, Libs?'

'There or thereabouts.'

'Reckon you can hit Christine's notes in *Phantom of the Opera*? Up for a duet?'

'Nooooooo,' Genevieve groaned. 'Don't make me listen to that, please.'

'I thought you liked listening to me sing. Isn't that why you fell in love with me?'

'Nope,' Genevieve said. 'It was the tight pants you wore in *Peter Pan*.'

'You're so romantic, Leung. Really.'

'You were in *Peter Pan*, right, Libby?' Ella asked.

Libby nodded. 'Chorus. I think that's where you and I first met, Gen.'

'Ah yes, my one and only attempt at being a star,' Genevieve said. 'What a nightmare that was.'

'But you got to look at my arse in very tight pants,' Ned said, slinging his arm around the back of her chair. 'So how bad could it have been?'

'How bad could it have been?' Genevieve said, poking him in the ribs. 'I was so thirsty for you it caused me actual physical pain, and I'm pretty sure you didn't even know my name until production week.'

'In my defence,' Ned said, ducking away, 'there were like fifty people in that show. Nightingale majorly overcast.'

'Fifty?' Ella said. 'How did you all manage to fit backstage?

Will showed me around there the other night, and those dressing rooms are tiny. And one of them is so full of old costumes you can't even go in there.'

Ned and Genevieve both snickered. 'No one goes in the Swamp to get dressed, trust me,' Genevieve said.

'Have you come up with any plans for the design yet?' Libby asked.

Everyone at the table looked at Ella. Libby felt her tense up, like she was a gazelle about to flee.

'You're thinking twenties, right?' she prompted her.

'Right,' Ella said, reaching for her glass and taking a drink. 'I talked about it with Will. They're all coming back from a war at the beginning, but it's such a frothy, sparkly sort of play that we wanted something fun, so ... twenties.'

'That's cool,' Ned said.

'Can I wear one of those flapper headbands?' Annalise asked.

'You've got to get in first,' Michael said.

'We've all got to get in first,' Ned said. 'God knows how this is all going to go.'

'Oh, please, I can tell you exactly how,' Annalise said. 'You're going to spend the next few months stage-kissing Caro in front of her boyfriend, and she's going to feel really weird about it, and she'll have some kind of breakdown and run off the stage in tears, and it's going to be a disaster.'

'Come on, Lise, that's mean,' Rashmi said.

'It's true, though,' Annalise said. 'Like, no shade on Caro—'

'—that was extreme shade.'

'But she's not cut out to be an actor,' Annalise said. 'Choreographer? Yes. Great. Loved what she did with *Rapunzel*. But we all know she's a stage disaster. You're going to end up saving her in every single show, Ned.'

'There's no guarantee I'm going to get Benedick.'

Half the table snorted.

'There's not,' Ned protested. 'I'd like it, obviously, but that guy who was in your group at callbacks was great, Rashmi.'

'His name's Roarke. I think, anyway. He wasn't a big talker.'

'The only person that for sure has a role sewn up is Caro,' Ned said. 'The rest of us have to cross our fingers and pray.'

'Will's taking his sweet time deciding,' Michael said. 'Any idea when we're going to find out, Gen?'

'You didn't hear this from me,' Genevieve said, 'but it should be tomorrow afternoon or tomorrow night.'

It was more than an hour – and a few drinks – later that they were called up to sing. The lights on the tiny pub stage were bright and Libby was blinded for a second as the bad karaoke backing track started.

For a moment, she was back onstage at Uni Rep, Nightingale's hand warm in hers as they took their curtain call on that one day she had been allowed to be a princess.

The kiss that had been a stage kiss, until it wasn't. The kiss that a braver girl – a smarter girl – would have raised hell about.

I've been thinking about you.

She forced herself to concentrate on the words scrolling across the screen. She should have missed her cue, but she didn't.

She squinted out at the crowd while Ned was singing the Phantom's verse. The Uni Rep crowd were enthusiastically booing him (they'd been gentler with her, she noticed – she wasn't surprised that she wasn't yet worthy of that level of enthusiasm). He stuck his middle finger up at them, still singing, and that was when she noticed that Roarke was there, leaning against the bar, watching her.

He caught her eye and raised his drink at her. She'd never been more embarrassed in her entire life.

'Nailed it,' Ned said, high-fiving her as they walked offstage to the sound of raucous booing. 'That wooden spoon is ours for sure.'

'It's been an honour and a privilege,' she said. 'I hope to serve with you again.'

'Oh, you will,' he said. 'Where have you been hiding that voice, angel of music? I know it's pub karaoke and the mics are shitty as hell, but you can seriously sing.'

'Thanks.'

'I mean it, Libby,' Ned said. 'If I'd known you could sing like that, then I would have promoted you out of the chorus ages ago.'

Libby refrained from mentioning that he'd heard her sing plenty of times before, and smiled in response.

'Hey, did you see whatshisface out there?' Ned asked. 'The Asian guy from auditions? He was at the bar with some blonde chick?'

'I saw him,' she said. 'I didn't see the girl.'

'I'm not sure he saw her either,' he said. 'He was staring at you. Like, *staring* at you.'

'Come off it, he was not.'

Ned waggled his eyebrows. 'It must be your turn to have a scandalous showmance, Libs. Maybe he can be the Claudio to your Hero, and—'

'How do you know he was staring at me? He could have been staring at you. If he's a theatre type, there's, what, a ninety percent chance he's gay?'

'Let's ask him.'

'Don't you dare!' Libby exclaimed, catching his arm.

Ned gave her an odd look. 'Are you okay, Libs?'

'Yeah, yeah, I'm fine,' she said, trying to recover her equilibrium. 'Just – if he's going to be in *Much Ado*, I'd rather not make it awkward before the show even starts, you know? Go and sit down. I'll go and buy another jug.'

Mercifully, when she got to the bar, Roarke was gone.

The next day, she tried to pretend she wasn't waiting for her phone to ring.

She sat at her desk. She diligently ploughed through her Torts and Con Law homework. She made some notes for an English essay due in a couple of weeks. She had one new ProofItLibby email – thankfully not from Nightingale – but it was only a short report, and it didn't take her long at all.

She tried to get ahead on her sociology reading. She tried to read for pleasure. She tried to watch Netflix.

'I'm going to an exhibition opening at the art school tonight,' Ella said. 'Wanna come? There'll be free wine and suspicious cheese.'

Libby shook her head. 'Gen said we'd hear back from Will about *Much Ado* today.'

'You can take the call at the gallery. It's not like the theatre. You don't have to be silent all the time.'

'Sorry.'

'All right, all right,' Ella said. 'This isn't my first rodeo. Wallow in your emotions. But text me as soon as you hear, all right?'

'I will. Eat all the suspicious cheese for me.'

Ella left. It got dark.

She didn't turn on the light. She couldn't read or pay attention to anything, so there didn't seem to be a point. She could feel her nerves like someone had turned them to metal, and they were jangling inside her skin.

Her mum had given her a few scented votive candles last Christmas that were supposed to be calming, so she dug one out, found an old saucer for it, and lit it, setting it on the coffee table. That killed a bit of time.

For all his faults, Nightingale would have called by now.

He'd directed the first show she'd ever done at Uni Rep. She and Ella had only been living in Terravale for a month, and they'd seen the poster advertising auditions for *Twelfth Night* in the student union building when they ducked into the campus convenience store to buy bread. 'You should audition,' Ella had told her.

'No,' she'd half-heartedly protested.

'Come on, Libs, I know you've got all that talent locked up in there,' Ella had said. 'I went to all your plays back home. I saw you get your Queen Margaret on. You'd be great.'

'I don't know.'

Ella reached over and ripped the tab with the theatre contact details off the bottom of the poster. 'You're doing it,' she said definitively. 'We said we were going to try new things when we moved, and you're going to try a new thing. The worst that can happen is that you don't get in, right?'

But Libby had made the mistake of fantasising. She'd gone over the script again and again and envisioned herself playing Viola. She'd prepared meticulously for her audition, and she'd gone in there confident.

She thought the audition had gone well. She hadn't been under the Nightingale spell then, but he still had that magical ability to make you feel like the only person in the world when he focused his attention on you. She'd been convinced that she was going to get the role.

'Hi Elizabeth,' Nightingale had said when he called her a few days later. 'Great news! I'm going to cast you in *Twelfth Night*. I want you to play a bunch of roles. Mostly non-speaking, though we might be able to give you a few lines here and there. It'll be a lot of fun. Sound cool?'

'Sounds great,' she'd said, although it'd felt like there was a golf ball in the back of her throat.

She'd swallowed it. She'd gone to rehearsal. She'd met people, made friends, and learned the way it worked. 'A bunch of us were in the uni theatre program when it got defunded two years ago,' Rosie Waters had told her one day, halfway through being fitted for one of her Viola costumes. 'Ned and I were only in first year, but Nightingale was, like, one semester away from finishing the major ... anyway, it was a mess. But the uni still owns the theatre, so Graham worked it out so we could have access to it for free if we were an official university society. Then we had to fight like hell to *become* a society, and then we had to work out how to make enough money to keep going, and then we had to work out how you even run a theatre company, and ... now we're bonded, you know? Being on the front lines for a fight like that makes you stick together.'

'I wish I'd been there,' Libby had said.

'No, you don't,' said Rosie. 'It was a lot of paperwork and going to student union meetings and angsting about money. It wasn't fun.'

Libby believed her. But all that fighting and meeting and angsting had made them into something, and God, she wanted to be part of it. A proper part, not just someone who blended into the background in the chorus.

That meant there were people she had to impress. Ned, for one.

Nightingale.

He was a nepotistic dickhead. She knew that. She *knew* that.

But despite that – despite the fact he mostly only gave roles to people he knew, and good female roles tended to go to whoever he was sleeping with – he'd given her a role in every show of his she'd ever auditioned for. *Twelfth Night. Peter Pan. Jack and the Beanstalk.* Surely that meant ...

No. She was not going to measure her self-worth by whether or not Nightingale had cast her in things. He was a terrible person.

Plus, he wasn't important, not anymore. He was gone. He wasn't making the decisions. He had no power over her.

What would he have decided, though?

Hi Queen Elizabeth, he would have said when she picked up the phone. *Good news for you. I've cast you as Beatrice. Is that cool?*

Yes, she'd have said. *Of course it is. Thank you.*

His voice would change. *I've been thinking about you,* he'd say softly. *Are you at home?*

Yes.

Can I come over?

No no no no no no. No. *No.*

That wasn't how it would have gone, anyway. *Hi Libby, it's me,* he'd have said. *Great news! I'm going to cast you in* Much Ado. *I want you to play a bunch of roles – mostly non-speaking, though we might be able to give you a few lines here and there. It'll be a lot of fun. Sound cool?*

And she'd have agreed that yes, it would be a lot of fun, because she had no spine.

Or maybe that night in the Swamp had been so terrible for

him that he'd just strike her out on principle. *Hi Libby, sorry, couldn't fit you into the cast this time. Lots of talented people and all that.*

Oh, she'd reply.

At least if Will didn't cast her, it wouldn't be because she was bad at sex. It'd just be because she was bad at acting.

She picked up her phone and scrolled through it, just in case she'd somehow accidentally missed the call.

She was halfway through a solo game of Words With Friends when her candle fell over and went out. She rescued it, burning her fingers on the hot wax. She blew on them before trying three times to re-light the candle. The fourth time, the flame caught too much of the match and she swore and dropped it on the table.

Her phone rang.

She dived for it, nearly going headfirst onto the floor. She knocked it off the table and had to scrabble for it behind the couch before she snatched it up, answering it after what seemed an inappropriately long time. 'Hi Will,' she said, doing her best to sound cool. 'Sorry, I was cooking in the other room and didn't hear my phone ringing.'

'No problems,' he said. 'How are you?'

'I'm good. How are you?'

'Also good. So: I have some news.'

Sorry, Libby, but we haven't been able to fit you in. You did wonderfully in the callback, but we had a lot of incredibly talented people audition, and the bar was set very high. You came close, but in the end, I'm afraid there just wasn't room for you.

That's all right, she'd say lightly. *I understand.*

Thank you for sending me Ella, though, he'd say. *And hey, we're always looking for crew, if you'd be up for that.*

'Okay,' she managed.

Your audition was very good, but—

I was impressed with your performance, but—

You're very talented, but—

'After a lot of deliberation, I've finished casting for *Much Ado*, and—'

I'm very sorry, but—

'—I'm very happy to tell you that you're in. I can't wait to work with you.'

She nearly melted into a puddle next to the ruin of her candle. 'Thank you, Will,' she said. 'That's fantastic news. I can't wait to work with you either.'

'So much enthusiasm, and I haven't even told you the best part yet.' She could hear the crooked grin in his voice. 'I've given it a lot of thought, and I want you to play—'

Hero.

Margaret.

Awesome genderbent Don Pedro.

'Beatrice.'

'What?' she said sharply.

'I want you to play Beatrice,' he said. 'Is that going to be a problem?'

'No,' she said, unable to restrain the smile breaking over her face. 'That's absolutely no problem at all.'

Interlude – Roarke

It was a new moon, and the world was very dark. The streetlights along the road had been vandalised. Roarke knew from experience that they usually went out if you kicked them hard enough, which was probably not the best thing when you lived in a street almost entirely populated by perpetually drunk uni students. Dimly, by the sweeping beams of the lighthouse, he could make out the windsock on the hill, snapping in the fierce wind whipping off the sea.

The air was freezing and salty, but he went out into the backyard anyway, shutting the screen door softly behind him. No matter how many windows he opened or fans he switched on, there always seemed to come a point when the house got too crowded, too close, too full of people and bodies and noise, and he had to get out. He was glad their sharehouse had a garden. He didn't know how he would survive without the sky.

He breathed the night air in deeply, drawing it round him like a cape. Even when there was no one in the house, he was never alone there. He could always feel his housemates, smell them, sense them, sticky wine glasses and laughter making him feel claustrophobic.

The memory of some people lasted longer than others. Some were robust, lingering on the palate for hours after they had gone. Some were less overt, and often he found himself thinking they had vanished minutes after their departure, but then he'd find them again, floating in dark corners like phantoms. Will, the last time he had been here, had been like a lion. Wherever Roarke had turned for days afterwards, Will seemed to be prowling and shaking his mane, demanding a response. *Audition,* the lion had growled. *I know how talented you are. Don't waste it.*

Celeste did not linger. She was his favourite housemate, because he could forget she had ever been there ten minutes after she had left. Sometimes he forgot her while she was still there, jumping three feet in the air when she put her hand on his shoulder.

He was the arsehole, he knew.

He couldn't see into her room from the backyard, but he could picture her, sprawled on her bed, hair spread around her like so much wheat, the dim light from her bedside lamp turning it to gold as she sobbed into her pillow.

Maybe he should go inside. Sit beside her. Stroke her hair. Tell her he was sorry.

He wasn't sorry, though. It had been the right thing to do.

Even if he hadn't meant to do it. He'd just got home from a dinner shift at the restaurant, and a minute later, she had knocked on his door (not unexpected) and he had let her in (expected).

He'd pulled her close for a kiss (like he always did, when the door was closed behind them), but she'd pulled back (which she rarely did). 'Roarke,' she'd said. 'I don't think I can do this anymore.'

Her eyes were willing him to reassure her (not unusual).

He committed nothing (as usual). 'What do you mean?'

'This, Roarke!' she'd said. 'Us! This – whatever this is! I – just – what is this?'

'What do you want me to say?'

'I want you to tell me what this is,' she'd said. 'What are we doing here? What is this? Am I your girlfriend? Are we friends with benefits? Am I anything to you at all? In your mind, what is this?'

'I don't know, Celeste,' he'd said. 'If you don't know, what makes you think I know?'

'What do you want this to be?'

He didn't know what to say.

'You mean so much to me, Roarke.' She was shaking, tears in her eyes, voice wavering. 'So much. But you don't give anything back.'

He'd given something back. He'd kissed her.

She'd pulled away almost immediately. 'No,' she told him. 'That's not what I mean.'

'I know,' he'd said. 'I know, Celeste.'

She'd touched his hand, running her index finger down one of his veins. 'Does this mean anything at all to you?'

'Of course it does,' he'd replied. 'But I just want things to be easy.'

'Then I'm going to make things easy for you,' she'd said. 'Do you want me to be your girlfriend? Yes or no?'

He hadn't wanted to answer. He'd wanted to sit there in silence and let her do the work.

But he thought of his mother: those few faded, perfect memories that his stepfather had not managed to stamp all over and smash into pieces. The ones that never lingered, no matter how much he wanted them to. She had named him after the romantic hero from her favourite book series. That Roarke, Book Roarke, the Roarke his mother had loved – he would not remain silent.

And this Roarke, the real Roarke, the Roarke his mother would have loved, if she'd lived – even he knew that he owed Celeste more than that.

'No,' he said.

'All right, then.' She'd stood up.

'Celeste, I'm sorry.'

'Don't be,' she'd said. 'I asked the question, after all.'

The door closed behind her. The room felt very small. He knew he'd done the right thing, because even though she was gone, she lingered.

He was almost grateful, really, when they asked him to leave. 'We've all agreed,' Janie said. 'The lease is up soon, and I think it'd be easier for all of us if you left and we looked for a new housemate.'

They were raring for a fight. He could see it in Tim's tensed shoulders, Janie's balled fists, the way they positioned themselves in front of Celeste, like he was going to leap at her and scream in her face.

A few years ago, he might have given them one, but he knew better now.

'That's fine,' he said. 'I understand.'

'It doesn't mean we're not still friends,' Janie said. 'And that we can't still hang out.'

'We'll come and see your play,' Tim said. 'Make sure you tell us when it is, all right?'

'I get it, you guys,' he said. 'Really. You don't have to worry about my feelings. I'm not fragile. I'll be fine.'

'Do you have somewhere to go?' Celeste asked quietly.

'Yes,' he said. 'I'll go to my brother's. He offered to let me move in with him ages ago. He could use someone to help him pay the rent.'

'Are you sure?' she said. 'I know things are complicated with you and your brother.'

'Celeste,' he said, 'please don't worry about me.'

Her expression didn't change. She cared about him, cared too much, and God, it made him uncomfortable.

Of course you can move in, Will texted back. *Thank you.*

Why are you thanking me? You're the one doing me a favour.

Rent isn't cheap. Between thesis / theatre / WDYT I don't exactly have time to get a job + my scholarship limits the number of hours I can work anyway + I know I can live with you.

Roarke knew exactly what Will meant when he said 'I know I can live with you'. He meant 'we've lived together before, so we know how to do it, and you won't be some stranger I don't know getting in my face when I need to work and taking all my *Beautiful Mind* equations off the wall'.

He wanted to deliberately misinterpret. *You can 'live with' me?* he wanted to send back. *Sorry to be such a burden.*

Will wouldn't text back. He'd call. 'You're not a burden, Roarke,' he'd say. 'Do we have to have this argument again?'

They would. It would end where it always did, with Roarke yelling, 'I didn't ask you to save me!' and Will saying, 'I wasn't going to leave you!'. Will would keep reaching out his hand, and

Roarke would keep slapping it away, and he would never, ever admit that he was afraid that Will would one day stop reaching.

His phone buzzed again. *Do you want to come round for dinner? You can check out the room + we can figure out when you want to move in.*

Ok, he sent back. *Can I bring anything?*

No, don't worry about it.

'How much is the rent?' he asked Will over dinner, sitting at the scratched dining table Will had inherited from his grandma, both of them drinking the beer he'd brought. Will had gone even more Russell-Crowe-in-*A-Beautiful-Mind* than the last time Roarke had been here. There had been half a wall's worth of equations pinned up in the living room then, but now the wall was nearly totally covered in papers with Will's scribbled numbers.

Will named a figure. Roarke raised an eyebrow. 'Is that how much you pay?'

'No,' Will said. 'I pay a bit more.'

'Fifty/fifty,' Roarke said. 'We split it fifty/fifty.'

'I have the master. It makes sense that I pay more.'

'Stop doing me favours.'

'How about you see the room before you make any decisions?'

'I've seen it plenty of times. Fifty/fifty or I find somewhere else.'

'Okay, okay, fine,' Will said. 'If you want to pay more than the room's worth, then go ahead.'

'Thank you.'

He took a swig of his beer, feeling vaguely like he'd achieved something, when Will said, 'I want you to play Benedick.'

He wanted to throw the bottle against the wall. *What did I just tell you?* he wanted to yell.

But that was what the husband his mother had once loved would have done, and if he became a man like that, it would break her heart.

He set the bottle down firmly on the table instead, right over the longest scratch, a deep groove that ran down its length. 'Will,' he said, 'I'm not your charity case anymore.'

'This isn't charity,' Will said. 'I'm way out of my depth, and I need at least one person I know and trust to do a good job in the trenches with me.'

Roarke had worked out a lot of lines of defence against Will in the years since the Callahans had fostered him, but this was the one that skewered him every time. *I need you.*

Will's phone rang. 'It's Caro,' he said. 'Do you mind ...?'

'No worries.'

He took a fresh beer with him and went out onto the balcony so Will could have privacy to pretend he wasn't three quarters of the way to breaking up to his girlfriend. The sun had set. The houses below were silhouettes dotted with lit windows, gradually giving way to the sprawl of the campus. The wind was cold and clean, the chill refreshing, the beer surprisingly good considering how cheap it had been, and for a few moments, looking up at the stars, Roarke was entirely, blissfully alone.

Chapter Four

The first time Libby had walked up the theatre stairs for rehearsal, she'd been a green eighteen-year-old, totally new not just to Uni Rep but to university and to Terravale. Even though she was slightly offended that she hadn't merited more than non-speaking chorus roles in *Twelfth Night*, she'd never felt more nervous. Everyone had seemed to know each other, chatting and hugging – and what if they were amazing actors? What if they were all so much better than her that they laughed at her?

She'd seriously considered just turning on her heel. *Oh, sorry,* she'd say breezily to Nightingale if he called to ask why she hadn't turned up. *Something else came up.*

Every time she'd walked up the stairs for the first rehearsal of a new show since then, she'd felt a little less nervous. Now she was one of the ones who was chatting and hugging everyone, and every so often, she'd catch the eye of a newbie on the outside, standing there awkwardly. She'd feel a bit sorry for them, but mostly grateful that she wasn't one of them anymore.

Not this time, though. She was a hundred times more nervous walking up the stairs on Saturday afternoon for the first read-through of *Much Ado* than she had been that first time, and more thrilled about it than she had been about – well, anything, really.

'Libby!' Ned roared, sweeping off her feet.

'Ned!' she said, laughing. 'Put me down!'

He obliged, but he didn't let go. 'I'm so happy for you, honestly,' he murmured into her ear. 'You deserve the hell out of this. You're going to smash it.'

'Thank you,' she said, as they separated. 'That means a lot, Ned, coming from you.'

'He's right,' Genevieve said, coming up and hugging her as well. 'You're going to smash this so hard there'll be shards all over the stage.'

'That's – weirdly violent? But thank you.'

'I just wish old mate here was going to be smashing it with you,' Genevieve said, draping Ned's arm across her shoulders.

'Excuse me, I am going to smash it plenty,' Ned said. 'I am going to make Claudio the most interesting character in the universe, and I defy any of you to stop me. By the end of the play, everyone's going to be all, 'um, Benedick who?' and be rooting for me to whisk Beatrice off her feet.' He nudged Libby with his elbow.

'I think Hero might be a little bit upset about that, given that she's your actual love interest and all.'

'Somehow, I don't think I'm going to be number one on the list of people Hero is upset with,' Ned said, looking pointedly across the room to where Caro stood beside Will, closer than a regular acquaintance would stand, but not touching him at all.

The group chat had blown up about half an hour after Libby got off the phone with Will. ('You're the first one I called,' he'd told her. 'I wanted to make someone happy before I let people down.') *Sooooo what did we all get?* Rashmi had posted. *Because I'm genderbent Don John & I can't WAIT to villainise all of your arses.*

I'm Don Pedro! Heidi had written back. *I guess our family had some confusing parentage, lil bro.*

If Denzel and Keanu can do it, so can we, Rashmi had replied. *Who else? Roll call.*

I got Margaret, Annalise had written. *IDK who that is???*

I'm Claudio, Ned had posted.

UM WHAT

Literally WTF Ned?!?!?!

Are you joking?!

Nope, Ned had written. *I'm Claudio.*

Who's Benedick, then?

Is it that new guy?

Maybe it's Bruni?

Not me, Michael had written back. *I'm Leonato. & Anthony's playing my brother, which isn't going to be awkward AT ALL.*

It's the new guy, Genevieve had confirmed. *Will just sent me through the full cast list.*

What's his name again?

Rourke, Rashmi had answered.

It's spelled Roarke, Genevieve had replied. *Roarke Rivera.*

So we all know Caro got Beatrice, Michael had written. *Who got that other chick role? Or is that one genderbent too? God knows this thing could use some gay love.*

Caro didn't get Beatrice, Genevieve had replied.

Libby had held her breath, watching dots appear and disappear on the screen as people tried to react appropriately.

Annalise got in first. *Who the hell did then?*

I did, Libby had posted.

Weirdly, she'd been scared. *What do you mean, you got Beatrice?* she'd imagined someone saying. *You haven't earned that.*

Of course they didn't. *OMG, Libby, congratulations!* Rashmi had written.

That's awesome!

So thrilled for you.

You deserve this so much, babe.

The fear had dissipated, but not all the way. *Of course they have to say that,* she'd thought to herself, and then, *Nightingale was always the one who was brutally honest.*

So what about Caro? Annalise had asked.

She's Hero, Genevieve had replied.

Huh, Annalise had written. *So it looks like I was right about you spending the next few months making out with her under her bf's nose until she has a nervous breakdown, Ned. Any bets on when it'll happen?*

Libby accidentally made eye contact with Caro across the room. She didn't want to look away, so she offered what she hoped was a friendly smile instead.

Caro stared at her for three full seconds before turning away and wrapping her arms around Will's waist.

'This is going to be awkward, isn't it?' Libby asked Ned and Genevieve.

'It's theatre, Libs,' Ned replied. 'We all get roles that other people want. It's not up to you to make yourself less shiny just because someone else is jealous.'

She made a noise of acknowledgement, privately thinking that it was very easy to say that when you'd been getting every role you wanted since you started wanting roles.

'Are you going to practice what you preach?' Genevieve asked Ned.

'I,' he said, 'am going to be a perfect gentleman to the new guy. Just you watch.'

Roarke chose that moment to lope up the theatre steps. He knocked lightly on the window for Will's attention, before miming the universal gesture for *smoke?*, tapping his wrist, and raising an eyebrow questioningly.

Will shook his head no. 'Okay, everyone, let's head upstairs!' he called. 'Let's get started.

They sat in a circle in the studio, in a cobbled-together assemblage of ratty couches and plastic chairs. Most of the faces were familiar – for all that *Much Ado* represented a shake-up, a lot of Uni Rep regulars were there – but there were more newbies than Libby ever remembered seeing before.

Or maybe it just felt like it, she thought, looking around and trying to count them. There were … three, including Roarke. Four if she counted Will. Maybe without Nightingale there, everything felt new and unfamiliar and alien.

For a single, traitorous second, she missed him so badly her whole body ached.

'Welcome to the first read-through of *Much Ado About Nothing*!' Will announced.

She forced the feeling away.

'First of all, congratulations on making it in. The competition was stiff, and I had a tough time making my choices, but I'm positive you'll all do a fantastic job.'

A platitude, sure, but it was true. There was stiff competition, and she'd beaten it. She was going to do a fantastic job or die trying and if – when – Nightingale heard about how good she was, he was going to feel *terrible*.

'I'm sure most of you know each other already, but we've got a few Uni Rep virgins, myself included,' Will went on. 'So we're going to start out with a basic icebreaker. We'll go round the circle, and I want you to tell me your name, who you're playing, where you were born, and something no one else in the room knows about you. All right?'

There was a chorus of vague affirmatives. They all knew this game. It had been one of Nightingale's go-tos. *It's time for the deep dark secret game*, he'd purr. *I want your name, your character, where you were born, and your deepest, darkest secret. Don't be shy, now.*

'Right, I'll start. I'm Will Callahan—'

I'm Nightingale Smith—

'—I'm the director—'

— I'm behind the desk on this one—

'—I was born in Leicester in the UK—'

—I was born to a pair of hippies right here in Terravale, because you can't get rid of me—

'—and my middle name, about which I am very embarrassed, is Earnshaw.'

He would look right into her eyes when he said it. *And I screwed Libby Lawrence senseless in the Swamp*, he'd say, *and she loved it*, and then he'd smile, and he'd wink at her, and the laughter would start around the circle: slowly, slowly, then all at once.

'I knew that,' Caro said.

'What?' Will said.

'About your middle name. You have to say something no one knows.'

'Right you are,' Will said. 'Let me think ... okay. One time I juggled knives in a carnival.'

'I knew that,' Roarke said. 'I was there.'

'It appears that I am an open book,' Will said, apparently oblivious to the amount of significant glances being exchanged around the circle. 'All right. When I'm nervous or anxious, I calculate pi to calm myself down. Because I am a huge mathematical nerd, and that is the kind of thing I do. Your turn, Roarke.'

Libby wondered if Roarke could feel everyone staring at

him. She hoped he could. She didn't have room to think or feel anything much, what with the space that, (a) Nightingale and (b) sheer joy at being cast, were taking up in her brain, but she hadn't been able to forget that feeling she'd had when he watched her at karaoke: that feeling that he could see right through her.

'I'm Roarke Rivera, I'm playing Benedick, I was born in Manila, and the last book I read was *The Fifth Season* by NK Jemisin.'

Even though he wasn't looking at her, she could somehow feel his eyes on her. *Go on, speak up,* he was daring her. *Tell them that you knew that already.*

She stayed silent. The game moved on. He still didn't look at her, but it felt significant, somehow.

'—and I can't ride a bike,' Ned finished.

'Bitch, literally everyone knows that,' Rashmi said.

'It's not my fault I've been here so long you all know my secrets,' Ned protested. 'Let's keep it moving, hey? You go, Libs.'

'Fine,' she said. 'I'm Libby Lawrence. I'm playing Beatrice – about which I am *so* unbelievably excited, let me tell you – I was born in a tiny town called Wimeena, which is in the middle of nowhere, and—'

I slept with Nightingale. It was a stupid decision, and I think I liked him, which is even more stupid, and if anyone finds out I will literally die.

'—and I have graphic fantasies about murdering my Constitutional Law professor,' she said. 'Seriously. I know we've only had one week of class so far this semester, but I've murdered him so many ways in my mind. He is so boring and his class is so dull and these fantasies are literally the only way I can deal with it.'

'Well, that's terrifying,' Will said. 'Please don't axe murder anyone. It would make my life very difficult.'

'I'll do my best,' Libby replied.

He smiled his crooked smile. 'Good.'

'I'm Caroline,' Caro said. 'I'm playing Hero, I was born in Terravale, and here's something no one seems to know: I'm a decent actor, even though I made a horrible mistake on stage one time.'

The pause lasted just a little bit too long.

'Right. Sal's?' Ned asked the company at large, after Will had dismissed them just before five ('go over your scripts, we've got a big week of analysis ahead of us!') and departed, Caro and Roarke following in his wake.

'Sal's,' Michael said, slipping his hand through Anthony's.

'I need grease,' agreed Rashmi.

Sal's was a little fish and chip shop down the road from the theatre, a couple of streets away from campus, located so close to the beach that king tides had been known to lap at their door. It was old but clean, threadbare yellow umbrellas like daffodils above painfully scrubbed plastic tables and aluminium chairs, the rust chipped carefully away. *Salvatorio's Milkbar* was painted in flaking orange paint above the door, the constant onslaught of the sea breeze revealing the worn weatherboard beneath.

Sitting at one of those worn tables eating chips smothered in chicken salt with a group of theatre people was one of the ways you knew you'd made it at Uni Rep. It had taken Libby until her third show to get an invitation. She had been at the bottom of the table that day, watching while Nightingale held court. He had been laughing, and the sunlight had made his dark hair shine, and something she'd only felt once before in her life, when Gerry Bloom had glanced sideways at her in English in Year Eleven, settled deep in her belly. For a second, it had been hard to breathe.

'So. Libby. Spill,' Annalise said when they were all sitting, three tables pushed together to make one long one.

'Spill what?' Libby said.

'What exactly did you do to get this role?' Annalise said. 'Or should I say … *who* did you do?'

'Shut up, Annalise,' Rashmi said. 'You were at the same readthrough as all of us. Libby's awesome. She earned this.'

'Rashmi, my darling, my love—' Michael said.

'Hey,' Anthony objected.

'—you and I and Lise and all of us know Libby deserves this, because she is a mighty and wondrous actor and we should all fall at her feet and weep at her excellence—'

'Um, thanks?' Libby said.

'—but we know this is not how this place works,' Michael said.

'That's so cynical, Bruni,' Heidi said.

'He's always this cynical,' Anthony said.

'I am not cynical,' Michael said. 'I'm right. What we have here is a puzzle, my friends. Our newly imported directorial dictator has someone to bone, and yet he did not cast her. I know he's the mathematician and all, but something does not add up.'

'I don't know what to tell you,' Libby said. 'I auditioned. I did the callback. I did the same things all of you did. If there's some deep dark secret behind me getting cast, I'm not in on it.'

'There is *totally* a deep dark secret,' Michael said. 'There has to be. Spill. Spiiiiilllllll.'

'Leave her alone, Bruni, or I might spiiiiillllllll this all over your head,' Ned said lazily from behind his sunglasses, waving a bottle of Diet Coke in Michael's direction.

'He's got a point, though,' Annalise mused. 'Sure, Libs, you're great, but Will is clearly not the righteous king of Righteouslandia. We all caught that thing where he and the new guy know each other, right? Like, they go way back?'

'The new guy's good, though,' Ned said. 'Sure, they clearly know each other, and I'm as curious as any of you about the backstory there—'

'Nepotismmmmmmmm,' Michael sang under his breath.

'But he's not not-talented,' Ned went on. 'I know it was only a readthrough today, but he was great. If I was directing, I'd cast him.'

'As Benedick?' Anthony said, raising an eyebrow.

'Maybe. He's got charisma.'

'I'm not disputing that he's good,' Annalise said.

'Can we all recognise the fact that he's so hot it hurts to look at him?' Rashmi said. 'I read against him in callbacks and I'm pretty sure I'm pregnant now.'

'But is he really better than you, Ned?' Annalise finished.

Ned held up his hands. 'Maybe he is, maybe he isn't. I've been in Will's shoes. Sometimes what you think as a director doesn't mesh with popular opinion, and you just have to deal with that.'

'I still think it's nepotism,' Michael said. 'They're clearly bros from way back, and then Will just *happens* to cast him in the lead? That's not a coincidence.'

'Maybe they're sleeping together,' Anthony said.

'Will's dating Caro,' Heidi said.

'Will could be bi,' Anthony said. 'I'd hit that – if I wasn't desperately in love with you, darling,' he added, as Michael pouted dramatically.

'Which brings us back to the question – why'd he cast you, Libby?' Annalise said.

'Maybe he's realised what we all already know – i.e. that Caro's the worst – and this is his passive-aggressive way of breaking up with her,' Michael said.

'If casting Libby as Beatrice was Will's diabolical way of sabotaging his own relationship,' Heidi said, 'then what was casting you two as old man dad brothers supposed to do to yours, huh?'

Michael and Anthony looked at each other. 'She's right,' Michael said in a dramatically hushed voice.

'It's over, isn't it?' Anthony said, mock sobbing.

'Oh, shut up, both of you,' Rashmi said. 'Food's here.'

They laughed and ate and threw chips at each other as the sun went down over the harbour. It was cold and the breeze was chilly, but huddled together, it was hard to notice. Pressed between Genevieve and Heidi, Libby had a sudden vision of what it would have been like not to get in, not to be here, and it made her heart stop for a moment.

Thank God Nightingale had disappeared. If people knew what she'd done, then there was no way she'd be sitting at this table now.

Of course you would be, she told herself. *Half the people at this table have slept with Nightingale.*

But if they worked out she'd been stupid enough to like him? They'd laugh. They'd laugh and laugh and laugh, and then she would have ended up like Caro.

There was a girl a few tables away, sitting with a friend, picking at a shared plate of calamari. She had blonde curls pulled back from her face, and for a moment Libby thought it *was* Caro, but then she turned to say something to her friend, and of course it wasn't.

'... sure you're okay?' the girl's friend was saying.

'I'm fine,' the blonde girl said.

She wasn't terribly convincing, Libby thought. Her shoulders were hunched and she wouldn't make eye contact. If she really wanted her friend to believe her, she could have made a bit more of an effort.

'It's for the best,' her friend said. 'You'll have some space, and some distance.'

'I know, I know.'

'Delete him from your phone. No contact. Clean break. Cut him out.'

'He's not skin cancer, Janie. He's my friend.'

'Really? Friend? That's what we're calling it?'

'We were never dating.'

Janie sighed. 'He's such an arsehole.'

'No, he's not.'

'Then why have you been crying over him for a solid week?'

'Because I made the mistake of getting wrapped up in it when it was never like that,' the blonde girl snapped. 'I don't want to talk about it any more, so can you just shut up and stay out of it?!'

Take a beat, Libby thought. *Give it one – two – three – and—*

'Celeste, I care about you,' Janie said, 'and I don't want to see you get hurt. Believe it or not, I care about him as well, and I don't want him to get hurt either.'

'Well, it's too late for that!' Celeste exploded. 'I'm hurt, and he's practically homeless now you and Tim have booted him out, and I might never see him again, so how about next time you decide to try and protect me from the big bad wolf you ask yourself if it's any of your business first?!'

Celeste turned on her heel and stormed away. Janie scrambled to her feet and chased after her. 'Wait!' Libby heard her calling.

There was silence for a moment.

'Well,' Ned said, 'how was that for impromptu theatre?'

'That was some proper soap opera shit,' Rashmi said.

'That last line could have been more effective, though,' Libby said. 'She got all screechy. It would have been way more powerful if she'd gone for quiet-angry.'

'Libs, this lead role thing has gone to your head,' Annalise said, snagging the last couple of chips. 'You're already spending too much time thinking about acting.'

Chapter Five

Her Monday Torts seminar ended at five and rehearsal started at six, which left her with an awkward hour to fill. Libby spent nearly twenty minutes crammed into one of the silent study carrels on the fourth floor of the library trying to make herself (a) understand and (b) interested in their reading for next week, but ended up spending the whole time wondering how long it had taken someone to carve *AMES + STEPH* into the desk. So she gave up, stuffed her textbook into her bag, and set off across campus towards the theatre, stopping in at the convenience store in the student union and buying a discounted cheese and garlic pull-apart for dinner.

Lucky we're only doing script analysis tonight, she thought, thanking the cashier, putting her wallet away, and then tearing off a (definitely going stale) bite. *Roarke would probably murder me if he had to kiss me with garlic breath.*

It wouldn't be tonight, but she was going to have to kiss Roarke at some stage. A lot of times.

The fact that he didn't like her was probably a good thing. He'd be professional, and keep the kissing as chaste and pretend as it was supposed to be.

The bread was like dust in her mouth. She forced herself to swallow.

She checked on her ProofItLibby flier, tacked to the union bulletin board. All the contact detail tabs had been ripped off, so she rummaged around in her bag for another. She did a lot of her advertising on student Facebook groups, but the analogue approach had driven a surprising amount of her business, so she usually kept one or two spares on hand.

She found one. It was slightly crumpled, but she pinned it to the board anyway and did her best to smooth it out. She'd forgotten to cut along the contact detail tabs at the bottom, and so she tried to tear them in straight lines.

'Libby?'

She jumped, slipping and accidentally tearing one of the tabs off. 'I know you say you're not an axe murderer, but you'd probably be really good at it,' she said. 'You can sneak up on people like nobody's business, Will.'

'I'm sorry,' he said. 'I didn't realise you were so intently focused on the bulletin board, or I would have stamped my feet or something – oh hey, it's you!'

'What?'

He tapped her flier. 'We meet at last, my bulletin board buddy.'

'I'm sorry, but I have no idea what you're talking about.'

'I'm hurt,' he said. 'Our fliers hang next to each other on nearly every bulletin board on this campus, and yet the glorious ProofItLibby doesn't recognise me?'

She blinked. He pointed to the flier next to hers.

Then realisation dawned. 'No way,' she said. 'You're Will Do Your Tax?'

'It is I,' he said. 'The Will, who does your tax.'

'That makes so much more sense now I know your name,' she said. 'I'm sorry to have to tell you that I've been judging you for having a boring business name for, like, a solid year now.'

'Ouch. My feelings.'

'But not anymore,' she said. 'Now I know it's a pun, I'm only judging myself.'

'This is good market research, though,' he said, helpfully holding her flier steady so she could continue to tear between the contact tabs. 'I should add that to my fliers. Like a subtitle. Will Do Your Tax – PS, it's a pun, my name is Will and I will do your tax if you pay me.'

'Perfect. Fixed it. No notes.'

She took another bite of her pull-apart and promptly choked. Will smacked her a couple of times on the back. 'You okay?'

'Yeah, yeah, fine,' she said. 'That'll teach me for buying day-old bread for dinner.'

He checked the time on his phone. 'We've got twenty-five minutes before we need to be at the theatre for rehearsal,' he said. 'You up for a little adventure if I can promise you something marginally more edible?'

'Wow, marginally more edible?' she said. 'How can I possibly resist an offer like that?'

They left the student union building. She normally headed straight down the main avenue to the theatre from here – it was only about a five-minute walk, if you did it in a straight line – but Will turned left before they reached the Psych building. 'I'm warning you, this is uncharted territory for me,' Libby said. 'I almost never come to this part of campus.'

'Welcome to the dark side, young padawan,' he said, as they cut through what she was about fifty percent sure was the Physics building. 'You're deep in science country now.'

They took another left on the other side of the building, only to find a sausage sizzle in full swing in front of the School of Mathematical Sciences. 'Welcome to my world,' Will said. 'The SPAM start-of-semester party.'

'SPAM?'

'Society for Physics, Astrophysics and Maths,' Will explained.

'The Uni Rep of the maths and science world.'

They joined the queue for sausages. 'I would have come to the dark side sooner if I knew it had catering,' Libby said. 'We very occasionally get a packet of biscuits in the theatre kitchen, and that's it. Even then, someone's usually eaten all the Kingstons.'

'One, I agree, the Kingston is the king of biscuits,' Will said. 'Secondly, Uni Rep must be the only student society that *doesn't* do a sausage sizzle. One of the first things I worked out when I started uni was that you can get a lot of cheap meals if you just figure out when all the sausage sizzles are.'

'How many are there?'

'I don't have my spreadsheet in front of me.'

'Please tell me that there is legitimately a spreadsheet.'

'I will neither confirm nor deny the existence of the spreadsheet. But I can tell you that you can make it to Week Four if you're smart and dedicated.'

'I'm smart and dedicated,' Libby said. 'And I have an awkward hour between class and rehearsal again on Wednesday. Who's offering the best sausage sizzle on Wednesday evening?'

'Well, I would have to consult the spreadsheet.'

'So it does exist.'

'Once again, I will neither confirm nor deny – stop trying, ProofIt. But I also have an awkward hour on Wednesday, so if you want some company ...'

'Sure,' Libby said.

Will smiled at her. There was a curl falling over his forehead, almost into his eye, and he tried to blow it away. She had the sudden intense urge to push it away for him.

Then his eyes refocused on someone over her shoulder. 'Catriona! Hi!'

'Hi, you,' Catriona said, leaning in to give Will a one-armed hug, carefully holding her half-eaten sausage sizzle away from him with the other hand. 'And Libby! I didn't know you two were ...'

She waggled her eyebrows.

'Oh – no!' Libby said, feeling herself flush bright red. 'We're not. We're—' She wanted to say *friends*, but it felt presumptuous.

'We're friends,' Will said. 'New friends, actually. I'm directing a play with the uni theatre company, and Libby's my leading lady. Onion or no onion, Libby?'

'Onion, please,' she said, finding her composure and grasping it as tightly as she could. 'Thank you.'

They got their sausages and moved out of the way of the queue. 'This is going to make designing the wedding seating chart easier,' Catriona said. 'I'll just stick you all on the same table. Are you still bringing Caro?'

'Yep, still bringing Caro,' Will said.

He really was a sausage sizzle expert, because he was eating his so tidily. Libby studied hers, trying to imagine a universe where sauce *didn't* end up all over her shirt.

'Serviette?' Will said, offering her one.

She took it gratefully.

'You're not bringing anyone, right, Libs?' Catriona asked.

She shook her head. 'Nope. Flying solo.'

'And Roarke isn't either?'

Libby narrowly avoided her second choking fit of the evening.

'Not that I know of,' Will said. 'He just broke up with someone. Well, *broke up* might be a bit generous. You know how he is.'

'Oh, I know,' Catriona said. 'But that works for me. Even numbers. There's eight people per table, and – sorry, I'm going to stop talking, because wedding planning is the most boring subject in the history of the world.'

'We have to go, anyway,' Will said. How had he kept his hands grease-free enough to check his phone? Was he a wizard? 'We have to get to rehearsal.'

Libby had a million questions running through her head as they walked towards the theatre – nearly all of them variations on *so, what's your deal with Roarke?* – but there was no universe in which she could ask them, so they talked about the play instead. 'I've been going through the script and marking all the things I want to look up,' she said, wiping her fingers as thoroughly as she could with the serviette and then lobbing it into a bin. 'Like Beatrice's first line, where she calls Benedick *Signior Mountanto*. What does that mean? I have no idea.'

'Two steps ahead of you,' Will said. 'I also got confused about that line, but I have already looked it up, because that's my fun new method of procrastinating from writing my Honours thesis. Apparently, it's a pun on some sword-fighting technique that's all unnecessary flourishes. She's calling him a wanker, basically.'

'Interesting,' Libby said. 'Is it *just* that, though?'

'What do you mean?'

'If it's all unnecessary flourishes, maybe there's a kernel of vulnerability there. Benedick's coming back from a war. Wouldn't unnecessary flourishes get you killed?'

'Oooh, good point,' Will says. 'And that would make sense, because—'

'Benedick and Beatrice have a history,' Libby said. 'There's that bit where she says *I know you of old* when they're having one of their banter fights, and then that bit with Don Pedro later, where she tells him that once Benedick won her heart from her with – what does she say?'

'False dice.'

'So it would totally make sense for Beatrice to be a little bit vulnerable while also calling Benedick a huge wanker,' she said, as they climbed the theatre stairs. 'Because even though she hates him, she still wants him to be all right.'

He grinned, holding the door open for her. 'I'm really glad you're getting into this. I knew you would, from the way you talked about the play in your audition, but I love that you are.'

'I love that we have a whole week of analysis before we start blocking and stuff,' Libby said. 'We've never done anything like this before. At least not in the shows I've done.'

'I'm big on understanding what you're doing before you actually do it, and not just making it up as you go along,' Will said. 'Maybe that's a very left-brained way to approach directing, but it works for me.'

'It sounds like a pretty excellent life lesson, to tell the truth,' Libby said. 'I wish I understood everything I did before I actually did it.'

'Oh my God, I totally forgot I was supposed to pick you up!' Ella said when Libby walked through the door after rehearsal that night. She was sitting on the living room floor with her hair in a half-collapsed topknot, one of her A3 notebooks open in front of her on the coffee table, the words *MUCH ADO – MASQUERADE CONCEPTS* scrawled across the top.

'It's okay. I didn't have to wait long for the train,' Libby said, throwing her handbag towards her bedroom.

It had still somehow been too long, though. She'd had a great night at rehearsal. Will had led them in a discussion of what would ultimately be the first half of the show before interval, picking apart meanings and motivations, and it had been fascinating. But then, while she'd been sitting at the station, waiting for the train, the messages had started to pour into the group chat.

What a pointless waste of time.

Total snoozefest.

Idk about you guys, but I work out my motivations by ACTING not TALKING ABOUT IT.

ugh. ugh ugh ugh.

I'm so BORED.

It wasn't all bad – *yep, how dare Will, wanting us to understand the words we're saying, what a monster,* Rashmi had written, followed by several eyeroll emojis, and a few people had agreed with her – but they were definitely the minority. *Just because Will doesn't know what he's doing doesn't mean the rest of us don't,* Annalise had written.

Libby had thought about responding. *I actually got a lot out of it,* she might write, or, *at the very least, us having a stronger understanding of the material can't hurt.* She'd even typed out the last message, her thumb hovering over the send button.

But then she'd deleted it. She might be Beatrice, but the wind at Uni Rep could change very fast. The last thing she needed was to be on anyone's bad side.

'You're rehearsing again on Wednesday, right?' Ella asked, taking her hair down then twisting it back up on top of her head. 'I want to come in with my tape measure and take some measurements so I can start on costumes.'

'Yep.'

'Hey.'

'Hmmm?'

'You've got that I-just-took-an-exam-and-I'm-not-sure-I'm-going-to-get-100% look on your face,' Ella said. 'What's wrong?'

Libby sighed and sank down on the floor beside her, leaning her elbows on the coffee table. 'I'm not sure I'm on the same page as everyone,' she said.

She relayed the saga of the rehearsal that she had loved and everyone else had thought was worthless trash.

'So what?' Ella said. 'It's one rehearsal.'

'Two,' Libby said. 'We're doing analysis of the second half of the show on Wednesday.'

'Two rehearsals, fine,' Ella said. 'What's the worst-case scenario? Everyone is annoyed again on Wednesday, and then the world explodes?'

'If they make Will's life annoying enough, he might quit.'

'So what if he did? They'd just find someone else to direct, right?'

'It's not like the pool of directors is that deep,' Libby replied. 'Ned and Nightingale have directed, like, eighty percent of Uni Rep shows between them. And with Ned *in* the show and Nightingale gone ...'

She hadn't thought of Nightingale all night, but now there he was again, fingers all over her thoughts. 'That might be the worst-case scenario,' she said. 'They find Nightingale, the whole money drama goes away somehow, and suddenly he's back directing.'

Sorry, Queen Elizabeth, but I'm going to recast, he'd tell her. *I think we both know you're not ready for the big leagues.*

Ella scoffed. 'You can't just steal eight grand and have that go away.'

'You never met Nightingale,' Libby said. 'If anyone could charm his way back in, it would be him.'

'Ugh,' Ella said. 'Men with charisma. It's such a red flag. If they *can* get away with something, you know they'll do it as soon as they can.'

Libby bit her lip.

This was the perfect opportunity. Right now. *Um, yeah, on that,* she'd say. *Nightingale got it in his head that he could do me. And he did.*

Oh my God, Libby! Ella would say. *Are you all right?*

Yeah, I'm okay. I just don't know how to feel about it.

Are you sure you're all right, though? It's not like you to do something so stupid.

'Here's an idea,' Ella said. 'How about we have a party?'

Libby blinked. 'What?'

'This whole rehearsal/group chat drama just sounds to me like people don't know each other very well yet,' Ella said. 'So they need a bonding exercise! And what bonds people more than being shut together in a small space with a lot of alcohol?'

'I don't know,' Libby said, having visions of herself posting, *so Ella and I are having a party, who wants to come?* to the group chat and no one responding. 'I don't think my social stock at Uni Rep is high enough for anyone to want to come to a party thrown by me.'

'Oh, shut up, Libby, everyone loves parties,' Ella said, waving a hand dismissively. 'Plus, you're the lead. I'm the production designer. If people don't come, I'll threaten to put them in hideous costumes. Easy.'

That was easy for Ella to say. People instinctively *liked* Ella.

'How about Sunday night?' Ella said.

'That's really soon.'

'Please, no one's busy on Sundays,' Ella said. 'Come on, Libs, it'll be fun. Besides, I don't know any of the Uni Rep people that well. I want to feel like one of the family.'

'All right, all right,' Libby said. 'But if no one comes, don't say I didn't warn you.'

'Can I ask you a question?' Libby asked Will on Wednesday evening, as they sat on the low stone wall outside the Engineering building. MESS – the Mechanical Engineering Students Society – had diversified a bit from the standard sausage sizzle, so they were both eating bacon and egg rolls.

'Is it *why do engineers always try to reinvent something that was already perfectly good*?' he asked, studying his roll suspiciously. 'The sausage sizzle is a classic for a reason.'

'Valid question, but no,' Libby said. 'It's ...'

He glanced over at her. 'What?'

'I'm trying to work out a way to phrase it that isn't passive-aggressive. Because it isn't. I'm genuinely curious.'

'Just say it, ProofIt,' he said. 'I'm a big boy. I can take it.'

'What are you doing at Uni Rep?' she asked. 'You're so different to everyone else.'

That was at the heart of the issue, she'd decided, after spending much more time than was sensible agonising over the whole Monday night rehearsal group chat debacle. Will's approach wasn't *bad*. It was just *different*.

Ella was right. She'd been catastrophising. These were just growing pains. And if she could figure out how to sort of smooth the way for Will and his approach a little, then ...

'Different in what way?' he said. 'Because if you mean 'can do basic maths', then yes, I agree with you. The state of the accounts makes it clear that no one who has any idea about numbers has ever been part of Uni Rep.'

'No, that's not what I mean.'

She took a bite of her roll to give herself some thinking time. 'Maybe it's part of it, though,' she said, swallowing. 'There are certain types of people you get at Uni Rep. Like, you can fit most theatre kids into certain boxes. They're not all the same box, but …'

'The boxes are adjacent?'

'Yep,' she said. 'We're nearly all Arts students. We nearly all want to act – like, even the people who do directing or musical directing or choreo or production are on the stage *sometimes*. We don't get a lot of … analytic types. You're this whole other kind of person.'

'So what is a boy like me doing in a place like Uni Rep?' he asked, meeting her eyes and raising his eyebrows.

'You don't have to answer,' she said, suddenly very embarrassed. 'It's invasive. Sorry.'

'No, no, it's fine,' he said, swallowing the last bite of his roll. 'It's not an interesting answer, though. I don't have some secret plan to take Uni Rep over on behalf of all the analytic types of the world and declare victory for the sciences over the arts.'

'Well, shit,' she said. 'I was thinking of defecting.'

Will wiped his fingers on his serviette and straightened his glasses. 'Really, I'm here because … well, because Caro asked me to be, but beyond that, because I've just always loved theatre. Ever since I was a little kid. My mums used to take my sister and I along to these pantos every school holidays, and I loved it. I know it's off-brand for me, but – it got me, you know?'

She nodded. She knew how theatre could get into your veins.

'I never wanted to be an actor, but I started dabbling in directing in high school,' he said. 'I directed Roarke in our high school musical, actually.'

'Roarke was in a *musical*?'

'Don't let his whole dark and tortured Heathcliff thing fool you,' Will said. 'He not only starred in the musical, but wrote all the music for it. He's just as big a theatre dork as anyone at Uni Rep.'

The group chat was going to be very disappointed when they found out that the Will/Roarke backstory was as simple as 'they went to high school together'. The theories about how they knew each other were becoming wilder every day. (*Hear me out: W & C were trying to spice it up in the bedroom, & R was the third they found on the apps, and now they're a full-blown throuple,* Anthony had written a couple of days ago).

'Anyway, I've experimented here and there with theatre while I've been at uni,' Will went on. 'Taken the odd out-of-faculty elective.'

'Like Graham's class.'

'Yep. And I've directed the School of Mathematical Sciences revue for the last two years.'

'I didn't know SMS had a revue.'

'It does,' Will said. 'We rent out the Uni Rep theatre space for it, in fact. That was how I met Caro. She was ushering.'

The group chat would also have capital-T Thoughts about that. The paid usher positions for the shows the theatre space hosted were highly coveted, and the fact that Caro had one was not at all popular.

'You know that you didn't have to wait until now to come and do stuff with Uni Rep, right?' Libby said, swallowing the last bite of her bacon and egg roll. 'You didn't have to limit yourself to the maths nerd revue. You could have done some stuff with us ages ago.'

'I know,' he said. 'And I thought about it, but then I met Caro, and she didn't exactly give Uni Rep a ringing endorsement.'

Oof.

Thankfully Will didn't let the silence linger for long. 'You ready to go? We should make a move if we want to make it to the theatre on time.'

He asked her about how she'd got into theatre – a much safer topic – as they walked over to Uni Rep. 'There was a little amateur society in the next town over from mine,' she said. 'I did a couple of shows with them, but they didn't have a youth company. It was mostly retirees. I liked it, but when you've already been pigeonholed as a nerd, spending most of your spare time with people in their sixties doesn't do great things for your social standing.'

'Ouch,' he said. 'High school is brutal.'

'It's all right, though. I had Ella. Plus, it all worked out. If we hadn't both been miserable, we wouldn't have uprooted ourselves and moved here, and you and I wouldn't be having this conversation, so – a net good, I think.'

'I agree.'

'Did I use 'net' right?' she asked, as he held the theatre door open to her. 'As I'm sure you've worked out by now, I'm not mathematical.'

'You did. Ten out of ten.'

There was a snort from the corner of the foyer that might have been laughter, or derision, or some combination of the two. Libby looked across, and her throat went suddenly dry.

'You're early,' Will said mildly.

'Thanks for telling me,' Roarke replied. He looked like David Bowie in *Labyrinth*, draped artistically sideways across one of the foyer chairs, one foot on the ground, one dangling over one of the arms. 'I never would have noticed otherwise.'

Will shot Roarke a look. Something Libby couldn't quite interpret flickered over Roarke's face. The moment stretched out.

Maybe the group chat was right. The relationship between Will and Roarke seemed a lot more intense than 'oh, we knew each other in high school'.

Thankfully, Ella came sailing in, bolts of fabric over her shoulder. 'Helloooo,' she sang. 'Can I borrow these two lovely actors of yours, Will? I have some measuring to do, and I'm sure you'll want them in rehearsal.'

'Of course,' Will said. 'Go right ahead.'

'Thank you,' Ella said. 'And you're coming to our party, right?'

'Your party?'

'Libby, didn't you invite them?'

Libby had quietly been hoping Ella would forget about the party, but no such luck. 'I, um, was going to make an announcement at the start of rehearsal,' she said. 'Ella and I are throwing a party on Sunday night at our place, for all the cast and crew.'

'You're both coming,' Ella said. 'No arguments.'

'Caro too, obviously,' Libby said to Will.

'Sure. We'll be there.'

'How about you, Roarke?' Ella asked him.

'I wouldn't miss it,' he replied, something that might have been half a smile playing over his lips.

The doorbell rang just as Libby was getting a tray of spring rolls out of the oven. 'Can you get that, Ella?' she called, balancing them awkwardly on top of the microwave. There were already two other trays taking up their meagre kitchen bench space, as well as a bowl of chips and three dips.

'I'm naked!' Ella yelled back. 'They're early!'

Libby looked at the microwave clock. Six thirty. 'Damn straight they're early,' she muttered, shaking off her oven mitts and brushing herself off, hoping she hadn't somehow managed to get anything on her jeans. Outside the kitchen window, the fairy lights they'd wrapped around their balcony railing were glimmering, but about a quarter of them were blown. She'd hoped to get time to fix them, but clearly she wouldn't now.

Nightingale always used to be early to parties. 'Fashionably late is so passé,' she remembered him declaring once, lounging at the head of the table at Sal's, one arm around Heidi, the other around Tessa di Angelo. 'Fashionably early is where it's at. That's when you can get into the good booze before anyone else has touched it.'

'Oh please,' Ned had said, detaching his lips from Rosie Waters' for long enough to reply. 'As if anyone can afford to bring good booze to our parties.'

What would she do, if Nightingale turned up on her doorstep right now? *Hi Queen Elizabeth,* he would say. *You never replied to my email, so I came looking for you. I can't stop thinking about you. Can I come in?*

She would slam the door in his face. Definitely. She would not let him in. He would not pass go. He would not collect two hundred dollars. Not when he'd already collected eight thousand.

She opened the door. She might have been less surprised if it had been Nightingale.

'Hi,' she said blankly.

'Hi,' Caro said. Her blonde hair was pulled back in a ponytail so tight it looked like it might be painful, and she was clutching a bottle of wine with a death grip, knuckles white. 'Um, this is for you.'

'Thanks,' Libby said. 'Make yourself comfortable.'

Caro handed Libby the wine and wandered to the middle of the living room, looking around. 'Nice place,' she said. 'I like the art.'

'Ella painted it all. My flatmate. The one who's designing *Much Ado*.'

'I know who she is.'

'She's an incredible artist. All of these are hers. The landlord won't let us put hooks in the wall, but we got some of those ones with the sticky backs and did the best we could, and – sorry, I should get back to the kitchen. I've got stuff in the oven.'

'Am I the first one here?' Caro asked.

'You're a bit early.'

'Will told me six-thirty.'

'Really?'

'No, I'm lying.'

Libby bit back a retort. 'Sorry,' she said. 'That wasn't meant to be an accusation. He must have got his wires crossed or something.'

'Maybe.'

There was an awkward pause. 'So where is Will?' Libby asked.

'Helping Roarke move. He's moving in with him.'

So their relationship *was* more than old high school acquaintances. Huh.

She wanted to ask for more details, but the moment was already uncomfortable enough. 'Do you want some wine?' she asked, at the same time as Caro said, 'You don't have to be nice to me.'

Another pause, even more awkward.

'You don't have to be nice to me,' Caro said. 'I know you hate me.'

'I don't hate you.'

'Yes, you do,' Caro said. 'Everyone hates me.'

'No, they don't.'

'Really? Ned doesn't hate me? Annalise doesn't hate me? Michael? Anthony? Rashmi? Anyone in the posse of cool kids?'

Libby had never in her life been accused of being in the posse of cool kids before.

'I can't speak for anyone else, but I don't hate you,' she said. 'I don't know you very well, but I don't hate you.'

Caro looked at her for a long moment. Then she exhaled. 'Were you serious about that offer of wine?'

'Absolutely,' Libby said. 'Come into the kitchen. I'll pour, and if you're game, you can help me put some of the frozen shit I whacked into the oven onto plates.'

Caro nodded.

'Ella, wine?' Libby called.

'Yes please!' Ella's voice came faintly back.

All three of them were more than a glass deep by the time the doorbell rang again. It was Rashmi and Heidi, bearing a bottle of wine each. Michael and Anthony arrived soon afterwards, bearing another one. Annalise arrived with two four packs of cruisers, Richard the techie with beer, and Ned and Genevieve with a four-litre cask of goon and a bottle of vodka, which Libby, in the interests of no one vomiting on the carpet, decided to hide.

Ella turned up the music and people started dancing. Libby hopped between conversations and kitchen, visions of the morning-after clean-up she'd gotten herself into becoming more and more terrifyingly clear in her mind.

But they'd all come. Ella had been right. She'd thrown a party, and people had come.

Maybe she really *was* one of the cool kids now.

'Hi,' Will said, polishing his glasses on his shirt and then putting them back on as Libby opened the door for what felt like the fiftieth time. 'Are we late?'

'Nope,' she said, smiling outwardly and wincing inwardly when she saw the two six-packs Roarke was carrying. 'Come on in, make yourselves at home. You can put the booze in the bathroom. The bath is full of ice. Just through – oh, okay.'

Roarke had already peeled off.

'Nice place,' Will said, calling her attention back. 'Are these paintings Ella's? I recognise her style.'

'Sure are.'

'There you are!' Caro said, leaning up to kiss Will hello. 'I've been waiting for you for ages. You told me the wrong time.'

Libby didn't wait to hear Will's apology.

Like Ella had predicted, the flat was way too small for all the people squashed into it. They ate spring rolls and party pies off paper plates, people perching on chairs and laps, squashed together on the couch, sitting cross-legged on the floor. They drank wine from plastic cups, sticky and sparkling, and they talked and laughed and laughed. 'So then Heidi walks over to the flat and picks up the bucket,' Ned said, waving a beer like a conductor's baton, 'turns around to go back to centre, and bam! straight on her head!'

There was uproarious laughter. 'It really hurt!' Heidi protested.

'It would have been really serious if the flat hadn't had doors in it,' Genevieve said, arm around Ned's neck as she sat on his lap. 'We all thought she was a goner. That thing weighed a ton.'

'You should have seen Nightingale run!' Michael said. 'He screamed like a girl!'

'Low-key sexist, Bruni,' Rashmi said. Michael flipped her off.

'Yeah, because it was three days till opening and there was no one to replace me,' Heidi said. 'God knows who he would have got to play Jill if I'd been pancaked.'

'That was one of the reasons I decided to do understudies in *Rapunzel*,' Ned said. 'You never know when someone's going to get murdered by the set.'

'Were you planning on me getting murdered by the set?' Annalise said.

'No, I was planning on Nightingale getting murdered by the set, but tragically the universe didn't help me out.'

'What happened?' Will asked Heidi. 'Were you hurt?'

'Not a scratch on her!' Michael announced. 'The doors opened around her, and she was fine.'

'Speak for yourself!' Heidi said. 'You try having a set piece that weighs a million billion kilograms fall on your head, doors or no doors, and see how you like it!'

'Who knows?' Rashmi said. 'Maybe it would improve his personality.'

'Oh, screw you, Rashmi.'

Libby started clearing some of the paper plates away as Michael and Rashmi went back and forth. Will caught her arm. 'Do you need a hand?'

She shook her head. 'I've got it.'

The party had not moved by the time she was finished, although they were considerably more drunk. Ned's retelling of Uni Rep stories from shows gone by were becoming more and more wild. Annalise was laughing so much she had to put her head between her knees. Michael and Anthony had apparently given up on listening and were making out, squeezed together in an armchair.

There was a smashing sound from the bathroom. 'Sorry,

Libs,' Heidi said sheepishly, holding the neck of a broken beer bottle. 'I hit it on the edge of the bathtub, and—'

'Don't worry about it,' Libby said. 'Here, take a fresh one. I'll clean up.'

She threw the broken glass into the bin, wiped up the beer, and then went into the kitchen to get a dustpan. The smell of cigarette smoke filtered in from the balcony on the other side of the kitchen window, and she wrinkled her nose.

'Can you just be nicer to her?' she heard Will say.

Instinctively, she crouched down behind the bench, dustpan clutched in her fist.

'I am nice to her,' Roarke said.

'Like hell you are, Roarke.'

'What do you want me to do? Serenade her with moonlight sonatas and bouquets of pink roses?'

'Just be civil to her.'

'I am being civil to her.'

'You haven't said a word to her tonight.'

'She hasn't said a word to me!'

'Roarke.'

'You're always like this, Will.' Roarke's words could have been whiny, but his register was low, the tone dangerous. 'You've always been like this. No matter what I do, it'll never be good enough for you.'

'That's not true.' Will's tone was equally dangerous. 'That's not true, and you know it's not.'

'I know what you're trying to do, and it won't work.'

'I want a leading man and a leading lady that get along. Is it so much to ask that you at least pretend to be polite?'

Libby's hand clenched tighter around the dustpan.

'When have you heard me say a harsh word to her?'

'You make her uncomfortable.'

'Well, maybe it's her you should be talking to.'

'Roarke, don't be a dick.'

'Will,' Roarke said, 'you can't socially engineer the world to make it more to your liking.'

'Boys, boys!' Rashmi's voice drifted out. 'Come back to the party!'

Their footsteps moved away. Their conversation ended. That left Libby, fists clenched, free to fume.

She wasn't quite sure what she was angry at, but she knew she was angry. In the bathroom, broken glass clattered into the dustpan so hard as she swept that it leapt right out again. It made a satisfying smashing noise as she dumped it into the bin on top of the rest of Heidi's broken beer bottle, and it made her want to reach into the bathtub, grab another bottle, and smash it as well, just to hear the sound.

So Roarke didn't like her? Fine. That was fine. She'd survived plenty of people not liking her in high school. She'd survive one more.

And what exactly was Will's deal? He'd clearly sent Caro to the party early tonight so she'd get some chance to – bond, or whatever. Was he trying to do that for her and Roarke now too?

How long had he been thinking about that? When he took her on his campus sausage sizzle tour, was it all to work out how he could fix her so Roarke would like her? Was the way he talked to her, all smiles and jokes and interested eyes, just to make sure she delivered the right performance, like she was some sort of machine he could cajole into working better by talking to her the right way?

He didn't want to talk to her. He probably didn't even like her.

He probably went home and curled up with Caro and laughed about her.

She grabbed a bottle of white wine from the bathtub. She looked around for her glass, but she couldn't remember where she'd put it.

'Screw it,' she muttered, and drank straight from the bottle.

'Whoa, Libby!' Genevieve exclaimed when she came out of the bathroom, bottle in hand.

Ned looked over, and a grin spread across his face. 'Here's to Libby –' he started singing.

'She's true blue,' just about everyone joined in – although not, she noticed, Will, who was absorbed in a conversation with Caro. Probably about her. Ugh. 'She's a pisspot, through and through. She's a bastard, so they say. She tried to go to heaven but she went the other way! Drink it down – down – down – down – down!'

Libby obligingly sculled from the wine bottle, and everyone cheered.

A while and half of the bottle later – well, it might have been more than half, but definitely not more than two thirds, no, no, no – she found herself on the sofa, and Roarke was beside her. 'Hi,' she said.

'Hi,' he replied.

He wasn't looking at her. His gaze was focused on some point in the distance – on Ned and Genevieve kissing, or Will and Caro arguing, or Ella pulling someone Libby didn't recognise into the hallway.

She felt like she was on fire, burning up from the inside, and it made her brave. 'Look, Roarke, I know you don't like me,' she said, holding up a finger before he could respond, 'and I want you to know that's all right.'

He was looking at her now, his face unreadable. 'What?'

'I mean it,' she said. 'You don't like me, and I'm cool with that. I don't need, like, all the people in the world to like me. I'm not going to break down in tears because you don't find me the most wonderful, inspiring person you've ever met, and it won't screw up the show. So don't feel like you have to pretend to coddle my feelings or anything, because I'm an *adult*, and I can deal with it when people don't like me.'

'You're drunk.'

'So what? I'm still right. Don't feel like you have to act around me, because nothing sucks as much as when people are pretending all the time.'

She saw a spark catch, somewhere beneath his implacable surface. 'No,' Roarke said. 'It doesn't.'

Chapter Six

Libby woke up the next morning to sun streaming gaily through her open curtains, a wide-open door, and a pounding headache. She was still wearing her clothes from the night before, her jeans digging into her skin. Everything was bleary. Everything was spinning. And there was ... Olivia Rodrigo coming from the kitchen?

She wanted to pull her pillow over her head, but she didn't think she could move. Or that she would ever be able to move again.

'Libby?'

Someone was shaking her shoulder. 'Nnngh?'

'Are you awake?'

She rolled over. It felt like someone was hammering nails into her skull. 'No.'

Ella's face swam into focus. She looked annoyingly perfect. 'Here. Water.'

Libby took the glass, gulped a few big mouthfuls down, and then promptly felt nauseous. 'Oh God.'

Ella sat on the edge of the bed. 'Big night, huh?'

'How did—' she swallowed. She was not going to let herself throw up. 'How did everyone get home?'

'You know, the usual way. Walked. Trained. Ubered. A few were sober enough to drive.'

'I didn't—' oh God, the last time she'd been even a tiny bit tipsy she'd ended up in the Swamp with Nightingale, and she'd gone so far beyond tipsy last night. 'I didn't do anything stupid, did I?'

Ella laughed. 'No. You were very high-functioning, apart from hugging everyone, like, a hundred times. You're a very affectionate drunk, did you know that?'

She made a vague affirmative sound and drank some more water.

'Anyway, we waved them all off, and then you went and fell face down on your bed, and you've been there ever since.'

'What time is it?'

'Just after eleven.'

Libby groaned. 'I have a Torts lecture at one.'

'Just listen to it online. That's what I'm doing with mine.'

'There's a seminar straight after, though. Then rehearsal tonight.'

'Then it's definitely time to get up and think about becoming human again. I'll fry up some stuff. Grease will make you feel better. Have a shower and then come eat something. Up you get!'

'I hate you,' she said, as Ella wrapped her fingers around Libby's wrists and hauled her out of bed. 'I really do.'

'Love you too,' Ella said, pushing her into the bathroom.

Ella was right. She did feel more human after a shower, although her hands were still unsteady as she tried to pick up her toothbrush and her head felt like her brain had liquefied in her skull. Her teeth felt hairy, like moss had grown on them overnight. *How much did I drink?* she wondered. *What did I say?*

Roarke's face swam through her mind. *You don't like me, and I'm cool with that.*

'Shit,' she said to her reflection.

Then Will. *I need you to be nice to her.*

She pulled her hair back severely from her face, pinning it back as tightly as she could manage without it hurting. Her jaw was clenched. She dug her fingers into the muscles near her ears to try and loosen it up, but it didn't work.

'Hi!' someone said as she stumbled into the living room.

Libby blinked.

There was a boy on the sofa. She didn't remember putting a boy on the sofa.

'Hi,' she replied.

'You probably don't remember me,' he said, standing and offering her his hand. 'I'm not surprised. I've done one or two Uni Rep shows before, but not for a few semesters – before your time, I think. I'm Paul.'

'Libby.'

'I know.'

'Um, okay. Where's Ella?'

'Kitchen.'

'Thanks.' She turned on her heel.

'Oh hey, you're up!' Ella said brightly, scraping eggs out of the frying pan onto a plate. The Thelma Plum song playing on her phone ended and a Spotify ad came on.

'What's that about?' Libby hissed.

'That's Paul,' Ella said. 'He's in the show. He plays Conrade.'

'What is he doing here?'

'You can get that judgmental slut-shamey look out of your eyes right now, Elizabeth Two, before I hit you with this frying pan.'

'I'm not – you can sleep with whoever you like!' Libby said. 'But do you have any idea how complicated theatre hook-ups can be?'

'Come off it, Libs, you're always telling me how everyone is sleeping with everyone else. If it was that complicated, there'd be no theatre company left.'

'I mean it! Rosie Waters was with Uni Rep since the beginning, until she hooked up with Nightingale and then – bam! suddenly she's gone.'

'Libby,' Ella said evenly, 'I know you're the one that knows Shakespeare and all, but he's playing a minor role, right?'

'Sure, but—'

'I'm the designer. The only one Will could find. Just say this does go horribly wrong. I'm not the one who's going to be replaced.'

Libby swallowed. 'Ella—'

'I know what I'm doing,' Ella said. 'It's fine. Everything's fine, everyone's fine. Now get out of my way. It's time for breakfast.'

Libby didn't think she could eat a thing, but Ella heaped scrambled eggs high on her plate, over two thick slices of toast, and she ate it all, forcing it through her clenched teeth, unsure if she was starving or if she wanted to throw up.

Surprisingly, she was vaguely grateful for the presence of Paul. He and Ella chattered brightly, and while every syllable felt like someone sticking pins in her eyes, it would have been worse if she'd had to carry on the conversation herself.

'Right,' Ella said eventually. 'I have to go to work. Are you all right to get to uni, Libs?'

'I can give you a ride,' Paul said.

'I'm fine,' Libby said. 'I don't need a babysitter. I'll take the train.'

'See you later,' Ella said. 'There's Panadol if you need it. Drink water. If you get really inspired before you go, there's an interesting stain on the hallway carpet you can take care of.'

Libby groaned. 'Okay.'

'Thank you,' Ella said, kissing the top of Libby's head. 'Feel better.'

'Hey, where's mine?' Paul said, standing and pulling Ella into a long, loud kiss.

Nauseous. She was definitely feeling nauseous.

'Bye,' Ella said, politely but firmly breaking free. The front door clicked shut behind her.

It took Libby a moment or two to realise that Paul hadn't gone with her. 'Let me wash up,' he said.

'No,' she said. 'I'll do it.'

'Please, I want to.'

'Okay. Whatever.'

She was about to go back to her bedroom and hope he'd take the hint when he spoke again. 'So, you're tight with Ned Riordan, right?'

'Lately I am. Why?'

'Just wondering. He must have been pretty pissed he didn't get the lead, hey.'

Paul mustn't be in the group chat. 'Not that he said to me.'

'If Nightingale was still directing—'

'Where is this going?' Libby interrupted.

Paul flashed her a smile, one that she immediately recognised as fake. 'Just making conversation. I'm really excited about the show. Are you?'

'Sure.'

'This is kind of my big break. Ned doesn't like me much, and neither did Nightingale, so I used to get shut out of a lot of shows. I think they were worried that if there was a third straight guy on the scene, I'd cut in on their territory.'

She raised her eyebrows.

'But now I get to do some real acting,' Paul continued,

oblivious. 'I'm so happy Will thought I had the chops for comedy—'

'Will thinks a lot of things,' Libby said, her jaw getting even tighter. 'Look, I've got to get ready for uni. Thanks for the offer to wash up, but you'd better go.'

'Oh, sure,' Paul said. 'See you at rehearsal tonight.'

'You play Conrade, right? Are you even in this scene?'

'Well, no, but I'm keen to see how Will runs his rehearsal room now we're actually going to be on our feet. I'm going to sit in.'

'Okay. Anyway, I have to go in a minute, so ... bye.'

'See you later.'

She waited a beat – two beats – three – after the door closed before she allowed the groan building up in her belly to escape her. She leaned her forehead against the wall. She wanted to sleep for a hundred years. She wanted to hit something.

She settled for washing up instead, working her jaw from side to side, trying to make it relax. She stood with her hands in the scalding water for a long time before she reached for the first dish, the burning sensation almost pleasant.

'Is he not approved in the height a villain that hath slandered, scorned, dishonoured my kinswoman?' Libby raged, clutching her script in one hand and slapping away Roarke with the other, as Benedick reached out to restrain Beatrice. The sound was harsh and loud, like a whip cracking, but it didn't make her feel any better. 'O, that I were a man! What! Bear her in hands until they come to take hands, and then with public accusation, uncover'd slander, unmitigated rancour—'

'Stop,' Will said. 'Let's try that again. Libby, you're getting too angry too fast. It gives you nowhere to go. Pull it back.'

'Fine,' Libby said. Her teeth were locked together so hard it hurt.

Will gestured at Roarke with his pencil. 'From line 298.'

'Is Claudio thine enemy?' Roarke asked.

'You better believe it,' Ned said. 'Libs, what do you say we add in a scragfight scene? You should totally come at me before you send Benedick to take me out. It'd be awesome.'

'Ned, not now,' Will said. 'Roarke, again.'

'Is Claudio thine enemy?'

'Is he not approved in the height a villain that hath slandered, scorned, dishonoured—'

'Stop,' Will said. 'There are commas there, Libby.'

'Fun fact,' Libby said, forcing the words out. 'Shakespeare didn't write with punctuation. It was all added in later.'

'Yeah, well, those editors weren't totally useless. Again.'

'Is Claudio thine enemy?'

'Is he not approved in the height a villain that hath slandered, scorned, dishonoured my kinswoman? O, that I—'

'Stop.'

Libby wanted to punch him. No, she wanted to tear him apart with her bare hands. She glared at him.

'Take five, everyone,' Will said. 'Libby, stay here, please.'

'Do you want me to stay too?' Roarke asked.

'No,' Will said. 'Back up here by half past, everyone.'

Libby walked over to the window. If she looked at him, she'd rip his head off.

The door of the studio snicked closed. 'Libby—'

'Sorry I'm not good enough,' she snapped.

'You're plenty good enough,' he said. 'I just wanted to see if you're feeling all right. You're a bit off your game.'

'I'm fine.'

'Is it Roarke?'

'What do you mean, is it Roarke?'

'I know he can be hard to get along with, but—'

'I don't have a problem with Roarke.'

'Then what's wrong?'

'Nothing.'

'What's he said to you?'

'Nothing!' she said, wheeling to face him. 'It's what you said to him!'

Will looked nonplussed. 'What, 'move further downstage'?'

'I heard you! Out on my balcony! *Oh, Roarke, you need to behave yourself around poor delicate Libby, because she's a porcelain doll and she'll break if you look at her wrong and the whole show will fall apart!*'

'Ohhhh,' he said. 'Libby, that's not what I meant at all.'

'You don't trust me, Will!' she exclaimed. 'You don't trust that I can do this!'

'Of course I trust you to do this. I wouldn't have cast you if I didn't think you could.'

'I don't need you to give people a script for how to interact with me. I'm not so incapable of interacting with other people in a normal way that you need to bully them into liking me just so the show works!'

'That's not what I think at all, I promise you. Will you listen to me?'

She looked at him, fully intending to snap back that she had listened to him, that was the problem. That he didn't have to pretend to listen to her anymore, to find her interesting, that she'd be just fine on her own.

Then she saw his face, and she didn't know how, but she knew he was telling the truth.

Her anger died as suddenly as a candle wick drowning in a pool of wax. For a moment, there was only the dim pounding of the remnants of her hangover.

Then the shame rushed in.

'Oh God,' she whispered. 'I'm sorry, Will.'

She'd just shouted at her director. Shouted. At her director. Who did she think she was?

'Please don't fire me,' she said. 'I've been so incredibly unprofessional, letting my emotions affect my performance. It won't happen again, I swear.'

'Of course I'm not going to fire you.'

'I yelled at you.'

'If that was a firing offence, I'd definitely have fired Roarke,' he said. 'He yells at me basically every day. And that's kind of the point, really.'

Will ran his hand through his hair and tugged at his curls. 'It wasn't about you,' he said. 'It was about him. I've known him for a long time, and he's prickly. He's not always good with new people. Considering how much time he has to spend with you in this play, I wanted to make sure that he didn't get prickly with you and make you uncomfortable. I know no one's getting paid, but this is your work environment, and no one should have to work like that.'

She sank down on one of the ratty studio couches. 'That sounds so reasonable,' she said. 'So incredibly reasonable. How is it that when you say it like that it makes so much sense?'

He shoved his glasses up his nose and sat down beside her. 'Will you do something for me?'

'Is it not to let my personal feelings affect my performance? Because it won't happen again.'

'Don't be afraid to yell at me,' he said, nudging her knee with his. 'If I've upset you, you never need to be afraid to tell me, or think that you're risking your role.'

Libby didn't know what to say.

'If something's making you uncomfortable – including me – you can tell me,' he said. 'I've heard the stories about the way this place has worked before, but it's not going to be like that in this show. I'm not some megalomaniac that you have to keep happy at all times or else.'

She could hear the unspoken name, as loud as if it were a church bell tolling in the middle of the room.

'You earned this,' he said. 'This role is yours, Libby. No one is taking it away from you.'

'Hi!' Paul appeared at Libby's elbow in the foyer after rehearsal like he'd teleported there.

'Hi,' Libby said, and turned back to her conversation with Anthony. 'Anyway, if you want to talk through how to structure it or anything, we could have coffee. I'm on campus for most of the day tomorrow.'

'Seriously? That would be great,' Anthony said. 'I'm terrible at essays. It's like I never learned in high school or something. I could really use the help.'

'No problems. Essays are my wheelhouse.'

'Is Ella in tonight?' Paul asked.

'She was earlier, but she left,' Libby said. 'How does eleven sound, Anthony? That place near the library?'

'Perfect.'

'She left?' Paul said. 'But she never even said hello.'

'Speaking of leaving, that's what I'm doing,' Anthony said. 'Peace out, Libs. See you tomorrow.'

'Bye.'

She looked around to see if there was someone she could grab a ride to the station from, but Paul interrupted her again. 'Are you sure Ella left?'

'Did she give you her number?'

'She forgot.'

'Look,' Libby said, 'don't take this the wrong way, but can I tell you something?'

'Of course.'

She hated this conversation. She never knew what to say, or how to put it. 'If she didn't give you her number, she doesn't want to see you again.'

'Does she have a boyfriend or something?'

'No, not anymore, but—' she sighed. 'Ella's not really a relationship person.'

'I just want to talk to her.'

'If she wants to talk to you, she'll find you. But – I'm not saying this to hurt your feelings, but she probably won't, okay?'

'Can you just tell her I'm looking for her? That I want to see her? Here, let me give you my number.'

'Dude,' Roarke said, 'leave before you embarrass yourself.'

Paul's mouth opened. Then it closed. He looked at Roarke, at Libby, then back at Roarke. Roarke gestured with his head to the door.

Wordlessly, Paul walked through it.

'Wow,' Libby said.

'He did an actual double take,' Roarke said. 'I didn't know they existed in the real world.'

'No, I meant you,' she said. 'You, like, out-alpha-ed him or something.'

Roarke didn't respond, and something about it stung. *In vino* there clearly wasn't *veritas,* because that drunken speech she'd given about not needing him to like her was not as true as she wanted it to be. 'Hey Will, are you leaving?' he said instead.

'In a second,' Will said, scribbling something on a piece of paper and handing it to Genevieve. 'Libby, do you need a ride?'

Her instinct was to say no, that she'd just walk, but she knew he'd insist, and she didn't have the energy for the argument. 'To the train station would be great, if it's not out of your way.'

'Not at all. It's on my way. Caro—'

'I'm going home tonight,' Caro said. 'I'll talk to you tomorrow.'

'All right,' Will said, and leaned down to kiss her, but she was already gone.

Libby chatted with Will on the ride to the station, trying to drown out the presence of Roarke actively not giving a shit about her in the back seat. 'So Catriona's wedding is next weekend,' she said. 'It's come up so quickly.'

'That reminds me,' Will said. 'Do you want a ride down? It doesn't make sense for us both to drive.'

'I wasn't planning on driving anyway,' Libby said, 'as I never learned—'

'You never learned to drive?' Will said incredulously.

'It was my form of rebellion growing up in a town where most people were driving tractors by the time they were, like, three,' Libby said. 'Anyway, Ella's giving me a lift down – she's going home for the weekend and it's not too far out of her way – but

I'd love a ride back so I could save her the inconvenience, if that's all right.'

'No trouble at all. The car is plenty big enough for the four of us.'

Four. Oh.

Her. Will. Caro.

And Roarke.

'Unless Roarke wusses out because he thinks Catriona is still in love with him,' Will said. 'In which case there'll be even more room.'

'Oh, shut up, Earnshaw,' Roarke said. 'You don't know what you're talking about.'

Will scoffed. 'Oh yes, I have absolutely no idea about how you operate,' he said. 'No clue at all. Never witnessed it.'

'I didn't know you dated Catriona,' Libby said, before the situation could become so awkward she had no choice but to fling herself out of the car.

'I didn't,' Roarke said.

Will scoffed again.

'We went out a couple of times, and now we're friends,' Roarke said. 'I was looking for her the night I met you in the bookshop.'

'Oh,' she said. 'I, um, didn't know.'

'How could you?' he said. 'It was pretty obvious you had your own shit going on.'

How did this boy she did not know at all manage to make her feel so incredibly stupid and off balance every time he opened his mouth?

It wasn't until later, when she was on the train, that she remembered what Will had told her when they'd realised they both knew Catriona. *She dated my brother for about five minutes.*

Were Will and Roarke *related*?

No. Surely not. Will's surname was Callahan. Roarke's was Rivera. Will was white. Roarke was Filipino.

It would explain some things, though. Their weird, tense, but clearly close relationship.

But – no. They knew each other from high school. The musical. Brothers would go to the same high school, though.

If they really were brothers, and the group chat found out, there would be uproar. *Can you even believe how nepotistic this is??!?!?!?!??* someone would write, and there would be an avalanche of furious agreement, almost all from people who had benefitted from Uni Rep nepotism before.

Ironically, the one person who might have defended them was Nightingale. *When someone's good, they're good,* he'd say, arm around whoever he'd cast in the lead, fingers stroking along the side of their neck, creeping up into their hair. *Can I help it if I recognise it off the stage as well as on it?*

Libby was trying desperately to get that image out of her head when she loped up the stairs to the second floor of her building to find Paul standing in front of her apartment door.

'Let me in, Ella!' he was saying, knocking furiously. 'Let me in!'

'Dude, what are you doing?' she exclaimed. The words were out of her mouth a second before she realised speaking was probably a terrible idea.

'Oh good, you're here!' he said. 'Can you let me in? I just want to talk to her.'

'Not a chance,' Libby said. Surreptitiously, she slid her keys between her fingers.

'Please.'

'No.'

'I just want to talk, I swear.'

'She's probably not even home.'

'She's not at the theatre, she's not here!' Paul said. 'There's another guy, isn't there?'

'Paul, I'm not talking about this with you,' she said, doing her best to keep her voice calm and even. God, she wished they were rich enough to live in a building with a security door! 'Please leave, or I'll have to call the police.'

'Please. Just let me talk to her.'

She wondered how fast she could get to her phone if she needed to. It was in her bag, probably buried under her Torts textbook.

'What do you want to say to her?' she said. 'I'll pass on a message.'

'I just want to tell her …' He paused. Even through the fear, Libby could practically see the wheels turning in his head. *Amateur*, she thought. *No wonder Ned and Nightingale never cast him.* 'Look, it's private. Let me talk to her.'

'Paul, I know it's hard and it's disappointing, but I told you the deal at the theatre,' she said. 'If Ella wanted to talk to you, she'd find you. Now please leave.'

He paused again. He was hovering on the edge of something, and for a moment, she wished desperately that Nightingale was there.

No. That she *was* Nightingale, that she could project that kind of charisma and aura that made people do whatever he wanted.

'Will you tell her I was here?' Paul said at last.

'Yes.'

'And that I need to talk to her?'

'I'll tell her. Now can you please go? It's late and I have to write half a Law assignment before bed.'

'If I could just come in with you and wait—'

She reached within herself. She reached not for Nightingale, but for Roarke, for the way he'd effortlessly made Paul leave with just a nod of his head. 'No.'

'Are you sure? I won't disturb you or anything.'

'Paul,' she said, 'I asked you to leave.'

'I just want—'

'Or I'll call the police. I mean it.'

'All right, all right,' he said. 'You don't have to be a bitch about it. I'm going.'

Libby waited until she heard his footsteps on the stairs. She opened and closed the apartment door as fast as she could, locking it immediately and throwing the deadbolt.

'Oh my God, *thank you*,' Ella said, throwing herself at Libby and wrapping her arms around her neck. Her skin was pale and clammy. 'He wouldn't go away.'

'How long was he out there?'

'Ten, fifteen minutes? I didn't know what to do. I thought about calling the police, but what if they thought I was overreacting? So I thought if I pretended I wasn't home he'd go away, but—'

'Hey, hey, it's okay,' Libby said, as Ella started to cry. 'He's gone. It's all right.'

She had to stand under a hot shower for fifteen minutes before she stopped shaking.

Chapter Seven

She still hadn't managed to fall asleep that night when Ella started screaming. She got up and ran across the hall. 'No, no!' Ella sobbed into Libby's shoulder, fingers clutching her pyjama shirt. 'Don't go, don't go, don't go!'

'It's okay,' Libby said, stroking her hair. 'You're all right. I've got you. I'm not going anywhere.'

Ella was apologetic the next morning. 'I really thought I'd finally grown out of the nightmare thing,' she said, as they both sat bleary-eyed at their table eating breakfast. 'I'm so sorry. But this whole thing with Paul has me really rattled.'

'Totally understandable,' Libby said. 'I'm not surprised a dude who is a literal nightmare gave you literal nightmares.'

Ella shuddered. 'Even the sex was a bit of a nightmare, to be honest,' she said. 'I mean, it wasn't terrible, but he has these weirdly smooth hands.'

Libby made a vague unimpressed noise.

Nightingale's hands hadn't been smooth. He had callouses on his fingers from playing the guitar.

'I'm so sorry about all of this,' Ella said. 'I thought he understood that it was a one-night thing. I had no idea he'd turn out to be such a stalker.'

'You don't need to apologise,' she said, reaching across the table and squeezing Ella's hand, squashing the uncharitable part of her that was saying, *you should have listened to me, I told you theatre hookups were complicated.*

Libby was scratchy-eyed and on edge all of Tuesday, but when that night passed without incident – and Wednesday night, and Thursday night – she relaxed. It was okay. It was just a blip. Everything was fine.

But then on Friday night, Ella woke up screaming again. 'I can't go to rehearsal tomorrow,' she sobbed into Libby's arms. 'I can't, I can't, I can't.'

'I'll have your back your whole time,' Libby promised. 'You won't have to see him or speak to him or anything.'

'I should just quit,' Ella whispered.

'You are *not* quitting,' Libby told her fiercely. 'I won't let you. You love this. You're good at this. He doesn't get to take it away from you.'

'Why am I like this?' Ella asked. 'Why can't I have my shit together like you?'

She nearly told her then. *I don't,* she nearly said. *I'm just as much of a mess as you. Worse, even, because I won't even admit it.*

But Ella didn't need her to empathise. She needed her to be strong.

'He's the problem, not you,' Libby said instead. 'I've got you. Everything is going to be all right.'

She made it sound as believable as possible. She needed it to be true as badly as Ella did.

When she finally went back to her own bedroom, she couldn't sleep at all for the rest of the night.

This wasn't the first time Ella had had nightmares. Three years ago, after her brother Emerson had died, she'd had them almost non-stop. Libby had experienced some of them firsthand, when Ella, unable to cope with the intensity of her mum and her nan's grief, had come to stay at Libby's for a week, and had woken them both up five nights running with her screams.

But then, Libby'd had her parents for help, and the knowledge that Ella's family was close by too. She couldn't remember anything quite as stressful as the first time she'd had to deal with Ella's nightmares on her own.

It had been just after they moved to Terravale, eighteen months ago. Things had been excellent for about a week, but then Ella's nightmares had started, night after night after night.

'I'm okay,' Ella had protested. 'I'm just homesick, that's all. I miss my mum, and I miss my nan, and … I miss Gerry.'

'Oh, Ella,' Libby had said.

'It's fine,' Ella had said. 'It's just still a bit fresh, that's all. I'll be okay. Sorry for waking you. Again.'

It had seemed reasonable. Of course she was homesick! Of course she missed Gerry! They'd been together for ages, and they'd only just broken up! And Ella had seemed otherwise fine as they partied their way through O-Week!

But then Libby came home from her first ever sociology lecture to find a note on the table. *Sorry Libs. Can't do this. Gone home. E.*

She'd panicked. She'd called Ella a million times, with no answer. She'd called Ella's mum. She'd even called her own mum. She'd started freaking out about the lease, and being on her own, and what if she had to get a new flatmate? She didn't want to live with someone she didn't know. What if they didn't like her? What if she couldn't cope on her own and she had to go back to Wimeena, a friendless failure?

She'd never been as relieved in her life as when she got a call at midnight from Ella's mum. 'I know it's late, but I thought you'd like to know that Ella's safe and sound here with us,' she said. 'We're going to keep her for a few days, but then she says she'll come back.'

Ella had never told her what had happened, not really, and Libby hadn't known how to ask. She'd plotted out a hundred hard conversations while Ella was away, but when she had come back, she'd been so sunny and breezy that Libby had been afraid to puncture it. 'Sorry for worrying you,' she'd said lightly. 'I guess the first week of uni just made it real, you know? I freaked out for a minute there.'

'Are you sure you're all right?' Libby had asked.

'I promise I'm all right.'

'Did you—' she'd hesitated. 'Did you see Gerry?'

Ella had nodded. 'We had a long talk. And ... I won't lie. It's hard being away from him. I still love him. Maybe part of me will always love him. We've been together in one way or another since we were thirteen. He was such a rock for me when Em died, and ... you can't just shake that off like it was nothing.'

Libby had bitten her lip. 'Do you ever feel like I roped you into this? Like getting out of Wimeena was my dream? And I made you come with me?'

'Absolutely not,' Ella had said. 'Getting out of that town is the best thing that has ever happened to me. It doesn't make it easy, but you, me, this, art school? This is where I need to be.'

She must have looked doubtful, because Ella reached over and squeezed her hand. 'I love Gerry, Libs,' she said, 'but if I'd stayed, I would have ended up a farmer's wife, and I would have *hated* it.'

Libby had watched her for a long time after that. Ella had been a little melancholy for a few days after their trip back to Wimeena for Emerson's memorial, and again after they went home for Christmas, but the nightmares hadn't come back. Ella said she was fine, and as far as Libby could tell, she was.

But if Ella wasn't fine ... what was she going to do?

Libby deliberately arrived at rehearsal ten minutes late the next afternoon. 'Sorry, sorry,' she said, rushing into the studio. 'The person taking the next shift at work was late, and I was by myself so I couldn't leave.'

'No worries,' Will said absently, barely looking up from whatever he was scribbling on his script. 'I'm not up to you yet anyway.'

She checked where Paul was sitting out of the corner of her eye, being careful not to make eye contact. *He's here*, she texted Ella. *Don't come in.*

Text me if he leaves? I'm going to go look at fabric, but I'll come back if he's gone.

Will do.

'What's up, Libs?' Ned said. 'You seem all stressy.'

'Hmmm?' she said, putting her phone back into her bag. 'Nothing. Long day at work. Tons of uni homework.'

Paul was looking at her. She could feel it. She busied herself with her script. 'What scene are we doing tonight again?'

'The second half of Act Four Scene One.' It wasn't Ned, but Roarke who answered.

'Cool. Thanks.'

'Is Ella in tonight?' he asked.

'She's not feeling well,' Libby replied.

'Let's pick it up from line 255,' Will said. 'Beatrice, Benedick, you're up.'

Obediently, she got up, careful to direct her gaze away from Paul, then immediately felt foolish for doing so. What was he going to do, leap up in front of everyone and demand to know where Ella was? Make an actual scene in the middle of their fake scene?

'Lady Beatrice, have you wept all this while?'

She blinked. 'Sorry, what?'

Now Roarke was looking at her too, judging her with his steely gaze, and she felt even more stupid. 'Sorry,' she said.

'It's fine,' Will said. 'Take a couple more steps towards prompt side, please. And turn away from Roarke. Remember, Beatrice is upset, and she's been crying.'

She nodded, turned her back, took a deep breath, and tried to focus.

'When you're ready,' Will said.

'Lady Beatrice, have you wept all this while?'

'Yea,' she answered, 'and I will weep a while longer.'

'I will not desire that.' Roarke's voice was deep, but not the dangerous depth she had heard in his fight with Will at the party. It was something else, something gentle, something protective. Something ... warm.

'You have no reason; I do it freely.'

She could feel Paul's eyes on her. But she could feel Roarke's eyes on her too, and she focused on those, on his footsteps as he walked towards her.

'Surely I do believe your fair cousin is wronged,' he said.

'Ah, how much might the man deserve of me that would right her!'

'Is there any way to show such friendship?' His breath was warm on the back of her neck, and his hand, as it came to rest gently on her shoulder, was warmer still.

'A very even way,' she said, using the shakiness, using the confusion, 'but no such friend.'

She turned to face him, and a shiver rippled through her,

starting from his hand on her shoulder and breaking over her whole body. He was standing so close.

'I do love nothing in the world so well as you.' He had dark eyes, but she could see now that there were lighter brown flecks in his irises, almost gold. 'Is not that strange?'

'As strange as the thing I know not.' Her breath was shallow. 'It were as possible for me to say I lov'd nothing so well as you; but believe me not, and yet I lie not—' Beatrice was almost as much of a babbler as she was, '—I confess nothing, nor I deny nothing. I am sorry for my cousin.'

She turned away hurriedly, but he grabbed her arm and pulled her back. 'By my sword, Beatrice, thou lovest me.'

'Do not swear, and eat it.'

'I will swear by it that you love me, and I will make him eat it that says I love not you.'

Roarke's presence was gravitational. When had his forehead touched hers?

'You have stayed me in a happy hour,' she whispered. 'I was about to protest that I loved you.'

'And do it with all thy heart?'

'I love you with so much of my heart that none is left to protest,' she said, and Roarke threw his script on the floor and kissed her.

It was nothing like when Nightingale had kissed her, and everything like it. It was chaste, impersonal, pretend, professional, and she felt like she'd been struck by lightning.

People were catcalling and applauding. 'Hot *stuff*!' Rashmi yelled enthusiastically.

'Good work,' Will said. 'Now let's run it again, from the top. Don't get so close in so quickly, Roarke. We'll lose some of the impact if we overdo it. Libby, good work on the shakiness in the beginning, but you can maybe dial it back a notch, okay?'

'Okay,' she said, without the faintest clue of whether she was capable of doing it.

When Will sent Libby and Roarke to the foyer to do character work later so he could spend some time working on the bits with Ned and Caro ('you two are looking fine,' he'd said to them, 'so I want to address the chemistry problem over here'), she felt strange and confused and a bit excited.

Which made her feel stupid, because it was a stage kiss, a proper one, and it meant absolutely nothing.

'So, um, I think that scene's coming along pretty well,' she said.

Roarke wasn't listening. He was looking at one of the pictures from past shows on the wall. 'Is this him?' he asked.

'What?'

'The guy you thought was me in the bookshop. Is this him? The one with the black hair?' He tapped his finger on Nightingale's face, beaming out from the photo from *Little Shop of Horrors*, one arm hooked around Ned and the other around Rosie Waters as the giant plant puppet opened its mouth behind them.

'Oh. Yes.'

Roarke looked closer. 'He doesn't look anything like me.'

'From the back he does. There's the hair, and he used to wear this coat kind of like yours, and ...'

'He's white.'

'I know, but— that night in the bookshop ... it had been one of those days, and—'

'I know what he did.'

She knew – she *knew* – he meant the embezzlement, but it didn't stop her throat drying up completely anyway.

'I'd have been furious too,' he said. 'I'm not sure it would have made me blind, but—'

'Are you ever going to let this go?'

It came out more snappish than she had intended, enough that he raised an eyebrow. 'Sorry,' she said. 'So, the scene. We should talk about it. I think it's going pretty well.'

'It could be better,' he said, folding himself into one of the foyer chairs. Libby wondered if he had dance training. He might, if he was as big a musical theatre dork as Will had told her he was. He moved like a cat.

'Obviously it could always be better. It's only the first time we've rehearsed it. But—'

'Libby?' Paul had followed them into the foyer.

If she was ever asked to write a list of adjectives to describe Roarke, *comforting* would not be in the top ten. But in that moment, she was very glad he was there.

'What do you want?' she said, keeping her voice even.

'I was just wondering whether Ella's coming in this afternoon,' Paul said.

'Shouldn't you be upstairs? Rehearsing?'

'I'm not in this bit. I really want to talk to her.'

'She doesn't want to talk to you. I don't know any other way I can put this to make you understand.'

'Did you give her my message?'

'Yes. She's not interested.'

'Could you give me her number?'

'No.'

'Please—'

'Leave. Now,' Roarke said.

For a split second Libby thought he meant her, but Paul's lip curled in something like a snarl before he turned on his heel and left.

She exhaled. 'Thanks.'

'What's his deal?' he asked, jerking his head after Paul. 'Why do I have to keep scaring him off?'

'His deal is he won't leave Ella alone,' she said, sitting on her hands to stop them shaking. 'He turned up at our front door on Monday night after rehearsal, and it took me forever to get him to leave, and – seriously, thanks.'

Roarke looked at her – or through her, maybe – for a long moment. 'You need someone to walk you to your door tonight?'

'It's all right,' she managed.

The moment stretched out. She could see the flecks of gold in his eyes.

Her phone buzzed. *Is he still there? I want to do some measurements, and I'm done at Spotlight, but I'll come back another time if he's lurking around.*

'It's Ella,' she said. 'Would you mind if we broke up this little character sesh so she could take some costume measurements from you?'

He shook his head.

'You stay here, and I'll go back upstairs and try and ferry people down to Ella so Paul doesn't realise.'

Roarke didn't answer. She turned her head. He was staring at her. 'What?' she said.

'Stay still.'

'What? Why?'

'Just stay still.'

He leaned over.

For one terrible, inexpressible moment, Libby thought he was going to kiss her again.

Oh, I know who you are, Nightingale whispered, breath warm against her lips. *You're the smart girl.*

Then his hand shot out and he cuffed the top of her head, hard.

'Ow!' Libby exclaimed, slapping his hand away. 'That – oh my God.'

Crawling limply on the floor by her feet, apparently stunned by the force of Roarke's blow, was an enormous huntsman spider.

'Is it safe?' Ella said, poking her head around the dirty glass door.

'From Paul, yes, he's upstairs,' Libby said. 'But look what was in my hair!'

Ella took two steps closer, then backed hurriedly away. 'Oh no no no no no. No thank you.'

'Do you want me to kill it?' Roarke asked.

'I think it's nearly dead anyway,' Libby said. 'I'm going to go back upstairs and smuggle some people down to you, Ella. Who do you need?'

'Ned and Caro, if you can get them. Rashmi and Heidi. Definitely not Paul.'

'I've got your back.'

'I won't leave you alone,' Roarke said, his voice almost – no, not tender, but gentle.

Libby paused on the stairs before she went up to the studio. She looked back, and met Roarke's eyes, dark, implacable.

She remembered his breath on her face. His hand in her hair. His lips on her lips.

She swallowed.

Slowly, deliberately, not dropping her gaze, he killed the spider with the heel of his boot.

'Great work this afternoon, squad,' Will said, snapping his notebook shut. 'We've blocked nearly the entire show now, and that's a real achievement. Obviously, there's still heaps more we need to do, but we have some great bones here. Well done.'

Everyone politely applauded.

'Okay, you can go home,' Will said. 'Paul, can I see you for a minute?'

If you leave now you'll be safe, Libby texted to Ella.

Already left, came the reply. *Do you mind catching a ride with someone? Didn't want to linger in case he saw me.*

'So you and the new guy,' Ned said, as they walked down the stairs.

It took her a minute to realise he was talking to her. 'Hmmm?'

'That was hot,' he said, waggling his eyebrows.

'Super hot,' Rashmi said, overhearing. 'What were you two doing all that time alooooooone in the foyer?'

'Just character stuff.'

'Is that what they're calling it these days?' Ned said. 'How many times did you 'do character stuff', hey?'

'Nine hundred and forty-three,' Roarke said, materialising in their midst.

Silence.

'Or maybe it was more,' he said, his tone mild. 'I lost count.'

There was another silence a beat too long before Ned laughed and everyone else followed suit. 'Treat her right, man, or we'll be having a chat,' he said, slapping Roarke on the shoulder. 'Now has anyone seen my girlfriend?'

The group disintegrated as people started to leave. Libby

turned to Roarke to thank him, but he'd already managed to vanish in that way that he had. She looked around for someone she could grab a ride to the station from when Paul came storming down the stairs and made a beeline straight for her.

'Bitch,' he said, so close she could feel his spit on her face.

Then he was gone, the glass door of the foyer slamming so hard behind him that two of the pictures hanging on the wall fell down.

There was total silence for a beat – one – two – three – and then—

'Clearly someone's jealous Libby's been making out with Roarke,' Ned said dryly.

Everyone laughed. Conversation continued. Libby wanted to sit down, but she also didn't want anyone to think this was a big deal, so she settled for breathing in and out very slowly.

'Are you okay?' Heidi asked her in an undertone.

'I'm fine,' she said. 'Excuse me for a sec.'

She elbowed her way past the Ritchie brothers. 'Can I borrow you?' she said to Will, just as he came down the stairs.

'Of course,' he said. 'Caro, I'll be back in a second. Wait for me. Libby, come back up to the studio.'

She followed him up the stairs. He held the studio door open for her so she could go in before him, and turned the lights back on. 'Will—' she began.

But he was already speaking. 'Libby, why didn't you tell me about Paul?'

She opened her mouth. Closed it again.

'It's not your problem,' she managed eventually.

'He was harassing you. You're in my show. Of course it's my problem.'

'Well, he was harassing Ella. I'm sure Roarke – that's where you got your info, right? – told you that. I was just sort of ... there.'

'Ella's part of my show too,' Will said. 'If anyone ever tries to pull this shit again, I want to know about it, so I can do something about it, okay?'

'What did you do about it?' she asked. 'Paul just stormed down the stairs and called me a bitch, so I assume you did something.'

'I fired him.'

She blinked. 'You fired him?'

'Yes. And I made it clear that he's not welcome back here ever again. I'll talk to Graham in the morning about getting him banned.'

A wave of something swept through Libby, and she felt almost weak at the knees.

'It's not that I think you can't handle yourself,' he said. 'Everything I said the other night is true. I know you're not a porcelain doll. But you or Ella or anyone shouldn't have to put up with that kind of shit. Not here, not anywhere. I'm in a position of power right now, and if I don't use it in situations like this, I'm abusing it. So please, never, ever be afraid to tell me if something like this happens again.'

'Will,' she said, 'thank you.'

'You don't have to thank me for doing my job,' he replied.

Chapter Eight

'Coffee?' Ella asked. It was the only word she'd said for ninety minutes.

They'd been on the road for four hours. The first couple of hours had been fine – they'd blasted Taylor Swift and sung along – but once they'd got further inland and the landscape had started to change, the houses getting sparser, the grass getting browner, Ella had fallen silent. Libby had tried to change the music or start nonsense conversations about uni or the show, but none of it had worked. She might be driving the car, but Ella was already somewhere else.

'Sure,' Libby said.

Ella pulled off the highway into the McDonalds carpark. 'Actually, maybe I don't want coffee,' she said, as they got out of the car. 'Maybe I want a cheeseburger. Or a sundae.'

'You can have them all, if you want,' Libby said.

They ordered and sat down at one of the laminate tables, the air smelling of grease and disinfectant. Ella took one bite of her cheeseburger and then put it down. 'Ugh.'

'You should eat something. It's a long way to Wimeena.'

'I know.' Ella toyed with some fries, but didn't eat them.

'Ella, I don't have to go to this wedding. I could come with you.'

'No.'

'I can tell Catriona I had a family emergency. I've never not been with you at one of these, and—'

'No, you're going,' Ella said. 'At least one of us is going to enjoy this weekend.'

'Do you want to talk about it?'

'Trust me, Libs, the last thing I want to do is talk about it. I just want to get through it and then forget about it until next year.'

'All right. If that's what you want.'

Ella sighed. 'I wish I was coming with you,' she said, taking the bun off her burger and peeling off the gherkin. 'I love weddings.'

'It's not going to be that fun. I hardly know anyone there, apart from a couple of bookshop people.'

'You know Will and Caro. And Roarke.'

'Just what I want. To get mixed up in their weird, intense dynamic.'

'Maybe it's a good thing,' Ella said. 'If you don't know anyone, you can meet people. Find a hot boy to hook up with. Get laid. Do me proud.'

'Oh yes, that sounds so much like me,' Libby said, in the best dry tone she could manage.

Ella sighed again and began to rip her burger bun into shreds. 'I'm sorry again about the Paul thing.'

'Ella, it's not your fault. You know that, right? Please tell me you know that.'

'Yeah, yeah, I know that,' she said. 'It's just ... all the stories you told me about Uni Rep kind of made me think it'd be a dream hook-up spot, you know? How most of the straight boys sleep around? How did I manage to stumble across the one who'd fall, like, obsessively in love with me straight away?'

'Who wouldn't fall in love with you straight away?' Libby

said, reaching over and taking the rest of the bun out of Ella's hand. 'You're the greatest.'

That drew the flicker of a smile.

'Anyway, Paul's gone, and you don't have to worry about him anymore,' Libby said. 'The new Conrade is (a) refreshingly normal, and (b) gay, so you're safe.'

'I can't believe Will did that for me.'

'Will and Roarke, I think,' Libby said. 'I wasn't the one who told Will, so ...'

'He's really cool,' Ella said, eating a fry.

'Will?'

'No. He's lovely, but I meant Roarke,' Ella said. 'We had a good chat the other day when I was measuring him for his costume. I like him a lot.'

Of course Roarke liked Ella. Would have a whole *conversation* with Ella. Will would never have to give him a lecture about being nice to Ella.

'He's ... interesting,' Libby said.

Ella lapsed into silence again once they hit the road. Libby rested her head against the window, staring out at the snow-covered mountains in the distance.

Since he'd fired Paul, Will had driven her home from rehearsal every night, even though it was way out of his way, and either he or Roarke had walked her to her door. It was nice, and she liked it, but part of her hated it as well, because she shouldn't need this. She should be able to deal with it on her own. She should be able to fix all her problems on her own. She was strong, and smart, and ...

And Ella needed her. What was she thinking, going to a wedding on this weekend, of all weekends?

'Ella, don't worry about the wedding,' she said suddenly. 'It's hours out of your way anyway. I'm coming with you.'

'You are one hundred percent absolutely not coming with me,' Ella said. 'I'm going to go and be miserable with my family on my own, thank you very much. You're going to go to this wedding, drink free wine, and lose your virginity. That's an order.'

It was the perfect opportunity to tell her. There would never be a better time to tell her. *It's a bit late for that,* she would say, and she'd tell Ella all about that night in the Swamp with Nightingale, and Ella would be stunned.

Oh my God, Libs, are you okay? she'd say.

Yes, I'm fine. I feel really weird about it, but I'm fine, she'd reply.

So … how was it? Ella would ask.

Um, okay, I think? Libby would reply, *like, I felt incredibly weird afterwards, but in the moment it was … fine, maybe? But I can't believe that I slept with him, and that I slept with him in the Swamp, like, that is objectively gross, and he's such an objectively gross person, what does it mean that I caved so easily?*

You know it doesn't mean you're gross or weak or anything, right? Ella would say, and they'd talk and unknot all the tangled knots inside Libby's brain, and Ella would have something else to think about this weekend instead of wallowing in years-old grief, and they'd both feel better.

She didn't say anything, though. The only sounds were the purr of the engine, the rushing of the other cars on the highway, and the smooth voice of the GPS occasionally interjecting with directions.

It was another couple of hours before they arrived at the hotel. 'Do you want to come in and have coffee?' Libby asked Ella, struggling to make the handle of her rolly bag work and eventually giving up and picking it up.

Ella shook her head. 'I should get going, or it'll be midnight before I get to Wimeena.'

'Are you sure?'

'No. But I should go anyway.'

'If you need me ...'

'I'll call. I promise.'

It was hard to watch her drive away into the distance. Libby knew she'd done the wrong thing, no matter what Ella had said. She'd stood beside her at Emerson's memorial every year for three years, and it wasn't like things were getting better.

What kind of awful, selfish person was she, going to a wedding when Ella needed her?

She exhaled. She wished there was someone in Wimeena she could call who would sub in and take over for her and be Ella's best friend for the weekend.

There is, she reminded herself. *Gerry'll be there.*

Will, Roarke, and Caro were just leaving the hotel check-in desk when she finally hauled her bag inside. 'Hi, Libby!' Will said. 'We're going to go and have a drink in the hotel bar. Want to come join us?'

'Sure,' she said. 'Let me just check in and I'll be down in ten minutes or so.'

It was more like twenty minutes. She talked herself in and out of calling Ella three separate times (*she's driving,* she finally reasoned with herself, *what if she answered her phone while she was driving and she crashed and it was your fault?*). The hotel bar was faux-English, all dark beams and whitewashed walls. There was a dark beam behind Will, and he was warm against it, the light glinting in his coppery hair. There was a white wall behind Roarke, and against it, he was a stark silhouette, dark and striking.

'Wine?' Will offered, as she slid into the booth next to Caro. 'We got a bottle. Do you like red?'

'Yes, and please.'

He poured. 'It's nice to see you,' he said.

'You too.'

Then no one said anything.

She should have stayed in her room. She should have gone with Ella. She should have made Ella come with her, so she had someone with whom she could carry on a conversation.

'I wonder why Catriona picked the snow to get married,' Will said. 'Do you know, Libby?'

'Not really,' Libby said. 'I've never asked her about it.'

'She likes the cold,' Roarke said. 'She told me.'

'Not me,' Will said. 'I hate it.'

'I love the cold,' Caro said.

'Do you?' Will said, surprised. 'I didn't know that.'

'You never asked.'

'So what's your opinion on this fascinating weather question, Libby?' Roarke said.

'I, uh, I'm not really into it,' she said. 'Where I grew up, it was considered an ice age if it got below fifteen.'

'That's where Ella is at the moment, isn't it?' Will asked. 'Your home town? I remember you telling me.'

'Mmm-hmmm,' Libby said, sipping her wine.

'Why didn't you go with her?'

'Well, you might have heard about this wedding that's happening.'

'Oh, of course,' Will said. 'But why didn't you wait and go together?'

'Will, stop prying,' Caro said.

'No, it's fine,' Libby said. 'Ella has a thing this weekend that she can't miss.'

'Is everything all right?'

'I wish you cared as much about me as you care about Ella,' Caro muttered, turning away to look out the window.

'Caro,' Will said, reaching across the table towards her, but not quite taking her hand, 'can we please not do this here?'

'Then when, Will?' Caro demanded, looking back at him. 'When?'

Libby wanted to reach for her wine and pour the entire glass down her throat, but that would probably be extremely inappropriate.

'Tell you what,' Roarke said, leaning over and picking up the bottle of wine. 'Libby and I are going to take this and go over there, and you two can come and join us when you've sorted your shit out, all right?'

Libby wasn't quite sure how it happened, but she found herself swept out of the booth and seated at another table before she was aware of it. 'Um, thanks,' she said.

'You thank people a lot,' Roarke said.

'Sorry.'

'Almost as much as you apologise.'

'Are you keeping some kind of spreadsheet of the things I say?'

'Then you ask defensive questions.'

'Do you study Psych?'

He smiled, a brief flash of white teeth. 'No. Top up?'

'Sure,' she said. 'Thanks. If I'm permitted to say that.'

He made a noise that might have been a laugh as he poured the wine. 'I'll allow it.'

'So if it's not Psych, what do you study?' she asked.

'Are you asking me that to fill the time, or are you actually interested?'

'Now who's asking defensive questions?'

'Touché,' he said. 'Cheers.'

She clinked her glass against his. 'So, you didn't answer the question. What do you study? Do you study? I don't think I've ever seen you on campus.'

'I study,' he said. 'Music/Economics. I'm terrible at the Econ, though. I'd have failed already without *Beautiful Mind* over there dragging me through.'

'That's like me and Law,' she said. 'I hate it.'

'Why do you keep doing it then?'

'Why do you keep doing Econ?'

'In the vain hope it'll actually get me a job one day. Do you want to be a lawyer?'

She nearly choked on her wine. 'Definitely not.'

'Then why are you doing it?'

She shrugged. 'So I'm not just doing an Arts degree, I guess.'

He raised one eyebrow. 'You're one of those Arts-degrees-will-only-get-you-a-job-at-McDonalds types?'

'No! Definitely not. It's just …' she tried to find the right words. 'It's just what it would look like, you know? High school dux comes home with nothing but an Arts degree.'

'Are you planning to go back to your home town?'

'I'd rather die.'

'Then why do you care?'

'Honestly? Habit, probably. Maybe you never stop worrying about what the people you went to high school with think.'

She felt stupid saying it. Roarke didn't seem like he'd ever worried about what another person had thought of him for a single second in his life.

He didn't laugh, though, just took another sip of his wine. 'You and Ella seem pretty close.'

He leaned back in his chair, swishing the wine in his glass around and around. Libby's breath caught in her throat at the picture he made, with the white of the wall, the black of his hair, the red of the wine.

'We've been best friends forever,' she said. 'Ever since we were two and our preschool was like, *you're both called Elizabeth, oh no, however will we deal with this insurmountable problem?*'

'She's a great costume designer. She showed me some of her designs the other day.'

'She's amazing,' Libby said. 'I wish she could have been here. Any other weekend and she would have been my plus one. I feel horrible that I'm not going home with her.'

'I'm not going to fish,' Roarke said mildly. 'If you want to be all mysterious, that's fine. No skin off my nose.'

'Sorry,' Libby said.

He raised an eyebrow.

'It's not like it's a secret or anything,' she said. 'Her brother – her twin, Emerson – died when we were sixteen, and her mum holds this big memorial service every year on the anniversary of his death. I've been with her every year except this year. I feel pretty guilty.'

'I'm not going to be your counsellor either.'

'Gee, thanks, Mr Sensitive.'

'I mean it,' he said. 'I don't do D&Ms. Not my style.'

'Well, I guess it's nice you know where your boundaries are.'

He didn't say anything. Something about the air felt heavy.

'So how are you going with *The Fifth Season*?' she asked him. 'In the market for the next one in the trilogy? I can put it aside at work for you.'

'I already bought it,' he said. 'But you can put the third one aside.'

It was about ten minutes of largely civil conversation later when Will threw himself down in another chair at their table. 'Is there any more wine?' he asked.

'No,' Libby said. 'We can fix that, though.'

She flagged down a waiter. 'Caro?' she heard Roarke ask in a low tone as she ordered.

'Don't ask,' Will said. 'Please.'

At the wedding ceremony the next day, the silence between Will and Caro was stony. Even though Will was his usual friendly self, and Caro behaved no differently than normal, Libby could sense a storm cloud hanging in the air between them. They stood close beside each other in the church, but never touched, their bodies always angled slightly away from each other, like one of them was going to leap away at any moment – hurdling over pews and people and knocking over sprays of roses and babies' breath in an effort to flee.

Will and Caro are fighting, she surreptitiously texted Ella as they waited for the bride to arrive.

Ella didn't reply. Libby wasn't surprised.

The wedding was lovely, the bride radiant, the vows heartfelt. Libby dabbed at her eyes and glanced at the people around her. Will, Caro, and Roarke were all staring straight ahead, completely unmoved. Will caught her looking, saw her damp eyes, offered her a smile. It wasn't comforting.

Hope you're doing ok, she sent to Ella as they left. *Wedding was gorgeous, but I miss you.*

No reply.

She escaped back to her hotel room before Will could make some painfully awkward suggestion that they all hang out together in the two hours between ceremony and reception. She took off her dark green cocktail dress, kicked off her heels, and flopped in an armchair watching SBS Food in her underwear. She'd brought her laptop, and she had a bunch of essays in her ProofItLibby inbox to work on, not to mention a giant pile of stuff to do for Torts and Con Law, but doing anything that required brainpower felt beyond her.

She looked in the mirror. Her makeup was still perfect, despite her tears.

She finally got a text from Ella just as she was about to leave for the reception, redressed and determined to stay as far away from whatever shitstorm Will and Caro had brewing as possible. *Things ok here. Memorial same as usual. Mum driving me nuts. Going to Crownie for drinks later.*

Have fun, she replied. *Caro & Will still not talking. Reception going to be SUPER awks.*

Just talk to Roarke, Ella texted back. *Leaving now.*

Wish you were here, she replied. It was a platitude, but she meant it.

Part of her dimly hoped that Catriona hadn't fulfilled her

promise to change the seating chart, but of course she was on the same table as Will, Caro, and Roarke at the reception, and the only other people she knew – the rest of the bookshop staff – were three tables away, barely visible behind the absurdly tall rose centrepieces.

Will seemed determined to pretend nothing was wrong, asking Libby question after pointless, trivial question, while Caro sat silently beside him, downing glass after glass of champagne.

'So you've done how many shows with Uni Rep?' he asked.

'This is my seventh.'

'And how long have you been in Terravale?'

'About eighteen months.'

'That's a lot in a short time.'

'Well, they weren't all as much work as this one. I did a lot of chorus roles. It takes a while to work your way up. There's a bit of a hierarchy.'

Caro drained her glass.

'Unless, of course, you're an acting genius, like Roarke here,' she added.

That drew a half-smile, and it felt like a capital-A Achievement. 'Top up?' Roarke asked.

'Please.'

'God, yes,' Will said. 'Caro, can you pass the—'

'Take it,' Caro said, shoving the ice bucket roughly in his direction. It nearly overturned, and the distant relative of the groom's who was sitting next to her gave her a sharp look.

'So what was your first show?' Will asked.

'*Twelfth Night*. Just bit roles, here and there. I had about three lines, all up. But I should have been grateful, because I didn't have any in my next two shows.'

'Which were?'

'*Peter Pan* – I was basically set dressing in that one – and – oh. Um.'

'What?'

'*A Chorus Line*,' Libby mumbled.

She regretted the words as soon as they came out of her mouth, but Caro gave no indication that she'd heard her. She was staring straight ahead into space, like she was a robot that had been powered down.

Will didn't seem to realise she'd made a massive faux pas either. 'So musicals as well as straight plays,' he said, toying with the stem of his champagne flute. 'Do you sing?'

Libby shrugged. 'I'm not bad.'

'She's excellent.'

'What?' she said, turning to look at Roarke.

'You're excellent,' he repeated. 'I heard you at karaoke.'

'As if you thought so,' she said, trying desperately not to blush. 'The way you glared at me, I thought you were trying to set me on fire with your laser eyes.'

'I wasn't glaring,' he said. 'I was listening.'

'That's just what his face looks like,' Will said.

Roarke flipped him off.

'Roarke?'

They all looked up.

'Roarke?' the girl said again. She had blonde hair, cascading down her shoulders in perfect waves. Libby knew she'd seen her somewhere before, but the champagne was fogging her mind and she couldn't quite place her. 'Can I talk to you?'

'I didn't know you were coming,' Roarke said.

He didn't move, but something about him changed completely, like he'd been blurred and all his sharp edges had suddenly come into focus.

'You didn't ask,' the girl said. 'Can we have a chat? It's been a while since I've seen you.'

'Of course,' he replied. 'I'll be back.'

Roarke followed the girl away. 'Ex-girlfriend,' Will said, though Libby wouldn't have dreamed of asking for an explanation. 'Kind of.'

Caro flagged down a waiter and got them to pop another bottle of champagne.

'So, singing,' Will said to Libby. 'Are musical leads as well as Shakespearean ones in your future?'

'We'll see. I definitely wouldn't say no if someone offered one to me, but there's no guarantee that'll happen.'

'Why wouldn't it?'

'Like I said, there's a hierarchy.'

'That makes no sense to me,' Will said, shaking his head. 'Why you wouldn't cast the most talented people in the roles they deserve—'

'Oh *shut up*, Will,' Caro said suddenly.

'Caro—'

'You want to make a point?' she snarled. 'Fine. Say it to my face. Don't pull this passive aggressive bullshit and sit there and pretend to be all innocent.'

'Caro—'

'Shut up. Just shut up, for once in your life.'

'Excuse me,' the man on Caro's other side said, 'but do you mind keeping it down? This is a wedding.'

'Sorry,' Caro said shortly.

'Thank you.' The man turned away.

'Let's not do this at the table, all right?' Will said.

'Just don't talk to me,' Caro said. 'Don't even look at me.'

Roarke slipped back into his seat. 'Caro, pass the champagne,' he said.

Caro stayed motionless. Will passed it instead.

'So we're doing this again, huh?' Roarke said, topping up his glass and then Libby's, although it was already mostly full.

'Not now, Roarke,' Will said distantly. 'What was that about?'

Roarke shook his head. 'You know Celeste.'

'Well, no, I don't. I only met her twice.'

'She wants me to know she still cares about me,' Roarke said, downing what looked like half his glass in one swallow.

'That's good, isn't it?' Will said.

'So I told her I had to get back to my date,' Roarke said, resting one arm along the back of Libby's chair.

That snapped Will back. 'You *what?*' he said, cutlery from the chicken-or-beef dinner clattering on the table as he turned sharply towards them.

'You heard me – cheers,' Roarke said, clinking his flute against Libby's. His arm was radiating heat behind her. She could feel a flush rising in her cheeks.

'Um, what am I doing?' she asked.

'You're helping me make it clear that I've moved on and so should she.'

'He wants you to help him be a dick,' Will said.

Libby looked from Will to Roarke, and back again. Part of her wanted to run screaming into the night.

Part of her was really enjoying the feeling of Roarke's arm on the back of her chair.

'Hi guys!' the photographer's assistant interrupted. 'Catriona and Vijay will be up to your table in a minute. Can I get you all ready for a picture?'

He didn't wait for an answer, but hustled them all over to a wall at the back of the function room, posing them in front of the carefully neutral background like mannequins. 'Now you just stand there,' he said, posing Libby in front of Will, '—and—'

'Wrong way round,' Roarke said, grabbing Libby's wrist and pulling her away. 'She's my date, not his.'

'Oh, sorry, sorry. You stand here, then, and—'

Libby watched as the wedding planner posed Will and Caro together, unsmiling, stiff as statues. 'And you two—'

'We've got it,' Roarke said, and his arm was around her, and she could feel the champagne fizzing in her veins and her breathing turned shallow and she prayed desperately that she wasn't turning red.

She could see Roarke's ex staring at them from a few tables away, a strange expression on her face. It wasn't hurt, exactly, but it wasn't happy either.

Will was right. She wasn't going to help Roarke be a dick.

Then she imagined what Nightingale would say if he could see her.

You had no effect on me, she would say, by putting her arm around Roarke's waist. *It meant nothing to me, and I'm fine.*

She put her arm around Roarke's waist. 'Fine, I'll be your date,' she murmured.

For a moment, there was nothing. Then Roarke leaned over and pressed a kiss to her temple, two seconds longer than would have been anything like platonic.

'Roarke,' she heard Will say warningly.

'Hello, hello, hello!' Catriona exclaimed, cheeks flushed red above the brilliant white of her lace dress. 'Look at you all! You all look so great! Sorry I haven't got across to say hi yet, it's been so hectic! Thank you so much for coming. Oh my God, Libby, you look gorgeous, I love that green on you! And I didn't know you knew Roarke!'

'Surprise,' Roarke said. 'You look great, Cat. Congratulations.'

Catriona and her new husband Vijay took their places and the photographer took the picture. 'And another one!' she said. 'Come on, smile! Especially you, little blonde girl. Look like you're enjoying yourself!' Caro didn't adjust her glare.

'Thank you for doing this,' Roarke murmured to Libby.

She looked up at him. He looked down at her. 'You're welcome,' she whispered back, and when the flash went off for the second time, she knew that even if everyone else in the photo was scowling, she and Roarke would be smiling at each other.

'Pass the champagne,' Caro said, when they got back to the table.

'Caro,' Will said, 'don't you—'

'Don't you dare tell me I've had enough. Don't even think about it.'

'Here you go,' Libby said, passing the bottle and then leaning back against Roarke's arm.

Will and Caro began to argue in low, venomous voices. Beyond them, the wedding photographer was setting up another photo against the wall. Roarke's ex was in it. Libby looked away before she got caught staring.

'You okay?' Roarke asked quietly.

'I'm fine,' she said. 'I'm an actor, remember? Fake wedding date isn't exactly a challenging role.'

'Oh, really?' he said, brushing his thumb along her cheekbone.

'Roarke!' Will said sharply.

'For God's sake, you can't even pay attention to me for *five seconds*!' Caro snapped, and stormed away.

'Caro, wait!' Will said, following her.

It took Libby another glass of champagne, a round of the Nutbush on the dance floor with her bookshop friends, and another ten minutes of conversation about nothing before she was bold enough to ask Roarke a proper question. 'So, prying, obviously, but what's the deal with Will and Caro?' she asked, as they swayed together to a slow song.

He raised an eyebrow, the same side of his mouth quirking upwards at the same time. 'Aren't you supposed to be smart? It's not hard to work out.'

'Talk to me like that again, fake boyfriend, and we'll be headed straight for a fake breakup.'

'That's what they're doing.'

'Breaking up, or faking it?'

'Both,' he replied, taking her hand and spinning her around before pulling her back gently into his orbit. He wasn't wearing a tie, and her eyes were level with the hollow at the base of his throat. She had a sudden overpowering urge to press her nose into it, to feel his skin against hers. 'Will's terrible at breaking up with people, so he fakes it for way longer than he should. You should have seen him with his high school girlfriend. It took him six months once he'd decided to break up with her to actually do it, because he was so terrified of hurting her feelings. He's too soft.'

'What, and you're the emperor of breakups? You don't seem to have done a very good job on your last one.'

She glanced over to where Roarke's ex was sitting. If it had been scripted properly, the girl would have been looking sadly back at them, a mournful look in her eyes, or maybe a jealous one, but she was talking to the person sitting beside her.

'In my defence,' Roarke said, 'we were never dating.'

'Oh, dude,' she said, making a face. 'Did she know that?'

'Yes. Of course she did. I'm not a total arsehole. No matter what Will's told you.'

'He hasn't told me anything. What would he tell me?'

'Well, I am, as you know—' he laced his fingers with hers, raising her hand to his mouth and kissing it, and he was *so* hot, and if Nightingale could see her now, God, if Nightingale could see her now, '—awful and mean, so awful and mean that I have to be ordered to be nice to you.'

'Did he tell you how angry I got with him about that?' she replied, wrapping both her arms around his neck. Her fingers brushed against his hairline.

She was frightened for a moment that he might pull away – *no, Libby, too much, too much, this is all fake, remember?* – but he just laughed. 'Oh, he did,' he said. 'Thank you for sailing in and defending my honour.'

'I didn't give a shit about your honour,' she said. 'That was about me. I don't like being played. I like it when people are straight with me.'

'In the interests of being straight with you,' he said, his forehead leaning against hers, 'I'm thinking about kissing you, if you'd be into it.'

'In the interests of being straight with you,' she replied, 'I probably would be.'

He was straight with her, and she was straight with him. 'You know this isn't a thing, right?' he said against her lips, pressing her up against the wall in the dark corridor, one leg between hers. 'You – me – this isn't anything.'

'Yes, I got it, you made it perfectly clear,' she gasped into his mouth.

His room was closer, so they stumbled there. They peeled each other's clothes off, peeled each other open.

There was a moment, after, her head resting on his chest, both breathing hard, when things weren't clear at all.

But then he got up to take the condom off, and she was alone, and as she picked up her green dress slowly and stepped back into it, she wondered.

He came back out of the bathroom. 'Here, let me get that,' he said, and zipped her dress back up for her.

Yes, things were perfectly clear.

Interlude – Ella

She had the music turned up as loud as it would go, but it still couldn't drown out the oppressive silence of the hot, dry land around her. She tapped her fingers against the steering wheel and wished Libby was there.

The green sign by the roadside read *Wimeena: 10 km*. A dead kangaroo lay underneath it, flies swarming around the bloody corpse, pulped into the bitumen.

He never made it home, Ella thought.

She'd been on the road for eight hours when she finally pulled up to the house. The roof glowed red in the dying sunlight, just like it always did. The paint was peeling just the slightest bit more than the last time she'd been here. Her mother was waiting on the verandah, just like she always was. She kissed Ella on both cheeks, her lips dry and chapped. 'Lovely to see you, darling,' she said. 'I've missed you.'

'I've missed you too, Mum,' she answered, permitting her mother's embrace.

'Nan's inside. She's desperate to see you.'

'Wait.' She grabbed at her mother's arm.

'What is it?'

'What time … is it?'

'Tomorrow at three. Same as always.'

She nodded silently and followed her mother into the house where nothing ever changed.

'Elizabeth!' her nan exclaimed, setting down her knitting on the side table beside her recliner. 'Sit down, my gorgeous girl.'

Ella obeyed, perching on the edge of the couch which was older than she was. 'It's lovely to see you, Nan.'

'It's always lovely to see you, my special one,' her nan replied. 'Tell me how you're going. Tell me everything. Are you finished with university yet?'

'No,' she said. 'Not for a while yet. I'm only in my second year. I've got eighteen months to go.'

'That's not so long.'

'And I might do Honours.'

'What does that mean?'

'Another year on the top, but I'd have a better degree.'

'Well, we'd miss you, but that would be nice, wouldn't it? Then you could come back here and live with us and start up a little gallery in town.'

Ella swallowed.

'No Libby this time?' her grandma asked. 'She always comes home with you for Emerson.'

'Not this time,' Ella said. 'She had a wedding to go to.'

'What a shame. She's a nice girl. Plain little thing, but sharp as a tack. How's your young man? You must have a young man, pretty girl like you.'

'No young man,' she said.

'Cuppa,' her mother said, handing her a steaming mug.

'Thanks.'

'I wish you'd stayed with that Gerry Bloom,' her nan said. 'He's such a nice boy. Then maybe you'd come home and see us more often.'

'I'm busy, Nan,' she said. 'Uni is a lot of work.'

'We know that, but we miss you,' her mother said. 'We'd love to see more of you.'

'I miss you too.'

It was only half a truth. She missed her mum. She missed her nan. She missed Gerry. God, she missed Gerry. But if she never had to visit this town again, she wouldn't shed a single tear, because there was no one she missed more than Emerson.

There was silence. Ella stared at the photographs on the mantelpiece. Her mother stared at her hands. Her nan stared into the empty fireplace.

Three generations of women, with nothing to say to each other.

She didn't wear black to the service. Black was the colour of adulthood, of a mature, grown-up grief that would eventually settle into melancholy, and then into peace. Her grief wasn't like that. It was a monster haunting a child's bedroom, an invisible spectre that could reach out and wrap its fingers around her neck at any moment. So every year, she wore bright colours instead, despite the disapproving looks her nan gave her.

There was a picture of Emerson propped on top of the small table that had been set up next to his gravestone. Ella had been in it as well, but she'd been cropped out. Emerson was grinning at the camera, sixteen years old, one arm around his invisible sister, young and alive.

A week later, he was dead.

The service was ending. She knelt and placed her bunch of gerberas on Emerson's grave.

It seemed small. But he hadn't been small, had he? He'd been tall, lanky, all elbows and knees.

She couldn't picture him clearly, even though the photo was right there. It felt like the worst kind of betrayal.

Someone laid a hand on her shoulder. 'El.'

She turned. 'Hi, Gerry.'

He was bigger now, broader, harder, stronger, but he was still the same Gerry, the Gerry who had been Emerson's best friend, the Gerry who had been her first kiss, first everything, and would have been her last if she'd let him. 'It's good to see you.'

'You too,' he replied. 'You look great.'

'Thanks. And thanks for coming. It means a lot.'

'I wouldn't miss it. You know I wouldn't. No Libby this year?'

She shook her head.

'Do you want to go for a drink tonight?'

She hesitated.

'Just you and me,' he said. 'One drink. Quiet. It'd be nice to catch up.'

'All right.'

'Tops,' he said. He kissed her cheek and ambled away. Ella knew he'd put Emerson behind him long ago.

She stood on the verandah later that afternoon, tapping her fingers against the railing. The sun was setting over the paddocks, turning the brown grass momentarily gold. The cows were luminous red blurs in the distance. It was a pastoral idyll, a rural Eden.

Of course Emerson was the one who found the snake.

From here, she could almost see the place where he'd died. It was an unremarkable spot, one she'd stomped past in thick black gumboots nearly every day in high school on her way to feed the chickens, but she'd never been back.

She wanted to. She knew, somehow, that she had to. But it would be too much like saying goodbye.

The Wimeena Crown had a monopoly on alcohol in town. If you wanted to drink, your options were the Crownie or nothing.

She hadn't been there in ages, not since she'd left school, but it hadn't changed. It had been the afterparty for the Year Twelve formal and she'd been lonely and sad and she'd had seven tequila shots and Libby had had to hold her hair back in the bathroom. She'd never had a hangover quite as bad since.

She spotted Gerry's dark hair at the bar. He was looking much more at home now than he had been at Emerson's memorial, back in a version of his normal clothes: jeans and a red flannelette shirt with the sleeves rolled up. She remembered one of the reasons why she'd been so lonely and sad at the formal as vividly as if she'd time-travelled back into her old life.

'Hey, El,' he said. 'Grab a seat. Can I buy you a beer?'

'Sure,' she said. She didn't usually drink beer, but things were different in Wimeena.

'It's good to see you,' he said, clinking the neck of his bottle against hers.

'It's good to see you too,' she said. 'How's things?'

'Oh, you know, same old, same old.'

He told her about working the farm with his dad. She nodded and pretended to understand as he spoke in a language she had deliberately forgotten.

'How about you?' he said, and she told him about Terravale, about art school, not knowing if he understood a single word either.

'And Libby?' he asked. 'You're still living together, right?'

'She's great,' she replied. 'She's doing really well at uni, and she's got the lead role in this play with the student theatre company. Shakespeare.'

'She hasn't changed, then.'

'She's still brilliant,' Ella said. 'And she's still my favourite person in the world. She could have gone to any university in the country but she chose to come with me, and I'll never, ever be able to repay her.'

Gerry took a long sip from his beer and said nothing.

'I worry about her, though,' she admitted.

'Why would you worry about her?' Gerry asked. 'If she's as brilliant and perfect as you say she is?'

'Because she spends so much of her time and energy holding me together,' Ella said. 'And no one does it for her.'

It was easier to admit that here, with Libby hundreds of kilometres away, but she was still somehow worried that she would overhear and instantly appear to protest. *You do hold me together,* Libby would insist, *stop calling yourself a bad friend, because that's garbage, and also, I'm fine, stop worrying about me,* and Ella would not be able to disagree.

'I could have held you together,' Gerry said. 'If you'd let me.'

The ache wasn't just in her heart. She could feel it in her whole body, down to her fingertips, down to her toes.

'Even if there wasn't a Libby,' she said, 'you and I wouldn't have worked, Gerry.'

'We'll never know, will we.' It wasn't a question.

'Libby wasn't the only one who wanted to leave,' she said. 'It was me too. I wouldn't have been brave enough to do it on my own, but I had to go. I couldn't stay here.'

'I know, El,' he said. 'I just miss you.'

'I miss you too,' she said.

He smiled at her, the same smile he'd smiled at her when

they'd been thirteen and he'd kissed her for the first time while Emerson had been in the bathroom. *We'd better keep this a secret,* he'd whispered, and *yeah, Em wouldn't like it,* she'd whispered back, and he'd kissed her again, and then they'd heard the toilet flushing and had sprung apart like magnets belonging to opposite poles.

It was the same smile Gerry had smiled when they were sixteen, and he'd found her standing in front of Emerson's grave, two weeks after the funeral. *What are you doing?* he'd asked her gently, and *I don't know, visiting,* she'd replied, trying to pretend she wasn't crying, and she'd caught a glimpse of that smile before he wrapped her up in those big, strong arms of his. *It's okay, El,* he'd said, *I've got you,* and she couldn't let go of him, and they were kissing, and then he was taking her back to the farm and they were kissing more and they were in his bed and he was so big, so strong, so solid, and afterwards he held her close to his chest and she could hear his heart beating and *I'm not going anywhere,* he was whispering, and then suddenly she was thinking about how Emerson's heart was never going to beat again, and she was crying, and *it's all right, El, it's all right, I'm sorry if I hurt you,* he was saying, but she couldn't say anything, couldn't do anything but cry.

'I think about you,' she told him. 'A lot, actually.'

That drew a smile. 'Yeah?'

She smiled back, nodding. 'Yeah.'

'I would have come with you,' he said. 'To uni. To the coast. If you'd wanted.'

'No,' she said. She took his hand and pressed his fingers to her lips before she let them go again. 'You belong here.'

They both drank. She looked at him through her eyelashes. He was muscled from all the work he was doing on the farm, and his face looked like someone had carved it out of rock with a chisel: all light and shadows, angles and planes. He looked solid, immovable.

Safe.

'Thanks for coming today,' she said.

'Em was my friend, you know?' he said. 'He meant a lot to me.'

'Thanks,' she said. 'For saying that.'

'I mean it,' he said, turning to look her in the eye. 'I loved him.'

She made a decision. It was a bad decision, but she made it anyway.

She drank the last of her beer. Gerry's was mostly empty on the bar in front of him. She picked that up and drank it too.

'Do you want to go somewhere?' she asked.

There was a pause, and suddenly the thought that he would say no was the most frightening thing in the world.

'Love to,' he said, taking her hand.

Her mum and her nan were home, and so were his parents, so he took her out into one of the back paddocks on his farm. His lips were warm on hers as he pressed her up against the side of his ute, her fingers nimble on the buttons of his shirt. His chest was hard, like the land, his arms strong as he laid her down on the tray.

She could see the stars, twinkling through loose strands of his hair. Was Emerson with the stars now? Where was he, now that he wasn't here?

She dug her fingers into Gerry's shoulders. She hadn't been able to pin Emerson down, but she had Gerry, warm and solid and safe, and he wasn't going anywhere.

At least until morning.

Chapter Nine

'Ready to go?' Will asked Libby in the hotel foyer the next morning. There were dark purple smears under his eyes, but he still made the effort to smile at her.

'Absolutely,' she replied.

They were the last words anyone said for three hours.

Will stared stonily ahead out the windshield, knuckles white on the steering wheel. Caro, who'd pointedly sat in the back and gestured at Libby to take the front passenger seat, was a storm cloud. And Roarke …

Libby rested her head against the window and thanked any higher power that might be listening that Roarke was sitting behind her, not in front of her, and then she didn't have to stare at the back of his head for hours and hours and agonising hours.

She felt sick. She wondered what would happen if she suddenly opened the door and catapulted herself out of the car.

Caro wouldn't care. Will probably wouldn't even move. Roarke wouldn't notice.

Someone was going to notice, though. Someway, somehow, someone would find out. *Did you hear?* they'd post in the group chat. *Libby and Roarke hooked up.*

OMG!

No way. Libby's a total prude. Everyone knows that.

Think whatever you want. She did Roarke like a crossword.

Hey, did anyone notice how she and Nightingale disappeared at that Rapunzel party?

The images blurred together in her mind. Roarke's long fingers on her skin. Nightingale's lips against her neck. Two memories. One memory. One mistake, made twice.

That was what stupid people did, wasn't it? They made the same mistake over and over and somehow expected things to turn out differently.

It wasn't a mistake, she told herself. *You were two consenting adults. You were clear about what you were doing. You had a good time. Tons of people hook up at weddings. He's not Nightingale. It's not a big deal.*

She exhaled slowly, then started worrying that Roarke would hear her, that the silence in the car was so oppressive that her exhale might reveal everything she was thinking to him, and soon he'd be asking someone else to be his fake girlfriend so he could send a message to her about how she meant absolutely nothing to him.

Maybe she needed to get in first. *Hey, that was fun last night*, she should say casually, if she got him alone. *Thanks.*

He'd look down at her, and she'd seem so cool and chill that he'd believe it. *Yeah, it was*, he'd say, and then, *maybe we should do it again sometime.*

You know I'm not your girlfriend, right? she'd say, and she'd be able to raise an eyebrow, just one eyebrow, the way he could. *This isn't anything. You aren't anything to me. Just so we're clear.*

Ha ha, he'd say dryly. *Very funny.*

Then he'd back her into a wall, and his knee would be between hers again, and—

Was that what she wanted?

She had no idea.

Things weren't any clearer a few hours later when they pulled up out the front of her building. 'Thanks for the ride,' she said to Will.

'My pleasure,' he replied. 'Roarke, give her a hand with her bag, would you?'

Roarke was half out of the car before Libby had time to protest. 'I've got it,' he said, when she tried to take the bag from him. 'Come on. I'll walk you to your door.'

They were up the stairs and outside her apartment before she managed to pull together the courage to speak. 'So we should probably talk.'

'What is there to talk about?' he asked.

She opened her mouth. She closed it again.

'Sorry. That sounded harsher than it was meant to,' he said, putting her bag down in front of her door. 'But it wasn't a thing, Libby. We agreed.'

'I know we did.'

'I'm not interested in a relationship.'

'Did I say I was?'

He raised an eyebrow.

'Sorry,' she said. 'I just – remember that talk we had about boundaries? I have one, and it's that I don't want my … my personal life spread around the theatre.'

He studied her. 'You really think I would do that? Go around telling everyone that we had sex?'

'No,' she said, running both her hands through her hair and closing her fists, pulling it tight against her scalp. 'It's just that it wouldn't be the first time something like that's got round the theatre, and I'd rather not be the butt of a bunch of jokes. Is that okay with you?'

'Of course it is,' he said. 'I wouldn't do that to you, Libby.'

'We're clear, then,' she said. 'It didn't mean anything, I've got no interest in being your girlfriend, and you're not going to tell anyone what happened. Ever. Deal?'

She put her hand out.

After a long moment, Roarke took it. 'Deal,' he replied.

She was glad Ella wasn't home yet. Ella would have taken one look at her face and known that something was wrong, and she wouldn't have stopped tugging at the thread until Libby told her the truth.

Though of course she could tell Ella. *Roarke?!* she'd say, surprised but delighted. *Get it, girl! How was it?*

Um, it was good, she'd say. *He, um, knows what he's doing.*

That's great! Ella would say. *Not many girls get a good first time, you know.*

But then *it wasn't my first time,* she'd have to say, because there was not telling someone something, and then there was lying to them, and *what?!* Ella would say, and the whole truth would come spilling out, and—

And it would be fine. It would be *fine.*

She made herself a cup of tea and wrapped her hands around the mug, even though it was really too hot to touch. Thunder rumbled in the distance. There was a storm coming, and she couldn't seem to get warm.

Her phone buzzed. It was Ella. *Hi lovely. Left W this arvo. Home 11ish. Love you.*

She looked at the time. It was only just after five. Six hours suddenly seemed like a very long time to be alone.

It would be nice to have someone she could call, so she

could pretend to be fine for a while until she actually felt fine. She opened the theatre group chat thread and thought about posting a message – *hey crew! anyone want to go for drinks?* – but the thought of no one replying was too much and she closed it again.

Thunder rumbled again, closer now. She made herself get up and get her laptop. All those essays in her ProofItLibby inbox weren't going away. If she couldn't think or behave like a normal person, at least she could get some work done.

She scrolled through, deciding which one to do first, and there it was, the email she still hadn't brought herself to delete.

She could reply. Right now.

Dear Nightingale –

Just so you know, you're not special. I slept with someone else, and he was way better than you.

Regards

Libby.

Though there was no way she'd come out of that interaction on top. *Oh, cute,* he'd send back. *Nice that you found someone else who'd do you. Good for you.*

She shook her head. 'Stop being ridiculous,' she told herself, but the line fell flat. She hadn't delivered it convincingly enough.

She put some Kate Miller-Heidke on and got to work. It started to rain outside, pattering faintly on the windows, and then harder, harder, harder. She was distracted, or maybe not distracted enough, so she put the TV on as well, *New Girl* clashing with the music and the rain and the rumbling thunder, but it was still so, so loud inside her head.

Lightning flashed. Thunder cracked, a sound like a giant punching their fist through a plank of wood. The lights flickered once, twice, out.

Silence fell like a bomb.

She took a deep breath, and another, then got up. Using the light from her phone, she rummaged around in the kitchen junk drawer until she found another of the votive candles her mother had given her for Christmas. She balanced it carefully in a saucer and tried to light it, but her fingers were shaking and the match wouldn't catch.

'Oh, for Christ's sake,' she said. Her voice felt much too loud in the darkness.

She got the candle lit. The flickering light seemed to emphasise the shadows, as if there was a monster hiding in every corner, under the table, behind the door.

She finished editing the essay. She worked her way through another one. She did the reading for Con Law, and took something that might have been notes, but her fingers wouldn't quite stop shaking, and her mind wouldn't quite obey her. Even though she was *fine*, and she was an adult, part of her was still afraid of the dark.

Her phone died. She thought about hooking it up to her computer, but she had a vague idea it would suck power away from the battery, and if her laptop died and she didn't have any work to focus on, she might lose her entire mind.

She wanted another cup of tea, and was halfway to the kitchen to make it when she realised she needed electricity to boil the kettle, and something about that was just so upsetting, and there were tears rolling down her face, and—

There was a knock at the door.

She broke out in goosebumps. She couldn't resist. She would open the door, and he would be there, and he would walk in, and he would peel her open all over again, and then he would laugh at her, and everyone would know what she'd done and how little it meant to him, how little she meant, and there would be nothing left of her.

She should just pretend she wasn't home.

No. Pretending hadn't got her very far recently.

She scrubbed the tears from her face. She set her jaw. She was Libby Lawrence, and she was clever, and she was strong, and she was going to be brave.

She opened the door.

'Hi Libby,' Will said, hair damp from the rain, her wallet in his hand. 'I tried calling, but you didn't pick up. You left this in my car, and I didn't want you to worry about – what's wrong?'

She wiped the tears furiously away. 'I'm fine,' she said.

'No, you're not.'

'I am,' she insisted, but she'd never been a worse actor in her life. 'Thank you for bringing my wallet back.'

'Libby, I'm not leaving you like this.'

She didn't say anything. If she did, she'd burst into full-fledged sobs.

'Unless you want me to,' he said. 'Do you want me to go?'

She shook her head.

He came closer slowly, asking her permission, and she wrapped her arms around him, burying her face into his shirt. He smelled like rain, and he was warm, and he was safe, safe, safe.

'Shhhh,' he whispered. 'It's all right. You're all right.'

He wasn't an actor, but she almost believed him.

'I'm sorry,' she said, what might have been seconds or minutes or hours later, as they sat together on the couch.

'What for?' he asked. His eyes were kind behind his glasses, illuminated by the flickering light of the candle.

'All of this.' She gestured helplessly at herself. 'You must think I'm so ridiculous.'

'Of course I don't.'

She wiped at her eyes again, even though they were dry now. 'I wish I could offer you a cup of tea or something, but until the power comes back on—'

'Are you all right?' he asked.

She didn't know how to respond.

'I absolutely understand if you don't want to talk about it,' he said. 'It's none of my business. What happens between you and Roarke is between you and Roarke, and—'

'He told you?!'

Her face was on fire. Her stomach plummeted, and her heart felt like it was going to jackhammer out of her chest.

'No, no, no,' he said. 'But I was there, Libby. I know I was wrapped up in my own shit, but it was hard to miss.'

Could you die of embarrassment? She was going to die of embarrassment.

'Can we please not talk about this?' she asked desperately. 'Like, ever?'

'Of course, of course, of course,' he said. 'Just tell me you're all right.'

'I'm all right,' she said. 'He and I are fine, Will. It's not going to hurt the show.'

'I don't care about the show,' he said. 'I care about you. I know he's my brother, but if he's done anything to hurt you, I'll do whatever you need. I'll replace him in the show. I'll—'

'Will, no,' she said. 'He hasn't done anything wrong. You don't need to worry.'

He didn't believe her, and didn't try to pretend otherwise. 'Libby, he said. 'You were crying.'

'Really, I'm fine,' she said. 'This is not about him. You don't need to, like, ride forth and defend my honour or whatever. I'm okay. He's okay. We're okay. The show's going to be okay. Everything's okay.'

'You're sure?'

'I'm sure,' she said. 'Thank you for caring, though. And for not laughing at me.'

'Why would I laugh at you?' he said. 'What kind of monster do you think I am?'

'Well,' she said, 'I do have a mounting pile of evidence that you're an axe murderer.'

He chuckled. 'Oh, ProofIt,' he said. 'I've fooled everyone else, but I couldn't get it past that lightning-quick brain of yours, could I?'

'Nope. This is a citizen's arrest.'

Then something he'd said finally registered. 'Wait, so Roarke *is* your brother?'

'... Yes?' Will said, clearly confused by the abrupt change of conversation topic. 'Didn't you know that?'

'No,' Libby said. 'Do you know how much speculation there is in the Uni Rep group chat about how you two know each other?'

'He's my foster brother,' Will said. 'He came to live with my family when he was fifteen and I was seventeen. His mother had died a few years earlier, and his stepdad was a racist abusive piece of shit, and ... it's a long, messy story, and it's not mine to tell, so—'

'Of course,' Libby said. 'I won't tell anyone.'

'I mean, you can tell them he's my brother,' Will said. 'That's not a secret. Everyone knows that.'

'I can assure you that they definitely don't,' Libby said. 'Otherwise they wouldn't be creating these elaborate headcanons about you and Roarke being in a dark and stormy passionate closeted romance, where Caro is your beard.'

She realised a moment too late – a moment after his face fell – that she'd said entirely the wrong thing.

'Oh shit,' she said. 'I'm sorry, Will. I didn't mean to put my foot in it.'

'You don't have anything to be sorry for,' he said. 'You're not the one that's screwed things up.'

'Did you and Caro …?'

He nodded.

'Can you fix it?'

He shook his head.

'I'm sorry.'

'So am I, believe me,' Will said. He leaned back and tipped his head to the ceiling. 'I wish it fixed things, me being sorry, but here we are.' He sighed. 'I feel terrible.'

'It'd be pretty surprising if you didn't,' she said. 'I don't think people generally come out of breakups dancing and singing and skipping around.'

'You know what the worst part is, though?' he said. 'Part of me is. Not dancing and singing, but relieved it's over. Which just makes me feel even more terrible, because I really care about her, and what does it say about me that I can be happy when I hurt her?'

'But you're not happy *because* you hurt her,' Libby said. 'That's not the same thing as being relieved that it's over.'

'I know, I know,' Will said, running a hand through his hair. 'But I still feel so incredibly shit. She's hurting, and it's my fault, and I've stolen half her life, and—'

'Half her life? What, have you been dating since you were ten?'

'No, no, no. Nothing like that. Not even a year. I mean Uni Rep.' He took his glasses off and started polishing them on his shirt. 'I told her I'd step down as director, but she wouldn't let me. She quit the show instead.'

'Oh.'

'So now I have to replace her, and that makes me feel terrible all over again, because I'm the interloper,' he said. 'Uni Rep was hers. She brought me into it. I was going to help her find her feet again. And now she won't stay, because of me. I was going to give it back to her, and instead I stole it.'

His voice cracked, and he covered his eyes with one of his hands, his glasses dangling precariously from the other.

'Oh, Will,' Libby said helplessly.

She didn't know what to do, so she sat up on her knees and wrapped her arms around him. 'I'm sorry,' she whispered into his ear. 'Will, I'm so sorry.'

He was still for a second, then he turned, and his arms were around her, holding her tight, and her shoulder was the one his face was buried in, and he was the one who was sobbing.

'It's okay,' she whispered. 'You're okay. It's all going to be okay.'

Chapter Ten

She woke the next morning to the sound of clattering and clanking. She was still dressed in her clothes from the night before, but she was in bed. Her shoes were neatly together on the floor.

She didn't remember how she'd got there. She touched a hand to her head. No hangover.

She heard the whir of electric beaters, and a weight lifted off her chest. The power was back, and so was Ella.

'Morning,' she said, shuffling into the kitchen. 'Welcome home.'

'Helllllooooo, Elizabeth Two,' Ella sang, standing over the stove, spatula in hand. 'What's the story, morning glory? I'm making pancakes, and you're going to help me eat them. I hope you're down with this plan, because you have no choice.'

'I am *very* down with this plan.'

She glanced at the clock on the microwave. It was just after ten. Still plenty of time to get to uni before Torts.

'How was Wimeena?' she asked, leaning her hip against the kitchen bench.

She asked the question deliberately lightly, and braced herself for the inevitable heavy answer, but Ella's demeanour didn't change. 'The usual,' she said, flipping over a pancake. 'The memorial was depressing. Mum and Nan are the same. I had drinks with some school people. That was nice. But enough about me. Let's talk about yooooouuuuu, Elizabeth Two.'

'What?'

'Don't you play coy with me, girl,' Ella said, pointing the spatula at her. 'It happened, didn't it? You finally got laid.'

Her mouth fell open. Was it really that obvious?

'Will's lovely,' Ella said. 'But doesn't he have a girlfriend?'

'Oh! Oh, Ella. No.'

'What do you mean, no?' Ella said. 'I come home to find you *literally asleep in each other's arms*, and you expect me to believe that nothing happened?'

'Sorry to disappoint you, but it's true,' Libby said. 'I accidentally left my wallet in his car and he came over to give it back. That's all.'

'I know when I return someone's wallet, I also end up draping myself over them and falling asleep. That's just a normal, everyday thing that happens to people.'

'He broke up with Caro,' Libby said. 'We were talking, and he was upset, and ... we fell asleep, I guess.'

'You fell asleep. Seriously.'

'Ella, I think that pancake's burning.'

'You know what else is going up in smoke? My dreams,' Ella said, rescuing it. 'He carried you to bed like you were a princess. It was adorable. I've already picked out names for three of your children.'

'Sorry to disappoint.'

'But just because nothing happened doesn't mean nothing *will* happen,' Ella said, a wicked gleam in her eye. 'You're single, he's single, you've already kind of slept together ...'

'Ella.'

'Ugh, you're no fun.' Ella poured more batter into the frypan. 'Anyway, tell me about the wedding. Anything epic go down? Apart from the big breakup, I mean?'

She thought about it. She really thought about it. *Actually, I did get laid,* she could say, and she could tell Ella all about it. Will hadn't laughed at her. Ella wouldn't either.

But she couldn't tell her about Roarke and then not tell her about Nightingale. And besides, she and Roarke had agreed, hadn't they? There was nothing to talk about.

'Nope,' Libby replied. 'Do you want some tea? I'll make some.'

'Well, I think that's all of us,' Will said at the beginning of rehearsal that night, after the Ritchie brothers drifted through the door. 'Before we start today, an announcement. I'm sorry to say that we've lost Caro.'

He paused briefly. Phones buzzed around the room, including hers in her handbag. Looking around, Libby could see at least three people with theirs in their hands.

'She sends her apologies, and she's very sorry to have to pull out like this, and I'm very sorry to see her go, but thankfully it happened now and not later when things were really complicated,' Will went on, seemingly oblivious to the fact that the group chat was blowing up. 'I'm going to recast Hero in the next week or so. Tonight, we're just going to have to manage as best we can. That might make things a bit tricky for you, Ned. I'm sorry about that.'

'No big,' Ned said, not looking up from his phone. 'I can handle it.'

'We're going to focus on the masquerade scene tonight,' Will said. 'I want you to get used to wearing masks in this scene, so we've got some cheap ones for you to wear for now. Apologies for the fact that you'll look like you're going to a four-year-old's birthday party. Your real masks will be much nicer, Ella promises. Genevieve, can you keep a track of Hero's blocking? I'll get you to stand in for her tonight, if that's all right.'

'Can do,' Genevieve said. 'Take a mask and pass them around, guys.'

'Hey Libs,' Annalise whispered, sliding over to Libby as the people who were in the beginning of the scene got up and the Ritchie brothers started arguing over where they were supposed to be standing. 'You were with Will this weekend, right? What happened?'

Libby shrugged, glancing at her phone. There were already eleven messages in the group chat, and she had DMs from four different people. 'No clue.'

'Come on,' Annalise said. 'Don't lie to me.'

'I mean it. I don't know what happened.' The masks came around. She took a zebra-striped one.

'Fine, fine, be that way,' Annalise said, taking a leopard-print mask and basically throwing the pile on to the next person. 'But will you do me a favour? Can you talk to Will for me?'

'About what?'

'Caro's gone,' Annalise said. 'I'd love to play Hero. This role I have is a piece of piss. I'd kill to trade up.'

'Sure, I get it,' Libby said. 'But why do you need me to get involved? Why not just talk to him yourself?'

Annalise rolled her eyes. 'Are you really going to be like this?'

'Be like what?'

'Libby, I'm not an idiot. He comes in here with a girlfriend, but bam! Suddenly you've got the lead role, and then bam! Suddenly the girlfriend's gone, on a weekend where you were away together.'

'Will and Caro breaking up has nothing to do with me.'

'Fine, whatever, you believe that if you want,' Annalise said. 'But any idiot could see that he, like, adores you, so will you ask him if I can trade up to Hero?'

'Libby,' Roarke said. 'We're up.'

His fingers closed around hers, and he hauled her to her feet. Surprised, she stumbled, and nearly fell into him, but he caught her.

His face was uncomfortably close to hers. 'Hi,' he said, the corner of his lips quirking up.

'Hi,' she said, stepping back and smiling politely. She put her zebra mask on, hoping that if she couldn't restrain herself from blushing, she could at least disguise it a little.

They waited for their entrance together in the corner of the studio. There wasn't much room, so they had to stand close together. Trying to project, *I am normal and cool and nothing out of the ordinary has happened to me ever* took a huge amount of her concentration.

'How are you?' Roarke asked quietly. His mask was tiger-striped, the orange bright against his dark hair.

'I'm fine,' she replied, focusing her attention on her script like a good, conscientious actor whose only worry was keeping her cue. 'How are you?'

'Also fine,' he said.

Then he didn't say anything, and it was so loud he might as well have been screaming in her ears.

It was such a relief when their cue came, and she could pretend to be someone else for a while. 'Will you not tell me who told you so?' she asked Roarke.

'No, you shall pardon me,' Roarke answered.

He was transformed behind the tiger mask. *You know this isn't a thing, right?* Roarke was gone, and in his place was someone playful, mischievous, with a roguish twinkle in his eye.

'Nor will you not tell me who you are?'

'Not now,' he said, and turned away.

She grabbed his arm, and pulled him back to face her. 'That I was disdainful, and that I had my good wit out of the Hundred Merry Tales,' she snarled.

'Pull that back, Libby,' Will said. 'Too much. Too angry.'

'Oops, sorry,' she said, plastering a smile on her face before Will could realise the anger was real.

Pointedly – or what felt like pointedly – Roarke removed his arm from her grasp.

'Sorry,' she said again.

'You don't need to apologise,' he said.

'Well, this was Signior Benedick that said so,' she pressed on, before she could think too much about it.

'What's he?' Roarke asked, and he was gone again, someone different in his place.

'I am sure you know him well enough.'

'Not I, believe me.'

'Did he never make you laugh?'

'I pray you, what is he?'

'Why, he is the Prince's jester,' she said, and keeping the edge of anger out of her voice was hard, so hard, because she knew she shouldn't be too angry, but she couldn't stop.

Oh God, she'd love to laugh at him. She'd love to beat him. She'd love to see his laughing face and smash her fist into it and splinter it into a million glittering pieces.

'I am sure he is in the fleet,' she said. 'I would he had boarded me.'

Thankfully, she wasn't required for Wednesday night rehearsal, but she had to go in early for one on Sunday afternoon, because Ella had a design meeting.

'Of course you're coming with me!' Ella said, when she protested. 'I need the moral support, Libs. What if Will hates my designs?'

'As if he'd hate your designs,' Libby said, but it was a fight she knew she had no chance of winning.

So she ended up sitting cross-legged on the foyer floor with Ella, Will and Genevieve forty-five minutes before rehearsal, three of her textbooks weighting down the corner of Ella's A3 set design sketch, and one of Will's, ominously titled *Calculus and Algebraic Methods,* on the fourth.

'This is great,' Will enthused, glasses nearly falling off his nose as he leant forward to study the sketch.

'You think so? Really?' Ella said anxiously.

'Really. These are brilliant. Designs of my dreams.'

'Seriously, we should've turfed Ackroyd ages ago,' Genevieve said. 'This is stunning, Ella.'

Ella beamed.

'The only thing I'm worried about is cost,' Will said. 'Is this going to come in under budget?'

'If we're creative,' Ella said. 'And if everyone pitches in to help. The biggest costs here are time and labour, not money.'

'I'll set up a working bee,' Genevieve said. 'How's next weekend? Saturday, before rehearsal?'

'Works for me,' Ella said. 'Another way we can probably save some money is if we rehab some old costumes instead of making new ones. If you don't mind, I'd love to go through some of the costumes in storage here and see what we have. Adapting'll be way easier and cheaper than buying or making.'

'Great,' Genevieve said. 'Any cost-saving measures you can come up with, Graham will be eternally grateful. Nightingale ripped the arse out of our bottom line.'

'I can make a start today, if you like,' Ella said. 'I'd love to go through – what's it called, Libby? The place that's, like, where costumes go to die?'

'The Swamp?' Genevieve asked. 'I'd wear a biohazard suit. Definitely wash anything you find in there. Several times. You don't know where it's been.'

'Is it really that disgusting?'

'Nightingale Smith's House of Hook-ups? Yes, it is absolutely that disgusting,' Genevieve said. 'There are probably layers in there that archaeologists should look at. The Swamp is way older than Uni Rep. Some of the stuff on the bottom might be from, like, 3000 BC. Or at least 1980.'

'What I'm hearing is hidden treasures,' Ella said.

'What you should be hearing is hepatitis, but if you're brave enough to tackle it, go ahead,' Genevieve said. 'I'll show you where it is.'

Libby focused on breathing. If she kept breathing, maybe she could keep her heart rate steady, and if she kept her heart rate steady, maybe she wouldn't turn the colour of an eggplant and give the whole game away.

'Hey,' Will said, as Ella and Genevieve disappeared through the auditorium doors. 'You okay?'

'I'm fine,' she said. 'Definitely less fragile than the other night. Not about to break down on your shoulder and cry.'

'Damn. I put on my most tear-absorbent jumper and everything.'

'Sorry to disappoint. How about you?'

'I'm okay,' he said. 'Not stellar, obviously, but I'm dealing.'

'Good,' she said. 'Because I didn't wear my most tear-absorbent jumper, so we might have been in trouble.'

'Thank you. For the other night, I mean.'

'You're welcome,' she replied. 'And thank you. It was ... nice, to have you there.'

'My pleasure.'

For a moment, as she looked at him, and he looked at her, everything was perfect and quiet and still.

Then he shook his head, and the bubble burst. 'So tell me about working bees,' he said. 'How well attended are they? What do I have to do to make people come?'

'Honestly? Buy them pizza,' she replied. 'People are much more willing to do shit if they're being fed.'

'I'll talk to Graham and see if the uni will pony up the money for it.' He sighed and took off his glasses, polishing them on his grey cable-knit jumper. 'That'll be a fun conversation. *Hey, your granddaughter just dumped me, give me cash.*'

'Some constructive criticism?' Libby said. 'Don't phrase it like that.'

'Thank you for that wise advice, ProofIt. I'll take it into consideration.'

'You know I've never actually properly met Graham?' she said. 'Not in a Uni Rep context, anyway. I took his class, but that's about it.'

'I've known him for a while, but I still don't really know what to make of him,' Will said, putting his glasses back on. 'When he got me to look over the books, and I told him how much money had been embezzled and who had done it, I thought he was going to leap into action. The way Caro talks about him, it was like his world had been shattered when the uni defunded the Theatre Studies major, and keeping Uni Rep afloat was his life. I thought he was going to be furious. But he just looked sad. Heartbroken, even. Then I suggested calling the cops, but he just sighed and said, *No, no, no, we're theatre folk, son. What happens in the theatre stays in the theatre. We deal with our own.*' He shook his head again. 'That's just mystifying to me, honestly.'

'The way people tell it,' Libby said, 'he had a real soft spot for Nightingale. He was one of the last students in the Theatre Studies program. It got cut right before he could finish the major. Maybe Graham feels guilty.'

'Maybe.'

'And Nightingale was one of the founding members of Uni Rep. That still means something to people here.'

'Caro was one of the founding members too, though, and people ditched her without a second thought.'

'That's different.'

'How?'

How was she having this conversation?

'Maybe it's not different,' she admitted at last. 'Graham didn't ditch Caro, and he didn't ditch Nightingale. But Uni Rep ditched Caro, and trust me, after he stole all that money, they've definitely ditched Nightingale too. He's, like, persona non grata now.'

'Yeah, but how long did it take to get there?' Will said, running his hand through his hair. 'When the SMS revue was in this theatre last year, I was talking with one of the ushers. She was one of the founding members of Uni Rep like Caro, but she told me this story about how she hooked up with Nightingale and basically got slut-shamed out of here.'

'Rosie?'

'You know her?'

'Not well, but we did a couple of shows together. There was more to the story, though. She was dating Ned at the time.'

'I know,' Will said. 'She told me. But how is it that she got basically chased out of here, and Nightingale didn't? How is it that Nightingale can steal eight grand and screw over half the girls in the company and people still have a secret little soft spot for him, but Caro messes up on one night in a show and everyone ices her out forever?'

'I ...'

He sighed. 'Sorry. It's really not fair of me to ask that.'

'You can ask,' she said. 'I just don't know how to answer.'

On Monday night, Will pulled Libby aside before rehearsal.

'We're doing some of the kissing scenes tonight,' he said, keeping his voice low so no one else in the foyer could here. 'Are you going to be okay with that?'

She nodded. 'Yes.'

She appreciated that he took her at her word and trusted her to do her job and didn't push her any harder. Especially because she wasn't sure if she was telling the truth.

So that night, Roarke kissed her, over and over again.

'Other side of her neck, Roarke,' Will said, scribbling something in his script. 'If you're kissing her on the downstage side, then you're blocking her face.'

'Right,' Roarke said, shifting his head. His breath was warm, his lips just barely brushing her neck. His hair was soft under her fingers.

'Actually, no, that doesn't work either, because it looks like you're a vampire,' Will said. 'Turn around a bit.'

She focused on her breathing as she and Roarke obediently shuffled. In. Out. In. Out. Keep your heartbeat steady, Libby. Keep your shit together.

'No, no, now you're blocking her completely,' Will said. 'I'll think about it. Let's move on.'

Roarke stepped back immediately, which was exactly what he should do. It stung, which it shouldn't.

'Have we got a Hero yet?' Ned asked at the end of rehearsal.

'Not yet, but we will have soon,' Will said. 'I promise.'

Annalise tried to catch Libby's eye. Libby focused very strenuously on the space between Will's eyebrows.

'Right, that's it for tonight,' Will said. 'But before you all go, Genevieve has an announcement.'

'Two announcements, actually,' Genevieve said. 'One is fun, and one is not so fun. The not-so-fun one is that we're going to have a working bee on Saturday before the rehearsal, and it would be killer if as many as you as possible could come along and help our excellent designer Ella out.'

'What are we doing?' Rashmi asked. 'Sets, costumes, everything?'

'Mostly costumes, because the Spruce Hall Players are on the stage right now, but hopefully we can get a few set pieces painted and stored ready for bump-in,' Genevieve said. 'That means you don't get a pass if you don't know how to sew, because there are still tons of jobs for you to do. I know it's a big ask, because I know some of you are required at Sunday rehearsal as well, but it would be a huge help if you could come. We start at nine am.'

There was a chorus of groans.

'Yes, yes, it's early, but (a) there'll be pizza for lunch, and (b) there's a reward,' Genevieve said. 'Time for the fun announcement. That day also happens to be my birthday, and because you're all going to work so hard at the working bee and then rehearse so hard at rehearsal, I want you to come to my party on Saturday night. We're going to the eighties nightclub, and my dad has sprung for a bar tab, so—'

'Sold!' Michael yelled.

'I thought that might grab your attention,' Genevieve said. 'Anyway, come one, come all. But please also come one, come all to the working bee, because Ella can't do this all on her own, and this show belongs to all of us.'

Despite Libby's best efforts, Annalise caught up with her as they filed down the stairs from the studio to the foyer. 'Hey, did you talk to Will for me yet?'

She thought about lying. 'Not yet,' she said instead. 'But I really think you'd be better off talking to him yourself.'

'Girl, he isn't interested in what I have to say,' Annalise said. 'If he was, he would have cast me as Hero or Beatrice or something in the first place, and not in this tiny-ass waste of space role.'

'Margaret's not a waste of space. The plot wouldn't work without her.'

'Yeah, fine, whatever, I'm on stage for like two seconds,' Annalise said dismissively. 'I want to do more, Libs. Just talk to him for me, okay?'

'I— all right.'

'Thank you,' Annalise said, and surprised her by hugging her. 'With all the bros in this theatre, we have to have each other's backs, okay?'

She didn't quite know what to say to that.

'Libby, want a ride?' Will asked, coming up behind them.

'Sure,' she replied.

Get it, girl, Annalise mouthed. Libby pretended she didn't see.

She couldn't stop herself turning red, though. She'd been grilled in the group chat over what had gone down with Will and Caro on the weekend away, and she knew her *I don't know*s weren't satisfying anyone. There must be dozens of spin-off conversations she was excluded from, speculating over what was happening. *He cast Libby over Caro, then he broke up with Caro while he was away with Libby. I know he's the mathematician, but I can do that maths.*

At least if people were speculating about her and Will, they had no idea about her and Roarke – or, God forbid, her and Nightingale.

'So how are the Hero recasts going?' she asked Will on the way home.

'I've got a couple of people I'm thinking about,' he replied. 'It's been tricky, to find someone who'll fit into the show as it stands now, but I'm going to meet with someone tomorrow. I'm not sure she'll want to do it, though.'

'Well, if she doesn't …' she swallowed. 'Have you thought about Annalise?

There was a scoffing sound from the backseat.

She swivelled her head around. 'What's wrong with Annalise?'

'She overacts and pulls focus,' Roarke said. 'She'd be terrible.'

'She's frustrated,' Libby said. 'She's used to having bigger roles.'

'So that makes it fine to throw a tantrum until she gets what she wants?'

'What did she ever do to you?'

'Nothing. I just think she'd be a shitty choice.'

'She's tried and tested,' Libby said. 'And she absolutely has chemistry with Ned. They've played opposite each other a million times.'

'I'll think about it,' Will said, pulling up and idling in front of Libby's apartment building. 'See you Saturday, Libby. Get Ella to let me know if there's anything she needs for the working bee.'

'Will do. Night.' She leaned over to hug him, then got out and closed the car door.

A second later, Roarke's door closed too. 'What are you doing?' she asked him.

'Walking you to your door.'

'I'm fine,' she said. 'You and Will put the fear of God into Paul. He's not coming back.'

He raised one eyebrow.

She rolled her eyes and walked away.

He followed her. 'I'm getting the impression that you're angry with me.'

'Would you care if I was angry with you?'

'Yes,' he said. 'Of course I would.'

How the hell was she supposed to react to that?

'Roarke, I'm not angry with you,' she said. 'You seem to be really angry at Annalise for some reason—'

'I'm not angry with her. I just don't think she's a very good actor. Do you?'

'I—'

'Seriously, do you?'

'I'm not answering that.'

'Libby,' he said, 'it's me. You don't need to worry about bullshit theatre politics.'

'I thought you didn't do D&Ms.'

'You answering a yes or no question isn't a D&M.'

'Fine,' she said. 'I think, as an actor, Annalise is fine. If she played Hero, she'd do fine.'

'Wow,' he said, grinning. 'Talk about damning with faint praise.'

'Shut up.'

'Gladly,' he said. 'See you Saturday. If we find some time, maybe we can work on that masquerade scene again. It didn't seem quite right.'

'Sure.'

He moved closer. It was strange, and tentative, and a bit ginger, but they hugged each other, and something that was almost a question began to bubble up inside her.

Then the front door opened. 'I thought I heard voices,' Ella said. 'Hey, Roarke. Do you want to come in for a bit?'

'I'd better not,' he said. 'Will's in the car. Thanks, though.'

He walked away, and the moment disappeared, and it wasn't a question she was even sure she wanted to ask.

Chapter Eleven

Will was sitting on the back steps when Libby and Ella got to the theatre on Saturday morning. 'Hey, you two,' he said, jumping up and taking the box out of Ella's arms. 'Good to see you.'

'Good to see you too,' Ella said. 'At least I'll have one person to help with all of this.'

'You'll have more than one,' Will said.

'Way more than one,' Libby said. 'Promise.'

Libby held the back door open and let Will and Ella through into the tiny theatre kitchen. Will dropped the box on the table. 'What's in here?'

'Fabric,' Ella said. 'Odds and ends. Bits and bobs. Things that might be useful.'

'She's been collecting things that might be useful since we were three,' Libby said.

'Oh, shut up,' Ella said. 'I've got a few more boxes in the car. Can you give me a hand, Will?'

'Sure.'

Ella and Will disappeared. Libby went inside and put the kettle on. She scrounged up some teabags from the jar, and sniffed the milk in the fridge experimentally before pouring it down the sink. She washed the mugs twice before she poured the boiling water into them. 'If we have time, we should do a clean-up of the kitchen,' she said over her shoulder, as Ella and Will came back with more boxes. 'I don't think anyone's cleaned in here since about 1994. It's gross.'

'We are absolutely not going to have time,' Ella said. 'I need everyone focused on my stuff today. Is that tea?'

'Yes. Although the teabags might date back to the founding of the university and the milk's off, so I hope you don't mind black.'

'I can run over to the student union and get some,' Will said.

'William Callahan,' Ella said, putting her hand on his arm, 'Libby and I both love you very much.'

'Is that a yes?'

'Yes,' Libby said. 'Thank you.'

'No problem.' Will disappeared out the back door.

Libby turned back to Ella. 'We both love him very much? What was that?'

Ella grinned. 'Nothingggggggg,'

Libby rolled her eyes. 'Is that all the boxes?'

'Yep,' Ella said. 'Can you start unpacking them? Sewing stuff in here, fabric in the annexe—'

'I remember the diagram,' Libby said.

'Cool. Sorry I'm being such a dictator. I'm just nervous. I want this to go well.'

'Chill out. You'll be fine.'

Ella's phone buzzed. She pulled it out to look at it, and a smile spread across her face.

'What?' Libby asked.

'Nothing,' Ella said. 'Well, not nothing. It's – ah – it's Gerry.'

Libby felt like someone had dropped ice down her shirt. 'Gerry?' she said, managing to keep her voice light. 'Your Gerry?'

Ella nodded. 'He's going to be in the city tonight. Some farm conference, or whatever it is you call it when a bunch of farm guys get together and talk about farming. He wants to have dinner.'

'Oh. Okay.'

'Do you want to come?'

'Definitely not,' she said, a little too quickly.

Ella raised her eyebrows.

'I'm already doing stuff tonight,' Libby said. 'There's rehearsal, and then there's Gen's birthday thing, remember?'

'Oh. Yeah. Apologise to her for me, would you?'

'It's at a nightclub. You could come after.'

She had a sudden vision of stumbling home late, only to find a note on the dining table. *Sorry Libs. I need Gerry, and Gerry needs me. Gone home. E.*

'Maybe,' Ella said, her voice airy. 'I'll see. I might be exhausted after today. I'm going to go upstairs and suss out the sitch in the storeroom before everyone gets here. Are you right down here?'

'I've got it.'

The kitchen was quiet when Ella left. It was strange to see it so still, so empty. Come show time, it was always crowded and chaotic and colourful, people perching on the counters, wigs askew, sculling honey and hot water and trying not to gag, dressers pinning frocks and coats and straightening collars, people attacking each other with slap foundation and heavy eyeliner, Nightingale governing the circus from his seat on the top of the half-size fridge, laughing at everything and everyone.

But he was only a ghost now.

Would her kitchen feel like this someday? Would she stand there in stillness, in emptiness, in silence, with Ella only a memory?

'Stop it,' she muttered to herself, as much to fill the quiet as anything else. 'You're being ridiculous.'

Ella and Gerry might have meant a lot to each other. But one night with him wasn't going to make Ella run. She had a life in Terravale now, a life that wasn't just Libby.

She felt better when Will came back, and gradually – a trickle at first, and then a flood – the theatre filled with people. Busy chatter filled the auditorium, the annexe, the kitchen, even the foyer, everyone talking and laughing as they sewed and painted and lifted and carried. Ella flitted from place to place like a butterfly, flannelette shirt tied knotted underneath her breasts, a smudge of paint along one cheek.

'I don't want you to take this the wrong way, Libs,' Michael said, while they painted a set piece together, 'because you know I sit on whichever end of the Kinsey scale is the gayest, but your friend is incredibly hot.'

'Don't I know it,' Libby replied.

There was a burst of sound from the bio box. 'Any requests for tunes?' Richard bellowed.

The only music kept in the bio box was soundtracks from previous shows, and soon, songs from the past few years of Uni Rep history were filtering through the building. 'Does everyone know all the words to these songs?' Will asked Libby as they sorted through a box of Ella's odds and ends in the kitchen.

'Pretty much,' Libby said. 'When you have to sing them week-in, week-out for a few months, they tend to stick.'

'What's this one from?'

Libby cocked her head to the side. '*Little Shop of Horrors.*'

'Were you in it?'

'Yep. Chorus.'

'Libby!' Ned yelled from the annexe. 'Get out here and understudy Audrey for me!'

'Duty calls,' she said to Will.

She didn't realise until she and Ned had finished their over-the-top rendition of 'Suddenly Seymour' that Will had followed her. He leaned against the kitchen door jamb and applauded.

'She's not half bad, huh?' Ned said, slinging an arm around Libby's neck. 'Libs, you would have killed as Audrey.'

'No, I wouldn't,' Libby said, extricating herself. 'Rosie did great. You know that.'

'Rosie Waters?' Will asked.

'Yeah,' Ned replied, going still beside Libby. 'You know her?'

'I do, actually,' Will said. 'I asked her yesterday to play Hero.'

'Oh no, man, you did not,' Ned said, groaning.

'I assure you, I definitely did,' Will said. 'She's going to do a great job. She'll be in for rehearsal tomorrow afternoon.'

Ned swore. 'She's my ex, man. That's going to be awkward as shit.'

'I know. She told me. But she seems to think it won't be a problem, so I have complete faith that you can do your job.'

'Does Gen know?'

'I haven't told her yet.'

'Do me a favour,' Ned said. 'Don't tell her till tomorrow. She hates Rosie, and I don't want to ruin her birthday.'

'Libby, I need you in the Swamp,' Ella said, running by. 'I found a box of boots in there the other day. Can you get it?'

She was gone before Libby had the time to make up an excuse.

'Do you need a hand?' Will asked her.

'No,' Libby replied. 'I've got it.'

It seemed quiet and dark backstage, even though the fluorescent working lights were blazing overhead, the music was still blaring, and she could still hear everyone talking and laughing and singing. She wanted to pause before she pushed aside the curtain to the Swamp, but she wouldn't let herself, because it was just a dressing room, nothing else, and pauses were for emphasis.

She waded into the costumes. They tried to suck her down.

Her underwear was in here somewhere.

It was just a dressing room.

What if Ella found her underwear when she was searching through here? They did their laundry together. What if she recognised it?

The box labelled *boots, misc* was on a shelf above her head. She put one foot on the top of a broken clothes rack half-buried in clothes, and grabbed the edge of the shelf, hoisting herself up, balancing carefully.

'Libby, do you need—'

Her hands slipped. She shrieked. Her heart rate escalated as she lost her footing.

'Whoa, whoa, whoa!' Roarke said, somehow managing to miraculously travel across the ocean of clothes and catch her before she fell entirely. 'Sorry. I didn't mean to scare you.'

She re-secured her grip on the edge of the shelf. 'I'm okay.'

'Are you sure?' he asked, hands still hovering at her waist.

'Yes, Roarke. I'm okay.'

'Good,' he said. 'Now can I help you? You're going to fall and kill yourself.'

'I'm not going to fall,' she replied. 'But here—' she reached up with one hand and pulled the box of boots to the edge of the shelf, '—catch.'

Ella was just about to leave when Libby got home after rehearsal. 'Hey, you're home!' she said, surprised, hooking a hoop earring through an ear with one hand while trying to do up the buckle on one of her strappy heels with the other, balanced precariously with a hip against the dining table. 'I thought you were going into town for Genevieve's thing.'

'I am,' Libby said, disentangling the red hairs from Ella's earring. 'I'm just getting changed first. Can't go to an eighties nightclub wearing grotty twenty-first-century clothes. You look nice.'

'Thanks,' Ella said, buckling her other shoe and picking up her black clutch. 'How's my makeup? Is anything smeared?'

'It's perfect.' *Not that Gerry would notice if it wasn't,* she wanted to add, but that felt like potentially perilous territory.

'If you can get ready to go in the next five seconds, I can give you a lift into town. You could come and say hi to Gerry for a minute.'

Libby shook her head. 'I have to have a shower. I'm all sweaty. I'll just take the train. Text me when you're heading back, though, and maybe I'll grab a ride home.'

Ella looked at her phone. 'Shit, I'm late. Catch you later, Elizabeth Two.'

Her heels clattered as she disappeared down the hallway. Libby looked after her, realising that she'd never promised to text her, or give her a ride, or even come home at all.

No, she told herself. *Stop.*

There was a text from Ella waiting when she got out of the shower. *Just had an idea,* she'd written. *There's a red minidress in my cupboard that I got at an op shop. It's super eighties. You should wear it.*

Don't text and drive, Libby sent back.

Her phone rang a few seconds later. 'I was at traffic lights,' Ella said, her voice tinny over the speaker. 'But you should wear that dress, Libs.'

'I've seen you wear it. It's not a dress. It's a shirt.'

'On me, sure, but you're shorter than me.'

'It won't fit.'

'Which of us is the costume designer here? Just try it on. Send me a pic.'

'Don't text and—'

'I'll pull over to look at it if I have to.'

Libby obeyed, taking a selfie of herself using Ella's mirrored wardrobe. 'See? Way too short.'

'Are you kidding? It's hot as hell.'

'It's ridiculous.'

'So were the eighties. You have great legs, Libs. Show them off.'

She hesitated.

'You're wearing it,' Ella told her decisively. 'If I come home tomorrow to find you didn't wear it, there'll be hell to pay.'

She hung up before Libby could protest.

If I come home tomorrow to find you didn't wear it, Ella had said. It wasn't a promise not to run off with Gerry into the sunset, but it certainly didn't sound like that was her *plan*.

Libby let out a breath and studied herself in the mirror. The dress was definitely way too short. But it did make her legs look good. And besides, what else was she going to wear?

'Bitch, you look amazing!' Genevieve exclaimed, when she walked into the nightclub. She was wearing an electric blue sequinned party dress and her hair was in a crimped side ponytail. 'Who knew you were such a stone-cold hottie, Libby Lawrence?'

'Right back at you,' Libby said, hugging her. 'You look great. And happy birthday. Can I buy you a drink later?'

'Sure,' Genevieve said. 'The way this crew drinks, the tab'll run out in about five seconds anyway.'

'You'll have to get in line, though,' Rashmi said. 'Michael has first drink dibs, and I have second. Can we talk about how hot you look? Damn, Libby.'

She ended up grabbing a drink and then dancing to 'Poison Arrow' with Rashmi and Heidi. She couldn't help but keep one eye out for Roarke, but she didn't see him anywhere, which she was glad about. As ... okay as she was with that whole situation, she didn't want to think about what him looking her up and down and then telling her how great she looked would do to her emotions.

Or – God – what if he didn't? What if he glanced at her, looked right through her, and didn't even notice? *Hi Roarke,* she'd say, and *not now,* he'd reply, and go back to a conversation with some other, hotter, less awkward girl.

Will was there, though, and he caught her eye from the bar. *You look great,* he mouthed to her.

Me? she mouthed back, putting one hand on her heart and pretending to be surprised.

He nodded, grinning, giving her two thumbs up.

He was wearing a shirt with a wide collar, unbuttoned two buttons more than normal. She pointed at him, tugged at her own neckline, then mimed fanning herself.

He laughed, licked a finger and pressed it to his exposed collarbone, miming a sizzle.

'So when's the wedding?' Rashmi asked her.

'What?'

'Or are you just going to keep us in suspense with all the flirting?' Heidi said.

'Oh,' she said. 'No, no, no – we're just ... playing.'

'Playing,' Rashmi said. 'Playyyyiiiiiiiinnnnnnnnnnngggggggg.'

'Is that what they're calling it these days?' Heidi asked.

Her traitor cheeks turned as red as her dress.

She was glad when the club filled up, because there was a much better chance of hiding in the darkness and in a crowd full of people stamping and howling the words to 'Tainted Love', and she could blunt the sharp edges of her nerves with alcohol. She got herself a vodka and orange and then let Michael and Anthony pull her out onto the dance floor 'You gotta know how to shake it in a dress like that, Libs,' Anthony told her solemnly, 'and we are here to teach you.'

It wasn't long until she was having fun, although she worried that her dress was going to ride up, and kept trying to tug the skirt further down, as if another inch of hem might suddenly materialise if she pulled hard enough. As predicted, the tab ran out by the time she'd had her second drink, so she bought a third, as well as one for Genevieve. She and Ned and Genevieve toasted, and she let herself get talked into a shot (but definitely not a second one, no matter how hard Annalise tried).

She was sweaty with a solid hour of dancing when she looked across the dance floor and saw Ella. 'Hey!' she said delightedly, elbowing her way across the floor until she reached her. 'I didn't think you were going to make it!'

'Gerry needed an early night!' Ella replied, yelling over 'Billie Jean'.

'How is he?'

'Fine! His girlfriend's pregnant!'

'What?' Libby yelled back, surprised, but not so surprised that she couldn't also be incredibly relieved. 'I didn't even know he had a girlfriend!'

'Neither did I! It's pretty recent, he said! The baby was a bit of a surprise!'

'When's the baby due?'

'Next February!' 'Billie Jean' turned to 'Love Shack' in the background. 'Gerry's going to be a dad! Isn't that the weirdest shit you ever heard?'

'You okay?'

'We've been broken up a long time, Libs! Of course I am! Where's the bar?'

'Over there! But didn't you drive?'

'I'll pick my car up tomorrow! Don't worry!'

Ella disappeared. Libby, looking after her, accidentally made eye contact with Roarke, who had turned up after all. He was all the way across the club, but his gaze was like a magnet.

He raised a hand in greeting. She realised about a moment too late that the cool, chill, normal thing to do would be to reciprocate.

'Hey, why so serious?' Ned came up beside her and spoke directly into her ear. 'You look like someone just killed your cat. Is something wrong?'

'No, no, no!' she said, tearing her eyes away from Roarke's. 'I'm fine!'

'Good!' Ned said. 'That's what I want to hear! You're always laced up so tight, Libs. Come and get down and boogie!'

She let him pull her out onto the dance floor. You didn't disobey Ned Riordan at a Uni Rep party, after all.

And it worked. She danced and she laughed and she had another drink or two. Ella came out onto the dance floor for a while and they got so into dancing to 'Africa' that they ended up almost crying with laughter and holding each other up. Someone wheeled out a cake for Genevieve, and she helped pass around the slices, and she danced some more, and she talked to some people, and she had another drink.

When it got to half-past eleven, Libby was sitting at a table at the edge of the dance floor, a half-full vodka and orange on the table in front of her. She'd been nursing it for a while now, and she'd come down from drunk to pleasantly tipsy. The DJ had got into the slow songs, and she watched the mirrorball spinning overhead, specks of light drifting around the room. She was happy and sore and content, and her mind was quieter than it had been for a long time.

'Sore feet?' Will asked, sliding onto the stool opposite her.

'Hmmmm?'

He pointed to the floor under the table. 'Your shoes.'

'Oh.' She barely remembered kicking off her heels. 'I don't think they're really meant for, you know, walking and standing and stuff. I'm pretty sure taking a step in them qualifies as an Olympic sport. Walking here from the station was a real adventure.'

'I hope the fact you've taken off your shoes doesn't mean you've stopped dancing.'

'I haven't danced this much for ages. Not since those eight-hour dance rehearsals Ned made us do in *A Chorus Line*.'

'I don't know if you've noticed,' Will said, 'but I'm screwing up my courage to ask the pretty girl to dance with me.'

'Where is she? Do you need me to ask her for you?' she said, pretending to look around.

He laughed. 'Come on, ProofIt. They're playing 'Lady in Red', and I'm pretty sure there's a law that says all ladies wearing red dresses have to dance when it's on.'

'I'm not putting my shoes back on,' she said, letting him pull her up. 'I don't care how disgusting the dance floor is.'

'If you need to, you can stand on my feet.'

'Right, because I'm five and I'm dancing with my dad at a wedding.'

'God, I hope not,' Will said. 'That would be weird.'

She laughed. He laughed too, and she could feel it the vibrations of it as she sank into him, chin on his shoulder. His heartbeat was slow and measured, like a metronome, the steady beat comforting. He was warm against her as he took one of her hands in his, his other resting between her shoulder blades.

'Do you think this is the cheesiest song of the eighties?' she asked.

'Solid contender,' he replied. 'But I think 'True' by Spandau Ballet might take the crown.'

'What's that one?'

'You don't know it?'

'I don't know. I might. Sing me a bit.'

'Not a chance.'

'Just do it, taxman.'

He turned his head so his lips were right against her ear and sang her a couple of lines, very off-key.

'Nope,' she said, smiling into his shoulder. 'This song is definitely the cheesiest one. I did a survey.'

'Oh really? Who did you survey?'

'A wide variety of knowledgeable people.'

'Yeah, well, I'm pretty sure there are deep flaws in your methodology.'

'Please. You don't know shit about my methodology. One of my majors is sociology, you lowly mathematician.'

'Making your comeuppance that much sweeter.'

'Comeuppance shomeuppance. What's your methodology?'

'Well, it has lots of numbers. Heaps. So many.'

'Is 'so many' a technical mathematical term?'

'Yes. And my methodology also involves dancing to 'True', and observing which is the cheesiest, through that process.'

'There's a technical term for that kind of method. We talked about in class last week.'

'No shit? I just invented sociology?'

'Well, not all of sociology. Maybe just deep participant observation.'

'Sounds dirty. Say it again.'

She turned her head, and his fingers were brushing her hair, and she was standing on his shoes after all, right on her tiptoes. 'Deep participant observation,' she whispered into his ear, and his hand tightened against the small of her back, and—

'Libby,' Rashmi said. 'I think you should come. It's Ella.'

It was like a bucket of cold water had been poured over her head. 'What happened? Where is she?' she said, pulling away from Will, abruptly wide awake and completely sober.

'Bathroom.'

'Thanks,' she said to Rashmi. 'Sorry,' she said to Will.

She didn't wait to hear his reply.

The tiles of the bathroom floor were cold under her bare feet. 'Ella?' she called.

'In here!'

She blinked. 'Roarke?'

'In here,' he said again, and there was the sound of someone retching.

Ella was on her knees, clutching the bowl of the toilet in the last cubicle. Her skin was pale and sweaty. Roarke was holding back her hair, which had come loose. 'Libby,' she groaned.

'Get out,' Libby told Roarke.

She expected an argument, but he obeyed wordlessly, so easily she felt momentarily guilty. 'Thank you,' she called over her shoulder, but he was already gone.

She scraped Ella's damp hair back. 'Hey, sweetheart,' she said, rubbing her back.

'Libby,' Ella said, her voice hoarse. 'I'm so stupid. I'm so stupid. Why am I so stupid?'

'Shhh,' Libby said. 'You're not stupid. You're fine. You're just a bit drunk.'

'No, no, no, I'm stupid,' Ella said, starting to cry.

'No, you're not,' Libby said. 'You're wonderful, and I love you, all right?'

Her only answer was more retching, punctuated by wrenching, hacking sobs. Ella clutched at Libby like a child clutching at a teddy bear, and Libby let her, ignoring the acidic smell of vomit.

Chapter Twelve

Libby had been up for three hours and had edited two essays from her ProofItLibby inbox when Ella emerged the next day. 'Hey,' she said croakily, red hair messy against the pink fleece of her dressing gown. 'Have we got any Panadol?'

'I ran out and got some this morning,' Libby said, getting up from the table. 'Gatorade, too. I'll get them for you. Sit down.'

Ella sat. 'My head is killing me.'

Libby popped two tablets out of the packet onto the table. Ella stared at them.

'Want me to make you breakfast?' Libby asked, putting the Gatorade next to the pills. 'It might help soak up all the alcohol.'

'No. If I eat anything, I'm going to throw up.' Ella groaned and buried her head in her hands. 'I'm really sorry. I know you probably didn't want to spend your night looking after me.'

'Ella, I'll look after you any time, any place. It's in the best friend contract. I read the fine print when we exchanged those necklaces when we were seven. Now take your pills and drink your Gatorade.'

Ella obeyed. 'God, that's disgusting,' she said, making a face. 'What's it made out of, lollies infused in sweat?'

'Full of electrolytes,' Libby said. 'It'll make you feel better.'

'Where'd you hear that?'

'Nightingale used to swear by it. You could tell when he'd had a big night, because he'd swan into rehearsal drinking it by the bucket.'

'Ugh. Gross.'

Ella took another swig. 'But it's what I deserve, I guess,' she said. 'I'm never drinking again. Ever. Ever ever ever.'

'Do you want to talk about it?'

'What's there to talk about?' Ella said. 'Alcohol is the devil. End of story.'

'You know that's not what I mean.'

Ella let her head thunk onto the table. 'I definitely don't want to talk about it.'

'We can, though, if you need to,' Libby said. 'It must be super weird, your ex-boyfriend having a baby with someone else.'

'Lots of people's ex-boyfriends have babies with someone else,' Ella said, forehead still on the table. 'They survive just fine.'

'I know, but—'

'It's not like I've been pining away for him or anything. Even if I was, there's no chance in hell he's ever going to leave Wimeena, and no chance in hell I'm ever going back.'

'You loved him, though,' Libby said, desperately shoving the immense relief she felt at *no chance in hell I'm ever going back* down into the recesses of her brain for later. 'It must be weird.'

Ella sighed and lifted her head. 'Yeah. It's weird. It's really, really weird.'

'I'm sorry.'

'Don't be,' Ella said. 'It's a good thing, probably. Maybe there was a tiny part of me still … like, clinging onto him. Can't do that now. Clean break, and all that.' She snipped the air with her fingers.

'That doesn't mean it's easy.'

Ella groaned again and let her head fall back onto the table. 'Why can't I be more like you, Libby?'

'You don't want to be like me,' Libby said. 'Trust me, you don't want to be anything like me.'

'Hmmm, let me think. Who do I want to be like? The girl crying and throwing up, or the one holding her hair back?'

'You've held my hair back before. Like when we had our party. You were the one putting me to bed and making me pancakes the next day.'

'It's not the same. You don't understand. You can't understand. You've never made a shitty decision in your life, and—'

'You think I've never made a shitty decision?'

'Name one,' Ella said. 'Name one shitty decision you've made.'

Libby hesitated. The words were on the tip of her tongue.

'See?' Ella said. 'You can't.'

'At least people *like* you.'

'People love you, Libs,' Ella said. 'I know high school was a bit of a shitshow, but look at you now. I was the one getting shitfaced at a party with your friends last night. Yours.'

'I never used to get invited to many of the parties, though. It's just because I'm Beatrice now. You wait. When the next show rolls around and the hierarchy is restored—'

'Oh, shut up with this hierarchy bullshit,' Ella said. 'We're not in Year Eight anymore.'

'Have you tried telling people at Uni Rep that?'

'Libby,' Ella said. 'You have friends. People there *like* you. And you know why? Because you're cool, and you're funny, and you're not a huge mess like me.'

'I am a mess, though,' Libby said quietly.

Ella snorted. 'No, you're not.'

'Yes, I am,' she insisted. 'I—'

She tried to say it. She *wanted* to say it.

'If I'm not a mess, then why did I cry on Will's shoulder for like ten solid minutes the other night because the power went out?' she finished lamely. 'Does that sound like something a sensible person would do?'

'Nope,' Ella said, taking a swig from her Gatorade. 'That sounds like a pretty sweet excuse to drape yourself all over him.'

She had a sudden flashback to the night before. *Deep participant observation,* she'd said, her lips just brushing his ear. His hand tightened on the small of her back, and—

'Will isn't interested in me,' she said. 'He broke up with Caro, what, five minutes ago?'

'Exactly,' Ella said. 'He's single.'

Libby rolled her eyes.

'If I were you, I'd be more worried about the thing where you spend all your time making out with his brother while he watches.'

'Ella,' she said. 'Will and I are not going to – wait, how do you know Roarke's his brother?'

Ella shrugged. 'One of the few things I remember from last night. We had a pretty good chat before, you know … the vomcano.'

'What else did he tell you?' Libby said, reaching across and taking a sip of Ella's Gatorade, trying to keep her tone casual.

'Oh, not much. He listened more than he talked, to tell the truth. Will you thank him for me? For looking after me?'

Libby nodded. 'Sure. I'll tell him.'

Libby intended to grab Roarke before rehearsal. *Hey, thanks for looking after Ella last night,* she'd say, coolly, casually. *No drama,*

he'd reply, and that would be the end of the conversation.

But she didn't get the chance, because she got grabbed by Ned first. 'Libs, I need a favour,' he said to her, seizing her arm and towing her into a corner the second she walked into the foyer.

'Of course,' she replied. 'What do you need?'

'I don't even know,' he said, taking off his beanie and raking a hand through his sandy blonde hair. 'It's just – Rosie.'

She glanced across to where Rosie was standing, talking to Will. Will caught Libby's eye and waved. She smiled and waved back.

'Don't look at her!' Ned said urgently. 'I don't want her to know I'm talking about her.'

'Ned, what are you asking me?'

He exhaled through his teeth. 'I told Gen this morning that Rosie was playing Hero and she lost her mind. Like, her entire mind. Can you help me run interference?'

'In what way?'

'I don't know!' he said. 'Just— you'll be doing a bunch of scenes with Rosie, I guess. I thought— never mind. Don't worry about it.'

'Don't worry about what?' Rashmi asked, coming up to them.

'Nothing,' Ned said. Libby felt like she'd failed some kind of test.

'How's Ella?' Rashmi asked.

'She's fine,' Libby said. 'She just drank too much.'

'How about you?'

'Also fine.'

'Come on, Libs, spill.'

'About what?'

Rashmi started humming *Lady in Red*.

'Ohhhhh, yeah, I forgot about that!' Ned said. 'Getting cosy with Callahan. Who knew you had it in you?'

'No,' she said firmly, knowing her face must be beetroot. 'Just no.'

'You're lying,' Rashmi said, grinning. 'Libby Lawrence, you are looking me in the eye and *lying* right now.'

Mercifully, Will – whether he somehow sensed that she was about to implode with embarrassment, or just had good timing – chose that moment to call everyone upstairs to the studio for rehearsal.

She lost track of the number of people who needled her about him. 'No wonder Caro quit,' Annalise said gleefully. 'She must be *livid*.'

'There's nothing happening,' she said. 'We're friends.'

'Yeah, yeah, sure, lady in red,' Michael said.

'Can you all just stop it? Please?'

'Not until you give us the goss,' Annalise said. 'Spill your guts, Libs. When did it start?'

The only respite she had from all of it was Rosie, who turned out to be a great scene partner. She asked questions, but they were about blocking, and character, and how Libby thought they should play various aspects of Hero and Beatrice's relationship. She only asked one question that might have been considered even vaguely personal, and it was whether Genevieve was still staring at her.

'Um ...' Libby said, looking across the studio to where Genevieve was glowering beside Will at the card table they were using as a production desk. 'Kind of? A little?'

Rosie exhaled.

The rehearsal revolved mostly around walking Rosie through all of Hero's scenes. As a consequence, Libby spent barely any time with Roarke at all. It wasn't until after rehearsal, when she (as usual, but provoking significantly more knowing winks than normal) got a ride home with him and Will, and he walked her to her door.

'How's Ella?' Roarke asked, a step behind her as they ascended the stairs to the second floor.

'She's okay,' Libby replied, feeling around in her handbag for her keys. 'Hungover, but okay. I wanted to thank you, actually.'

'You don't need to thank me.'

'No, I do. I was really rude to you in the bathroom last night—'

'You were worried about her. I get it.'

'—and I've been super weird lately, and I'm sorry about that, I'm just in a really weird headspace, and— Gerry?'

'Libby?' Gerry scrambled up from where he'd been sitting on the hard cement of the walkway, leaning against their front door. 'Do you know where Ella is?'

'Is this the guy?' Roarke asked sharply. 'Ella's Gerry?'

'She told you about Gerry?' Libby asked, taken aback.

'Bathroom floor breeds honesty. Is this the guy?'

'Yeah,' Gerry said. 'I'm the guy. Where's Ella?'

Roarke punched him.

It was so sudden, so sharp, that Libby barely had time to scream Roarke's name before Gerry was back on his feet, and punching Roarke with a fist that looked like a ham hock. Roarke reeled backwards, slamming into the bricks, blood pouring from a cut on his eyebrow, before he rebounded and tackled Gerry with his shoulder. They smashed into the door, and Libby was screaming and screaming – screaming both their names. She tried to get between them, but Gerry pushed her aside, and 'don't touch her!' Roarke bellowed, and swung for Gerry again. He missed, momentum carrying him forward. Gerry grabbed his head and smashed it into the door.

Roarke teetered for a moment, then slid slowly to his knees.

'Roarke!' Libby exclaimed, kneeling beside him. 'Roarke, are you okay?'

''m okay,' he slurred, then spat blood out of his mouth. It stained the concrete like a firework.

'Gerry, get out!' she yelled.

'He started it!' Gerry said, shaking out his knuckles. His left eye was starting to swell. 'Now where's Ella?'

'Don' talk to her,' Roarke said. 'Don' even look at her!'

Gerry ignored him. 'Libby, I have to see Ella. I have to explain—'

'What is there to explain?' Libby demanded. 'She's not your girlfriend anymore, Gerry. Your girlfriend is the one having the baby. Now get out.'

'If she'd just talk to me—'

'Get out!' Libby screamed.

Gerry got out.

A door opened down two apartments down, and one of the girls who lived there stepped out. 'Oh my God,' she said, covering her mouth with her hand in shock . 'Do you want me to call an ambulance? Or the police?'

'No!' Roarke said.

The girl looked at Libby.

'Will,' Roarke whispered.

'It's okay,' Libby said. 'I've got this.'

She scrabbled for her phone.

Will was there so quickly it felt like he'd teleported. 'What happened?' he demanded, running down the walkway and kneeling beside Roarke in a motion so fluid it almost looked like he was doing a rockstar slide across the concrete. 'Was it Paul?'

'No,' Libby said. 'It was this guy I know from my hometown. Ella's ex.'

'Will,' Roarke said, and there was an edge of need Libby had never heard in his voice before: not when they were talking, not when they were acting, not in that brief hour that they'd been in bed together.

'I've got you, buddy,' Will said, pulling a bloody clump of hair off Roarke's forehead. 'We need to get you to hospital. You need stitches.'

'No.'

'Shut up. No arguments. Libby, have you got a bag of peas or something? Anything frozen?'

She nodded and disappeared into the apartment.

She wasn't sure how it was decided that she was going with them. It was like she blinked, and she handed Will the peas, and then she blinked again, and the three of them were struggling down the stairs towards Will's car, she and Will each with one of Roarke's arms looped over their shoulders. Will's fingers were brushing hers, just a little, and Roarke was a dead weight between them, pulling them down into the ground.

'This is ridiculous,' Will said, getting up abruptly and starting to pace. His shoes squeaked on the linoleum of the emergency room floor.

'I'm okay,' Roarke said. 'I just need stitches, Will, not surgery. I can wait.'

'God knows how much blood you've lost,' Will said. 'And you could have a concussion.'

'It looks worse that it is,' Roarke said. He was lisping slightly past his swollen lip, but he'd regained most of his lucidity. 'Libby, get those peas away from me.'

Will snatched the bag out of her hand and pressed it to Roarke's eye himself, even though it had long since unfrozen. 'Stop. Talking,' he snarled.

There was an edge in Will's voice that suggested he would not take disobedience lightly, and a glint in Roarke's eye that suggested he was about to disobey.

'How about I get you some water?' Libby said.

'Thanks.'

She looked at Will. He shook his head wordlessly.

Her body was stiff from the hours of sitting beside Roarke in the emergency room. Some of his blood had dried on her shirt, stiff and a little sticky.

Nightingale had started a fight with fake blood in the annexe once. They had all screamed and squealed and hurled it at each other until they were all plastered with it. He'd grabbed her around the waist and smeared blood across her face. It hadn't been personal – he'd just reached for the person closest to him – but it had been the first time he'd touched her, and the blood had tasted like chocolate on her lips.

She'd kept the shirt, folded, unwashed, in a plastic bag in the bottom of her cupboard. She'd told herself that it might come in useful at a set painting day sometime.

When she got home, she was going to take her shirt off and throw it away, and she was going to dig that shirt out and throw it away too.

'It's not very cold,' she said, handing Roarke the plastic cup of water. 'Sorry.'

''s all right.'

'Are you sure you don't want anything, Will? They have coffee machines. I'm sure the coffee they make is abysmal, but—'

'Roarke Rivera?' a nurse called.

'Finally,' Will growled. 'Come on, Roarke.'

He tried to sling Roarke's arm over his shoulders, but Roarke pulled away. 'I can walk,' he said.

'Are you family?' the nurse asked.

'I'm his brother,' Will said.

'You are not,' Roarke said.

Libby's phone rang. 'Excuse me.'

It was Ella. 'Libby, where are you?' she said. 'I just got home from picking up my car, and there's blood on the floor outside our flat, and our front door is all dented.'

'I'm at the hospital,' Libby said.

'The hospital?' Ella almost screeched. 'Are you all right? Was it Paul?'

'I'm fine. All good. Not Paul. No need to worry.'

She gave Ella a brief sketch of what had happened. 'Oh my God,' Ella said. 'Oh my God, oh my God, oh my God.'

'It's all right,' Libby said. 'I'm all right, Gerry seemed like he was all right. Roarke – well, he's going to need some stitches, but he's all right. We're all all right.'

She glanced over at Will. He'd clearly lost the battle, because Roarke was gone. He was hunched forward in his chair, staring at the ground, his fingers twisting together, over and over again.

'I'm going to kill Gerry,' Ella said. 'I'll chase him all the way to Wimeena if I have to, but I'm going to kill him.'

'Ella, no,' Libby said. 'He didn't – I don't want to say he didn't do anything wrong, but he didn't throw the first punch, either.'

'No, I need to have it out with him,' Ella said. 'He wanted to talk to me, and now he's absolutely going to have to talk to me.

Are you okay to get back from the hospital?'

'Yeah. I'm here with Will.'

'Bye,' Ella said, and hung up.

Libby stared at her phone and sighed, before sticking it back in her bag. She went back over to the water cooler and filled a couple more plastic cups with water. 'Here,' she said, handing one to Will. 'Drink something.'

He took it, but didn't drink. 'I need you to tell me about this Gerry guy.'

'There's not much more than what I told you,' Libby said, sitting beside him. 'He's Ella's ex. They dated for years in high school, but now he's knocked up his new girlfriend, and I guess Ella told Roarke, and he was … I don't know, defending her honour or something.'

'So you know him,' Will said.

'Yeah, I know him.'

'Will he press charges?'

'What?'

'Do you think he's litigious?' Will said. 'Roarke threw the first punch, right? He could probably press charges.'

'I doubt it,' Libby replied. 'Roarke definitely came off worse. Gerry's, like, six-foot four and built like a brick— Will, you're shaking.'

She took his cup of water before he spilled it. 'I'm sorry,' he said. 'I hate seeing him like this. He promised he'd never do this again, and—' He swore under his breath.

'He's going to be okay, Will. It's just stitches. Everyone's had stitches.'

It turned out not to be just stitches. Roarke had a concussion, so they kept him in hospital overnight. He didn't want to stay.

'I hate hospitals, you know that,' he protested to Will. 'Talk to someone. Get me out.'

'No,' Will said shortly. 'I can't even look at you right now.'

'I'm fine.'

'No, you're not. You promised, Roarke.'

Roarke turned away. The seven stitches holding the cut on his forehead closed looked like train tracks against his face.

'Want to tell me why you thought it was a good idea to start a fight?' Will said.

'No.'

'Roarke.'

'The guy was a dick.'

'So are you, nine days out of ten.'

'I'm not having this argument with you.'

'You have had this argument with me,' Will said. 'And you promised me that you'd never do this again!'

Libby slipped out of the hospital room, feeling the way she did sometimes when she and Ella watched *Married at First Sight*, like she was seeing someone's dirty laundry, laundry that they probably didn't want her to see.

It was about fifteen minutes before Will emerged. 'Hey,' he said tiredly, running his hand through his hair. 'You didn't need to wait.'

'I wasn't going to leave,' Libby said.

'You could have gone ages ago.'

'I didn't want you to kill him,' she replied, strangely hurt, 'which you really seemed like you wanted to do.'

He sighed. 'I'm sorry. That was rude.' He ran his hand through his hair again. 'I just worry about him.'

'I get it,' she said. 'I worry about Ella.'

'She likes to get in fights too?'

'Oh yeah,' Libby said. 'You should see her right hook. Lethal.'

That drew a weak smile.

'Hey,' she said. 'Come here.'

It took him a second. She wrapped her arms around his torso and he wrapped his around her shoulders and rested his chin on top of her head, and they stood like that in the hospital corridor for a long time.

'Will,' she said, 'I think you should take me home with you.'

He drew back so he could look her in the eye. The Adam's apple in his throat worked as he swallowed. 'Libby—'

'Not like that!' she said hurriedly, stepping all the way back. 'That wasn't a proposition. Sorry. I should think about what I say before I say it. I just meant – you're clearly shaken up, and, honestly, I'm a bit shaken up as well, and … well, I don't think you should be alone right now, that's all.'

He looked at her for a long time. The lines of his face were taut, tense.

'Unless you want to be alone,' she said. 'Because I'd totally get that.'

'No,' he replied, his shoulders relaxing, just a little. 'I don't want to be alone.'

Interlude - Will

When Will Callahan was nine years old, someone had given him a book of stories about King Arthur and the Knights of the Round Table.

For three weeks, his whole world had been Camelot. He'd charged around the backyard using half a broken broom handle as his Excalibur, rescuing damsels in distress from their precarious perches in tree branches and his mothers' hanging pot plants. His sister hadn't been very impressed when she discovered he'd been using her dolls as his damsels.

As childhood phases do, it faded away. He opened the book from time to time – he liked the story of Sir Gawain and the Green Knight the best, because Gawain had won his wife with logic, and mathematical Will liked things to be logical – but the world had other things in it that demanded his attention.

It did, however, leave one indelible mark on him. Will Callahan couldn't seem to stop himself from trying to save people.

Why do you always have to try to fix everything? fifteen-year-old Roarke had screamed at him once in one of his rages, just after he had first come to live with Will and his sister and their mums.

That question had troubled Will for years. He had crusaded into Roarke's life, decided what was best, and made it happen. He'd seen the kid at school getting into fights all the time, figured out he was getting the shit beat out of him at home by his stepdad, told his mums, and reported it to the school principal, even though Roarke had begged him not to. He'd dismissed Roarke's opinion, because he was in the middle of the situation and he was too emotional – not like Will, who was logical. There was a right, and there was a wrong. And wasn't doing what was right the right thing to do?

Once could have been an accident, but it wasn't just once.

There was Roarke. There was Susie, Will's first girlfriend, whose rich parents were piling so much pressure on her to succeed that she was being slowly crushed. There was Caro: cold, prickly, defensive Caro, so desperately alone behind her walls. All he'd wanted was to help her tear them down.

They weren't the only ones. Friends and acquaintances and lovers and theatre companies, he couldn't help himself – he had to rescue them. Sometimes it felt almost like being possessed, like he was nothing more than a passenger in his own body, while Sir William sallied forth to save the day.

Then he'd met Libby Lawrence.

She'd seemed unremarkable, that first time he'd met her. If he'd walked past her on campus, he wouldn't have remembered her. She'd been nervous, fidgeting, a blush creeping slowly up her neck. He'd said her name, and she'd replied with a monologue apologising for it.

But then he'd asked her about Shakespeare, and her eyes had lit up. This time, when she apologised and he told her not to worry about it, he meant it.

Nothing had stuck with him so much from that frantic, busy weekend of auditions (when he'd met actor after actor after wannabe actor) as her eyes lighting up.

'I can't cast you in the lead,' he'd told Caro that night,

shrugging into his jacket as they got ready to go to dinner with her grandpa. 'You know that, right?'

'Of course I know that,' she'd replied, her back to him as she put on her lipstick.

'It'd look too much like nepotism.'

'Will,' she said, still not looking at him. 'You don't need to explain.'

He wished he could explain. There were so many things he wished he could have found the words to explain to Caro.

But if he'd found the words, he never would have taken the desperate Hail Mary pass that was the directing job. He never would have set foot in Uni Rep, because it was Caro's.

He'd been trying to save it – the slowly dying thing that was him and Caro – because that was all he knew how to do. But one thing that King Arthur and his knights had never taught him was that sometimes, trying to save something was the worst thing you could do. All it did was prolong the end, elongate the death, until the thing you were trying to save was rotting in your hands.

He cast Libby as Beatrice. She was objectively the best, he told himself, just like Roarke was objectively the right choice to play Benedick, even if he was his brother. He was Will Callahan, and he was logical, and he knew what was right.

Nothing had felt as right to him in a long time as going to those two student society barbecues with her. It felt right when he started driving her home after rehearsal, even though she lived well out of his way. It was because of the Paul thing, of course, and he'd do it for any member of his cast in a similar situation, but it still felt *right*.

He started buying Caro flowers. Lots of flowers.

'What are these for?' she'd asked him suspiciously, after the third bunch.

'No reason,' he'd replied. 'You deserve flowers, that's all.'

She'd turned away. He hadn't known what to say next. It wasn't the first time.

Caro had been the one to finish it in the end, during that last, vicious fight at the wedding. Sir William wasn't brave enough to put the wounded, dying animal of their relationship out of its misery. She was braver than he was. He was proud of her, in a strange sort of way.

He was proud of her, and he was relieved, and he was furious with himself, because he was a coward, and a thief, and worst of all, he was a liar.

He hadn't realised when he was buying Caro all those flowers. He hadn't realised that night after he and Caro had broken up, when he'd gone round to Libby's, and she'd been crying, and then he'd cried too, and they'd fallen asleep, and he'd carried her to bed while Ella struggled not to laugh. He hadn't even realised when she was kissing Roarke right in front of his face – Roarke, who he knew she'd slept with! – and he was giving them instructions on how to make it look more believable.

It happened during the working bee. Ned had pulled her out into the annexe and they'd started singing some song from a musical that he didn't know.

Libby Lawrence wasn't beautiful. She wasn't even pretty, though she passed for it when she tried, like on the night of Genevieve's party. But she was laughing and singing, and a ray of sunlight caught her hair, and she was the loveliest thing he'd ever seen.

Something in him shifted, and clicked, and screamed *her, her, her.*

It was all kinds of wrong. He'd only just broken up with his girlfriend. She'd slept with his brother. He was a director, and she was an actor, and he'd heard all the stories about how Uni Rep worked. He wasn't going to be the kind of guy that abused his power like that, not a chance in the world.

But still: *her.*

He'd never felt better and worse in his whole life.

He looked at her now, sitting beside him on his couch, drinking tea, the light from the lamp beside her catching her hair, illuminating it against his wall of equations. Her shirt had been smeared with Roarke's blood, so he'd given her one of his, the grey show T-shirt from the SMS revue two years ago. He hated how much he liked looking at her wearing it.

He liked it more than the red dress she'd worn to the nightclub, and he'd loved the red dress. He'd loved it enough that even though he knew, through the haze of a few drinks, that it was a terrible idea, he'd asked her to dance, and even though he knew it was a terrible idea, he made her whisper those words, *deep participant observation,* right into his ear, and even though he knew it was a terrible idea, he would have turned his head and kissed her if Rashmi hadn't interrupted.

He needed to remember that it would have been a truly, truly terrible idea. He needed to remember Caro. He needed to remember Roarke. He needed to remember not the way Libby had felt against him, but the way she'd jumped back in the hospital corridor. *That wasn't a proposition.* He needed to remember her saying it.

It was so hard to remember, though, with her sitting here on his couch, wearing his shirt. She'd plaited her hair tightly down her back, but wisps were escaping, and all he wanted to do was reach out and push them behind her ears. To put his hand on her cheek and kiss her – just once, just lightly, just a peck, because sitting on his couch in his shirt with him on Sunday night while some bullshit late-night TV played in the background was the kind of thing she did all the time.

'Hey,' she said, nudging him with her elbow. 'You're quiet.'

'Sorry,' he said. 'Just thinking.'

'Anything I can help with?'

'No. Just worried about Roarke.'

He shook his head, trying forcefully to clear it. 'I'm sorry if he scared you. He hasn't gone off like that on anyone since he was in high school.'

'He might have just misread the situation,' Libby replied. 'Gerry's a big guy, and he was pretty aggressive. He was all WHERE'S ELLA?, and Roarke might have thought I was in danger or something.'

He needed to remember that right when Caro was breaking up with him, Libby had been sleeping with Roarke. He needed to remember that even if it had only been a tipsy wedding hook-up, even if she and Roarke had just got carried away with the whole fake dating thing, even if Libby's breath had been hot against his ear when she whispered *deep participant observation* – she wasn't interested in him.

Will, I think you should take me home with you, she'd said.

He would have done it. Despite Caro. Despite Roarke. Despite the fact he was a director and she was one of his actors. He would have done it.

He wasn't a knight. He was a monster.

'But you don't need to worry,' Libby said. 'Ella found Gerry. She texted me before. She said he laughed when she asked him if he was going to go to the cops.'

He exhaled. 'That's something, I suppose.'

'I'm really sorry, Will.'

He looked at her sharply. 'Why on earth are you sorry?'

'Lots of reasons,' she said. 'It was my door that Roarke got smashed up against. Gerry's – well, he's not my bullshit per se, but he's from my life, not yours. Maybe if I'd found another way to defuse the situation, or if you had walked me in and not Roarke, or ... I don't know. I just feel like this is my fault.'

'None of this is your fault,' he said. 'You're not the one who did the punching. You're fine, ProofIt. You're perfect.'

'Oh dude, I am not perfect,' she said, hugging her knees to her chest. 'I'm the least perfect person in the universe. I might not punch people, but I do my fair share of incredibly stupid shit.'

He wanted to do some incredibly stupid shit. He wanted to lean across the couch and kiss her, and forget all about Roarke, and all about everything.

'For example,' she said, 'do you know I had the most ridiculously out of control crush on him?'

'Roarke?'

'No, no, no, no. I know that certain incidents might make it look that way, but not Roarke. Gerry. In high school.'

'Oh.'

'I've never told anyone this before,' she said. 'Not even Ella. Obviously not Ella, because she and Gerry were hot and heavy and head over heels and all the H words. But I used to look at the way he'd hold her hand, or he'd brush the hair out of her eyes, or even the way he'd just look at her, and I knew it was the stupidest shit in the world, but I used to imagine what it'd be like if it was me.'

So many things he wanted to say. So many things he wanted to do. So many things that were wrong, wrong, wrong.

'I guess I wasn't very subtle about it, because some of the other kids at school caught on,' she went on. 'I was already pigeonholed as the smart kid, and I didn't have many friends beside Ella, so it was brutal. I was the laughing stock of the entire school. I denied it and denied it and denied it, and no one believed me. Probably not even Gerry, honestly.'

She sighed. 'But Ella did. I went up to her, and I apologised, and I lied to her face and I told her it wasn't true, and she said, 'Libby, I know, of course it's not true' and hugged me. And that was, like, two, two and a half years ago, and I've never told her. Or anyone. So before you go around calling me perfect, remember that I'm stupid enough to fall for the worst person in the world for me, and shitty enough to lie about it.'

Libby Lawrence had mastered the art of crying prettily. Two single tears slipped down her face, sparkling like crystals.

'Sorry,' she said, wiping them away. 'I came over to be your support person, and here I am, crying on you again.'

He wanted to press. *If you're stupid, I'm stupid too*, he wanted to say. *Because even though it's wrong for so many reasons, I can't stop thinking about you.*

But then she'd draw back. *I told you I wasn't propositioning you*, she'd say. *It's not like that, Will.*

So he was a coward, and he let it go. 'You can cry on my shoulder any time you want, ProofIt,' he said, and resigned himself to being the saviour once again.

He dropped Libby off at her place on the way to the hospital the next morning. 'Are you sure you're going to be all right?' she asked him. 'I know I probably wasn't much help last night, but if you need me to go with you ...'

'No, it's all right,' he said. 'I'm used to looking after Roarke. Thank you, though.'

She hugged him. He hugged her back. If this was all they could have, all he could offer her, he'd take it. He'd take it and pretend to be a knight, when really he was a coward.

'Call me if you need me,' she said, 'although I can't imagine why you would.'

He didn't need her. He knew that his life would go on without her. But as she walked away from the car with the sunlight in her hair, he wanted her, he wanted her, he wanted her.

Roarke was silent nearly the whole way back from the hospital. 'How are you feeling?' Will asked him eventually.

'Fine. I could have come home last night. There's nothing wrong with me.'

'Roarke, you got in a fight. Again. You promised.'

'I know what I promised,' Roarke said. 'But I couldn't stand the way he was treating her.'

There were a million things Will should have said, but he didn't.

'I'm sorry I put you through this again,' Roarke said.

'I know,' Will replied. 'You're always sorry.'

The second they got home, Roarke went out again. Even though he knew he should stop him, Will was glad, and he didn't even feel bad about it. He couldn't stand to look at him.

His own damn brother. Who hadn't really done anything wrong, except sleep with Will's girl (not Will's girl, not Will's girl, he'd only just broken up with Caro, FFS!) and sally forth to defend her.

The day after Roarke had moved in with him, they'd been sitting together on Will's balcony in the setting sun, drinking beer, and Roarke had tried to explain to Will how people could still be in a room even when they were gone. 'Say I'm talking to Janie,' he'd said, gesticulating with his bottle, a few drops falling on the concrete, 'and then a few hours later, I'll feel like she's still there, watching me. Do you get that?'

'No.'

'You've never felt it? Like the walls are closing in on you, like you're standing in a crowded room even when you're completely alone?'

He hadn't understood what Roarke was talking about. Instead, he'd tried to solve the problem like an equation. *It must be because of his stepdad,* he'd thought. *Of course you'd always be looking over your shoulder if you grew up with someone like that. Then when he came to live with us, he must have been terrified that we were all watching, waiting for him to screw up so we could send him away again. x+y=feeling like the walls are closing in on you. If x is equal to—*

'Will?'

'Never,' he'd said. 'I've never felt like that.'

He got it now, though.

Roarke had been living with him for more than a month now, and he couldn't feel him anywhere. Caro had spent heaps of time here, and there was no trace of her, even though they'd only been broken up for a fortnight.

Libby had spent one night on his couch, and now everything was saturated with her.

She was in every room, on his walls, the floors, the ceilings. Everywhere she had been, everything she had touched, everywhere her gaze had flickered, there she was. The kitchen was hers. The table was hers. The couch was hers. The equations on the walls, the heart of his Honours work – they were all hers now too.

He closed his eyes. He was hers.

But it didn't matter. It couldn't matter.

Resolutely, he made himself coffee, black and strong. He took his most recent set of equations down from the wall, gritted his teeth, and started to work.

He worked and worked and worked. He loved maths. It was clean and clear and didn't leave room for anything else in his mind, didn't let him be distracted – oh God, there she was again, the smell of her hair as she buried her face in his shirt, the sound of her voice, the way she'd whispered *deep participant observation*. And there was a ringing in his ears and a numbness in his mind, and he could feel her, draped around him like a cloak.

No, wait. There really was a ringing. He wasn't imagining it.

There, sitting on the coffee table, was Libby's phone.

It was an unknown number. He almost walked away, but then he realised it was probably Libby calling from someone else's phone, so he picked it up.

'Hello?' he said.

'Um, hi,' the person on the other end said. 'Who's this?'

It wasn't Libby. It was a dude, one whose voice he didn't recognise.

'Will Callahan,' he said. 'This is Libby's phone. She left it here. Can I take a message?'

'Will Callahan,' the dude repeated, drawing out the L sounds. 'Willlll Callllllahan.'

'Yes, that's me. What do you want me to tell Libby?'

There was a pause.

'Tell her,' the dude drawled, 'that Nightingale called.'

The line went dead.

Will stared at the phone in his hand for a long time.

Nightingale? Nightingale Smith? The Nightingale that had managed to skim eight grand from Uni Rep before anyone had noticed? The Nightingale that Caro had once described to him as 'having charisma ... no, wait, it's pronounced chlamydia'? *That* Nightingale was calling Libby?

What?

Why?

She didn't have his number saved in her phone. They clearly weren't in regular communication.

Although wouldn't Nightingale have got a new phone when he left Terravale? And maybe Libby hadn't saved his number in case Graham finally did decide to call the police and her phone was seized for—

No. None of that was logical. Why on earth would Libby protect Nightingale? He clearly hadn't liked her much, if he'd relegated her to the chorus all the time, and Caro had told him that Nightingale cast his shows mostly with his boner, and *why was he calling her?*

He might have hold of some old cast list. Maybe he was calling down it, trying to find someone who'd talk to him and give him the lay of the land.

Whatever it was, it was none of his business.

He put the phone back down again. He told himself not to think about it.

Instead, he threw himself back into his equations – into the pure world of mathematics, where there were problems he could solve.

Chapter Thirteen

After Will took her home, Libby stood in the hallway outside her apartment for nearly two whole minutes, staring at the ground. Someone – Ella, maybe? – had wiped the blood splatter away, and only the faintest of copperish smears was left on the concrete, but there was no wiping away the giant dent in their front door.

Would she and Ella have to pay for it? It wasn't their fault that two dudes had happened to get into a brawl right outside their front door. Technically speaking, anyway.

She traced her finger down the middle of the dent. Whitish flecks of paint dust came away.

She'd pretended to get punched on stage once. In *Peter Pan,* one of the many roles she'd played was a random pirate, and someone – she didn't remember their name now, they'd never done another show at Uni Rep – playing a random Lost Boy had fake-punched her in the big fight scene. They'd swung their fist and bumped her cheekbone, while she slapped her upstage leg and dramatically recoiled.

It clearly hadn't been her finest performance, because a real punch sounded nothing like that. It had been ... crunchier. Squelchier. And the sound when Gerry had regained his balance and punched Roarke back – it wasn't possible, but she felt like she'd heard Roarke's skin tear as that cut had opened up on his forehead.

If she asked Will, he'd make Roarke pay for the door. Or he'd do it himself. She knew he would.

She couldn't believe she'd told him about Gerry.

Ella was sitting on the couch, but she scrambled up when Libby came inside. 'Oh my God, Libs,' she said, immediately folding her in a hug.

'I'm okay,' Libby said, hugging her back.

'I know you are,' Ella said, drawing back. 'You're always okay.' She hugged her again, so hard Libby could feel her fingers digging into her shoulder blades. 'I'm not okay, though. Oh my God.'

A part of Libby too loud for her liking was annoyed, but she squashed it down. 'How late were you up with Gerry?' she asked, letting the hug go on a few moments longer than she really wanted.

'Late. We had a ton of shit to work through. Like ... a ton.'

'Is he gone?'

Ella nodded. 'Yeah. He headed back to Wimeena this morning.' She sighed. 'Back to his pregnant girlfriend.'

'How's his face?'

'Swollen. Technically, he's got a black eye, but realistically, one whole side of his face is purple. How does Roarke look?'

'Probably worse,' Libby said. 'Black eye, puffy lip, stitches – the works.'

'Will he have a scar?'

'I don't know. Maybe.'

'I can't believe he just hit Gerry like that,' Ella said.

'Well, it wasn't out of nowhere, exactly,' Libby said. 'I was like, *um, hi Gerry*, and Roarke was like, *um, Ella's Gerry?*, and then Gerry put his angry pants on and was like, *yeah, that's me, now where's Ella, tell me or else*, and he took a step toward me, and then – pow.' She mimed a punch.

'Roarke thought Gerry was threatening you?'

Libby shrugged. 'I've seen him do it before. Paul cornered

me in the theatre foyer a couple of times to ask about you, and Roarke came over all, like, threatening bodyguard and ordered him out.'

'But he didn't punch him.'

'No, but ...' She exhaled. 'I don't know how his mind works, Ella. I don't understand why Roarke is the way he is and does the things he does.'

Ella opened her mouth. She closed it, then opened it again, then made a face.

'What?' Libby asked.

'I-might-have-an-idea,' Ella said, the words all running together.

'What do you mean?' Libby said, surprised. 'Are you, like, secret best friends? Have I been turfed?'

'No, no, no,' Ella said. 'But like I told you, we had a really good chat that night in the bathroom at Genevieve's party, even though I was off my face. Probably because I was off my face, honestly. I told him about Gerry, and our whole sordid history, and all about the pregnant girlfriend—'

'I gathered.'

'And I told him that Gerry and I hooked up the other weekend.'

'What?!'

'See, this is why I didn't tell you!' Ella said. 'I knew you'd react like this. I knew you'd be all judgey, and—'

'Not judging! One hundred percent not judging! I'm just surprised, that's all.'

'You want surprise?' Ella said. 'I'll give you surprise. Imagine how surprised I was when after what was honestly a really nice time that made me happy, I get a call from Gerry, and he's like *I'm in town, wanna have dinner?* and I'm like, *sure!* and I get all excited, and I think maybe we can have another really nice time, and then he's like, *sorry, babe, girlfriend's preggers.*'

'Please tell me he didn't say it like that.'

'Of course he didn't say "sorry, babe, girlfriend's preggers".' He's not a total arsehole.'

'I think he might be,' Libby replied. 'He slept with you *knowing* that he had a pregnant girlfriend?! That's hugely arseholic.'

'In his defence, he didn't know she was pregnant then.'

'He still had a girlfriend! What if he'd got you pregnant too? Or what about STIs? Or—'

'We were safe, Libby. I'm not that much of an idiot.'

'I'm not suggesting you are,' Libby said. 'God, Ella, I would never suggest that you are. I'm just furious.'

'You know what the worst part is?' Ella asked. 'It's not even about the sex.'

'What do you mean?'

Ella ran her hand through her hair, shaking it out. 'If we'd gone to the Crownie for a drink,' she said, 'and it'd all gone exactly the same way – if I'd be like *hey Gerry, wanna go somewhere?* and instead of *yeah, babe, always*, he'd been like *nah, El, I can't, I've got a girlfriend*, I think I'd still feel exactly the same.'

A tear welled up in Ella's eye. 'It's not that he didn't tell me,' she said. 'It's that he's gone. He was mine, and now he's *gone.*'

'Oh, honey,' Libby said.

More tears spilled over Ella's eyelashes, but she wiped them away hurriedly. 'I'm not going to cry about this,' she said determinedly. 'I'm not going to cry about someone that I broke up with eighteen months ago.' She wiped more tears away with her sleeve. 'Let's forget about my love life. Let's talk about yours.'

'I don't have a love life,' Libby said.

'Um, sure you don't have a love life, girl who was out all night,'

Ella said, plucking at Libby's sleeve. 'This shirt is definitely your size.'

'My shirt had blood on it. What was I going to do, sit around in it all night?'

'Please tell me you spent at least some of the night wearing no clothes at all.'

'Will was all shaken up. He was worried about Roarke. And he lives up near campus anyway, I wasn't going to make him take me all the way home! We're friends, Ella. Good friends, but just friends. Plus he just broke up with his girlfriend.'

'Excuses, excuses,' Ella said. 'Just rip the band-aid off, Libby. You can't hang onto that V-card forever. He's so nice. Plus, he's a couple of years older, so he probably knows what he's doing, and—'

Libby had her mouth open to tell her the truth when Ella's phone buzzed. 'Oh, I need to go out,' she said, glancing at it. 'Then I should get to uni. I'll stop by the IGA on the way home and get something for dinner. I'll leave it in the fridge for you for after rehearsal.'

'Shit, uni!' Libby said. 'I totally spaced that it was Monday. I've got Torts all afternoon and I haven't done the reading.'

'Please, if anyone can fake it til they make it, it's you,' Ella said. 'Later, Elizabeth Two. Don't think this Will subject is closed, because it isn't.'

'Yes, it is,' Libby replied. For once, it wasn't a lie.

Will gave her phone back that night before rehearsal. 'You left this at my place.'

'Oh, thank God,' she replied. 'I've been looking for this everywhere.'

'I hope you weren't expecting any important calls or anything. The battery died at some point.'

'Well, I was expecting Hollywood to call and offer me a role in their next blockbuster, but I'm sure they'll call back. How's Roarke?'

'Banged up, but he's okay. We'll have to make do without him tonight, though.'

They ended up having to do without Roarke at rehearsal all that week. Libby half-expected the Uni Rep crew to be angry about it – and there were a few annoyed messages in the group chat – but he wasn't the main focus of everyone's ire.

'Ugggggggggggghhhhhhhhhhhhh,' Genevieve groaned, as they sat down at Sal's after the Saturday afternoon rehearsal. The sea breeze whipped her hair in her face. The salty sea air seemed to merge with the chicken salt smell from their chips. 'Why is Will torturing me like this?'

'Babe, it's not that big a deal,' Ned said, putting his arm around her. 'You have nothing to worry about. Rosie and I have been over for forever. You know that, right?'

'Of course I know that,' Genevieve said, taking an elastic offered to her by Rashmi and tying her hair up. 'If I did have something to worry about, you'd have two less balls and I'd have two new earrings.'

'You might have to fight me for the earrings if I found out that old mate here ditched you for his role-stealing ex,' Annalise said. 'I can't believe Will gave her that role.'

Libby suddenly became very interested in the chips.

'I can't believe you're all being such bitches right now,' Rashmi said. 'Rosie's great as Hero. She's off-book for the first two acts already, and she's way better than Caro was.'

'No,' Genevieve said, pointing her finger at Rashmi. 'I don't want your fair. I don't want your reasonable. I just want you to agree that I am being unjustly tortured.'

'Agreed,' Annalise said. 'We hate her. Why couldn't Will have just given Hero to me?'

Libby considered trying to slip under the table and disappear.

'You know what I don't get?' Anthony said. 'Hero and Margaret are supposed to look alike, right? So they can pull off that thing where Claudio thinks Hero's making out with Conrade even though it's really Margaret?'

'Right,' Annalise said.

'I don't mean this the way it sounds, but Lise, you're white and Rosie's Black,' Anthony said. 'How's that going to work?'

'I don't know how you meant it to sound, but it came out racist,' Rashmi said.

'You know what I mean, though, don't you?'

Rashmi shot him a look.

'Did Will consult anyone on the production team when he cast Rosie?' Annalise asked.

'No,' Genevieve said. 'He's a lone wolf.'

'Couldn't you have leaned on him harder, Libs?' Annalise said.

'I tried,' Libby said. 'But I don't have any say in what he does.'

'Sure thing, lady in red,' Michael said.

Libby threw a chip at him. 'I wonder how Caro's doing.'

'Nice attempt at changing the subject,' Ned said. 'Subtle, Libs. Ten out of ten.'

'She seems fine,' Genevieve said, running her hands through her hair and then shaking her head like it was a magic eight ball she was trying to reset. 'She was at the committee meeting a couple of days ago. Will was doing a report on the progress of the show and they were perfectly civil to each other. It was kind of disappointing, really. I was hoping for fireworks and explosions. Maybe some light chair-throwing.'

'Say what you like about Nightingale,' Michael began.

'He's the worst person to ever be born?' Heidi suggested.

'—but he brought the drama. Will is so tame by comparison.'

'What, you think him breaking up with his girlfriend and her quitting mid-rehearsal period is tame?' Rashmi said.

'Not to mention when he fired that dude Paul for, like, no reason?' Heidi added.

'There was a reason,' Libby said.

Everyone looked at her. Ned raised his eyebrows.

'He was harassing Ella,' she mumbled. 'Will found out, and … you know.'

'One, that's gross, and I'm going to kick Paul in the dick if I ever see him again,' Rashmi said. 'Two, Will is way more interesting than Nightingale. We haven't even begun to figure out whatever his weird deal is with Roarke.'

'And we have all this will-they-won't-they stuff,' Heidi said, grinning wickedly at Libby.

'You guys, it's nothing,' Libby said. 'Seriously. We're friends. Nothing has happened, and nothing is going to happen.'

'I vote we lock them in the Swamp till they bone,' Anthony said.

'If only the Swamp was lockable,' Genevieve said.

'I hate all of you,' Libby said, her face so hot she was pretty sure her head was a second away from bursting into flame. 'Every single one. Please. Stop.'

'Okay, okay, we'll lay off,' Rashmi said. 'If you say you're not interested, we should at least pretend to believe you.'

The conversation shifted back to the great Problem of Rosie Waters. They laughed and talked and ate and drank, and Libby did too, making sure they couldn't tell a single thing that she was thinking.

She'd thought that being one of them would feel a bit more rewarding.

Ella was out when Libby got home that night. *Hey, where are you?* she texted, dropping her handbag on her bedroom floor and sitting down on the corner of her bed.

Met with some groupwork (ugh) people for this project thing we have to do for uni, then went to dinner with a mate, Ella sent back. *Have a nice night. xx*

It was probably a good thing. Her Torts and Con Law textbooks were taunting her, and there was the Sociology lecture she'd skipped in the interests of sleeping in, and she'd never get through it all with Ella distracting her. Especially because she wanted to be distracted.

She made it through the Sociology lecture, lying on her belly on her bed in her pyjamas and playing it from her laptop while she nominally made notes (although realistically played several solo games of Words With Friends on her phone). It seemed like she blinked and Ella was screaming.

Blearily, she groped for her phone. Two am.

There was also a missed call from a number she didn't recognise, but then Ella screamed again. 'Emerson!'

The adrenaline hit, and she jumped into action, nearly tripping over as she ran into Ella's room. 'Ella?!'

'Emerson!' Ella screamed. 'Emerson – don't – don't! Don't go! Emerson!'

'Ella!' she said, shaking her shoulder. 'Ella, wake up!'

Ella came awake the way people did in movies: her eyes

snapping open, her breath a desperate gasp. Her chest heaved. 'Lib-Libby?'

'It's me,' she said. 'It's just me.'

'I— I— I—'

'I'm here,' she said. 'I've got you. You're all right. You're safe.'

Ella was still panting like she'd just run a marathon. 'Libby, I— I— I'm sorry.'

'It's all right,' Libby said. 'Come on. Get up. Walk around a bit. Shake it off.'

She led Ella out to the kitchen. 'Thank you,' Ella said, when Libby handed her a glass of water. She drained it in two big gulps.

Libby took it back and refilled it. 'Are you all right?'

'Yeah,' Ella said. 'I mean, no, but I will be.'

'Are you sure?'

Ella nodded. She was halfway through the second glass of water, and some splashed onto the floor. 'I'm sorry for waking you.'

'You don't need to apologise,' Libby said. 'It's just ... what can I do, Ella? How can I help?'

'Unless you can go to the library and dig up *How To Deal With Your Dead Brother, third edition*, you can't do anything.'

Libby didn't answer.

'Shit, I'm sorry,' Ella said. 'But seriously, don't worry. It's probably all this shit with Gerry stirring things up in my brain again. I just need to ... find my balance or something. No big deal.'

Her tone was light, but there was an edge in her voice that warned Libby not to pursue the subject any further.

'Okay,' she said, feeling like the worst sort of coward. 'Come on. Let's go back to bed.'

Libby usually never skipped her Arts tutorials, but Tuesday morning, when she should have been in a Nineteenth-Century Lit seminar, she was sitting at the dining table. Nominally, she was working on a backlog of Law homework, but realistically, she was staring into space.

Ella had told her not to worry, so she wasn't going to worry. Everyone was entitled to one nightmare when the love of their teenage life knocked someone else up. It was probably a reasonable and sensible reaction.

Sure, it came on the heels of the series of Paul nightmares, but who wouldn't have had nightmares after that? And that Gerry/Roarke incident had been so violent! That might have triggered the same fight-or-flight responses. Better that it came out in nightmares than in Ella actually running away, right?

Everything was fine. Everything was *fine*. Except for her, because she was being ridiculous. As usual.

She forced herself to read the next sentence in her Con Law textbook. None of the words made it into her head.

She tried reading it again, and again, and again, and maybe once more (or maybe a hundred times more), when there was a knock on the door.

She opened it, and blinked. 'Hello,' she said, after a pause that was a second too long.

'Hi,' Roarke said.

Something about it felt like a dream. In fact, she might have had a dream like this. Nightingale or Roarke or some amalgam of the two had turned up at her door, and she'd stared at him and he'd stared at her, and then without a word he'd slammed her back against the wall and kissed her like he wanted to devour her whole.

'What are you doing here?' she said.

'Ella,' he replied.

'What about her?'

'She asked me to come around.'

'Oh. Okay,' Libby said, realising it must be for a costume fitting. Ella had had people in and out of their apartment all week. 'She's at uni, but if she told you she'd be here, she must be skipping some classes. She'll probably be back soon.'

'Cool.' He scratched at the shiny new skin just underneath the line of his stitches.

'Come in,' Libby said, much too late for it to be anywhere near natural. 'Sit down.'

Roarke obeyed, taking the chair opposite hers at the table. 'Thanks.'

'Can I get you anything? Water, tea ...?'

'No thanks. I'm fine.'

She took her seat. She wasn't sure whether she should look at him or her laptop, or whether she should pick up her computer and take it elsewhere, or insist on making him tea, or throw herself out the window.

'Shouldn't you be in class?' he asked her.

'What?'

'Ella said you had class.'

'Oh. I'm skipping today. Ironic, but I'm up to my eyeballs in uni work and if I don't get some of it done, I'll be in deep shit.'

'I know the feeling. I'm surprised you do, though.'

'What?'

'I thought you were a model student. All those people whose essays you edit must be so disappointed.'

'I've been too busy editing their essays to work on my own stuff. Especially when it's Law, and I'd rather pull my own fingernails out.'

'You know no one is making you do that degree.'

'Yeah, yeah, I know.'

Silence.

More silence.

'If you have work to do, don't let me stop you,' he said, gesturing to her laptop at the same time as she said, 'So I should thank you.'

Roarke raised one of his eyebrows, just a little. 'For refusing to let Will do that stupid thing he wanted to do in the masquerade scene? Because I was looking out for myself there. You were only collateral saving.'

'No, for, uh...' She shouldn't have brought this up. Why on earth had she brought this up? 'For the thing with Gerry.'

'Libby, don't thank me.'

'I'm not thanking you for punching him. That was stupid. And frightening, honestly. But thanks for standing up for Ella. And for me.'

He stood up and walked away, but the apartment was only small, and there was nowhere he could really escape to. He stood at the screen door, staring out onto the balcony.

'I don't understand why you're even speaking to me,' he said. 'Let alone thanking me.'

'If it makes you feel any better, I could un-thank you.'

Roarke exhaled audibly and turned around. 'Look, we should talk about that night at the wedding.'

'All right,' she said, her throat suddenly dry. She pulled one of her feet up onto her chair and hugged her knee into her chest.

'I'm sorry.'

'For what?'

'I pulled you into my bullshit,' he said. 'That whole fake dating thing – I didn't even ask you, and then we both got carried away.'

'And it was a mistake,' she finished.

'Is there any question about that?'

'I'm sorry.'

'Don't apologise!' he almost spat. 'God, how have I twisted this around so you're the one apologising?'

'Roarke, I've been the one who's been eighty different kinds of weird since.'

'But I made it that way,' he said. He let out a long breath and pinched the bridge of his nose. 'I just about bit your head off with that whole I-don't-want-a-girlfriend thing.'

'I didn't make it any better when I was like never-tell-anyone-ever,' she said, letting her foot fall to the floor and folding her arms, resting her elbows against the table.

'I haven't,' he said, dropping his hand and looking at her in the eyes. 'I hope you know that.'

'Will knows,' she replied. 'He figured it out.'

'He figures everything out, when it's other people's bullshit. Terrible at his own, though.'

Libby didn't know what to say to that.

'I want you to know,' Roarke said, sitting back down opposite her at the table, 'that it's not like I regret that night, exactly. I had a good time. We both had a good time. I think, anyway. Don't answer that.'

'I had a good time, Roarke.'

'It was just … a bad idea.'

'Can I make a suggestion?'

He raised an eyebrow.

'It didn't happen,' she said. 'We don't have to talk about it. We don't have to think about it ever again. Because it didn't happen.'

'Libby,' he said, leaning forward, elbows on the table, mirroring the way she was sitting, 'it did happen.'

'We agreed that night that it wasn't a thing,' she said. 'So we can take that agreement a step further, if you want. It really wasn't a thing. Because it didn't happen.'

He looked at her for a long moment. 'Are you sure?' he asked her at last.

She nodded, just as the front door opened.

'Libby!' Ella said, surprised. 'What are you doing here?'

'Wagging,' she said. 'I have so much Law homework I'm drowning in it.'

'Sorry I'm late,' Ella said to Roarke.

'It's all right,' he replied.

Libby picked up her laptop. 'I'm going to go and work at the café down the road and leave you two to your costume fitting,' she said. 'They don't have any WiFi. I might actually get something done.'

'Costume fitting! Yes!' Ella said. 'Have fun, Libs. Roarke, I've got a bunch of stuff I want you to try on for me. Two secs. Take your clothes off.'

Ella disappeared into her room. 'I'd better do what the lady says,' Roarke said.

'I would,' Libby said, slinging her handbag over her shoulder.

'You—' He stopped, and she was surprised, because she wasn't sure she'd ever seen Roarke hesitate before. 'You meant it? You're sure?'

'Yes,' she said. 'I meant it. I'm sure.'

Chapter Fourteen

Roarke didn't speak to her in rehearsal the next night, except when they were Beatrice and Benedick. The most he gave her was a tight-lipped smile while they waited for their cue together.

It should have made her feel awkward, but it didn't. She had no idea if things had turned out the way she wanted, but she felt the way she did when she put her bag down after she'd been lugging her Law textbooks round all day: sore, but relieved.

Tonight, for whatever reason, it was easier than it had ever been to slip into Beatrice's grounded, witty, laughing shoes. They'd only been totally off-book for a couple of rehearsals, and everyone was still a little uncertain, but she didn't drop a single line. She was in the right place at the right time doing the right thing. Everything was easy, and certain, and sure.

'You're killing it tonight, ProofIt,' Will said to her when they took a break in the middle of rehearsal.

'Thanks,' she said, taking a swig from her water bottle. 'It felt good. I'm just in a good mood today, I guess.'

'Anything in particular that's got you so chipper?'

'What, do you want me to burst into tears on your shoulder?'

'My week isn't complete until you do. It's in my diary and everything.'

'Oh, shut up,' she said, punching him in the arm, and then immediately regretting it when she saw Michael and Anthony with their heads together, watching and laughing.

'Oi Libs!' Ned yelled across the studio. 'Karaoke's on again on Saturday night. You in?'

'Sure,' she called back.

She turned back to Will. 'Want to come to karaoke with us?' she asked.

'I probably shouldn't,' he said.

'Oh,' she said. 'Okay.'

'All right, everyone!' he called. 'Back to it. Wedding scene. Make it happen. Make it glorious. Make me proud.'

The second half of rehearsal wasn't as good as the first. She made all her cues, and she didn't drop any lines, and when Roarke was being Benedick, it felt real and natural and right. But their parts in this scene were secondary, and hardly anyone else could keep it together.

'Oh, what men dare do!' Ned exclaimed dramatically, falling to his knees. 'What men may do! What men daily do!'

Everyone laughed. Next to Libby, Rosie rolled her eyes.

'Too much, Ned. Pull it back,' Will said.

'What men may do!' Ned pressed on, clearly on the verge of bursting out laughing. 'What men daily do!'

'Further back,' Will said.

'Sorry, sorry,' Ned said, wiping his eyes. 'Back up, Bruni.'

'As freely, son, as God did give her me,' Michael said, so solemnly that Libby could tell he was on the verge of losing it again.

'And *hwat*,' Ned said, drastically over-pronouncing the words, 'have I to give you back, whose worth may counterpoise this rich and precious gift?'

'Nothing,' Michael said, 'unless ...'

He grabbed the script Rosie had in her hands, the only one on the stage. '... you render her again,' he finished, reading.

'Sweet prince, you learn me noble thankfulness,' Ned said, stepping so close to Michael they were nose to nose.

Then he grabbed Rosie by the wrist and sent her cannoning into Michael so hard and fast that they both fell over. 'There, Leonato, take her back again!'

It was a dramatic, slapstick fall. Everyone started laughing, except for the people who didn't.

'What the hell, Ned?' Rosie said, scrambling up. 'That's not the blocking.'

'I was just trying something out.' He offered her a hand up, but she ignored it.

'Ned, don't ever let me see you do that again,' Will said.

He didn't shout. He didn't need to. Everyone stopped laughing.

'You know this scene,' Will said. 'You know your lines. You know your blocking, and you know what I've told you to do. And what I didn't tell you to do was injure the other people with you on stage.'

'Will, we all know how to take a fall,' Ned said, in a tone like he was explaining something to a child. 'And we all know how to take a joke, and—'

'I didn't think it was funny,' Rosie said.

'Sorry,' Ned said. 'Did I hurt you? I didn't mean to.'

'I've heard that one before.'

'Rosie,' Will said, 'are you all right?'

She nodded. 'Fine.'

'Michael?'

'No worries, bro,' Michael said lightly, dusting himself off.

'Ned, if I ever see you do something like that to her, or to anyone in this cast, again, your arse is grass,' Will said. 'Is that clear?'

'Will,' Ned said, 'it was a joke.'

'We have three weeks until this show opens,' Will said. 'You will take this seriously. Am I understood?'

'Yes! Fine!'

'Good,' Will said. He must have heard Ned mutter *your majesty* under his breath, but he ignored it. 'Now go back to the top.'

When rehearsal ended, Libby hung back in the studio instead of clattering downstairs to the foyer with everyone else. 'Hey,' she said to Will. 'You all right?'

'Fine,' he said, stacking chairs, not looking at her.

'You sure?'

'Yes,' he said. 'I'm sorry, I can't give you a ride home tonight. I lent Roarke my car and he's already disappeared somewhere, so I'm walking.'

'That's okay. I'll find my way.'

He kept stacking chairs.

'There's always one rehearsal like this,' she offered. 'It's better everyone gets it out of their systems now rather than when it's really crunch time, like production week or something.'

He didn't reply.

'Nightingale used to call it a Bundy run. You know, a run where everyone behaves like they're drunk. Though I don't know why he thought everyone would be choosing Bundy to get drunk on.'

'I don't care what Nightingale did.' The chairs clattered as he practically threw another one on top of the stack.

A lump was starting to develop in her throat. 'Okay,' she said. 'See you Saturday.'

'No, Libby, wait,' he said, just as she'd reached the door. 'I'm sorry. That was rude.'

'It's fine, okay?' she said. 'Everyone behaved like little shits tonight. You were entitled to be pissy with them.'

'That's not what I'm apologising for. Or who I'm apologising to.'

He looked at her, right in the eyes, and for a moment she felt like she couldn't breathe.

'It's all right,' she said at last. 'You don't need to explain.'

But there was an explanation. The next day was Thursday, and Ella had shooed her out of the flat so she could do more costume fittings ('undressed people don't appreciate an audience,' she'd said, practically shoving her out the door). She'd decided to work in the uni library. She was walking through the fourth floor, trying to find a spare carrel, when she spotted him slumped over an obscenely large stack of papers right at the end.

She walked away.

Five minutes later she came back. 'Hey, taxman,' she whispered in his ear.

He jumped, then looked up at her, bleary-eyed, his glasses crooked on his nose. 'Is that coffee?' he said, his voice hoarse.

'I got them to put an extra shot in. You look like you need it.'

He took it from her, eyes closed as he inhaled. 'Will you marry me?' he asked. 'I'm serious. I'll give you a good life.'

'You have ink on your face,' she said, reaching over and trying to rub it off. His skin was scratchy. He clearly hadn't shaved. 'You're a mess.'

'What I am is behind,' he said. 'The theatre is sucking up my whole life. I'm way behind on my Honours thesis, and I've got this report thing due that I keep trying to write but I'm not sure it's even in English, but everywhere I turn, there's *Much Ado* stuff, and –'

'Shhhhh!' someone hissed at them.

'Come on,' Libby said, grabbing his wrist and hauling him to his feet. 'Let's get you out of here. You're coming with me into a place with natural light, and you're going to eat something and drink some more coffee, and I'm going to help.'

'I have all the respect in the world for your intelligence, ProofIt,' he said as she pulled him away, fingers still closed around his wrist, 'but unless you know things about partial differential equations—'

'You're on your own with that, but I can proofread your report, and I can probably help with *Much Ado* stuff, and most of all, I can make sure you don't turn into an overworked, overstressed hermit marinating in your own filth in a dark corner of the library.'

'I guess that's a no to my marriage proposal, then.'

'Sit,' she said, pointing at a table in the sun. 'I'm going to go grab us lunch. I'll be back in a few minutes. Drink your coffee and turn your brain off for a second.'

'You don't have to—'

She put her finger against his lips. 'If you're as busy as you say you are, you definitely don't have time to be arguing.'

Will had no reply to that.

'This is really good,' Libby said half an hour later, dunking one of the last chips in the aioli.

'Yeah, it is,' he agreed. 'You were right. I needed to eat.'

'No, I mean your report,' she said. 'I've marked a few things in here you can sort out, but I don't know what you were so worried about. It's fine.'

'You understand it?'

'Well, no. Not my area. But I can follow your argument, even if I don't understand the numbers. You have a nice writing style.'

'Thanks,' he said, smiling his crooked smile at her.

As always, she couldn't resist smiling back. 'Is this based on your Honours stuff?'

'Not my thesis. This is for my coursework Stats unit, and – sorry. I won't talk maths to you. It can't be very interesting.'

'Sure it is.' The sun was warm, soaking into her skin, highlighting faint freckles on his cheeks. 'Is that what you want to do? Maths?'

'When I grow up? Yes. My mums would love me to do a CPA and be an accountant and make a ton of money, but my heart belongs to the environmental mathematical modelling stuff I've been doing for Honours. Which means a PhD, probably. What about you?'

'What do I want to be when I grow up?' she asked. 'Good question.'

'You don't have to decide right now.'

'I know,' she said. 'But it's one of those things I know I should think about, and I don't even know where to start. All I know is that I'm three-and-a-half semesters into a Law degree and I don't want to be a lawyer.'

'Why are you doing it, then?'

She had a brief moment of déjà vu. 'Because I'm the smart girl,' she said. 'That's my whole identity. And the smart girl should come away with more than an Arts degree.'

'Nothing wrong with an Arts degree.'

'I know that, but—'

'And you're much more than the smart girl.'

'Thank you? I think?'

'Although you are clearly a smart girl, don't get me wrong,' Will said. 'But – take it from a mathematician who occasionally dabbles in theatre – that doesn't have to be your life. Do what you want. At least you won't be miserable.'

'It sounds so simple when you put it like that.'

'It should be that simple. If you want something, you should do it.'

'There's one big problem,' she said. 'I have no idea what I want.'

One of the things Libby had done a lot when she was in high school was make lists. She'd managed her Year 12 study program rigidly, checking off every item as she did it, because she wasn't taking any chances: she was getting out of Wimeena. She'd made them for Ella too – they'd researched art schools together, and she'd made her a list of everything she needed to do to get in. Even though Ella tried to run away from it and give up more than once, she'd made sure that every item on it got crossed off too.

The lists had fallen to the wayside when they'd moved to Terravale. They'd been a means to an end, and the end had been achieved. She'd got out. She'd got them both out.

Working in the bookstore on Thursday night, reorganising some of the shelves, she tried to make a list of what she wanted.

(1)   She wanted *Much Ado* to be a smash. In particular, she wanted everyone to be so wowed by her performance that they fell at her feet and worshipped her.

(2)   She wanted to be sure that Ella was okay, and that she would stay.

(3)   She didn't want to do her Law homework. Ever again.

(4)   She wanted to be really, truly cool with Roarke. She wanted to be one of those people who could be around people they'd slept with and have it not be weird.

(5)   She wanted not to feel like the ground beneath her feet was as thin as an eggshell, like she could fall through it at any moment.

(6)   She wanted to stand firm. She wanted to be steady. She wanted to be an immovable object. She wanted to be an irresistible force.

It wasn't the right list, and it didn't have everything on it yet, and she had no idea how she'd be able to check some of the things off. But it was a start.

'Excuse me?'

She turned around, pasting on her customer service smile. 'Hello. How can I help you?'

It was an unusually busy Thursday evening, but by half-past seven, the rush had petered out and she was alone in the shop. She processed a delivery from that afternoon and entered all the new orders into the system, but by eight, she'd done every task Catriona had asked her to do. She wasn't supposed to read at work, but – against store policy – she allowed herself a glance at her phone.

It was a terrible mistake.

Her list went out the window, and she had no idea what she wanted. She was praying that no one would walk into the shop and see her freaking out.

But at the same time, what wouldn't she give for the comforting presence of another person? For Ella to walk in and see her, and go, *God, Libs, what's wrong?* and to listen while she finally told her the whole story. For Will to walk in, and listen, and say *you know what you want, and it's not this.* Even for Roarke to walk in, like he had that first time – yes, maybe Roarke would be best, actually, because he was the closest thing to Nightingale there was. He wouldn't want to hear the story at all, but if something really threatening happened she could probably rely on him to punch it in the face.

She swallowed, then opened the email that had just come in to her ProofItLibby inbox. She was just going to skim it, she told herself, and delete it.

Hi Queen Elizabeth –

I know you must be angry with me. I'd be angry at me.

But I can't do this any more. I can't stop thinking about you & there's a few things I need to explain.

I'm playing a gig at the Arms on Tuesday next week – you know that pub a few streets away from campus? I really want to see you. I'll put your name on the door. Please come.

(I'm not playing under my own name, for obvs reasons, but I promise Blackbird Jones is me.)

Time for a request that makes me sound like a huge creeper: don't tell anyone from Uni Rep. I promise this isn't a COME ALONE, GIRL, SO I CAN MURDER YOU type request! It's just things are messy with Uni Rep at the moment (but I'm working on it! one of the things I need to explain!).

& besides: I don't want to see them. I want to see you.

Nighty xxx

PS. Heard you got the lead in Much Ado. Proud of you, girl. Always knew you could do it.

She knew exactly what a smart girl would do.

A smart girl would laugh. A smart girl would see straight through his bullshit. A smart girl would probably take a screenshot of this email and post it to her Instagram and tag in everyone from Uni Rep. A smart girl would make sure Graham and the Uni Rep committee knew Nightingale was trying to reach out.

A smart girl would erase it not just from her phone but her

brain, because a smart girl would know that he was not worth her time. A smart girl would know that he was just trying to get the dirt on Uni Rep, and would see that he'd identified her as an easy target (she'd gone to the Swamp with him so easily, after all, he'd barely had to ask).

A smart girl wouldn't feel anything when she read the line *I can't stop thinking about you ...* She'd shrug *proud of you, girl* right off, because there was nothing in his behaviour to suggest that he'd known she could do it all along.

You're much more than the smart girl, Will had told her.

He'd been wrong. She wasn't even that.

The bell above the door jangled. 'Good evening, welcome to Terravale Terrace Bookshop,' she said, forcing her face into a rictus customer service smile. 'How can I help you?'

The customer had a complicated question, but she answered it. She was competent, and she was good at her job, and if she could find obscure books, she could delete Nightingale from her brain.

She wasn't going to go to his gig. Of course she wasn't going to go. Nightingale wanted her to go, and if nothing else, she wasn't going to let him get what he wanted.

What if she didn't go, though?

What if he turned up at her door?

What if he turned up at the theatre?

What if he turned up at the theatre, and announced to everyone that she'd slept with him?

She could hear the laughing. It wasn't even the Uni Rep people laughing – it was everyone she went to high school with, every single person she'd grown up with, every person she'd ever met in her entire life.

No. That was ridiculous. Ella wouldn't laugh. Ella would listen.

But then she'd realise that Libby wasn't the rock she'd pretended to be all this time, that she wasn't strong, that she wasn't sensible, and she'd start having more nightmares, and ...

Will would listen. He'd nod, and he'd say all the right things, and then he'd be weird and distant and they'd never have lunch in front of the library ever again.

Blackbird Jones. She'd slept with someone who was using *Blackbird Jones* as their secret stage nom de plume.

(7)   She wanted not to have been so stupid.

(8)   She wanted not to care.

'Are you all right?' the customer asked. 'You look a little bit pale.'

'I'm fine,' she replied. 'No need to worry about me.'

Chapter Fifteen

She made a decision.

If she wanted not to care, then she needed to act like she didn't care.

OMG you won't believe what happened, the version of Libby that didn't care would post in the group chat. *Nightingale emailed me – out of the blue! – and he was all like, 'gurl, I need to see you,' and tried to manipulate me into going to some gig he's playing at one of the bars near campus so he can pick my brain about Uni Rep, and *get this* he's calling himself BLACKBIRD JONES.*

Everyone would turn up at that gig. Literally everyone. Nightingale would be lucky to escape with his life.

But he'd get close, so close to her that it would be like they were in the Swamp again. *Was it good for you?* he'd ask. *Honestly, it was pretty ordinary for me.*

Then everyone would forget about murdering Nightingale, because they'd be too busy laughing at her.

So no. She couldn't be that version of Libby that didn't care. If there was one thing in the world she wanted, the true number one on all of her lists, it was that she never wanted to be the object of ridicule ever again.

But maybe there was another version of Libby that didn't care. A mature one. A professional one. One that was a little set apart from the insular incestuous tangled web of Uni Rep. The one that quietly told the people that needed to know that Nightingale was back in town.

She could tell Graham. She'd never talked to him before, and this would be an awkward first conversation, but he'd be impressed with the fact that she hadn't taken it to the group chat. *You are a clever, poised young woman,* he'd say. *An asset to this theatre company.*

But what could he do? Turn up at the bar, be one thousand years older than everyone else there, then politely ask Nightingale for the money back? *Um, no,* Nightingale would say. *How did you find out I was here, Dr Lewis?*

Then he'd work out she'd told Graham, because she was the only one that knew, and he'd tell Graham about the Swamp, and even though Nightingale was the one who stole the money, she'd be the one who paid the price.

There was only one person she could tell, really. One that she could trust to keep her name out of it, if she asked. Who wouldn't press her hard to ask her why, who wouldn't be terrified that she wasn't as strong as she seemed and run away, who'd actually try and make sure Nightingale paid some kind of price.

Her Saturday morning shift at the bookshop finished at half-past twelve. She didn't need to be at the theatre for rehearsal until two, but she jumped on the first possible train and went straight there.

She was so early that the dirty glass front doors of the theatre were still locked. But when she went around the back, Will's car was there, parked between Genevieve's and someone else's. When she tested the kitchen door, it was open.

She came back ten minutes later and went in. The kitchen was empty, and so was the annexe, but lights were on in the little office, visible through the half-closed door.

'Hello?' she said, tapping on it. 'Will? I brought you— oh. Hi.'
Will was sitting behind the desk. Perched on the corner,

legs crossed, only a foot or so away from him, was Caro.

'Sorry,' Libby apologised. 'I didn't know you were in here with anyone. I just brought you ...' She gestured at the coffee tray in her hands.

'You didn't have to do that,' Will said.

'I know,' she said, taking one of the coffees out of the tray and putting it on the desk in front of him. 'But you've been working so hard, and I know you're tired. Hi, Caro. Sorry. Hi.'

'Hi, Libby,' Caro said.

'Coffee?' She offered her the tray.

Caro gave her a strange look. 'I'm not drinking your coffee, Libby.'

'Okay. I, um, I'll leave you to it,' she said, and ran away.

'Are you all right?' Roarke asked her later, as they paced awkwardly through the dance sequence that would come at the end of the show.

'Hmmmm?'

'You haven't said a word to me all day,' he replied. 'I thought, after the other day ...'

'It's not you. I'm just distracted.'

'Not like that, Libby,' Caro said. 'You're doing it wrong. Lean back into it. Stop being so stiff.'

Caro demonstrated what Libby should be doing. That had been why Will was talking to her, it turned out – he'd asked her to choreograph the final dance scene, and she'd said yes.

Her hair was a blonde waterfall down her back. Libby had never noticed before that Caro was beautiful.

'Caro, can you come show me that?' Rosie called. 'I have no

idea what I'm doing wrong, but it's not working.'

'You're not the problem,' Caro said. 'It's Ned.' Her heels clacked on the ground as she walked over to them.

Dancing with Roarke came surprisingly easy. Caro only had to yell, 'Libby, what did I tell you? Trust your partner!' at her once. When she spun away from Roarke, she knew he'd be there when she spun back.

If nothing else, they looked good by comparison.

'Oh for God's sake, Ned, can you just listen to her?' Will snapped. 'It's not that hard.'

'I'm trying!' Ned protested.

'I know you can dance, Ned,' Caro said. 'I've seen you do it. What's your problem?'

Ned opened his mouth to say something, then saw Will glaring and thought better of it.

'Let's try it again,' Rosie said.

The dance rehearsal went on for another laborious hour. 'Look, you've all got the basic steps down,' Caro said. 'I've done what I can. I'll be back next weekend. Make sure you meet on your own time to practice. Especially you, Ned and Rosie.'

'How about we all thank Caro?' Will said.

The applause was, at best, lukewarm.

Libby watched Will as he walked Caro out. His fingers brushed the small of her back, casually but not accidentally. She said something to him, and he laughed, then kissed her cheek and hugged her goodbye.

'I'm going to run across the road to the Psych cafe,' Roarke said. 'Want anything?'

She shook her head. Drinking that coffee had been a terrible idea.

'Have it your way.'

'Thanks, though,' she said, but he was already gone.

She sighed. 'Get it together, ProofIt,' she murmured to herself.

'Libby!' Ned called. 'Get over here! We need to work out what new horror we need to sing tonight to win the wooden spoon!'

She looked over. Genevieve was sitting on Ned's lap on one of the studio couches. Annalise was braiding Rashmi's hair, while Rashmi braided Heidi's. Michael and Anthony were laughing together about something.

'Just a second,' she called back, and then went over to the other side of the studio instead, where Rosie was sitting alone, cross-legged on the floor.

'Hi,' she said, sitting beside her.

Rosie blinked. 'Hi.'

'What's up?'

'Not much.'

'Cool.'

She floundered for something to say. How was it that she'd lived in the world for nearly twenty years, and she still didn't know how to have a conversation?

'So, Caro was pretty tough on you, hey?' she tried.

'Not really,' Rosie replied. 'She was just doing her job. We needed to do better.'

'At least we still have a couple of weeks to go before we have to do it for real.'

'What do you want to know?'

'Um ... what's new? What's going on?'

Rosie rolled her eyes. 'Come on, Libby, I know you're friends with Ned and Genevieve,' she said. 'What are you trying to find out? If I'm crying myself to sleep at night and making secret plans to win Ned back?'

'What? No!'

'Because I'm not. You can report that back to base command.'

'I'm not – that's not – let me start again.' Libby took a deep breath. 'I'm not here as, like, a spy. I just didn't want to see you sitting by yourself.'

'Libby, I don't need your sympathy, and I definitely don't want your pity.'

'I'm not suggesting we exchange friendship bracelets! I just ... there's no reason for you to be all isolated, just because you dated someone and it didn't work out.'

Rosie laughed, a short, sharp laugh devoid of amusement. 'It was a bit more complicated than that.'

'I know, but ... look, I don't know you that well, Rosie, but I respect you. You're a good actor, and I'm sure when you're not accusing me of being some kind of secret agent you're probably cool, and there's no reason why we can't be friends. Friendly. Civil acquaintances.'

Rosie looked at her for a long moment.

'I'm really sorry for the way everyone's been treating you,' Libby said.

Another pause.

Then, 'thanks,' Rosie said.

'That's all right,' Libby said. 'I just think we can get through this show without the girls' dressing room being a war zone, you know?'

'Oh, I don't think we can,' Rosie said, looking over Libby's shoulder.

Libby turned her head and followed her gaze, to where Ned, Genevieve, and her whole circle of friends were staring at them.

'Count yourself lucky that you're in Ned's friend zone,' Rosie said, sighing. 'At least with Nightingale you knew you were only going to get screwed, not screwed over.'

Ella was sitting on the couch when Libby got home, holding her red mass of hair on top of her head and looking at herself in her phone camera. 'Do you think my hair looks weird like this?' she asked.

'Your hair looks great. It always looks great.'

'I hate to say this to you, Elizabeth Two, because you know I love you more than life, but your hair does not look great right now,' Ella said. 'What have you been doing? Rolling around on the floor?'

'It's been a long day,' Libby said. 'Work, and then dance rehearsal, and then regular rehearsal ... my brain is fried. Clearly it fried my hair too.'

'Make sure you do something to it before you go to karaoke.'

'I don't think I'm going to go. I just want to have a shower and go to bed.'

'No! You have to go. You loved it last time, remember?'

'I'm so tired I might cry. And I have to help *someone* build a set tomorrow, remember?'

'I don't believe what I'm hearing,' Ella said. 'How many times have you come home all sad that you didn't get invited to theatre people events? Now you are getting invited, and you're what, sitting it out?'

Libby rubbed her eyes. 'Today was just really weird, Ella.'

Ella turned towards her on the couch, crossing her legs. 'What happened?'

'Just – ugh, a bunch of stuff,' Libby said. 'We had dance rehearsal, and Caro's choreographing, so that was weird—'

'Weird, hey?'

'Stop grinning,' Libby said. 'Not like that. It's just that no one likes her, so that always adds a level of tension. Then no one likes Rosie much either, and she was sitting by herself when we were on break, and I was like, *hmmm, I remember many occasions when I was the one sitting by myself,* so I went and talked to her, and now I don't think anyone is talking to me.'

'What, they're not talking to you because you had one single conversation with someone they don't like?'

Libby shrugged.

'One, that's batshit,' Ella said. 'I guarantee you that's not what's happening.'

'You weren't there. You don't know.'

'You know what I do know? You. And I know that you always think that people hate you when probably they don't actually think about you that much.'

'Wow, I sound great,' Libby said. 'That's like five different insults wrapped into one.'

'Two,' Ella said, ignoring her, 'just say they *are* offended that you dared to have a single conversation with Rosie. You're only going to make it into a bigger deal if you don't go to karaoke. If you do go, and act like it's all cool, then chances are it will be.'

Wheels started ticking over in her mind. She'd promised to sing with Ned, hadn't she? And if she didn't turn up – if she deliberately snubbed him – then what would he think? What would everyone think?

If she made an enemy of Ned, she'd never get cast in anything again. Ever.

'You're right,' she said. 'I should go. Want to come with me? Be my moral support?'

'Can't. I've got things to do. A whole day of set con and bump in to prepare for. But if you get ready fast enough, I'll do your hair for you.'

She was as good as her word. Libby's brain might be a fried, scrambled mess, but at least, she thought, checking herself out in the train window as she headed back into town, her hair – piled on top of her head, inspired by Ella's – looked great.

Ella was right. If she acted like she'd committed some mortal sin, then everyone would treat her that way. If she acted like she was cool, then ...

'Hey guys,' she said, walking into the pub, borrowing a bit from Beatrice's effortless self-possession. 'Anyone want drinks? I'll buy this round.'

'Yaaaaassssss,' Rashmi said.

Libby collected drink orders and went to the bar. She managed to duck under a burly arm and flag down a bartender almost straight away, a rare achievement; and didn't accidentally put her elbows in any sticky patches on the bar, a rarer achievement still. She was in the middle of congratulating herself on her extremely simple scheme for looking cool when Genevieve popped up beside her. 'So what was that about today?'

'What was what was about?' Libby said, infusing her voice with deliberate innocence and willing the bartender to pour their jugs faster.

'You were talking to Rosie for ages.'

'I was just being nice,' Libby said lightly. 'Plus, we had some character stuff I wanted to talk through. Here, can you carry some glasses?'

Genevieve took them. 'Did she say anything about Ned?'

'Did who say anything about Ned?' Ned said, appearing and taking the glasses out of Genevieve's hands.

'Rosie,' Genevieve said.

'Babe, I think she said everything she wanted to say about me when she fell into bed with Nightingale,' Ned said, as they walked back to the table, taking the long way around to avoid the crowd of footy bros.

'Who do you think she slept with to get the Hero role?' Annalise asked, taking a jug out of Libby's hands and a glass out of Ned's and pouring herself a beer.

'She one hundred percent did not sleep with anybody,' Libby said, setting the other jug down on the table. 'Will cast her because he thought she'd be good. End of story.'

'And you know that howwwww?' Annalise said, grinning.

Libby closed her eyes and exhaled.

'Come on, Lise, leave her alone,' Rashmi said.

'Thank you,' Libby said.

'Will was totally wrong, though,' Annalise said. 'She's not good. Did you see dance rehearsal today?'

'That wasn't all her,' Ned said. 'A lot of that was me.'

'Ned, just admit it,' Annalise said. 'Stop trying to be a gentleman. She's the worst.'

'She's not.'

Libby didn't realise until about two seconds after she'd spoken – when everyone looked at her – that she'd said it. 'She's not the worst,' she said, trying to sound as nonchalant as possible, pouring herself a drink, forcing herself not to turn red. 'She's good as Hero. And, I don't know, she seems cool.'

'Libby, she hooked up with Nightingale!' Genevieve said, smacking the edge of the table twice for emphasis, nearly spilling everyone's drinks.

'So has half of Uni Rep,' Heidi said.

'They weren't dating Ned at the time!' Genevieve said.

'Babe,' Ned said quietly.

'And they aren't draping themselves all over him every chance they get!'

'If it helps, she told me that she has zero interest in getting Ned back,' Libby said.

'I thought you just talked about character stuff.'

Libby dug her nails into her thigh. 'I don't want it to be weird backstage,' she said. 'I know you're not her biggest fan, Gen, but you won't be in the dressing room with her. We will. It'll be easier if we at least vaguely get along.'

'Would you have thought the same thing if it was Caro?' Genevieve demanded, smacking the table again. 'Would you have been all *oooh, she's not so bad!* if she was in the dressing room with you, and she was still sleeping with the dude you'd kill to be sleeping with yourself?'

Silence.

'Gen,' Ned said, 'that's enough.'

'Don't,' Genevieve said. 'Don't you dare, Ned.'

She pushed her chair back and strode away from the table. 'Shit,' Ned said, almost falling over as he chased after her. 'Gen. *Genevieve!*'

No one cared enough to chase after Libby.

Probably no one even noticed that she'd left, to tell the truth. And even if they had, why would any of them have been worried about her?

A train was just pulling into the station as she got there. She folded herself into a corner seat and leaned her head against the window.

This wasn't her first rodeo. She'd spent basically her whole life in social Siberia. She knew what it was like to have zero friends in the world apart from Ella. She'd done it before. She'd survive it again.

And she wouldn't have zero friends. She'd have Will. She'd have Roarke, kind of, and maybe she could be friends with Rosie, and ...

She wanted to groan aloud, but she was in the quiet carriage, and she probably shouldn't make complete strangers hate her too.

Music was pumping out of the apartment next door when she got home. She closed the front door behind her and shuffled inside, intending to head straight to her bedroom and flop face-first on the bed and potentially never emerge again.

She stopped dead.

She felt like she was in a movie and someone had just pressed the pause button. One hand held her keys, about to drop them on the table. Her handbag dangled loosely from the other. Her feet were rooted to the ground, and the world was a tunnel, with only one thing visible at the end.

Ella and Roarke were tangled up on the couch, kissing. She was on top of him, and her hair was loose and dishevelled. One of his hands was tangled in it, and the other was on her hip, pulling her into him, so closely pressed together that Libby couldn't see where one stopped and the other began.

She felt lightheaded, like she was hovering above herself. There were the two of them, together, and her, on her own, and the rushing of the blood in her head was louder than even the pumping music next door.

'Oh, shit!' Ella exclaimed, sitting up hurriedly, pulling her shirt back together. 'Libby, I didn't think you'd be home!'

Roarke turned around, and he was looking at her, and he must be able to read everything she was thinking from the expression on her face, and she was going to die if he looked at her for even a second longer.

'Um, don't mind me,' she said, 'carry on,' and fled to her bedroom.

Chapter Sixteen

About fifteen minutes later, she heard the sounds of a murmured farewell and the front door closing.

It took another fifteen minutes before Ella tapped on her bedroom door. 'Libby? Can I come in?'

She'd used that half hour well. She'd breathed in deep and cleared her mind and steeled her nerves and she'd made a list in her mind of things that she knew.

Ella would never hurt her. Not on purpose.

Ella would never go near Roarke, not if she knew.

She and Roarke had agreed it wasn't a thing. They'd agreed it hadn't happened.

She didn't want it to be a thing. She didn't want Roarke.

It had happened, though.

But that didn't matter. That couldn't matter, because there was a 6) on that list, and that was that she could never, ever tell Ella that it had happened, so she prepared exactly what to say.

'It's open,' she called back.

Ella opened the bedroom door, but she didn't come in. Instead, she leaned against the doorjamb. 'So ...'

'That was a surprise,' Libby said, in her lightest tone.

'I'm sorry you had to see that. I didn't think you'd be home.'

'I figured.'

Ella sighed. 'Okay, out with it. Get it over with.'

'Get what over with?'

'The lecture!' Ella said. 'Theatre hook-ups are complicated.

I know. I'm on the rebound. I know. I'm making your life awkward, and this is a terrible idea—'

'Why do you always think I'm going to lecture you?'

'Because you do!'

'I do not!'

'Well, it feels like you do!'

Libby said nothing.

Ella groaned. 'I'm sorry, Libs. That's not fair. I'm, I don't know, projecting or something.'

'Come in,' Libby said. 'Sit down.'

Ella obeyed. She sat on the edge of Libby's bed. Her hair was a mess, half falling down around her shoulders.

At Catriona's wedding, Roarke had run his hands through Libby's hair too, biting her bottom lip as she arched against him.

She tasted bile in the back of her throat.

'Do you want to tell me about it?' she asked.

'I don't know what there is to tell,' Ella said. 'It's new.'

'How new?'

'Very.'

At least he hadn't been sleeping with them both at the same time. That was something.

'I was going to tell you,' Ella said. 'As soon as I knew what it was. As soon as he knew – we knew – what it was.'

'Do you know what it is?'

'Something. I think it's something.'

Ella sighed, running her hand through her dishevelled hair. 'I know it's a bad idea, Libs. I don't need you to tell me that. But it just kind of happened.'

'When?'

'After the Gerry thing, I guess? We had that chat at the

party, and he really made me feel better, and then, when Gerry actually turned up … no one's ever done anything like that for me before.'

'What, punched someone?' It came out sharp.

'Yes. No. Kind of,' Ella said, tugging at her hair again. 'It's not that I expect people to be running around punching people in the face to defend me. That's not even the reason. We've been chatting for a couple of weeks now, and he just … he gets me, Libby. I know I should do the sensible thing, and take some time, and really work through all this Gerry shit, but … there he is.'

Oh God. When Roarke had turned up at the door the other day. When he'd been like *so, that thing we did was a mistake, hey?* and she'd been like *what thing? I don't remember a thing*, and then Ella had come home and told him to take his clothes off.

She was so stupid. She was the stupidest person in the whole universe, not to be able to see what was happening right under her nose.

'Are you angry with me?' Ella asked.

'No,' Libby said. 'I'm surprised, and I wish you'd told me, but of course I'm not angry with you.'

'It's weird, though. I know you're friends, and I asked him not to tell you until we knew what it was, and he hated that, trust me, and … you have to kiss him! All the time! That's very weird! And I don't want to make your life weird, because I do that enough already, and—'

'Ella, don't worry about me, okay?'

'But I'm sorry,' Ella said. 'I know it's messed up, with all the Beatrice and Benedick stuff.'

'You don't have anything to be sorry for. It's fine. That's just – theatre.'

'You're okay with it, then?' The words spilled out of Ella like water, and Libby loved her and hated her and wanted to hug her and wanted to punch her right in her beautiful face and knew she would die if she ever lost her, all at once.

She made herself laugh instead. 'Ella, this isn't *Pride and Prejudice*. You don't need my blessing. You can do whatever you want.'

'But I want it to be okay with you,' Ella said. 'I like him, and I think he likes me, but if it's too weird for you—'

'Don't be silly,' Libby said. 'I just want you to be happy.'

That bit, at least, was true.

Later, when Ella was gone, Libby sat on her bed in the dark, hugging her knees. The performance had exhausted her, and there wasn't much she could do apart from staring numbly at the wall.

A single tear snaked down her cheek. She wiped it away angrily. She'd been trying to muster up the single tear of angst on cue for all the time they'd been rehearsing *Much Ado*, and she hadn't been able to manage it. Of course it would turn up now.

She was going to punch Roarke in the face. Then kick him in the balls. Then punch him in the face again before he could ask why she was beating him up, so she didn't have to think of a coherent answer.

Of course he wanted Ella. People always wanted Ella. Gerry had only had eyes for Ella, and everyone had killed themselves laughing at the mere idea that he might want Libby.

She buried her face in her hands, digging her fingers into her browbone.

She was all right. She didn't want Roarke. It wasn't a thing, and it hadn't happened. They'd agreed. None of this was a big deal, not really. Maybe it was even a good thing, if Roarke could help Ella get over Gerry, and keep her safe from creeps like Paul ... and keep her tied to Terravale.

She wished any of that felt true.

Her eyes felt heavy the next morning, but the set had to be built, and the show had to be bumped in to the auditorium. She had to keep going. If she wasn't going to care, she had to *act* like she didn't care. If she was going to be cool, she needed to *be* cool.

Of course, that was the advice Ella had given her to get her out of the house so she could spend the evening ripping Roarke's clothes off, so maybe she should take it with a grain of salt.

Will and Roarke were both waiting on the back stairs of the theatre when she and Ella got to the theatre. 'You okay?' Will asked her, as they hefted boxes out of the back of Ella's car.

'Just tired,' she said. 'I didn't sleep well.'

'Can I buy you a coffee?'

'No, I'll go. Want one?'

'Always.'

'I'll go with you,' Roarke said.

'No,' Libby said. 'You help Ella. I'll go on my own.'

Roarke's hand had brushed hers as they unloaded the car. It had felt like spiders crawling over her skin.

How was she going to do the show with him? How was she going to do the kissing scenes? He'd kiss her the same way he always did, like it was no big deal, like it wasn't a thing at all. And even though it wasn't a thing, because they had *agreed* that it wasn't a thing, she was going to throw up in his mouth.

There was a poster on the door of the café next to the Psych building. *Tuesday at the Arms,* it read. *Blackbird Jones.*

She wasn't going to survive today. She should just leave now, walk down the street, and not stop walking until she hit the beach, and then still not stop walking until the ocean closed over her head.

She went inside instead, because she'd somehow got herself into a position where not only did she have to act normal around Roarke, she also had to buy him coffee.

Well, fine. She had no idea what kind of coffee he liked, but she could guess, and he was going to get totally the opposite. She was going to fill it with sugar, and—

'Hi, Libby.'

'Oh,' she said. 'Hi Gen.'

Genevieve looked about as good as Libby felt: hair dishevelled, dark smears under her eyes. 'Coffee?' she asked.

'Um, yeah,' Libby replied. 'Just grabbing some caffeine before bump in. Long day and all.'

'No, I mean, can I buy you one?'

'I'm buying for a few,' she said. 'Will. Ella. Roarke. Don't worry.'

'I'll buy them all,' Genevieve said. 'But will you sit with me for a minute?'

She didn't wait for Libby's answer, just slid into one of the chairs at the nearest table. Libby, not knowing how to extricate herself, followed.

Genevieve tapped her fingernails against the edge of the table several times before she finally spoke. 'I owe you an apology, Libs,' she said, eyes downcast. 'I'm so sorry for what I said to you last night. That was out of line.'

'It's okay.'

'No, it's not,' she said, lifting her gaze to meet Libby's. 'I was a bitch. I know you're just trying to be a team player. Ned read me the riot act, and ... I'm sorry. I'm so, so sorry.'

'I, um – thanks?'

'Are we cool?' Genevieve said. 'Please don't hate me.'

'Yeah, we're cool,' she replied, because there was no other possible answer. 'But can I ask you a question?'

'Sure.'

'Why do you hate her so much?'

'Rosie?'

Libby nodded.

'Isn't it obvious?' Genevieve picked up one of the sugar packets and started twiddling it between her fingers.

'I get that she's Ned's ex, but—'

'But don't I trust Ned?'

'Well, yeah.'

'Of course I do,' Genevieve said, gaze fixed on the sugar packet. 'In my head, anyway. But then I look at them standing together on stage, and they look so perfect, and then I remember how long they were together, and how much he loved her, and I want to smash things.'

'She really doesn't want him back, if that makes you feel any better.'

'It doesn't. The problem isn't her. It's not Ned, either. It's me. I'm the psycho.'

'You're not a psycho. You're allowed to be bothered by stuff like this. I am.'

'Oh, shut up,' Genevieve said, putting the sugar packet down with an audible smack of her hand. 'Stop lying. You never have this kind of drama. You're, like, the chillest person I know.'

'Trust me, I'm just as big a disaster as everyone else,' Libby said. 'I just hide it better.'

'Can you teach me how?'

'To hide it?'

'I hate being like this, Libby.' Genevieve picked up the sugar packet again, ripping it open and letting the crystals spill onto the table. 'I know Ned doesn't want to touch her with a ten-foot pole.'

Libby picked up a sugar packet of her own.

'But then I think about what a strong reaction that is,' Genevieve went on. 'About how much she hurt him when she cheated on him. It's only people that you really love that can hurt you like that. And I really love him, and I think about what it would feel like if she took him away from me, and ...' She closed her eyes.

'She's not going to,' Libby said. 'And Ned wouldn't go, not even if she tried.'

'Oh, he might. If I keep behaving like such a psycho bitch and yelling at people like you, just trying to do their job, he might.'

'Gen, you're forgiven. It's okay.'

'Thanks. I'm so sorry, though. It's just ... Ned's everything to me.'

Genevieve sighed. 'God, doesn't that sound tragic. *My boyfriend's my whole world, and if he even looks at another girl, I'll literally die.*' She picked up another sugar packet. 'If you'd told me when I was in Year Ten that I'd be obsessed with anyone, let alone Ned Riordan, to the point where I was throwing hysterical tantrums in public, I would have laughed you out of the room.'

'You knew him before Uni Rep?'

'I've known him forever. Kind of, anyway. He was in the year above me at high school. Totally different social circles. I never paid attention to him until Uni Rep. And to begin with, I honestly only really paid attention to his arse.'

'The *Peter Pan* tight pants. I remember the story.'

'I remember the moment it all changed, though,' Genevieve said. 'I was standing in the foyer after one of the *Jack and the Beanstalk* shows. The show was over and I was waiting for all of you guys to come out. Heidi was out first and she came over and she tried to ask me something like four times and I didn't hear her, because I was just watching the doors. I didn't realise it, but I was waiting for Ned.'

Genevieve ripped open the second sugar packet and picked up a third. 'It was like this lightbulb moment. Choirs of angels singing in my mind, you know? Then he came out the doors, and he was still covered in makeup and he was all sweaty, and I just didn't give a shit about anything in the world except for him.'

'That's really nice,' Libby said.

'It might not mean anything, in the long run. Not if Ned dumps me for being crazy.'

'He won't.'

'He might,' Genevieve said. 'I'm not an idiot. It's maths. Economics. Supply and demand. This is a theatre full of straight girls. He could have basically anyone he wants. Why on earth would he want me?'

That phrase kept echoing around her head all day. *Why on earth would he want me?*

She knew exactly how Gen felt. She felt like that all the time. She knew, intellectually, that she wasn't the first person to have felt like that, but it was still strange to think of confident, take-no-prisoners, no-bullshit Gen feeling like that too.

Kneeling between Rashmi and Heidi, painting one of the set

pieces, Libby watched as Ned and Will and some of the other boys hauled a flat into place. It was hot under the working lights, so they'd stripped off their shirts, and they were glistening with sweat, muscles working under their skin.

As if he could feel her gaze, Will's eyes swung around toward hers. Hurriedly, she started paying extremely close attention to what she was painting.

'Libs, can you come help me for a sec?' Ella asked. 'I need an extra set of hands.'

'Sure,' Libby said, resting her paint roller in the tray and scrambling to her feet.

Ella needed her to hold some chipboard steady so she could use a jigsaw to cut out one of the more ornate set pieces. 'Are you sure you don't want someone stronger to hold this for you?' Libby asked.

'You'll be fine,' Ella told her, finishing off the pencil line.

'I can cut it for you, if you want,' offered Roarke, who had been deputised to hold the other side.

'Roarke,' Ella said, 'if you're one of those dudes that insists on being the one to use the power tools, then this thing with you and me is going nowhere.'

She pulled her beautiful hair up into a knot on the top of her head then picked up the jigsaw. 'Hold it steady, kids. Mama's going in.'

The wood vibrated under Libby's hands. She pushed down as hard as she could, but it was almost impossible to stop the shaking.

Her eyes met Roarke's across the chipboard. He jerked his head towards the open side door of the theatre.

She shook her head firmly, as Ella came between them with the saw.

She was pushing so hard into the wood that she almost fell when the two halves gave way. 'There,' Ella said, switching the jigsaw off and dusting herself off. 'Perfect. Do you doubt my prowess now, boy?'

'I wouldn't dare,' Roarke replied.

'Good,' Ella replied, smiling up at him. As if he couldn't help himself, he smiled back.

Libby escaped to the kitchen, which was blessedly empty. She put the kettle on and rummaged around until she found the jar of tea bags.

'I brought some milk in with me this morning, if you want it,' Will said from behind her.

'Good thinking,' she said. 'Do you want one?'

'Sure.'

He'd put his shirt back on, but he hadn't buttoned it up, and she could see a sliver of his chest in her peripheral vision. 'I had an interesting chat with Roarke last night,' he said, leaning beside her, next to the sink. 'About Ella.'

'That must have been fun,' she said, willing the kettle to boil faster.

'Not half as much fun as it must have been for you to come home and find them together.'

'Oh, it was a rollicking good time. Ten out of ten.'

He made a noise that might have been a laugh.

She cracked. 'It was weird, Will. The whole thing is really, really weird.'

'I can imagine.'

'It's not that I'm heartbroken or anything,' she said. 'Because I'm not. It's just ...'

'Weird.' Their elbows were brushing. She could feel his warmth, even through his shirt.

'Weird,' she repeated. 'And awkward, because Ella doesn't know about – the wedding – and I obviously can't tell her.'

'Why not?'

The kettle bubbled aggressively. 'Because I don't want to hurt her,' she said, pouring hot water into their mugs. 'It's not like I have a prior claim or anything. Technically, no one's done anything wrong, and I don't want to make Ella feel like she has. But ...'

'Is there anything I can do to help?'

'You can drink this cup of tea with me,' Libby said, handing him his mug. 'You can tell me that it's okay to feel weird about it.'

'It's definitely okay to feel weird about it,' Will said, blowing across the top of it and then setting it down on the counter to cool. 'And I'll drink a cup of tea with you any time you want, ProofIt.'

There was something hot and tight in the pit of her stomach, and right behind her eyes. 'Thank you,' she said, although those weren't the right words, not yet.

She wrapped her arms around his torso and pressed her ear to his collarbone. His skin was warm and a little sticky against hers, and he smelled like sweat and sawdust, but she didn't care.

His arms came around her too, and he pressed his lips to the top of her head. 'Whenever you want, Libby,' he said. 'Whatever you want, I'm there.'

Libby was sore and exhausted by the time she and Ella got home later that evening, but at least the exhaustion had quieted her mind down. 'I'm going to have a shower and go to bed,' she told Ella. 'Mind if I go first?'

'Go ahead,' Ella said. Despite the fact that she was also sweaty and covered in dirt and dust and paint, she still looked gorgeous.

Libby scolded herself for being jealous as she washed her hair. She'd been down this path before when she was a teenager, and she wasn't doing it again. She wasn't going to feel sorry for herself because Ella was so beautiful. She was better than that.

It didn't help, though, that when she got out of the shower, dressed in an extremely classy ancient T-shirt, pyjama pants, and no bra, Roarke was sitting beside Ella on the couch.

'I'm going to jump in the shower,' Ella announced, pecking Roarke on the cheek, apparently not noticing that Libby wanted to die. 'I defrosted some frozen soup. Libs, do you mind heating it up?'

'Sure,' she said, because she couldn't say no.

Ella disappeared, and they were alone.

'Libby,' Roarke began.

She turned on her heel and walked into the kitchen.

He followed her. 'Libby, we need to talk.'

She dug a saucepan out of the bottom drawer, making as much noise as possible, pretending she didn't hear him.

'Libby.'

'What, Roarke?' she snapped, as the shower started in the background. 'What is it that you would like to say to me, Mr I-Don't-Do-D&Ms and I-Don't-Do-Relationships?'

'I—'

'Because you don't need to apologise,' she said, pouring soup into the saucepan. 'It wasn't a thing, remember? It didn't happen?'

'Libby, when I was here that day, I thought you knew about me and Ella,' he said. 'I didn't realise she hadn't told you. I thought, when you said that we could agree that it didn't happen, that you knew, and that was why.'

'Nice of you to check. Nice of you to be all *so, now that we've agreed that was a mistake that didn't happen, do you mind if I start sleeping with your best friend?*'

She'd forgotten to turn the gas on. She turned the knob, and it sparked to life.

'I didn't do this to hurt you,' he said.

'Let me guess. It just happened.'

'Yes. Kind of. I promise you, I had no idea that Ella hadn't told you until it was too late.'

'I love how that's her responsibility,' Libby said, implements in the cutlery drawer rattling everywhere as she searched for a wooden spoon. 'Really. Super into that.'

'Why wouldn't it be? She's your best friend.'

She went very still.

'Why wouldn't I assume that she'd told you she was seeing me?' he said. 'Why wouldn't I assume you knew?'

Her knuckles clenched around the wooden spoon.

'Although maybe you're right, and I'm the idiot,' he said. 'After all, you never told her about me.'

She slapped the wooden spoon down on the kitchen bench so hard it made a sound like a whip crack. 'Stir the soup,' she snarled. 'Tell Ella I went to bed.'

At least he didn't follow her. That was something.

She knew, theoretically, that she was tired, so she turned out her light and lay down, but her jaw was clenched so hard her teeth felt like they might snap. She hated him. She hated him. *She hated him.*

How was she going to do this show with him? She was a good actor. She knew she was a good actor. But she wasn't that good.

How was she going to pretend to fall in love with him night after night for two weeks when she all she wanted to do was murder him?

The first half of the show, when Beatrice and Benedick were at each other's throats, was going to be very convincing. The second half – the half with all the kissing – was going to be so spectacularly bad no one would ever give her another role at Uni Rep again. Everyone in the cast would be furious with her for ruining the show, and no one would ever speak to her again. Especially Will, because he'd believed in her, and she'd made him look ridiculous.

All she'd have would be Ella. But wherever Ella was, Roarke would be too, saying shit like *after all, you never told her about me.*

She smacked her hand against her doona. Why couldn't Roarke just steal eight thousand dollars and run away with it, so she never had to see him again?

She heard Ella's bedroom door snick closed. She heard their footsteps, the rustle of clothing and bedding, their voices.

They were laughing together. Ella was laughing. *He* was laughing.

She pulled her pillow over her head and pressed it against her ears, as hard as she could.

It wasn't hard enough to drown out the sound of Ella screaming.

'No! No! Em! No!'

Libby snapped awake. 'Ella? Ella?!' she heard Roarke saying.

'No, Emerson! Don't! Don't!'

She didn't think. Her body simply galvanised itself into

action. She was running, and she threw Ella's door open so hard it smashed into the wall. Roarke was kneeling next to Ella on the bed, and she shoved him away with one hand on his shirtless chest as she scrambled towards her. 'Get out,' she ordered him.

Ella was breathing in sobs and gasps, sweaty strands of red hair stuck to her forehead. 'Don't! Don't!'

'Come on, Ella, wake up,' Libby said, shaking her. 'I've got you.'

'No, no, no, Emerson!'

Libby caught her flailing hands. 'Ella, I've got you. You're all right.'

Ella was panting. 'Libby?'

'I've got you. You had a nightmare, but I've got you, all right?'

'Don't go,' Ella begged her. 'Please don't go.'

She folded Ella up in her arms. 'Never,' she promised. 'I'm never going anywhere.'

She wasn't sure how long it was until she smoothed the covers over Ella and delicately extricated herself, careful not to wake her. Ella made a small sound that might have been a sob, and Libby froze, but then Ella sighed and snuggled deeper into the pillow.

Libby wanted to cry. She closed the door quietly behind her instead.

Roarke was sitting on the couch, but he scrambled to his feet when she came out into the living room.

She didn't say anything. Neither did he.

'What was that?' he asked at last.

'She has nightmares sometimes. About her brother who died.'

'Is she all right?'

'She's sleeping,' Libby said. 'You should go. I don't want you to disturb her.'

'I'll stay out here.'

'Do whatever you want. I don't care.'

'Wait.'

She turned. 'What?' she said. 'What could you possibly have to say to me, Roarke?'

'I'm sorry.'

'Is that all?'

'No.'

She raised her eyebrows. God, she wished she could raise just one, like he did.

'Thank you,' he said.

'Don't you dare thank me for doing something for her.'

Something was cracking inside her. Something was erupting, and her veins were full of lava.

'I don't care if she tells you things she doesn't tell me,' she said. 'I don't care if you're kindred spirits, or you just get each other, or whatever the hell your deal is. She's my best friend and I love her more than anyone in the entire world, so don't you *ever* act like I'm doing you a favour by looking after her.'

'That's not what I—'

'Do you want to know what I would have said?'

He was silent.

'Do you?' she demanded. 'If you'd actually asked me? If you'd been like *hey Libby, we're cool now, mind if I start something with Ella?* – do you know what I would have said?'

'It seems like you want to tell me.'

'I would have said that she's fragile,' she said. 'I would have said, *hey Roarke, you know she's fragile, because the reason she started telling you all her deep dark secrets in the first place was because she was making herself sick over her ex, so don't be that guy that swoops on in, hey?* I would have said, *look, you're not a relationship guy, and her biggest fear is people leaving her, so maybe it's not a good idea.* I would have said, *Roarke, this ends in one of two ways, and one is with her cutting and running so you can't do it to her first.'*

Her fists were clenched. She was breathing hard and fast.

'What's the other way?' he asked.

'The other way,' she said, 'is that you leave her, and you break her again. And if you do that, Roarke – if you hurt her – I'll kill you.'

'Libby, wait,' he said again, but she didn't listen this time. She turned on her heel and left him standing there, like they were in a play and he was the jilted lover, the one left behind.

She was really proud of that exit.

She didn't always know what she wanted, but when she did, she would work hard to get it. It was one of the few things about herself she knew for sure. She would always (1) look after Ella, and (2) fight for what she wanted, when she knew what it was.

The next night at Monday rehearsal, she knew exactly what she wanted, which was to do a good job at being Beatrice, no matter what else was going on. She wanted to be strong, and fearless, and unshakeable.

'Libby, great job,' Will said, when he gave everyone notes at the end. 'There were a couple of places where it was maybe a little too intense – I know Beatrice is going through some real shit after Claudio ditches Hero, but pull it back a touch – but overall, that was awesome. Well done.'

Out of the corner of her eye, she could see people exchanging glances. She wasn't sure if she *wanted* not to care so much that she was tricking herself into thinking she *didn't*, or if she actually didn't care.

'Ned, it's getting there, but we need a bit more at the beginning,' Will said. 'That moment when Claudio sees Hero for the first time needs to feel like the heavens have opened and all the angels are singing to him.'

'Okay,' Ned said.

He was sitting with Genevieve on one of the studio couches, their hands laced together, Genevieve's head leaning on his shoulder. Rosie was standing a little way behind them, leaning against the wall, scribbling notes in her script, paying no attention to them.

Libby turned her focus back to Will, who was giving notes to Rashmi and Heidi. His glasses were crooked on his nose.

I have no idea what I want, she'd said to him when they had lunch outside the library.

Last night, when she'd told Roarke that if he hurt Ella, she'd kill him, she'd been sure.

She needed to be sure again.

It was a terrible idea, she told herself the next morning, as she stared into her cupboard, trying to decide what she would wear.

It was a terrible idea, she told herself, waiting in the queue in the student union to grab a quick bite of lunch after her Sociology lecture.

It was a terrible idea, she told herself in her Nineteenth-Century Lit seminar, and in her Con Law lecture, when she really should have been paying attention.

Hey, I'm going to be late tonight, she texted Ella, even though it was a terrible idea. *Group project for Sociology. We're going to work late in the library. Don't wait up.*

No probs, Ella texted back. *Roarke and I were going to go to his place tonight, but if you're not going to be home, we'll stay at ours ;)*

That only hardened her resolve.

She did go to the library, but it was to change into the outfit she'd brought with her in the bathroom. She wished she had Ella to do something to her hair, but – no. She had to do this on her own.

Because she had to be sure.

She stared into the mirror. This was *such* a terrible idea. She should text Ella back and tell her that oops, everyone cancelled, typical groupwork, I'm probably going to have to do it all myself. She should go home and put on pyjamas and try and focus on her Law textbooks and go to bed early and ignore the sounds of Roarke and Ella in the next room.

This wasn't her. She didn't do stupid shit like this. She was cautious. She was armoured. She was smart.

But maybe this *was* her. She'd let Nightingale lead her into the Swamp with not a word of protest, after all.

The gig didn't start till eight, so she sat in the library for a couple of hours, editing essays from her ProofItLibby inbox, correcting mistake after mistake. She decided she was just going to work late there. She had heaps to get through, after all.

At seven forty-five, she slid her laptop into her bag and walked out.

It was a short walk from campus to the Arms. Too short, really. If it had been longer, she would have had more time to lecture herself about what a bad idea it was.

But it seemed like she blinked and she was there. *Live music,* someone had scrawled on the chalkboard outside. *Tonight only: Blackbird Jones.*

That name, if nothing else, should have made her realise she was in the process of making a truly awful mistake.

'Love? Are you coming or going?' the bouncer asked.

'Coming,' she replied, handing him her ID. 'I'm on the list.'

The pub was full. She was glad. This would be so much easier if she could make it fast. She just wanted to look at him: to look at his face, hear his voice, and to be sure.

'Can I get a glass of your house white, please?' she asked the bartender.

'Sure,' he said. 'You here for the show?'

'No,' she replied. 'Just grabbing a quick drink.'

She took her wine and found a spare table. It was much closer to the stage than she wanted, but it was in a corner, and it was dark.

She remembered that moment in her *Rapunzel* show when the lights had shone down on them and his tongue had touched her lip.

She closed her eyes, but it didn't make it go away. *I know who you are*, he whispered. *You're the smart girl.*

His hands slipping under her shirt. His mouth on her skin. His breath hot against her ear. *Shhh. Someone will hear us.*

This was a terrible idea. She had to go.

She opened her eyes, and there he was.

She'd imagined a dramatic entrance – him striding onto the stage, flying on the wings of applause as he was introduced. He should have walked out and seen her, and his eyes should have widened with surprise or excitement or anticipation or *something.*

It wasn't dramatic at all. He was standing about three metres away, back to her, tuning his guitar. He hadn't even seen her.

Which was good, of course, because she didn't want him to see her, didn't want him to know she'd caved, but – it should have been theatrical. It should have been explosive.

It should have been more than this.

He was smaller than she remembered. Roarke must have an inch on him, and Will another three or four.

'Good evening, everyone!' he said, but his microphone wasn't on. He tapped it a couple of times and looked at it curiously before finding the switch. 'Let's try that again. Good evening, everyone! Are you all having a good night?'

There was an apathetic murmur.

There should be more than this. Surely, *surely*, there should be more than this.

'I'm Blackbird Jones,' he said. 'You can call me BJ, if you like. I like.'

No one laughed.

'I'm going to get us started with one of my own songs. Don't worry, we'll get to the shit you all know soon enough. This one's about a girl I knew in high school, who I never quite got out of my head.'

His fingers strummed the guitar, fingers that had once touched her, and people went back to their conversations as he started to sing.

Why had she come here? She was smarter than this. She *was* sure: that she was stupid. She was *so stupid*.

And then he saw her.

Interlude – Nightingale

Nightingale hated playing cover songs, but people wanted covers, people cheered for covers, and, moreover, people paid for covers, and it was his job to give people what they wanted. When you gave them what they wanted, they were much more likely to give you what you wanted. He allowed himself only one concession to artistic sensibility: he always opened a set with one of his own songs.

The song about the girl from high school was a new one, and he thought it was pretty good. It wasn't about a real girl, but it sounded like it could have been, and it made him seem dreamy as hell.

Not that it was working this time. This crowd was barely listening to him. They were drinking and laughing and talking to each other, and he was on stage singing his goddamn heart out, all alone.

He'd only taken this gig to please his mother. 'I miss you, Nighty,' she'd said when she called him a few weeks ago. 'Won't you come home for a visit?'

'Maybe,' he'd replied half-heartedly. There was a crash from the opposite room, then laughter, then moaning. He hoped his mum couldn't hear his flatmate getting his *Fifty Shades* on through the wall. 'I'll think about it.'

'Or we could come up and visit you! You could show us the Harbour Bridge and the Opera House and we could have a lovely time.'

'I've got nowhere for you to sleep.'

'Your father and I aren't fussy, Nighty, you know that. The floor would be fine.'

The thought of his parents asleep on the threadbare, beer-stained grey carpet made his heart stop beating for at least ten seconds. 'Owen emailed me about a gig at the Arms,' he said, snatching at the first thing that came into his mind. 'I wasn't going to take it, but it'd be a good excuse to come and see you.'

'Oh, Nighty, yes, take it! You can invite all your friends from the theatre! They must miss you. If you like, I can get on the phone to Graham right now, and—'

'Oh, no no no, I'll invite them myself,' he said hurriedly. 'Don't worry, Mum.'

'Well, at least let me put up some posters for you.'

'No, no, Mum, really, that's not necessary.'

'Nonsense. I want to.'

'I'm not singing under my own name any more,' he said, because he knew even if he made her swear not to do it, she'd do it anyway. 'It's – um – Blackbird now. Blackbird – ah – Jones.'

Now here he was, playing and singing under the worst fake name in the history of the world in the town he used to own, and the only person he had actually invited hadn't had the decency to show up.

He didn't even remember how the bet had happened, though probably it was about Rosie. (Really, the whole thing was about Rosie, when it came down to it.) 'Hey mate,' he'd said. He slapped Ned on the back and slid into the seat next to him in the seating bank at *Rapunzel* after-show drinks on the first Saturday. 'All alone?'

Ned had looked at him sideways. 'What do you want, Nightingale?'

'Just bringing you a beer,' he'd replied. 'Cheers.'

Ned had waited a long time before he'd clinked the neck of his bottle against Nightingale's, but he'd done it, and something about that made Nightingale feel like Leo in *Titanic*, screaming *I'M THE KING OF THE WOOOOOORLD!* into the wind.

'How's things with Gen?' he'd asked.

'Keep her name out of your mouth.'

Nightingale had followed his eyes down to the stage, where Gen was dancing with Annalise and Heidi and whats-her-face with the tits and whats-her-name with the legs up to her eyeballs. The Leo feeling intensified.

'I thought we were past this,' he'd said. 'I told you, mate, Rosie came onto me. And it's for the best, isn't it? You and Gen—'

'If you don't shut your mouth right now, I'm going to drop one of the lights on your head in the middle of your solo during the matinee tomorrow,' Ned had said. 'I'm not kidding.'

'All right, all right, calm your farm,' he'd replied, leaning back and spreading his arms along the backs of the seats. 'Just because I'm irresistible doesn't mean I'm going to steal your girl, Neddy.'

Again, he'd thought, smiling to himself.

Ned had snorted. 'Irresistible. Cute. You keep thinking that, if it helps you sleep at night.'

'Want me to prove it? Pick a chick. Any chick.'

'What are you talking about?'

'Pick a chick,' Nightingale had repeated. 'Any chick in this building I want, I can have. Pick one, and I'll prove it.'

'I'm not picking a girl for you to crack onto, Nightingale.'

He'd shrugged. 'Guess it'll be Gen, then.'

Ned had made this sound that was part sigh, part exasperated groan, but Nightingale could hear what was behind it. Ned had loved Rosie, and Nightingale had taken her from him like it was nothing.

He'd started to grin. He was Leo, screaming into the wind.

'Fine,' Ned had said. 'Libby.'

He'd blinked. 'The shy nerdy one who edits essays and shit?'

'Is there another Libby I don't know about?' Ned had taken another swig of his beer. 'She'd never go near you. You know it.'

'I wouldn't be so sure about that,' he'd said. 'She's got, like, *Dirty Dancing* hungry eyes.'

'Whatever you say, mate,' Ned had said, not paying attention to him and watching Genevieve dance instead. 'Whatever you say.'

But Libby had gone with Nightingale willingly. She'd let him lay her down in the bed of costumes in the Swamp. She'd let him win.

God, he'd wanted to rub that in Ned's face. *Mission accomplished*, he'd texted him later that night, and *oh yes, I totally believe you*, Ned had texted back, followed by like a thousand laughing emojis.

It was stupid, he knew. It was incredibly, intensely, aggressively stupid, because if he'd judged it even a little bit wrong, then Libby would have told everyone he was playing this gig, and a whole mob of Uni Rep people would descend on this bar, and he'd have to hope they'd rip him limb from limb, because that'd be easier than having to answer their questions.

If he'd judged it a lot wrong, then the mob wouldn't turn up, but Graham would, and he'd have to deal with the disappointment in his eyes. *Nightingale, I fought for you*, he'd say. *We built Uni Rep together, from the ground up. How could you do this?*

It was stupid, but he needed to know. He needed to know whether people knew he'd taken Libby to the Swamp. He needed to know if Ned knew that even though he was gone, he was still the king. That he could have any chick in that place he wanted.

This was probably the best-case scenario, he told himself, finishing the song and launching into 'Eagle Rock'. Libby hadn't turned up, but she hadn't sent a bunch of people after him either, or dobbed him into Graham. No harm, no—

There she was.

A smile spread across his face. He still had it. Holy shit, he still had it.

When his set was over, he took his time. He went to the bar. He chatted with the bartender. He got a couple of drinks. He had a laugh with the girl beside him. He could feel Libby waiting, feel her eyes on him. He hadn't felt like this for a while, and it felt so good.

He delayed a little longer at the bar, trying to think of cool opening lines, but when he finally went over, he decided to keep it simple. 'Hey, you,' he said smoothly, sliding a glass of white wine across the table to her. 'Fancy seeing a girl like you in a place like this.'

'Hello, Nightingale,' she said. Her voice was cool – icy, even – but those dark eyes of hers were as hungry as ever.

He leaned over and kissed her on the cheek, letting his lips linger a second longer than was polite. He felt her shiver, and goddammit, why had he taken that money? Why had he left? Why had he run away from Uni Rep when he could still do this to people?

'Long time, Queen Elizabeth,' he said, sitting down. 'I'm glad you came.'

She didn't say anything, but he saw the way her tits rose and fell as she drew in and let out a deep breath, and he knew he had her.

He let his fingers brush against hers, and met her eyes with his wickedest smile. 'Of course, if you're interested in coming again, I could make that happen.'

She pulled her hand away.

Shit. Okay. Not the right tack.

'Sorry,' he said. 'I'm sorry, Libby. It's just you look so hot – like, *so* hot, girl, damn – and I've missed you.'

'You've missed me,' she said. 'Really.'

It clearly wasn't a question, but he decided to pretend that it was. 'Of course I have. I've tried calling you a couple of times. And emailing. You're the only one I invited here, aren't you?'

'Because you knew I was the only one stupid enough to come.'

'Hey,' he said. 'Look at me.'

She obeyed, because he was Nightingale Smith, and any chick he wanted, he could have.

'Don't let anyone tell you you're stupid,' he said, keeping his voice gentle, sensitive, low. 'Because you're not.'

'Yes, I am,' she said. 'I really, really am.'

'No, you're not,' he said, taking her hand again. 'If I know one thing about you, Queen Elizabeth, it's that you're the smart girl.'

He knew he'd said the wrong thing almost immediately. She yanked her hand away and stiffened and shoved her phone back into her bag. 'I have to go.'

'Wait!' he said. 'Please wait. I know you must be angry with me, but hear me out, all right?'

'What is there to hear out?' she said. 'You're a complete shithead, Nightingale. If I didn't know it before, I sure as hell know it now. You stole from us. You screwed us all over. You—'

'Were you a virgin?' he asked.

Oh shit, that really was the wrong thing to say. He wanted to redirect the conversation, to butter her up, to tell her how much he cared about her, how he was sorry he'd had to leave her, all about his feeeeeeeelings, because it seemed like a much easier jump from there to *hey, so did you tell anyone about our frolic in the Swamp?* than it was from *so let me explain why I stole eight thousand bucks.*

But now her eyes were flashing, and her face was flushing, and it definitely wasn't because she was hot for him. 'Go to hell, Nightingale,' she snarled, pulling the strap of her handbag over her shoulder.

'It's all right if you were,' he tried. 'It's an honour. Please sit down. I didn't mean that the way it came out. I'm sorry.'

'I'm not interested in your apology.'

'Then why are you here?'

She didn't sit down. But she went silent, and she didn't move, and that was something, that was something.

'There's something that you want from me,' he said, pitching his voice low, soft, sexy. 'There's something that you want, or you wouldn't be here. Tell me what it is.'

She took another deep breath, in and out, like they were doing vocal warm-ups before a show, then she put both her hands on the table and looked him dead in the eye.

'There's nothing I want from you, Nightingale,' she said. 'Nothing at all.'

He put his hands on the table too. He leaned forward, close enough that it wouldn't take much for him to kiss her if she offered even the smallest sign that she'd be into it. 'Are you sure?' he said. 'Because I'm here. You're here. No one would ever have to know.'

'Of all the people in the world,' she said, 'why would I want anything from you?'

He spent a long time turning that phrase over in his mind after she left, all through his second set, and his third. *Of all the people in the world, why would I want anything from you?*

Who was he, now he couldn't go back to Uni Rep again? What was there that anyone would want from him, ever again?

But then he forced it away. He still had it, he thought, catching the eye of a pretty girl at the bar and watching her blush when he winked at her. He was still the king. And one day, he was going to find a way to rub Ned's nose in it.

Chapter Seventeen

It wasn't a long walk, but it felt like a marathon and a sprint all at once.

There's something that you want from me. His voice had been like a purr, a vibration she could feel on all her skin, and it had made every hair on her body stand on end. *There's something that you want, or you wouldn't be here. Tell me what it is.*

If she wanted, she could be with Nightingale right now. She could have let him lead her to some quiet place, let him slide his hands under her clothes, feel his breath against her skin, the nudge of his tongue against her bottom lip.

She had to stop and put her hands against a tree until she was sure she wasn't going to throw up or pass out or both.

Her phone buzzed. *Are you still coming around?* Will asked. *Do you need me to come + pick you up?*

I'm fine, she replied. *On my way. There soon.*

She wasn't sure what the biggest mistake she'd made tonight was – going to see Nightingale, or sending that text to Will the second she'd left the pub. *Are you busy? I'm around campus, and I thought I might drop by if you're free.* ☺

Never too busy for you, ProofIt, he'd replied, less than a heartbeat later.

She should text him back right now. *Actually, don't worry about it!* she should say. *Just jumped on a train home. See you at rehearsal!* It would be nothing, and he would think nothing of it, and she could go home and scream into a pillow for an hour and put herself back together. This didn't have to be a thing.

She kept walking.

'Hey!' Will said, opening the door to her ten minutes later. 'Nice to— are you okay? You're shivering.'

'Just a bit cold,' she said.

She knew how this scene should go. She should burst into tears, and he should put his arms around her, and he should tell her that everything was all right, and then somehow everything would be all right, because he said it would be. She would look up at him, and he would look down at her, and his eyes would go dark, and his fingers would be gentle against her cheek, and she wouldn't need to talk.

'Come in,' he said. 'Sit down. Let me make you some—'

'I just saw Nightingale,' she blurted out. 'At the pub. I'm so stupid, Will, I'm so stupid.'

He reached around her and pushed the door closed. 'Are you all right?' he asked. 'Did he hurt you?'

'No, no, I'm okay,' she said. 'But I'm— Will— I'm—'

She should be crying. Why wasn't she crying? Why couldn't she just burst into tears and let that do all the work for her? Why was she left only with words?

'Sit down,' Will said. 'Let me make you some tea. Then you can tell me whatever you want me to hear, all right?'

'All right,' she said. 'All right.'

For the second time that night, she sat, waiting for a man to bring her a drink. The first time had been nerve-wracking, but the second ...

She wondered if Will would let her go if she just bolted out of the apartment now. She could see the piles of paper on his dining-room table, the maths textbooks in stacks four high, the pinned-up equations spilling off one wall onto a second. Maybe she could convince him that he dreamed it, that she'd never been there.

She was actually considering gaslighting one of the best people in the entire world. Not even convincingly.

'Will, I should go,' she said, standing up as he emerged from the kitchen. 'You're so busy. You don't need to deal with my bullshit.'

'Libby,' he said, 'if you want to go, of course, go, but ... don't. Please don't. Sit down. Have a cup of tea with me. Talk to me.'

She sank back into the couch, because there was nothing else she could do. If she made a break for the door, her legs might give out underneath her.

He sat beside her and handed her a cup of tea. 'It's hot,' he said. 'Be careful.'

She wrapped her fingers around it anyway. He was right – it was hot – but at least that feeling wasn't ... this.

'I'm sorry,' she said. 'I'm so sorry, Will.'

'What are you apologising to me for?' His voice was gentle, like Nightingale's had been, and it made the hairs stand up on the back of her neck, like Nightingale's had, but it was so different, so, so, so different, and – why had she come here? Why was she doing this to herself?

'For wasting your time.'

'I'm plenty good enough at wasting my own time. If you think all that shit on the table is a sign I've been productive tonight, then you are very wrong.'

'Not just tonight,' she said. 'All of this. This whole time. You think I – you think I'm this – you've got this idea of me that's all wrong, and I'm sorry.'

'Libby,' he said, 'not a single second of the time I've spent with you has been wasted. Do you know why?'

She bit her lip.

'Because I spent it with you.'

For the second time that night, a man reached out and took her hand. His fingers curled through hers, and he looked her in the eye, and he raised her knuckles to his lips, and—

'No!' she exclaimed, snatching her hand back like it was on fire. 'No no no no. Please. Don't.'

Will closed his eyes. A furrow appeared between his eyebrows as his head fell forward. 'I'm sorry,' he said. 'I thought— maybe—'

'I slept with Nightingale.'

His head snapped back up.

'I told you,' she said. 'I'm not the person you think I am, Will. I'm not even the person I thought I was.'

'Tonight?'

'What?'

'Did you—' His Adam's apple bobbed as he swallowed. 'Did you come straight from him to me?'

'No,' she said. 'Well, yes, I came from him to you, but it didn't happen tonight. It was months ago. Right before he left.'

Will exhaled. 'You nearly gave me a heart attack.'

'Aren't you listening to me?' she demanded. 'You know what a terrible person he is. I knew what a terrible person he was. And I did it anyway. He didn't even have to try, because I *wanted* to.'

Silence, for several long heartbeats.

'Libby,' he said, 'what do you want from me?'

There were so many words in her, so many thousands and thousands of words, and she couldn't think of any of them.

'Do you want me to tell you that you're a terrible person?'

She dug her fingernails into the fleshy part at the base of her thumb.

'Do you want me to shout at you? Do you want me to tell you to leave? To never speak to you again?'

Her heart felt like a jackhammer in her chest, one operated by someone who'd never used one before, fast, erratic.

'Because I won't do that,' he said. 'If you came here looking to be punished, I can't help you.'

'I want you to ask me why,' she whispered.

'All right,' he said. 'Why?'

'I just wanted him to see me,' she said. 'It was before I knew about the money or anything like that, but I still knew who he was. I knew he was a terrible person. I knew all that, but I still wanted him to *see* me. To look at me. To approve of me.'

Will's eyes were dark, and his gaze was steady.

'I'm supposed to be smart,' she said. 'I'm supposed to be so smart, but he made me stupid. There was this one show in *Rapunzel* where I got to play the lead, and it was like suddenly, finally, he *saw* me, and I ... I knew it was stupid, but I did it anyway, and he didn't even have to *try*.'

He didn't look away.

'I tried to talk to him about it a couple of days later,' she said. 'But he just brushed me off like I was nothing. He's this terrible person – this objectively awful person – and I was nothing to him.'

'Libby,' Will said, 'you're not nothing.'

'I might be, though,' she said. 'I used to be so sure about things. I used to be so sure about myself and who I was, but it turns out I wasn't her after all. I might be nothing.'

'Libby,' he repeated, 'you're not nothing.'

'Whatever I am, it's not smart,' she said. 'I'm pretty sure I slept with Roarke just to try and get Nightingale out from under my skin, but it didn't work. He invited me to this gig at the pub tonight, saying he needed to see me, and I knew I shouldn't go. I knew it was a terrible idea. But I did it anyway. I had to look at him. I had to ... check.'

'Check what?'

'I don't know!' she said. 'I thought it might make me feel better – give me closure or something? – but it made me feel worse. I could see the wheels turning in his mind. I could see him trying to say the right thing to get me to do what he wanted. I could see that it was all an act. And you know what the worst thing was? You know why I could see it?'

'Why?'

'Because I do it too! All the time! I pretend to be this person I'm not. I pretend to be smart and tough and certain. But I'm not any of those things. I'm just like he is. I'm not even a real person. I'm just a character that I play.'

Will was quiet for a long time. After everything, that was what finally made tears spring to her eyes.

'There's one thing I don't understand,' he said at last.

'What?'

'Why did you come here?'

'I'm sorry,' she said. 'I'll go.'

'No, no, no,' he said, catching her wrist. 'That wasn't what I meant. Why did you come here, to me? Why not tell Ella?'

'I love Ella,' she said. 'More than anyone. But she's fragile. She needs to think that I'm strong.'

'You are.'

'Weren't you listening?' she said, the first tear finally spilling over her lashes, hot against her cheek. 'I'm not.'

'Of course I was listening,' he said, letting go of her wrist and lacing his fingers through hers. 'I listen to everything you say.'

Her breath was coming shakily, in and out. There was a rock in her throat, and it felt like it was on fire.

'Why me?' he asked again. 'Why did you need me to know this? Why tell anyone at all?'

'Because you're a real person,' she said. 'And you need to know that I'm not one, before ...'

'Before what?'

She shook her head, more tears spilling down her face.

'I didn't know you before Nightingale,' he said. 'I only met you afterwards. I've only ever known this version of you, the one you think isn't a real person. She's smart, and she's strong, and she's my favourite person to talk to.'

'Don't,' she sobbed. 'Please.'

'Just because someone made you feel like nothing doesn't mean you are.'

The rock in her throat was growing. There was lava in her belly, and she was going to throw it up, right in his lap.

'You're not nothing,' he said. 'You're everything.'

She looked at him. He looked at her.

It wasn't a lightbulb. It was an explosion. She was a volcano, one that had been dormant forever. Now she was full of lava, and it felt like all of summer had happened to her at once.

She let go of his hand. She went up on her knees on the couch, and reached across to him, running her thumb across his cheekbone.

'Libby,' he whispered, covering her hand with his.

'Don't talk,' she said. 'Please.'

Slowly, she closed the space between them. His breath was as uneven as hers, and as her lips brushed his, gently, tentatively, once, twice, his hand came up to cup the side of her face, and—

'No,' he said.

The word was like a blast of icy wind in the face. Her heart stopped beating, and there was a moment – just a moment – where what he meant wasn't quite clear.

But then—

'Oh shit,' she said. 'Oh no. I'm sorry.'

She fell away from him, burying her face in her hands. She was such an idiot. She was *so stupid*. Of all the people in the world, why would he – why would she—

'Hey, hey, hey,' he said. 'ProofIt. Look at me.'

She shook her head. 'I'm sorry. I'm so sorry, Will.'

'Please,' he said. 'Please look at me.'

The thought of looking at him – of seeing the pity in his eyes, of seeing the kindness, of him being *nice* to her – made her want to die.

'It's not that I don't want you,' he said softly. He wasn't touching her, but she could feel him there, a heartbeat away. 'Because I do. So badly. But not like this.'

She was going to throw up. She was definitely going to throw up.

'Not when you're exhausted and you're emotional and you're crying,' he said. 'I don't want this to just ... happen. I want to choose it. I want you to choose it. I want you to choose me.'

The lava in her was hardening into rock. Every part of her felt heavy, frozen.

His fingers gently feathered against her hair, and then she felt the brush of his lips, just behind her ear. 'You mean too much to me, Libby,' he whispered. 'This means too much for us to mess it up.'

Chapter Eighteen

She spent the night on Will's couch, but she left early the next day, before he woke up. She left him a note, and she agonised for nearly fifteen minutes over what she was going to say, but in the end, she just wrote, *thank you, taxman. x*

The thought of having to see him again made her want to go down to the beach, walk into the icy grey waves, and let them close over her head.

The thought of not seeing him again was unimaginable.

But it wasn't like she had a choice in the matter, unless she wanted to quit the show, change her name, and move continents. It was tech rehearsal that night, and there was no way she could miss it.

She skipped her Wednesday Con Law and Sociology classes and went home, but it was a mistake, because it meant her brain had nothing to focus on. She tried to distract herself with editing work, but it swam before her eyes. All she could hear was Will's voice – *what do you want from me?* All she could feel was the gentle brush of his lips against the skin behind her ear.

She tried cleaning the apartment instead. Vacuuming, scouring the kitchen, scrubbing the bathroom, anything to occupy her mind, anything that wasn't *this*.

Maybe she should turn up late to rehearsal. Minimise the amount of time she'd have to spend in his presence.

But if she wasn't there, he'd worry, and he'd call her. If he called her, she'd have to talk to him, and if she talked to him, words and words and more words might come spewing out of her mouth, and she might say – she might say—

She sank down beside the washing machine. 'What are you afraid of?' she asked aloud. 'What the hell are you so scared of?'

The spinning clothes didn't reply.

'You look like shit,' Ella said, coming home later that afternoon to find Libby fitfully dozing on the couch. 'Are you feeling all right?'

'I'm fine,' Libby replied, batting away Ella's hand as she tried to feel her forehead. 'I just need a shower.'

'Seriously, though, are you sure you're not getting sick? You're all pale and sweaty.'

'I didn't sleep well.'

'Join the club.'

'Ella, I don't want to hear about your love life.'

'Wow. Okay.'

'Sorry,' Libby said, sitting up and hugging her knees to her chest. 'That came out way bitchier than I meant it to. I'm just tired. Stressed.'

'It's cool, don't worry,' Ella said. 'I've lived with you during Production Week before, Elizabeth Two. I know how you get.'

'Sorry anyway.'

'I wish I wasn't getting any sleep because I was getting laid,' Ella said, dropping her bag on the floor and flopping back on the couch beside Libby. 'Guess which handsome young gentleman got subjected to a full Elizabeth Grey night terror last night?'

'Oh my God, I'm so sorry I wasn't here. Are you all right?'

'I'm fine, don't worry,' Ella said. 'Roarke handled it like a pro.

It took him a while to, you know, wake me up, but then he was great about it. He made me tea—'

She could feel the burn of the teacup against her fingers. *Sit down. Have a cup of tea with me. Talk to me.*

'—and then he stayed up and watched Netflix with me.' Ella smiled. 'It was ... great, actually.'

Suddenly, she was furious, fire rushing through her veins. She had to grit her teeth to keep it from pouring out of her mouth.

'It's a lot, you know?' Ella said, still smiling, oblivious to the fact that surely, *surely* all the blood vessels in Libby's eyes were bursting. 'All the shit with my nightmares would send a lot of people fleeing for the hills. But not him. He just ... rolled with it.'

'That's great,' she forced out.

'He asked me to be his girlfriend. Like, formally. Officially. Exclusively.'

'What did you say?'

'I said yes.'

'I— um—'

'Yeah, it's hard to know what to say to that, hey?' Ella said. 'Do you say congratulations? Well done? You have a man now, you're fulfilled in life?'

She made herself laugh.

'It's weird,' Ella continued. 'The whole thing's weird. I haven't been anyone's girlfriend but Gerry's, so that's, like, a mental shift. Then there's the thing where he's going to spend the next couple of weeks making out with you—'

She made a noise that she hoped was open to interpretation.

'But it's nice,' Ella said. 'I'm happy.'

How is it so easy for you? Libby wanted to shriek. *How do you just know what to do?*

'Where were you last night, anyway?' Ella asked. 'You missed my latest scream spectacular.'

'I finished up late at uni,' Libby said. 'Will let me crash on his couch.'

Her first instinct had been to lie. What did it say about her that her very first instinct was to lie to her best friend?

She's smart, and she's strong, and she's my favourite person in the world to talk to.

She was a good actor. At least she had that.

She did her best to make sure she was always with someone at rehearsal that night. She stuck so closely to Ella when they first arrived that they were nearly attached at the hip. She almost ran through backstage on her way to the girls' dressing room, then jammed herself into a corner, just in case Will suddenly decided to break theatre protocol and poke his head in.

'You okay?' Rosie asked. 'You're all jittery.'

'I'm fine. Just nervous energy.'

'For the most boring rehearsal of them all?' Annalise said, sticking her head between them at the mirror so she could do her eyeliner. 'If you're nervous now, Libs, you're going to be a disaster when opening rolls around.'

Oh God. She was going to have to be in the building with Will *every day* for the next three weeks. She was going to have to see him every single day, and eventually, they were going to have to say words to each other.

Was it possible to die of embarrassment?

You're not nothing. You're everything.

No. Not embarrassment. Not quite.

'Drink some water,' Rosie said, quietly, so the other girls in the dressing room couldn't hear. 'Here.'

When the cast finally got summoned out to the stage for the beginning of the actual rehearsal, she positioned herself behind Michael and Anthony, hoping that if she could hide behind them, she could somehow evade Will's notice. 'We're not going to run the show in its entirety,' Will announced. 'That'd take too long. Instead, we're going to go cue to cue. I want you all out here in the seating bank and paying attention so you don't miss anything.'

The seating bank. Great. And she was going to be required for so many cues! She'd have to sit down the front, just like Will, and she'd always be able to see him out of the corner of her eye.

What if he suddenly decided to sit next to her? What if his hand brushed hers and her entire brain short-circuited and exploded?

'We're going to start in ten minutes,' Will said. 'Remember, I want to keep this snappy so we're not here all night. Make sure you're paying attention.'

He didn't even look in her direction. He clearly wanted to be in her presence as little as she wanted to be in his.

Tears pricked the corners of her eyelids. She blinked them away and hurried back to the dressing room to fix her mascara.

When the run started, she positioned herself in the front row at the very end of the seating bank, as far as she could from Will. She couldn't help looking at him, but he didn't seem to know she was there. 'Cue one!' he yelled up to Richard in the bio box. 'I want it to look like champagne, like we talked about. Can you show me?'

'How's this?' Richard yelled back, bringing up a wash of light.

'Any chance you can make it warmer?'

'I can add in some pink! How's this?'

'Better! Okay, cue one! Beginning of show! Actors! Get in place!'

Libby sat beside Rosie on the picnic blanket that Gen had spread from them, right in the middle of the stage. She looked up. Her eyes met Will's.

For a second, everything stopped.

I want to choose it. I want you to choose it. I want you to choose me.

It seemed so difficult, but it wasn't, really. *Will,* she could say, *I want this. I want you.*

He'd smile his crooked smile. *I want this too, ProofIt,* he'd say, and his fingers would brush against hers, his nose would brush against hers, his lips would brush against hers ...

And someone would catch them. *I knew it!* they'd shriek. *I knew Libby was hooking up with Will!*

'Can we start from blackout and bring in the audio cue?' Will called, looking away from her and craning his head back towards the bio box. 'I want to make sure we've got the timing perfect.'

The lights went down. The auditorium went pitch-black. In the darkness, Libby felt fingers curl lightly against hers, and then squeeze comfortingly.

It was Rosie. She *knew* it was Rosie. But she was back on that couch with Will last night, feeling him press his lips against her knuckles, and then springing away and basically screaming *no no no no no* in his face, and it was so hard to breathe she thought she might suffocate.

There was a version of last night where she'd let Nightingale touch her again. She knew how she felt about that.

But there was a version of last night where she'd gone up on her knees on the couch, and she'd closed the space between them, and she'd brushed his lips with hers, once, twice, and then, *Libby,* he'd said, *yes,* and he'd kissed her back, kissed her properly, and she'd fallen back under his weight, and one of his hands was on her hip and one was tangled in her hair, and—

'Okay, looking good! Program that one, Richard, and let's move on to the next cue!' Will called. 'Let's go to where Don Pedro and co enter.'

His eyes skated right over her. She was right in the middle of the stage, and he still wouldn't look at her.

'Are you sure you're all right?' Rosie whispered to her, when they finally, about ten cues later, got the chance to escape from the stage. 'You and Will—'

'What?' she said, way too quickly.

'Don't worry,' Rosie said, lowering her voice even further. 'It's not obvious. Not to everyone, anyway. But I've been in your shoes, Libby. If you need someone to talk to—'

She shook her head.

'I get it,' Rosie said. 'But if you change your mind, no one understands how weird and awkward theatre hook-ups are better than me. I'm a sympathetic ear. And a discreet one.'

There's nothing going on, she nearly said. That instinct to lie was so strong.

'Program that, and let's move on!' Will called up to the bio box. 'Okay, Act Two! Top of the first scene!'

She just wanted him to look at her.

He didn't.

Will didn't look at her that night, or at any of their rehearsals for the next five days. He didn't speak to her either, unless he was giving notes at the end of the run. 'Beatrice, that moment where Don Pedro hits on you is good, but you're making it a little bit too weird,' he said. 'Play it lighter instead. Almost like she's joking. Spare her feelings.'

He didn't say her name. It was always 'Beatrice'. Then his eyes would slide past her to Heidi – 'Don Pedro, you can lean into a little harder: you really do like her, so you can give us that moment of vulnerability' – and everything in her whole body would ache.

'Benedick, same note to you,' he said to Roarke. 'During that bit where you're in the mask and Beatrice is insulting you to your face, you can be a bit more genuinely wounded.'

'How much more?' Roarke asked. 'If I overdo it, won't she guess it's me?'

Ella was leaning back against him. He had his arms around her waist, and his chin resting on her shoulder. It was casual and comfortable and easy, and Libby forced down the swell of anger that was becoming way, way too common every time she saw them together.

'Just a little more,' Will said. 'You're armoured, but she's got a dagger in through your defences. It stings.'

That was how it felt every time he didn't look at her. Another dagger. Another sting.

I want to choose it. I want you to choose it. I want you to choose me.

All she had to do was choose it, choose him, and then—
And then ...

She spent so long tossing and turning in bed that night that she overslept the next morning and ended up having to sprint down the street to get to her Thursday shift on time. 'Sorry, sorry,' she said, making it into the bookshop with one minute to spare.

'It's all right, you made it,' Catriona said. 'Big day? Your play opens tomorrow, right?'

'Everything's chaos,' Libby said. 'Everything.'

'Vijay and I are coming to see it on Saturday. We're so psyched. Will you be ready?'

'I hope so.'

'You'll be great,' Catriona said warmly. 'Anyway, it's been super quiet, so I'm going to head off and take my lunch break now. Will you be all right on your own?'

'Yep.'

Catriona left. Libby took a few minutes to get her breath back, then started reorganising the shelves. Alphabetising. She could do alphabetising. She understood how that worked.

The bell above the door rang. 'Hello, welcome to – oh. Hi.'

'Hi,' Roarke said.

He was wearing the same grey overcoat as the first night he'd come into the bookshop, the one that looked like Nightingale's, but there was no mistaking him now for anyone but himself. 'I want to buy a book,' he said.

'Catriona's on her lunch break,' she said. 'If you come back in an hour or so, she can help you.'

'No,' he said. 'I want to know what you'd recommend.'

She walked back behind the counter, grateful to have the solid barrier between them. 'What are you after?'

'I finished that Jemisin trilogy. I liked it. What should I read next?'

'Depends what you liked about it. You could try R.F. Kuang. Maybe Tamsyn Muir. Nnedi Okorafor. Octavia Butler, if you want to go classic.'

'I've read Butler. And Okorafor and Muir, but not Kuang. I'll try that one. Thanks.'

'The first one's *The Poppy War*. It's in SFF. Behind you.'

He turned, tilting his head to the side to scan the spines, just like he had that first night.

She was gripping the edge of the counter so hard her knuckles were turning white. She tried to make herself relax, but with limited success. 'So you're a big spec fic reader.'

'I don't know about big,' he said, finding the book and taking it off the shelf. 'Medium, maybe. I was named after a spec fic hero.'

She blinked. 'Really?'

'Well, kind of spec fic, kind of romance,' he said. 'You know JD Robb? *In Death*?'

'Yes,' she said. 'Well, no, I've never read them, but I know of them. You know JD Robb is—'

'Actually Nora Roberts, big time romance author, yes, I know,' he said. 'I read a couple of the ones she writes under that name, but they weren't really my scene. But I started reading some of the *In Death* ones when I was a teen, and now here we are.'

She studied him. 'You,' she said at last. 'You've read romance novels.'

'I don't blame you for being surprised.'

He turned back towards her, putting the book on the counter. 'I know I've treated you like shit, and I've given you absolutely no indication that I'd be any good at relationships,' he said.

'Telling me that you didn't want a girlfriend about forty-seven times was a bit of a tip-off.'

'But I really care about Ella,' he said. 'I'm serious about her.'

'I meant what I said. If you hurt her, I'll kill you.'

'I'm not going to hurt her.'

She looked him dead in the eye.

'I promise you,' he said. 'I know you have no reason to trust me, and lots of reasons not to. But I promise.'

Libby bit her lip.

'She told me she had a nightmare the other night,' she said at last.

'Yeah,' Roarke said. 'She did.'

'She said you were good with her. Helped her.'

'She's not the only person in the world who's had nightmares. I've done my time.'

There was a heavy, still moment.

'You keep being good with her,' she said at last, 'then you and I, we're good.'

'Libby,' Roarke said. 'I promise.'

His eyes were dark, serious, sincere. In that moment, he didn't resemble Nightingale in the slightest.

'Good,' she said. 'So are you buying that book or what?'

She offered him the eftpos machine. He tapped his card. 'Are you sure you put this through right?'

'I know how to do my job, Roarke.'

'I know, but I thought it would have added up to more.'

'I put it on staff discount. Do you want a bag?'

'No. Staff discount?'

'I can charge you more if you like.'

'No. That's cool. Thanks.' It sounded almost like an apology.

'If you're going to kind of be my brother-in-law, then you probably qualify as friends and family,' she said.

She passed him the book. Their fingers brushed. She didn't feel anything – desire, revulsion, love, hate. Just a fleeting moment of physical sensation, which passed.

'Libby,' he said. 'About the brother-in-law thing?'

'We've been over the rules,' she said. 'If you're good to her, then you're good with me.'

'No. Not that.'

She raised her eyebrows.

'Don't break his heart,' Roarke said.

The Opening Night nerves started early the next morning. They began almost as a welcome distraction from what Roarke had said to her, but soon it was all mixed together, a cocktail of stress roiling in her stomach. 'It's the big day!' Ella said to Libby over breakfast at their dining table. 'How are you feeling?'

'Like I'm not ready,' Libby said, picking up a piece of toast, looking at it, and then putting it down again.

'Pfft, don't be silly, of course you're ready,' Ella said, taking the toast, adding an extra layer of peanut butter, and then handing it back. 'Here you go. Protein. Keep your strength up.'

She did her best to keep herself busy, but the downside of tying herself in knots for the last few days over that night with Will and Nightingale meant that most of the busywork she'd normally do to distract herself from Opening Night nerves was already done. The apartment was sparkling. Her ProofItLibby inbox was empty. She was even up to date on all her Law homework.

'You're ready,' she told herself fiercely, looking in the bathroom mirror as she combed out her newly washed hair. 'You can do this.'

She was getting worse at acting, because it wasn't remotely believable. She had no clue what she was doing.

She was going to walk out on stage that night. She was going to look up, into the blinding whiteness of the stage lights, and she was going to open her mouth, and nothing was going to come out.

Or maybe too much would come out. Maybe *no no no no no* was all that would come out, and she'd run offstage, and everyone would be so angry with her, and she didn't have Caro's connections to keep her foot in the door, and no one would ever speak to her again, and Will would be so, so disappointed in her. *No,* he would say again, if she ever got up the nerve to tell him she wanted this, she wanted him. *You had your chance, and you ruined it.*

'Libby?' Ella called, knocking on the bathroom door. 'Are you psyching yourself out in there?'

'No!' she called back.

'Stop lying!' Ella said. 'Roarke's going to be here in a few minutes. He said he'll run lines with you if you want!'

Roarke. Another person she couldn't look in the face. What was she supposed to say to *don't break his heart*?

The nerves only grew, and by the time she and Ella walked into the theatre kitchen that evening, they were a hot ball of electrified barbed wire in her stomach, sending fizzing currents through her whole body. 'Sign in!' Gen barked at them. 'You're late!'

'Are we?' Ella said, checking her phone. 'You said the two-and-a-half-hour call, right?'

'Oh. I did. Sorry,' Gen said. 'Reflex.'

'I probably should have been here sooner, though. I have a million things to do,' Ella said. 'Libby, head up to your dressing room. I just need to do a few tiny adjustments on the Don John costume, and then I'll start on your hair.'

Libby nodded and obeyed.

She sat down at the dressing-room table, its mirror surrounded by lights. The girl who looked back at her was not the kind of person that anyone would look at and think 'leading lady'.

She wasn't anything. She was a mistake. She was nothing.

'Don't psych yourself out,' Rosie said, sitting down next to her and pulling out her makeup bag. 'That's a classic Opening Night mistake.'

'I don't think I can do this,' she said.

'Of course you can,' Rosie said. 'It's just stage fright. Everyone gets it. Put your makeup on. Having an inch of foundation on your face always helps. War paint, you know? Gives you something to hide behind.'

They did vocal warm-ups at the one-hour call. Libby's stomach was clenched so tightly she felt like it was about to explode. 'Red leather, yellow leather, yellow leather, red leather,' she repeated obediently, but her hands were shaking and she wouldn't have been surprised if her voice was wavering too.

'We have a full house!' Will announced.

That meant 120 people were going to watch her play at being Beatrice tonight. Black dots swam in front of her eyes.

After vocals, she sat herself down in a corner of the girls' dressing room and tried to calm herself down by taking deep breaths.

'Stage fright?' Rashmi asked, hidden behind her enormous bunch of flowers.

'A bit,' Libby replied.

'I don't get it. Everyone is freaking out, and I'm, like, fine. What's that about?'

Libby wanted to kill her.

'Fifteen-minute call,' Genevieve said, sticking her head into the dressing room. 'House is going live.'

Libby made her way down to the prompt-side wing at the ten-minute call, legs feeling unsteady beneath her. Michael and Rosie were already there. Genevieve was quietly lecturing one of the crew members. He was holding the picnic blanket Libby and Rosie sat on in the first scene, and he nodded and walked out onto the stage to lay it out.

She could hear the audience outside on the other side of the curtain, talking, laughing, eating. In the quiet blackness of the wing, she felt suffocated.

Genevieve touched her headset. 'Five-minute call,' she announced.

Libby's knees felt like they were going to give way. She was going to faint. She was going to die.

'Libby,' Will whispered, touching her shoulder.

She jumped. 'Shouldn't you be out in the audience?'

'I heard you were nervous.'

'I can't do it, Will,' she said.

'Yes, you can.' His face was close to hers so she could hear his whisper in the darkness, and she could feel his breath against her skin. 'Of course you can.'

'I really can't.'

'You're a fantastic actor, and there's no chance you're going to fail tonight. I'm a mathematician, and I'm telling you that it is statistically impossible.'

'But what if I do?'

He tucked a stray strand of hair behind her ears. 'You won't,' he said softly. 'You're going to go out there, and you're going to be awesome, all right?'

She was still shaking.

'And even if something goes wrong,' he said, leaning in to whisper in her ear, in a voice so low that no one else could hear it, even in the quiet of the wing, 'even if you freeze – even if you forget every single one of your lines – it doesn't change a single thing.'

The ball of barbed wire in her stomach caught fire. Every single part of her buzzed with electricity.

She wanted to scream. She wanted to cry. She wanted to press her face into the crook of his neck, and not move for a long, long time.

But she had a job to do. He had chosen her. He was trusting her. And she couldn't ruin her makeup.

'Thank you,' was all she could say.

He pressed his lips to her hair in that same spot, just behind her ear. 'Break a leg,' he breathed, and then he was gone.

Beginner's call went around. 'Chookas, everyone,' Genevieve hissed. 'Places.'

She made herself keep breathing, in and out, in and out. She could do this, she told herself as she and Rosie walked out onto the dark stage and sat down on their picnic blanket. She could do this. She was going to do this. She was ready.

The lights came up.

'Strike up, pipers!' Roarke declared, waving an arm expansively, and as the music began and they launched into the dance, Libby was sure she could feel her heart literally swelling in her chest.

She held onto Beatrice until the very last second, when Roarke dipped her nearly to the floor and kissed her, but when they went offstage in the blackout, she couldn't remove the silly, very un-Beatrice grin from her face.

'Great work, team!' Ned whispered, barely audible above the applause, high-fiving Heidi and Rashmi. 'Listen to them! They love us!'

The curtain call began. The secondary roles filed on, to a lot of cheering, and then the cheering got even louder when Ned and Rosie walked out onto the stage, leaving Libby alone in the wings with Roarke.

'You did great,' he told her.

'Thank you,' she said. 'So did you.'

He caught her hand and squeezed it. Together, they walked onstage.

The applause broke over Libby like a wave. Her grin only got wider. God, this feeling. This *feeling*.

Roarke wasn't holding her hand any more. He gestured to her, and she bowed, alone, before doing the same for him.

Will and Ella were sitting together in the centre of the front row: applauding, smiling. Libby tried to freeze their faces in her mind. She never wanted to forget this.

It wasn't done to squeal with joy in the wings after a show, because the audience might hear you. But that amount of joy and excitement couldn't be suppressed by silence. Annalise held out her arms dramatically the moment they got back to the dressing room, and all of the girls hugged – all of them, even Rosie – bound together in the knowledge that they'd just done something a little bit magical.

'That was awesome,' Rashmi said. 'Oh my God, that was *awesome*.'

'We killed it!' Heidi exclaimed.

Libby couldn't speak. She wiped away her makeup, but she couldn't wipe away her smile.

'Hey,' Rosie said, nudging her. 'You were great, Libby.'

'So were you.'

'I hope we can do this again together sometime. I've really liked working with you.'

'Me too,' she said, and meant it.

There was more applause as the cast walked out into the foyer together. Someone pressed a plastic flute of champagne into Libby's hand. 'Congratulations!'

'Thank you,' she replied automatically, but sincerely.

'Libby!' Ella said, launching herself at her. 'You were amazing! I'm so proud of you!'

'Oh my God, Ella,' she said, half-crushed by the hug.

'Didn't I tell you you'd be fantastic?'

'Libby!' Ned roared, coming up behind her and lifting her off her feet. 'Lady of the hour!'

'Dude, put me down!'

He obliged, but didn't let go. 'You're never going back to the chorus, Libs,' he said into her ear. 'Not if I have anything to do with it.'

'Thank you,' she replied.

'Elizabeth?'

She turned. 'Oh! Hello, Dr Lewis.'

'Call me Graham, please,' he said. 'I wanted to congratulate you on a job well done. I haven't seen Beatrice done so well in many years.'

'Thank you.'

'You have a wonderful stage presence,' Graham told her. 'And clearly a sharp mind. I remember your writing from last semester, and I see your astute skills of interpretation extend to the stage. I hope we see more of you at Uni Rep.'

'That's so nice of you to say,' Libby said. 'And don't worry. I'm not going anywhere.'

When Graham drifted away to talk to someone else, she allowed herself a moment to believe it.

The foyer was loud around her, but the ground beneath her feet was still and certain. It wasn't going to crack, and neither was she.

'Cheers, Libby,' Roarke said.

She clinked her champagne flute against his. The sound the plastic made wasn't very satisfying, but it didn't matter. 'Cheers.'

They drank together in silence, but it wasn't an awkward one.

'So now you've officially lost your Uni Rep virginity,' she said.

That drew a sound that might have been a laugh. 'That's one way of putting it.'

'Will you do another show here, do you think?'

'I don't know. It depends.'

'On what?'

'A lot of things,' he said, looking across the room to where Ella was talking with Genevieve.

'I hope you do,' Libby said. 'I'd like to do another show with you.'

He turned his head and studied her for a long moment. 'Why would you say that to me?' he asked at last.

'Because we work well together,' she said. 'You're a good actor. And if nothing else, we've proven that even when we're going through incredibly awkward personal shit we can keep it off the stage.'

A corner of his mouth quirked upwards. 'I'll drink to that.'

They drank again, then she nudged him with her elbow. 'Go kiss your girlfriend. And congratulate her on her amazing designs.'

'All right, all right, you've twisted my arm.'

He didn't go, though. He paused for a moment, and then he leaned down and hugged her. 'Thank you,' he said.

'You're welcome,' she replied, though she wasn't entirely sure what he was thanking her for.

He threaded his way through the crowd towards Ella. Libby looked after him for a second.

Then she saw him.

He was near the glass foyer doors, talking to Caro. 'Thank you for coming,' Will said.

'Of course,' she said. 'I wouldn't miss it.'

'And thank you for choreographing. It looked great.'

'I know.'

He smiled.

'I have to go,' Caro said. 'Congrats again.'

He hugged her. She hugged him back. 'Goodbye, Caro.'

'Goodbye, Will.'

He turned his head as Caro walked away, and then he saw her too. Will was looking at Libby, and Libby was looking at Will, eyes locked across the space between them, and something happened, something shifted, and she didn't give a shit about anything in the world except for him.

Chapter Nineteen

She didn't do anything about it.

She was going to. She was going to walk over there, and say, *I know what I need to say to you now.*

She would say it, and something would change: something intangible, something unnameable, but something completely irresistible. He would look at her, and he would smile, and *I've been waiting so long to hear you say that,* he would say, and then he would lean down and kiss her.

And everyone would be watching. People would start cheering and jeering and catcalling, and everyone would see – everyone would know—

Someone started talking to him. Someone started talking to her. The moment passed.

She could have found him afterwards. It would have been easy. He would have let her pull him aside, into some dark corner, or up into the studio, or into the Swamp. She could have said what she needed to say, and then, *I think you should come home with me,* he would whisper, and his voice would have been hot against her ear, and—

And someone would have flung open the curtain to the Swamp, and then everyone – everyone—

She groaned, turning over and punching her pillow. Of course everyone was going to see them. Of course everyone was going to know that they were together. That was – well, not the whole point, exactly, but some of it, surely? You found someone who *saw* you, who *knew* you, and then you went out into the world holding hands, and everyone saw you and knew that you were together, and *why did the thought of people knowing what she wanted make her want to throw up?*

This would be so much easier if she never wanted anything.

'Hour call,' Genevieve said, knocking and sticking her head into the dressing room before the matinee next day. 'Time for vocals.'

Libby tried to covertly study Will while Ned led vocal exercises. The unbuttoned flannelette shirt he was wearing was half tucked, half untucked. She was pretty sure the T-shirt he had on underneath it was back-to-front. His jeans had a hole in the knee. His glasses were crooked, there were dark smears under his eyes again, and his curly hair was clearly out of control. He was the best thing she'd ever seen in her whole life.

He could be hers. Her best thing. All she had to do was force the words out of her mouth.

When vocals were over, she went back offstage to the dressing room, just like everyone else.

The Saturday matinee didn't go as well as Opening had the night before – second show slump was one of theatre's inevitabilities – but it didn't go badly. 'You were fine,' Will reassured Heidi, as the whole cast and crew sat around a table at Sal's in the break between the end of the matinee and the call for the evening show. 'Trust me, if you were awful, I'd let you know about it.'

Libby wanted to ask what he thought about her performance, but she was – completely irrationally, she knew – too frightened of the answer.

'Hey, well done, Libby!' Catriona said, hugging her in the foyer after the show that night. 'I had no idea you were so amazing!'

'Yeah, that was great,' her husband Vijay said. 'Full disclosure: I was pretty prepared for this to be boring, but it wasn't.'

'High praise,' Libby said.

'Congratulations,' Vijay said, shaking Will's hand as he came up behind Libby.

'Thanks,' Will said, shaking back, then leaning over to kiss Catriona on the cheek. He brushed against Libby and she nearly spontaneously combusted.

Catriona and Vijay waved goodbye. Gradually, the rest of the Saturday night audience filtered out as well.

The gap between then and their Wednesday show suddenly yawned in front of Libby like a chasm. How was she going to cope without seeing Will for so many days?

She watched him slide into the front seat of his car. She could fix this. Right now. She could run over and jump into the passenger seat and say *take me home with you.*

Roarke got into the passenger seat. They drove away.

'Are you okay, Libs?' Ella asked on the way home. 'You're quiet tonight.'

'Just tired.'

She rested her head against the cool glass of the car window. She couldn't go on like this forever.

She glanced across at Ella, who was tapping her fingers against the steering wheel and humming off-key to the radio. Ella had lost more in her life than Libby ever had, and she wasn't scared. She'd taken Roarke's hand and dived straight in: no fear, no second-guessing.

Why was she so terrified? What was *wrong* with her?

She slept late on Sunday. Ella went off somewhere with Roarke, and so Libby sat at the dining table by herself, compulsively refreshing her ProofItLibby inbox.

On Monday, Ella still wasn't back. Libby took an early train to uni. She sat through her Torts lecture and seminar and did her best to pay attention. She went to the library afterwards, and she worked until she ran out of things to work on.

She went in super early on Tuesday, even though her Sociology lecture wasn't until ten am. She went to the fourth floor of the library, looking for a carrel with a powerpoint, and saw Will's curly hair down the end of the row.

She fled.

She nearly collapsed at the table where they'd had lunch that one time, but – what if he'd seen her? What if he'd chased her out? He'd sit down across from her and there'd be no way she'd be able to escape having the conversation then. She'd have to say something, and he'd say something back, and the best thing that had ever happened to her might start – would start! – and she might actually die.

This was ridiculous. She was ridiculous.

She sank down on a bench around the corner and buried her face in her hands. Why was she such a joke of a person?

She wasn't sure how long she sat there until she took out her phone. *Hey, are you on campus today?*

Yep, Ella replied. *In class until 11, but free after. Want to have an early lunch? Feel like I haven't seen you for days!*

You haven't, Libby sent back. *I missed you. And yes. Lunch would be great.*

She skipped her lecture and went over to the food court in the student union early. She bought herself tea from the coffee cart, but they hadn't made it right, and it tasted weak and watery.

'Hey,' Ella said, sliding into the seat opposite a while later. 'Sorry I'm late. Class ran over.'

'That's all right,' Libby said, and burst into tears.

She had classes she needed to go to. Ella had classes she needed to go to. But Libby only offered up the slightest of protests when Ella bundled her into her car and took her home.

'Hey, handsome,' Ella said, her phone on speaker as they headed away from campus. 'Change of plans. I'm staying at mine tonight.'

'All right,' Roarke said. 'I can take the train down, if you like. Grab dinner.'

'Not tonight. Libby and I are having a girl's night, okay? I'll see you tomorrow.'

When they got home, Ella went straight to the kitchen and got the ice cream out of the freezer. She put it on the dining table, took the lid off, and handed a spoon to Libby.

'Okay,' she said, twirling her own spoon in her fingers. 'We have all the proper arrangements. Now talk.'

Libby scraped some ice cream off the top. 'I don't know what to say.'

'Libs, you're scaring me. I've never seen you like this. Not once. Not even the day before Year Twelve results came out and you were so nervous you spent eight hours pacing around your backyard.'

She put the spoon in her mouth. Her throat seemed to close up, and she wasn't sure she was going to be able to force the ice cream down.

'Is it the show?' Ella asked. 'Did someone review it? Was it bad?'

'No.'

'What is it then?'

She did her best to swallow. The ice cream felt like a huge, cold rock sliding down her throat.

'Is it Will?'

She broke. She buried her face in her hands.

'What did he do?' Ella demanded, dropping her spoon so she could wrap her arms around Libby. 'What happened?'

'Nothing!'

'Bullshit. I've seen the way you two look at each other. So has everyone. What did he do to you?'

'He hasn't done anything to me! It's me. I'm the problem. I don't know how to do this!'

'Don't know how to do what? Come on, Libs. Talk to me.'

'How do you do it?' Libby said. 'How do you go up to someone and say, *hey, you're wonderful, I want to be with you?* See, that's terrible. I'm useless.'

'I know you don't like talking about your feelings,' Ella said, prying Libby's hands away from her face. 'But here is some knowledge, from me to you. No one's good at this. There's no protocol. There's no script.'

'A script wouldn't help. It's not even the words. It's— I'm so scared.'

'What are you scared of? What's the worst thing that could happen if you just asked him out?'

'He could laugh at me.'

'He is absolutely not going to laugh at you. And if he did, I'd cut off his nuts and beat him to death with them.'

Libby scrubbed her hands across her face. 'I know. I know he won't laugh. That's not even what I'm scared of, though. It's ...'

'It's what?'

'He's going to say yes!' she exploded. 'The second I say, *you and me, Will, how about it?* he's going to say yes.'

'Libby,' Ella said, reaching across the table and taking her hand, 'I know I've been teasing you about him for ages, but if you really don't want to be with him ...'

'I want to be with him. So much.'

'Okay. You want to be with him. You know he wants to be with you. What's the problem?'

'I don't even know how to put it in words.'

'Can you try? For me?'

She took a deep breath.

A drop of ice cream melted and ran slowly, so, so slowly, down the side of the container. She watched it fall.

Slowly. Just a drop.

'I had a crush on Gerry in high school,' she said.

Ella sat back, blinking. 'What?'

'I had a crush on Gerry,' she repeated. 'In high school.'

'No, you didn't,' Ella said. 'I know there were all those rumours going around, but it was bullshit. You told me.'

'I lied,' Libby said.

The ice cream droplet met another drop, a bigger one. They merged.

'I didn't want to upset you,' she said. 'I knew if you knew that I liked Gerry, you'd feel weird about it, so I lied. I lied to you, and I lied to everyone, and then I just ... never stopped lying.'

'This is about ... Gerry?'

'No,' Libby said. 'It's about me. And why I am the way I am.'

'Do you need me to forgive you?' Ella asked. 'Because obviously, yes, I don't love that you lied to me, but we all did dumb shit in high school. And I get it. It would have been weird.'

'I don't understand how you do it.'

'Do what?'

'Want things,' Libby said. 'I don't know how to be in the world, wanting things, and having people know that I want them.'

'What are you saying?' Ella asked. 'That you're afraid to start something with Will because then people will know that you like him?'

The drop of ice cream picked up another drop. It was rolling faster now.

'Because newsflash, Libs, everyone already knows that you like him. And that he likes you. Why do you think everyone's been making fun of you about it?'

She clenched her fingers around the spoon, so hard that her nails dug into the fleshy part of her palm.

'I don't want smart things, Ella,' she whispered. 'I'm supposed to be smart, but I never, ever want smart things.'

'Oh, please,' Ella said, waving her hand. 'Wanting Will is plenty smart. He'll be a beautiful boyfriend. If I was going to custom design a boy for you, I couldn't do any better.'

'It's not him!' Libby said. 'It's me! I never like things that are good for me! I liked Gerry.'

'You can't control the way you feel!' Ella said. 'Plus, you know why I liked Gerry – and why I bet you liked him too? He was a really good dude.'

'He slept with you while he had a girlfriend, Ella! A pregnant girlfriend!'

'I'm not saying he necessarily grew up into the best dude! But at the time—'

'That's not all!' Libby said, an angry fire beginning to burn in her belly. 'I was head over heels for Nightingale. Did you know that?'

Ella laughed, and Libby felt that laugh like a needle in every cell of her body. 'Don't confuse someone being hot and charismatic with being into them.'

'I slept with him.'

Ella stopped. 'You what?'

'I slept with him,' Libby repeated. 'He looked at me, winked, called me Queen Elizabeth, and then it was on. Just like that.'

'And you didn't tell me?'

'How was I supposed to tell you?'

'Using words! Like, *oh God, Ella, I think I've done something really stupid, I just slept with Nightingale!*'

'See!'

'See what?'

'Stupid!' Libby said. 'It was stupid and *I'm not supposed to be stupid!*'

'Okay,' Ella said. 'Okay okay okay. Let's slow this down for a minute. There are some things I need you to tell me. Number one: did you go and get yourself tested? Because God knows where that boy has been.'

'Yes. I did all the things you're supposed to do. Don't worry.'

'But I am worried!' Ella said. 'Shit, Libby. I would have gone with you. Held your hand. Done whatever you needed.'

'I know,' Libby said. 'I know you would. I just— I couldn't—'

'I still would, you know,' Ella said, reaching over and touching her hand. 'Anything you need. Want to make Nightingale voodoo dolls and stick them full of pins? I'm your girl.'

'I know. I know.'

'There's another thing I need you to you,' Ella said. 'And it's that you understand that dicks don't get to define you.'

Libby nodded.

'Because they don't, Libby. Sleeping with dickheads doesn't make you some weak, terrible person.'

She didn't say anything.

'I'm so sorry I made you feel like you couldn't tell me any of this,' Ella said. 'I love you so much and – God, it kills me that you couldn't tell me this. So I need you to know that I love you. That I'm here for you. That you can tell me anything. That nothing is ever going to change any of that.'

'Are you sure?'

'What do you mean, am I sure? Of course I'm sure! What the hell did I ever do to make you think otherwise?'

Libby took a deep breath. 'Nightingale wasn't the only one.'

'Okay,' Ella said. 'If you're waiting for me to slut-shame you, Libby, you're going to be waiting a very long time.'

'It's bad. It's really, really bad.'

'How bad could it possibly be?'

'It was Roarke.'

A moment.

A heartbeat.

Everything fell apart.

'... what?' Ella said.

'It didn't mean anything,' Libby said. 'He and I talked, and we both agreed it was nothing. But it ... it happened.'

'How?' Ella said, sounding dazed. 'Can you tell me how, please?'

'Catriona's wedding. Will and Caro were fighting, and so Roarke and I spent a bunch of time together, and then his ex was there, and we were both a bit drunk, and a lot stupid, and I was such a mess over all the Nightingale shit, and – please, Ella, please, no, don't cry.'

'You slept with my boyfriend,' Ella said, her voice hollow, stunned.

'No!' Libby insisted. 'He wasn't, then. He wasn't anyone's.'

'You have to kiss him,' Ella said, tears trickling down her face, running into each other, gathering momentum, running faster, faster, faster. 'All the time.'

'But it's fake! I don't want him, Ella! Remember where we started? I want Will. Only Will.'

'You didn't tell me. *He* didn't – he'd – with you – and then – he didn't tell me.'

'Because it wasn't anything! Him and me, we agreed that it wasn't anything! I don't want him. He doesn't want me. I want Will. And Roarke wants you!'

'That doesn't matter!'

'Of course it matters!'

'No, it doesn't! You know what matters? The fact that *you didn't tell me*!'

'I'm sorry!' Libby said. 'I'm so sorry, Ella. I've been a shitty friend, and I know that. But I love you. You're so, so important to me. So please: what do I do? How do I fix it?'

Silence. A long one.

'I love you more than anyone in the world,' Ella said, raking a hand through her hair. 'I know you'd never do anything to hurt me on purpose.'

'Of course I wouldn't.'

'But you didn't tell me,' Ella said. 'I— I just don't think I can look at you right now, Libby.'

The tears would never come when she needed them. For a long time after Ella's bedroom door snicked shut behind her, Libby sat at the dining table, staring. She sat there so long that the ice cream melted into a sticky puddle and started dripping off the edge of the table onto the floor.

Ants. They were going to get ants.

Ella didn't come out.

Libby broke eventually, and went to bed. She slept badly, and when she woke up late and stumbled out to the kitchen to find the note on the table where the puddle of ice cream had been, she thought for a second that it was a nightmare.

Sorry Libs. Not you. It's me. I love you. Gone home. E.

Chapter Twenty

She forced herself to do the sensible things. She sat down at the table and took deep breaths until the initial burst of panic subsided. She made herself a cup of tea. She tried calling Ella thirteen times and sent her seven texts that all read, *please tell me you're ok*.

When that didn't get any response, she called Ella's mum in Wimeena and let her know that Ella was on her way there. 'Is everything all right?' Ms Grey asked.

'Nothing you need to worry about,' Libby lied. 'She's having a bit of a rough patch with her boyfriend. She just needs a couple of days to get her head back together.'

'I didn't know she had a new boyfriend. What's he like?'

She ended that conversation as soon as she could.

She scrolled through her phone. She wasn't Facebook friends with Gerry, but he didn't have very tight privacy settings, so she sent him a message. *Hi Gerry. Sure you're not very interested in hearing from me, but Ella's on her way up to Wimeena and she's a bit of a mess. Thought you should know. L.*

She thought long and hard before she hit send, then decided it was better he have some kind of warning. Who knew where Ella's head was at?

What if she never came back?

It was raining outside, a steady mist of drizzle. She looked at her phone.

She tried calling Ella eight more times.

She looked at her phone again, for several long minutes, before she put it in her coat pocket and went out into the rain.

'Libby!' Will said surprisedly when he opened his front door about forty minutes later. 'Hi. You're soaked. Can I—'

'Is Roarke here?' she asked, before Will could say anything too— much.

He blinked, but, 'yes,' he said. 'Come in. What were you doing outside in weather like this?'

It had gone from drizzling to pouring as she was walking from the station to Will's place. Of course it had.

'I didn't want to do this over the phone,' she said.

'Are you all right?'

'I'm fine,' she said. 'It's Ella.'

'What?' Roarke said, appearing suddenly as if summoned by her name. 'What is it?'

Wordlessly, she handed him the note.

His brows furrowed as he read it. 'I don't get it.'

'She's gone,' Libby said.

'What do you mean she's gone?'

'She's gone back to Wimeena. I don't know for how long, or what she's thinking. She just left.'

'What? Why?'

'Because I told her.'

Roarke looked at her. His eyes were steely. 'You *told* her?'

Libby nodded, painfully aware of Will standing behind her.

'Why the hell did you do that?'

'I—' she fought to keep her voice steady. 'I had to.'

'You had to?' he demanded. 'What, she had you tied to a chair? Bamboo under your fingernails?'

'Roarke,' Will said warningly.

'Why didn't you at least tell me you were going to do it?'

Roarke said. 'You could have given me some warning, Libby.'

'I— you know what, I'm not sorry,' she said. 'She deserved to know. I came over here because I thought you should know where she is and where her head's at, and I thought you should hear it from me. Message delivered. Goodbye.'

'Where is it?'

'Where's what?'

'The town you're from. Her house. Show me on Google Maps. I'm going to go and get her.'

'Roarke, you can't. It's a six-hour drive.'

'I don't care. Will, give me your car keys.'

'Roarke, come on,' Will said. 'Think it through. If she wanted to see you, she would have told you. Give her some time to cool down.'

'She does this sometimes,' Libby said. 'When she's scared, or upset, she runs. But she comes back. She— she always comes back.'

'You told me that her deepest fear is people leaving her,' Roarke said. 'You might be happy to leave her there—'

'Don't you dare accuse me of not caring about her!' The anger was sudden, white-hot.

'—but I'm not. I'm going to get her. She's the one person I've ever met who doesn't make me feel like the walls are closing in on me whenever she gets close to me, who doesn't make me feel like she's expecting something of me that I can't deliver, and— damn it, Will, give me your keys!'

'Roarke,' Will said, 'we have a show tonight.'

'I don't care about the goddamn show!' Roarke roared. 'I care about my girlfriend!'

'Slow down,' Will said. 'Just think about this for a minute.'

'No! I don't want to think! Everything's always thinking with you – thinking and thinking and never actually doing anything! How's that turned out for you?'

'How's this going to turn out for you?'

'Will, listen to me for once in your life. I am going to get Ella. This is something I need to do. Give me your car keys.'

Will looked at Roarke for a long moment.

Then he picked up his car keys from the table. 'Be careful,' he said, handing them to Roarke. 'Stop every couple of hours and get coffee. Don't speed. Don't be an idiot.'

'You're my brother, not my mother,' Roarke said. 'Libby. Give me the address.'

Libby glared at him.

'What do you want me to say?' he said. 'That you love her best of all? Fine. You do. No one loves her more than you. You win. But I need to do this. I *need* her.'

'You have to promise me something.'

'Fine. Yes. Whatever.'

'You have to promise me you'll bring her back.'

Her voice cracked on the wrong syllable. It should have been the last one, but it cracked in the middle, and the last few words were barely audible.

'Libby,' Roarke said, 'of course I'll bring her back.'

She gave him the address.

After Roarke left, Will sank down on the couch, like his bones had melted away. He swore, his voice muffled by his hands.

'I'm sorry, Will,' she said. 'I'm so sorry.'

Don't be, she wanted him to say.

'Roarke drives like a maniac when he's upset,' he said instead. 'If he crashes the car—'

Then I'll never speak to you again, Libby.

'I've never seen him like this over a girl before,' he said. 'I don't want to know what'll happen if she breaks his heart.'

It'll be your fault, Libby.

'I'm sorry,' he said, looking up at her. 'I worry so much about him, but – you. Are you okay?'

'No,' she said. 'I'm not.'

She sat down on the couch beside him. 'I can keep it together,' she said. 'I can pretend. I'll be okay for the show. But—'

He swore again. 'What the hell are we going to do about the show? How do you do *Much Ado* without Benedick?'

She hesitated for a second.

Then: 'You know it,' she said.

He looked over at her. 'No.'

'You do, though,' she said. 'Well enough to manage for a night. I could probably carry you through some of the scenes. Pick up any lines you drop, that sort of thing.'

'No!' he said, his eyes wide with panic. 'I can't do it, Libby! I don't know have the faintest clue how to act!'

She set her jaw. She took all the worry over Ella, all the fear, and shoved it down, because she had a job, and she was going to do it.

'I do,' she said. 'I'm going to help you. Where's your script?'

'Okay,' she said a couple of hours later, sitting cross-legged on his couch. 'I think I know what the problem is.'

'The problem is that I suck,' Will said, face in his hands. 'I'm not an actor. I belong on the other side of the desk. The one where you tell people what to do instead of doing it.'

'You're trying to play it exactly like Roarke does. No one wants to see Will pretending to be Roarke pretending to be Benedick.'

'No one wants to see Will at all,' he muttered between his fingers.

'No time for moping,' she said. 'Only time for fixing. You've got to play it like you would do it. Find the Benedick within.'

He groaned.

'And it's going to be really hard, because you have an afternoon to do it, instead a semester. But you can, Will.'

He sighed. 'How about we go into the theatre? Maybe this'll click once I'm in the space.'

While he changed his clothes, she tried calling Ella again. She expected it to go to voicemail, but Ella picked up on the fourth ring. 'Hey.'

'Ella, oh my God!' Libby said. 'How are you? Are you all right?'

'Yeah.' She sounded tired.

Libby swallowed. 'Are you at Gerry's?'

'No,' Ella replied dully. 'I'm at home.'

'Good. Good.'

'Mum says you called her. Told her I was coming.'

'I did, yeah.'

'She says thanks.'

'No problems.'

'And Nan says hi.'

'Hi to her too – look, Ella, I'm so sorry.'

There was no response.

'I should have told you about all of this ages ago,' Libby said. 'You deserved to know.'

'You couldn't tell me, though,' Ella said. 'I made it so you couldn't.'

'No. Of course you didn't. It was me.'

'You couldn't tell me about Gerry,' she said. 'You couldn't tell me about Nightingale. You were going through all of this on your own, because you couldn't tell me. Because I'm a terrible, shitty friend.'

'No you're not.'

'Yes, I am!' Ella said. 'You spilled your guts to me last night, and what did I do? I made it all about me. I'm selfish, and greedy, and I rely on you way too much.'

'No,' Libby said. 'You're the best friend in the world. You might be the best person in the world. I haven't met every single person, sure, but I'm pretty sure you're right up there, and – please don't cry, Ella. You'll make me cry, and I really don't have time to cry right now.'

'I'm sorry,' Ella sobbed.

'Don't be— look,' Libby said, fighting to get control over her face as Will came back into the room. 'I just called because I wanted to make sure you were okay, and to tell you that I love you, and to let you know that Roarke is on his way up to you. He'll be there in a few hours.'

'No. I can't see him. Not yet. Not now.'

'He's still coming.'

'No. I don't want him to. And the show—'

'Will's going to do the show,' Libby said, meeting his eye across the room. 'We've been rehearsing, and he's going to do great. Nothing's more important to Roarke than you, all right?'

Ella said nothing. She could hear her ragged breathing on the other end of the phone.

'Just ... be okay, okay?' she said. 'I need you to be okay, Ella.'

'I don't think I am,' Ella whispered.

When she finally hung up, she put the phone down on the

table, put her hands on her knees, and took a couple of deep breaths.

She should have jumped when Will's hand came down on the small of her back, but she didn't. 'You all right?' he asked her.

'Nope,' she replied. 'You?'

'Not even a little.'

She straightened, and as she looked at him and he looked back at her, she knew they were getting close to somewhere, and there was no turning back.

But they were exhausted, and they were emotional, and this meant too much to mess it up. 'Come on, let's go in to the theatre,' she said, taking his hand. 'I want to make sure you've got the dance routine down.'

'Um, *what*?' Annalise exclaimed, when Will told them the news at the ninety-minute call.

'Are you serious?' Ned said.

'They're both really sick,' Will said.

'We can deal without Ella, but Roarke better be on his deathbed,' Ned said.

'Trust me, there's no way he can perform,' Libby said. 'Neither of them can move, let alone speak. This isn't a runny nose and a sore throat.'

'If he's conscious, he should be here,' Ned said.

'Well, he's not,' Will said, 'and we're just going to have to deal with that. I've been working with Libby and I'm going to play Benedick. There are a few scenes I'd like to run with people, so we're going to do vocals early and make them short today. Libby, do you want to lead?'

'Sure.'

She surveyed the cast's faces as she led them through vocal warm-ups. There was some anxiety in the mix, but mostly, they were incensed. This was not going to be pretty when Roarke got back. What had happened to Caro was going to look like a walk in the park.

'Libby, give me the real story,' Ned said, grabbing her arm as they went back into the wings. 'What's going down with Roarke?'

'It's like Will said,' she said. 'He's really sick.'

'That is such a pissweak excuse,' Ned said. 'I've done shows with broken bones and no voice and dead family members—'

'Ned, ranting about it isn't going to fix it,' Rosie said. 'He's not here. Deal with it.'

Ned gave her a hard look before turning on his heel and stalking away. Libby exhaled and pressed her fingers to her temples.

'Come on,' Rosie said. 'Let me help you with your hair.'

By the time the ten-minute call rolled around and she headed down to the wing to wait for her first entrance, Libby was as wrung out as a limp rag. The thought of doing a whole show was almost unimaginable. She was going to fall asleep the second that she and Rosie sat down on that picnic blanket.

Maybe when she woke up, the awful scene with Ella would have been a dream. Maybe she'd have a chance to plan it out, script it, do it properly. Find a way to tell her that wouldn't send her running for the hills, a way that would make everything all right.

'Libby,' Will whispered.

'Hey!' she said, forcing her feelings back down. 'You should be on OP side, not here. What are you doing?'

'I don't— I don't know how to do this,' he said, his voice cracking. 'I'm going to humiliate myself in front of a hundred people.'

His hands were shaking. She took them in hers, and made sure hers weren't.

'You can do this,' she said, making her voice certain. 'You've been living this play for months now. You've got this.'

'I really don't,' he said. 'I'm going to humiliate myself in front of— in front of you.'

She caught his face between both her hands, made him look at her. 'Will,' she said. 'You could never, all right?'

She could feel the eyes of the other people in the wings on them. They weren't being subtle. Everyone knew what was happening here. Everyone.

'I'm here with you,' she told him. 'Every step of the way. Even when I'm not on stage with you, it's just you and me, okay? I've got you.'

'You and me,' he repeated, dazedly. 'You and me.'

Time stretched. Every scene seemed to take twice as long as usual. She was hyper-aware of every second, jumping at any pause from Will that was even slightly too long. 'God keep your ladyship still in that mind!' he said, his tone light, but his eyes panicked.

'So some gentleman or other shall scape a predestinate scratched face?' she replied, seeing his shoulders slump ever-so-slightly with relief when she turned his dropped line into a question. 'Scratching could not make it worse, an' twere such a face as yours were.'

Time stretched, but it also contracted. The seconds were long, but the minutes were short. It was like she blinked, and it was the second half of the show, and she was onstage in Hero's broken wedding, watching as Ned shouted and railed and eventually stomped away.

'Lady Beatrice, have you wept all this while?' Will asked, coming up behind her.

'Yea,' she replied, 'and I will weep a while longer.'

She was lucky she'd done this scene so many times before. If she was in Will's shoes, she definitely would have forgotten all her lines.

'I do love nothing in the world so well as you.' Will's voice was low and gentle. 'Is not that strange?'

Her heart was beating so fast.

'As strange as the thing I know not,' she said. 'It were as possible for me to say I lov'd nothing so well as you; but believe me not, and yet I lie not; I confess nothing, nor I deny nothing.'

In this scene, at least, he'd taken her advice. This was nothing like playing this scene with Roarke.

There was part of her – a large part – that wanted to pull a Caro and run offstage. This was not how she wanted this to happen.

He was so close to her now.

'I will swear by it that you love me,' he said, and she could feel his breath against her skin, 'and I will make him eat it that says I love not you.'

Oh God oh God oh God. She was going to have a heart attack right here on stage. Or a panic attack. An attack of some kind.

He touched her cheek, just like Roarke had done a thousand times. But his fingers were not steady, like Roarke's. They were shaking.

He knew, like she knew, that they were not on solid ground.

'You have stayed me in a happy hour,' she said, covering his trembling hand with hers. 'I was about to protest I loved you.'

'And do it with all thy heart?' Roarke always played that line with a wry smile, but this wasn't Roarke. This was Will, and this was – this was—

'I love you with so much of my heart that none is left to protest,' she said, and they were kissing.

It was a stage kiss. Simple. Chaste. Pretend. Looking like way more than it was. There were no fireworks, no trails of flame scorching up her spine, no heatwave breaking over her. It was nothing like the time Nightingale had kissed her as the lights went down in *Rapunzel*.

But it was something – something that was so much more than nothing, and it changed everything.

She stayed in the dressing room long after everyone had gone out to the foyer, using about a dozen more makeup wipes than normal to take off her makeup.

'You okay?' Rosie said from the doorway.

'I—' she sighed, throwing the wipe she'd been fiddling with away. 'No. Not really.'

'It's been a big night,' Rosie said, twirling her car keys around her fingers. 'If you don't want to deal with it, we can sneak out the back way. I'll give you a ride.'

'No. I need to deal with it. I just need to make myself get out of this chair.'

'There's a bottle of scotch stashed in the kitchen,' Rosie said. 'Ned brought it in for the first Uni Rep show ever because he heard it was good for your voice, and I hid it after he accidentally went on stage drunk. Want to take the edge off first?'

'Yes,' Libby said, slipping the strap of her handbag over her shoulder. 'Very much so.'

Nightingale was in the kitchen.

Chapter Twenty-One

Her mind struggled to compute it. It utterly refused to parse the scene in front of her.

Nightingale was in the kitchen, sitting in his usual spot on top of the half-sized fridge, leaning back against the wall the same way he had a thousand times before.

'Rosie!' he said, in that lazy, charming voice of his. 'Libby! Long time, ladies.'

'Nightingale, what the hell?' Rosie said. 'Get out before anyone sees you, you idiot.'

He jumped down, landing lithely on his feet like a cat. 'Nice to see you too, Rosie-Posie.'

He reached out to tap the end of her nose with his index finger. Rosie slapped his hand away.

He turned, and suddenly the full force of his smile was directed at Libby. 'Queen Elizabeth!' he said. 'We meet again.'

She resisted the urge to step back. 'Nightingale, get out,' she said. 'No one wants you here.'

'Oh, I think they will when they see what I've brought with me,' he said. 'Spoilers: it's a cheque. A big one.'

'You can't just buy your way back in,' Rosie said. 'It doesn't work like that.'

'Babe,' he said, 'I thought you knew about the size of my cheque. It's enormous. Stupendous. Gargantuan.'

Rosie rolled her eyes.

'Libby gets it,' he said, and winked at her.

She tasted bile in the back of her throat.

'No,' she said firmly. 'No, you don't get to come back, Nightingale.'

'That's not your call,' he said. 'It's Graham's. And I'm pretty sure he's here, because I saw his car outside, so if you'll excuse me—'

Nightingale tried to push past her, but she stood her ground. He raised his eyebrows.

'Let's say this stunt of yours works,' Libby said. 'Let's say you manage to buy off Graham and convince him to let you back into Uni Rep. It doesn't mean anyone's ever going to cast you in anything. Ever again.'

'Honey,' he said, 'you might have sucked someone's dick to get bumped up to a principal role, but it doesn't work like that for me.'

Libby shoved him in the shoulders, hard.

'God, you're a piece of shit, Nightingale,' Rosie said, shaking her head.

Nightingale laughed and chucked her under the chin. 'You love it.'

'Don't touch her,' Ned said quietly from behind them.

The grin that spread across Nightingale's face was bigger than the Cheshire Cat's. 'Too late.'

'Get out,' Ned said. 'Before I throw you out.'

'Ooooh, big man. I'd like to see you try, Neddy.'

'I would too, actually,' Rosie said. 'I'd like to see what it looks like after your face smashes into the back stairs, Nightingale.'

'Me too,' Libby said. 'Please, Ned, feel free to do some throwing.'

'I've got something I need to tell you, mate,' Nightingale said, ignoring Libby and Rosie and talking to Ned instead. 'I won the bet.'

'What bet?' Ned said. 'What are you talking about?'

'You remember,' Nightingale said. '*Rapunzel*. I told you I could have any chick in this place, and you told me I couldn't, that I couldn't have her.' His hand fell heavy on Libby's shoulder. She shrugged it off as violently as she could 'And guess what, mate? I did.'

'Don't touch me,' she snarled.

'That's not what you said last time. How long did it take before you spread your legs for me? Five minutes?'

There was something inside Libby that was like a steel bar. For years, she'd been piling things on top of it: wanting, yearning, guilt, embarrassment, frustration, shame.

She looked at Nightingale – looked at that awful, smug grin on his face – and it broke.

'You think you're coming back?' she demanded. 'Okay. You're coming back. Come and say hello to everyone.'

Nightingale, while not a big man, was bigger than Libby. But a dam had burst inside her, and she was full to the brim of adrenaline and emotion and rage ... so much rage. She could not resist him that day in the Swamp, and he could not resist her now.

Her fingers closed around his wrist, and she yanked him bodily through the annexe and out through the auditorium, kicking the doors to the foyer open. 'Look who's here!' she announced to everyone. 'Guess who's back to pick up right where he left off? Aren't we all just so excited?'

There was silence. Some of the patrons looked confused. She was probably going to lose Uni Rep a bunch of ticket sales.

She should care about that, if she ever wanted to get cast in anything again. But the floodgates were open and that fear poured right out of her, a surging froth of white water.

'Apparently he's got a big cheque for all the money he stole from us,' she said. 'Isn't that right, Nightingale?'

'More than,' he said, fixing his charming smile back on his face. 'Ten grand, baby.'

'Oh good! That makes it totally fine, then!'

'I was always going to pay it back. I love this place. It's my home.'

'Lucky that's how exactly how it works!' said Libby.

'Look, I made a mistake,' Nightingale said, addressing the room rather than her. 'But I'm man enough to try to fix it. I promise you – all of you, here tonight – that I'll do everything I can to make it right.'

'How nice. How are you going to fix the thing where you make bets on which of the girls here will sleep with you?'

His face changed. The grin morphed – not a big change, really, it should have been bigger, given how many pantos Nightingale had done – into a sneer.

'So what if you were a bet, Libby?' he said. 'You liked it. I didn't hear you complaining.'

'You've never been very good at listening,' she said. 'If you were, you would have realised that no one wants you here.'

'I'm going to make it up to you,' he said, addressing the foyer again. 'I've been an arsehole, I know, but I'm going to work hard to make sure—'

'Oh my God, Nightingale, shut up,' Rosie said. 'No one wants to hear your bullshit.'

'I seem to remember you being very interested in hearing my bullshit, once upon a time.'

'Dude, you need to leave,' Ned said. 'Get out now or I'll throw you out.'

'I'll help,' Michael said.

'Me too,' said Rashmi.

'I know you're all angry with me,' Nightingale said, softening his tone. 'You have every right to be. But if you give me another chance, I'll—'

'No, son,' Graham said heavily. 'There aren't any more chances for you here.'

'Graham, I can fix this,' Nightingale said, 'I know I've screwed up so badly. I'm so sorry, but – please.'

'If you're really sorry,' Graham said, 'you'll give me that cheque you were talking about.'

Nightingale looked at him, for a long moment. He was trying to plead with his eyes, Libby realised, because his words weren't working. But he wasn't doing a very good job, because Graham's gaze remained steady.

'I'll fix this,' Nightingale said, 'I swear,' and walked out the door.

Immediately, there were a million hands on her, a million hands asking her if she was all right, *God, Libs, that was brutal, can I—*

She shoved them all away. 'Did you bet on me?' she asked Ned. 'Did you actually bet on me?'

'Libby, no,' he said. 'Not really. It was a throwaway comment. I never expected that he— and I never expected that you—'

'That'd I'd fall for it? That I'd sleep with him?'

'I'm so sorry.'

'Is that why you started being so nice to me all of a sudden? Because you felt guilty?'

'No,' Ned said. 'Yes, but no. You're cool, Libby. I just had to get to know you better.'

Someone came up behind her. He didn't touch her, but he was close, and she didn't need to turn to know exactly who it was.

'Ned,' Will growled.

She put a hand on his chest. 'No, Will,' she said. 'I've got this. I can do this on my own.'

By the time the theatre was finally, totally empty, it was after midnight.

The adrenaline and emotion that had carried her through the day and night had finally left her system, leaving her a wobbly-legged, shaking, emptied-out mess. Part of her felt like she should be in the office with Will, who was talking to Graham about a contingency plan for if Nightingale turned up again. But she had nothing left to give. Instead, she sank into a seat in the third row of the seating bank and closed her eyes.

Her phone buzzed. *Me and R leaving tomorrow morn,* Ella had texted. *Home afternoon-ish.*

Great, she texted back.

She hesitated.

Then, *I miss you,* she sent. *I love you. Can we talk when you get back?*

The pause seemed interminably long.

Yes, Ella sent back. *I love you too.*

'Hey,' Will said.

She hadn't heard him enter. He stood on the stage in front of her, looking totally out of place.

He'd managed that evening, but he wasn't an actor, not at all.

'Sit with me?' Libby asked.

He did. She was sitting in an aisle seat, but he didn't bother clambering over her. Instead, he sank down beside her on the stairs, long legs stretched out in front of him.

She reached over and took his hand. For a moment, she just held it, feeling the weight of his fingers in hers, and then she pressed his knuckles to her lips.

His chest rose and fell. 'Libby—'

'I know what you're going to say,' she said. 'You're going to say that it's late, and we're exhausted, and we're emotional, and we should do this properly. But I need to get this out, Will. I'm so bad at saying what I want, and if I don't say it now, I might never, so – please.'

'Yes,' he said. 'Of course.'

'Every time I thought about how I was going to say this to you, all I could come up with was a spectacle.' Her voice was barely above a whisper, but she made herself keep talking. 'A speech. Interpretive dance. Puppets. A laser show. A chorus of fifty dancers. Some way I could – I could distance myself from it somehow. Make it a performance.'

His thumb was drifting back and forth across her knuckles. She never wanted him to stop touching her.

'But I don't want to perform it,' she said. 'I just want to say it. Which is hard for me, because I'm so unbelievably bad at talking about my feelings. I got this idea in my head at some point that the world is playing an elaborate joke on me and if I ever reveal how I really feel about something, someone's going to rip the carpet out from under my feet and everyone will laugh at me.'

'Libby—'

'No. Don't speak. Let me say this.'

He nodded.

'Will, I like you. So much. I like you, and I trust you, and I want you, and I want to be with you, and I hope that's okay.'

There was a long pause. It would have been three heartbeats normally, but it felt more like thirty, because her heart was beating so fast.

'Can I say something now?' he said.

'Please.'

'That was the best speech I've ever heard in my life.'

She'd spent every last reserve of emotional energy she had that night, but somehow she wanted to cry and laugh all at once.

'I'm a numbers person, not a words person, so my speech isn't going to be as good as yours,' he said, shifting and angling his body towards hers, his thumb still stroking her knuckles. 'But just saying hello to you makes me happy, ProofIt. Every day I get to see you is automatically better than the days when I don't.'

She leaned her forehead against his, twining her fingers in his curly hair. 'Can I ask you something?'

'Of course,' he said, his free hand coming up to cup the nape of her neck.

'Will you kiss me? I might die if you don't.'

He didn't make her wait again.

This was not a stage kiss. Not even close. He clutched at the collar of her shirt like he was drowning, and she clung to him so that if they did drown, they'd go down together. There was nothing in the world except this, nothing in the world except the feeling of his lips against hers. Nothing in the world but Will, her wonderful, beautiful Will – and the only person laughing at her was herself, for taking so long about it.

Chapter Twenty-Two

'I want to go and see the uni counselling service,' Ella said. 'It's free, right?'

'Pretty sure it is, yeah,' Libby said. 'Do you want me to look up how to make an appointment?'

'No,' Ella said. 'I can do it.'

'Do you want me to make you a cup of tea?'

'Yes. Please.'

Her phone buzzed while the kettle was boiling. *Hey,* Will had sent. *How's Ella doing?*

She's a bit of a mess, but we're getting there, she replied. *We had a long talk. How's Roarke?*

Heartbroken. Not that he'll say it.

I'm sorry.

It's not your fault. Give you a ride in to the theatre tonight?

Please. x

xxx

It was just a row of kisses – the kind you might send to someone totally platonically – but she still felt her cheeks go red.

'Here you go,' she said, putting the tea down next to Ella.

'Thanks,' Ella said. 'I made an appointment. Tomorrow afternoon.'

'Do you want me to come with you? I could sit outside in the waiting room.'

'I'm not sure. I might need to do it on my own, but – God, I might need you, Libs. Is that okay?'

'Of course it is,' she said. 'Always.'

Ella picked up her tea, but she didn't drink it. Instead, she held it to her mouth, both hands wrapped around the mug. 'Did I do the right thing?' she asked. 'Taking some time apart from Roarke?'

'I can't answer that for you,' Libby said, picking up her own mug. 'All that matters is what you think, and what you need.'

'I'm going to miss him. I already miss him. It feels like someone's punched me in the gut.'

Ella closed her eyes. Libby wondered if she should reach across and save her tea before she spilled it.

Then she opened them again. 'But I need to sort my own shit out before I drag someone else into it. And between Emerson and Gerry and, well, everything ... there is so much shit to sort out.'

'Whatever you need, I'm here for you.'

'I know, Libs. But I can't rely on you for everything.'

Ella put down her tea and sighed. 'That was why having Roarke was good, honestly. The whole reason we bonded is because we both understand what it's like to have so much shit. And to have someone that you owe everything to, and no way to pay them back.'

'Ella, you don't owe me anything.'

'I owe you a real friendship,' Ella said. 'One where you can tell me all the shit that's going on in your life. And I owe Roarke a real girlfriend, one he doesn't have to worry is going to fall apart and run away at the drop of a hat.'

'I don't want to put any pressure on you,' Libby said, 'but I don't think Roarke is interested in this magical real girlfriend. I think he just wants you.'

'I know. He told me. He wouldn't let me break all the way up with him, even though I tried. He told me he'd wait. He told me he'd do anything. But I can't do that to him. I can't be some fragile little damsel that he needs to save all the time. That *you* need to save all the time.'

'I get it. Though if you ever need saving ...'

'You'll always be the first person I call, don't worry,' Ella said. 'I couldn't do to you what I did to Roarke, Libs. I need you. It's probably unhealthy how much I need you.'

'I need you too, Ella,' Libby said. 'You have no idea how much.'

Ella sighed again. 'Is Roarke going to be in trouble with everyone? For skipping the show?'

'Look, it's going to be rough,' Libby said. 'But after all the Nightingale fireworks, it might just blow over.'

It didn't blow over, of course. Perhaps Nightingale had never been as powerful as she'd thought.

'I see you've deigned to show your face today,' Annalise said, as Roarke signed in on the sheet in the kitchen.

'Yes,' Roarke said shortly. 'Excuse me.'

'You don't sound like you were sick,' Gen said, blocking the doorway.

Roarke just looked at her. 'Could you move?'

Gen glared, folding her arms across her chest. 'You abandoned us yesterday,' she said. 'Do you have any idea the position you put us in? Oh wait, no, you don't, because you're a selfish arrogant prick, who—'

'Gen,' Ned started.

'Don't you dare speak to me right now, Ned Riordan!' Gen exploded, turning to face him. 'Don't you dare!'

'Gen—'

Roarke slipped out the door. Libby followed him, as eager to be in a place Ned wasn't as anything else. 'Roarke?' she called, tapping on the door of the boys' dressing room. 'It's me. Can I come in?'

He grunted. She took it as a yes. 'Hey.'

'Hey,' he replied, pulling his shirt over his head.

'You okay?'

'You're brushing up against the D&M rule. I've already had to have one with William Earnshaw, and I can't cope with two in a day.'

'Yeah, well, Will isn't about to play opposite you in front of a hundred people. I just wanted to check how angry you are with me.'

'I'm not angry with you,' he said, buttoning up his first costume shirt. 'I'm as fine as I can be, under the circumstances. I'll be the same old Benedick onstage. End of story.'

'All right,' she said. 'Break a leg. See you out there.'

'Hang on.'

She turned back.

'Is Ella ...?'

'She's going to be okay,' she said. 'She's not there yet, but she will be.'

'Tell her ...'

'Tell her what?'

Roarke shook his head. 'Don't tell her anything,' he said. 'She asked for space. The least I can do is give it to her.'

Despite wanting to more than anything, she didn't see Will for more than a few minutes after the show that night. 'I'm sorry,' he said, his breath warm against her lips as they stole a moment together under the seating bank in the dark auditorium while the rest of the cast was in the foyer. 'But I have to get Roarke out of here.'

She kissed him. 'Of course,' she whispered back. 'We've got all the time in the world. There's no rush.'

It was probably for the best, anyway. Roarke needed Will, and Libby needed to be with Ella.

She went with Ella to uni the next day. She didn't go to the counsellor's office, but she worked through some ProofItLibby essays in the library until Ella texted her that she was done. 'How was it?' she asked on the car ride home.

'Terrible,' Ella said. 'I seriously considered throwing myself out the window at, like, eleven different points.'

'If this counsellor isn't working out for you, we can find you another one.'

'It's not that. It's just ... hard. Talking about shit. Sometimes you just really don't want to do it, you know?'

'Trust me, I know,' Libby said. She had an appointment of her own booked for after the show closed, even though the thought of someone prying away at all the walls and dams she'd built in her mind made her feel nauseous.

'But we're going to do more of it,' Ella said. 'You and me. We're going to talk about all the stuff. Good stuff, bad stuff, happy stuff, sappy stuff, messy stuff, sexy stuff – everything.'

'I'd like that.'

'And we're going to start with the last one. Right now. Tell me about you and Will.'

Libby hesitated. 'Are you sure you want to talk about this?'

'Yes,' Ella said. 'I'm sure. Now that I've put my own love life in the freezer, I'm going to live vicariously through yours. This relationship already has a fandom. Give me all the details.'

She went in early for the show that night to grab some quiet time with Will. 'I can't wait for next week,' he said, nuzzling her hair with his nose, as she sat on his lap in the theatre office, the door locked behind them.

'Hmmm?' she said, tracing her fingers along the curve of his shoulder.

'When all of this is over,' he said, kissing her temple, then her cheek, and then a long line down her jaw. 'When we have the time to go on a proper date. Spend time together.'

'It'd be nice to have some time to Netflix and chill.'

He made a sound deep in his throat. She smiled against his lips and kissed him.

By the time she emerged, she was late for her call time, and she had to rush her whole hair and makeup routine. 'How's Ella?' Annalise asked, as they tried to make space for each other in front of the mirror. 'Still sick?'

'She's getting better, but she's not there yet,' she replied, nearly poking herself in the eye with her mascara.

'So Roarke really was sick?'

'Of course he was. He didn't just not show up because he felt like it.'

'Hmmm,' Annalise said. 'Here, babe, you need this.'

'What?'

'Concealer. For that hickey on your neck.'

'What? Where?'

A grin spread across Annalise's face in the mirror. 'So you and Will, hey?' she said. 'When did it start?'

'Um—'

Rosie put her compact down loudly. 'What are you trying to prove, Annalise?'

'Excuse me?'

'You heard me.'

'Doesn't mean I knew what you meant.'

'Oh, come off it, Lise,' Heidi said. 'Yes you did.'

'What did I mean, then?'

'You've been doing this for ages,' Rashmi said. 'Insinuating that Libby slept her way into this role.'

'I have not.'

'You kind of have,' Libby said.

'Well, was I wrong?' Annalise said. 'You hooked up with Nightingale, didn't you? You've got form.'

'Annalise, if you want to talk to someone who hooked up with Nightingale specifically to get something, you can talk to me,' Rosie said. 'Otherwise, you can shut your mouth.'

Annalise looked from Rosie to Heidi to Rashmi to Libby, and back to Rosie again. 'I'm going to go and do my makeup in the kitchen,' she announced, and left.

Libby unscrewed the lid of her water bottle and took a few sips, trying to calm her racing heart.

'Libs,' Rashmi said, 'you know none of us think you hooked up with Will just to get this role, right?'

She nodded.

'If we were going to slut-shame you for sleeping with Nightingale, we'd have to slut-shame basically every girl here,' Heidi said. 'Hell, I'm woman enough to admit it: I hooked up with him once. It was very ordinary. Extremely not five stars.'

'Thank you,' Libby said, voice wavering.

'Don't cry,' Rosie told her. 'You don't have time to redo your makeup. Want a hand with your hair?'

It was a relief the next night to know it was the last time she'd have to do this, but when she signed her initials in the last column on the sign-in sheet on Closing Night, she was glad that relief wasn't all she felt. Nightingale had taken a lot from her, but he hadn't taken Uni Rep. He hadn't taken that jittery, urgent energy of Closing Night, that bittersweet sadness tempered with joy. Even after everything, she still loved this place, and it would still be hard to say goodbye to Beatrice.

'Libby?' It was Ned. 'Can I ... can I talk to you for a second?'

She drew the pause out as long as she could – and then a few beats longer – before she nodded, just one single jerk of the head.

'I think you know what I want to say. I'm so, so, so sorry.'

She didn't respond.

'I never thought Nightingale would take what I said so seriously,' he said.

'You still said it.'

'I know. I shouldn't have. I'm sorry.'

Ned ran his hand through his sandy hair. 'Gen's not speaking to me,' he said. 'If that makes you feel any better.'

'It doesn't.'

'I'm so sorry, Libby. Please. You need to believe me.'

'I believe you, Ned,' she said. 'I don't think I'm ready to forgive you, though.'

'That's fair,' he said.

When he left, she had to put her hands on the kitchen counter and breathe deeply for a few seconds, until she could be sure she wasn't going to cry.

The back door swung open. 'You're not sick, are you?' Ella asked. 'You're all pale.'

'Ella!' she exclaimed, turning. 'You came!'

'I didn't want to miss the last show,' Ella said. 'I figure I should finish at least one thing I started.'

On their way from the kitchen to the dressing room, they ran into Roarke, because sometimes life was as inconvenient as theatre. 'Ella,' he said.

'Roarke,' she replied.

'How are you?'

'I'm all right. And you?'

'All right too.'

Libby knew, and she knew Ella knew, that he was lying.

The girls in the dressing room – well, most of them – were excited to see Ella. 'Are you feeling better?' Rashmi asked, as Annalise stalked back to the kitchen

'We were all worried about you,' Heidi said. 'Libby made it sound like you were dying. What did you have, anyway?'

Ella grimaced. 'It was pretty unpleasant,' she said. 'You don't want the details.'

Libby recognised the dodge as one of her own manoeuvres.

'I'm sure I don't have to remind you to keep it professional until after the audience is out of the auditorium,' Will said, standing on one of the seats in the front row of the seating bank as the cast gathered on stage at the one-hour call. 'Just because it's Closing Night doesn't mean we don't have to deliver an awesome show. So go out there and smash it. Who wants to lead our last round of vocals?'

Libby volunteered. His hand was warm in hers as he helped her up onto the seat beside him. He tried to restrain a smile, but he was much worse at concealing his feelings than she was.

She went down to the wing at the ten-minute call with Rosie. It was the last time she'd ever do any of this – stand here, walk on stage, be Beatrice.

God, she'd loved being Beatrice. Who knew if she'd ever get another role like this again?

But it was time for it to end. Performing was exhilarating, but it was exhausting. This couldn't be every day.

'Libby,' Will whispered from close behind her.

'Hey,' she whispered. 'Get back to the audience, taxman. You're not supposed to be here.'

'I know,' he said, 'but it's closing, and I couldn't not see you.'

This was her new everyday, right here. And even though she knew the shine would wear off and the sparkle would dim, she couldn't imagine being with him ever being less than extraordinary.

He lifted her off the ground as he hugged her. 'I want to kiss you,' he murmured, 'but I'm sitting with Ella, and I suspect there'll be consequences if I ruin your lipstick.'

'Look at you,' she whispered back, 'always looking out for number one.'

He put her down, and, very carefully, kissed the corner of her mouth. 'Break a leg, ProofIt,' he said.

She turned to find Rosie, Gen, and half the crew watching. She felt her face turn red, and hoped the fifty-seven layers of stage foundation would hide it.

Closing, she'd once heard Nightingale say, *is like doing a show on an acid trip.* She'd never been on an acid trip – and Nightingale probably hadn't either – but for once, she agreed with him. All her memories of Closing Nights were bright but blurred, as if she were seeing them through a glass of champagne. They were fizzing euphoria, and afterwards, they could feel like a dream.

The Closing Night of *Much Ado* wasn't exactly euphoric, but it was dreamlike. She remembered it in moments, in bright flashes. 'If he hath caught the Benedick, it will cost him a thousand pound ere he be cured,' she remembered laughing, and later, she recalled quipping, 'He that hath a beard is more than a youth'. The dancing at the end was imprinted on her memory, those final seconds of the show as Roarke spun her around and dipped her low.

She didn't remember Roarke telling her that he loved nothing in the world so well as her. But that was probably not so strange.

She did remember being in the wings with him, though, as the audience applauded at the curtain call.

'Roarke,' she said. 'Thank you.'

He hugged her. She kissed his cheek. He didn't say anything, but it was enough, and they walked out on stage together.

She bowed alone. He bowed alone. Then together, they walked over to the front row and pulled Will and Ella up onto the stage.

'No,' Ella said, as they grabbed her hands. 'No, no, no. I can't.'

'You can,' Libby said. 'Take a bow. You've earned it.'

Someone had wrestled Genevieve onto the stage too, and pulled the crew out from the wings. Together – cast, crew, production team – they bowed for the last time.

Bowing in front of an applauding crowd, one hand in Will's, one in Ella's, was a moment Libby would never forget.

Directors often made speeches on Closing Nights, but Will wasn't that kind of director, wasn't that kind of person. Instead, even though they were in a crowd of people, he just looked at Roarke, and then at her, and that was enough.

She squeezed his hand in hers, tight. He squeezed back.

Everyone raised their arms in the air for the last time, and together, they took their final bow. The show ended.

Meanwhile, something new for Libby Lawrence and Will Callahan was just beginning.

That Thing I Did

Allayne Webster

After Taylor Kennedy makes a fatal Facebook error and is dumped by his best friend, he's befriended by his eccentric next-door neighbour. Cravat-wearing, Chupa Chup addicted aspiring pornographer Chip drives a funeral hearse and talks to dead people. And he wants Taylor to help him create a body-positive Instagram account, Hotties of the Northern Burbs.

But mild-mannered prison escapee Jackson Rollock has other plans for them. Soon after he leaps Taylor's backyard fence, they're liberating Jackson's beloved, mouthy grandmother from her nursing home and hitting the road to fulfil her dying wish. And sardonic, black-clad stranger Chloe, who has her own reasons for getting out of town, hitches a ride.

They'll break the rules, bare their souls … and make a shitload of questionable jokes, while inadvertently exploring sexuality, consent, the dark side of social media, mental health and friendship.

Frank, fearless and taboo-breaking, *That Thing I Did* is a rollicking road trip with a serious side.

If you do only one thing this year, read That Thing I Did. *I loved this book.* – Erin Gough

A wild ride from start to finish: it's witty, hilarious, hectic, manic and unabashedly irreverent! – Holden Sheppard

Sunburnt Veils

Sara Haghdoosti

Girl meets boy, ghosts his text messages, then convinces him to help her run for the student union. Just your typical love story with a hijabi twist.

Tara wears hijab even though her parents hate it, and in a swipe right world she's looking for the 'will go to the ends of the earth for you' type of love. Or, she would be, if she hadn't sworn off boys to focus on getting into med. Besides, what's wrong with just crushing on the assassins, mages and thieves in the fantasy books she reads?

When a bomb threat on her first day of university throws her together with totally annoying party king and oh-so-entitled politician's son Alex, things get complicated. Tara needs to decide if she's happy reading about heroes, or if she's ready to step up and be one herself.

Sunburnt Veils *is an insightful and powerful exploration of what it's like growing up in a minority group and being constantly pigeonholed as something you're not. It is also about finding power in what makes you feel scared or angry and using your voice to create change.*
– Mischa Parkee, *Books & Publishing*

Road Tripping with Pearl Nash

Poppy Nwosu

The summer is finally here, and Pearl Nash is on a mission to save her slowly disintegrating friendship with a whirlwind end-of-year road trip that is definitely, absolutely, most positively going to solve all her problems.

Except, instead of her best friend Daisy's feet on her dash, suddenly Pearl ends up stuck in the middle of the desert beside Obi Okocha, a boy with a mega-watt smile and an endlessly irritating attitude. Tasked with delivering him to the most epic end-of-year party ever, located in a beach shack in literal middle-of-nowhere woop woop, Pearl Nash is certain that nothing could be worse than this.

She's wrong.

Add in a breakdown, multiple arguments, an AWOL nana and a kiss that was most definitely a huge mistake, and suddenly Pearl has the perfect ingredients for the perfect disaster.

Road Tripping with Pearl Nash is a story about home and family, about breaking apart and fusing together, and, of course, about love.

I had a wonderful time reading this – the building romance between Pearl and Obi is so perfectly, beautifully complex, original, authentic and sexy. I'm head over heels in love with Obi. – Jaclyn Moriarty

www.ingramcontent.com/pod-product-compliance
Lightning Source LLC
Chambersburg PA
CBHW030917050726
47498CB00003BA/784